GOVERNMENT INTERVENTION

Jamie Waterman's phone buzzed. Jamie tapped the phone's keypad. The face of the president of the Navaho Nation appeared on the flat screen mounted on the wall to his right.

"Ya'aa'tey," Jamie said, dipping his chin slightly.

"Ya'aa'tey," she replied. It is good.

"Everything goes well for you?" Jamie asked.

"Almost everything."

"Almost?"

With a shrug, she replied, "The Anglos are trying to buy more of the reservation's land. If we don't sell they say they'll go to court and take the land anyway. There's plenty of open land in other places," the president said, "but they're putting a lot of pressure on—"

The phone buzzed once more, interrupting her. Jamie touched the keypad and his wall screen split into two images. The new one showed C. Dexter Trumball, in his office high up in one of Boston's financial district towers.

"Morning," Dex said curtly.

"How are you, Dex?"

"You haven't seen the news?" Dex asked. "This morning's news from Washington?"

"No," said Jamie.

"The president's zeroed out the Mars program."

Jamie felt it like a sharp blow to his heart. "She zeroed out . . . ?"

"What does that mean?" asked the Navaho president.

"It means the U.S. government will stop funding us when the new fiscal year starts."

"She can't do that!" Jamie protested.

"She's done it."

"Congress won't let her get away with it," he insisted, but he knew he was clutching at straws.

Dex's expression was halfway between a sneer and a scowl of disgust.

The Navaho president said, "Other nations fund the program, too. Maybe—"

"America puts in the lion's share," Dex said. "Once Washington pulls out the others will do the same."

"But—"

"We're sunk," Dex growled. "Screwed. Dead in the water."

Not while I breathe, Jamie said to himself. Not while there's a beat left in my heart.

TOR BOOKS BY BEN BOVA

*Forthcoming

MARS LIFE

BEN BOVA

TOR®

A TOM DOHERTY ASSOCIATES BOOK
NEW YORK

This is a work of fiction. All of the characters, organizations, and events portrayed in this novel are either products of the author's imagination or are used fictitiously.

MARS LIFE

Copyright © 2008 by Ben Bova

All rights reserved.

A Tor Book
Published by Tom Doherty Associates, LLC
175 Fifth Avenue
New York, NY 10010

www.tor-forge.com

Tor® is a registered trademark of Tom Doherty Associates, LLC.

ISBN-13: 978-0-7653-5724-3
ISBN-10: 0-7653-5724-0

First Edition: August 2008
First Mass Market Edition: July 2009

Printed in the United States of America

0 9 8 7 6 5 4 3 2 1

To Barbara, my favorite columnist; to Maria and Mike Cote, my favorite editors; and to the memory of Carleton S. Coon, an early victim of political correctness

I do not feel obliged to believe that the same God who has endowed us with sense, reason, and intellect has intended us to forgo their use.

—GALILEO GALILEI

MARS LIFE

PREFACE

This is a work of fiction. I have striven to make the scientific background of this story as accurate as possible. All the descriptions of the conditions existing on Mars are based solidly on the observations made by satellites in orbit around that planet and rovers trundling along its rust red sands.

However, I have not been constrained by the facts. I have created a scenario to explain the current conditions on Mars that is purely my own invention. While many scientists hope to find bacterial organisms living deep underground on Mars, there is no evidence that the red planet was once inhabited by an intelligent species. That speculation can only be disproved by a thorough exploration of Mars, an exploration conducted by human beings, in addition to robotic craft.

The description of the greenhouse flooding on Earth is also based on actual climatological data, although I have accelerated the timescale somewhat. With a little bad luck, many of us will live to see such flooding. Alas!

The political results of massive greenhouse flooding will be, I fear, to accelerate a trend toward ultraconservative religion-based governments almost everywhere on Earth, a trend that is already evident in much of the world, including the United States. With coastal cities flooded, productive farmlands parched with drought, and the electrical power grid collapsed, millions will be displaced from their homes and their livelihoods. They will demand safety and order, even at the price of individual liberties. History has shown all too often that people turn to authority when faced with disaster, and willingly surrender their freedom.

BEN BOVA
Naples, Florida
July 2007

BOOK I
DYING TIME

Listen to the wisdom of the Old Ones.

*The red world and the blue are brothers, both born of
Father Sun. Separated since birth, bombarded by
fiery Sky Demons, they found their own paths through
time and space. The blue world grew large and rich,
deep with water and teeming with life. The red world,
farther from Father Sun, smaller, colder, also
bore life—for a while.*

*The Sky Demons returned to both brother worlds, howling,
burning, destroying with terrifying hammer blows. Many
creatures of the blue world died under their mindless fury.
On the red world almost all life was annihilated.
Almost all.*

*Man Maker brought The People to the blue world,
where in time they flourished. Strangest of all,
Coyote—the Trickster—led The People back to the
red world. In time.*

DATA BANK

∎

Mars is the most earthlike planet in the solar system. But that doesn't mean that it's very much like Earth.

Barely half of Earth's size, Mars orbits roughly one and a half times farther from the Sun than Earth does. It is a small, cold, seemingly barren world, a frozen desert of iron-rust sands from pole to pole.

Yet Mars is a spectacular world. The tallest mountain in the solar system is the aptly named Olympus Mons, a massive shield volcano three times higher than Everest, with a base as wide as the state of Idaho. The main caldera at Olympus Mons's summit could swallow Mt. Everest entirely. Other huge volcanoes dot the Tharsis highlands, all of them long extinct.

Almost halfway across the planet is Hellas Planitia, an enormous impact crater nearly the size of Australia and some five kilometers deep, gouged out when a huge meteor slammed into Mars eons ago.

Then there is Valles Marineris, the Grand Canyon of Mars, a gigantic rift in the ground that stretches farther than the distance between Boston and San Francisco, a fracture that is seven kilometers deep in some places and so wide that explorers standing on one rim of it cannot see the other side because it is beyond the horizon.

The atmosphere of Mars is a mere wisp, thinner than Earth's high stratosphere. It is composed mostly of carbon dioxide, with traces of nitrogen, oxygen, and inert gases such as argon and neon. The air pressure at the surface of Mars is about the same as the pressure thirty-some kilometers up in the high stratosphere of Earth's atmosphere, so thin that an uncovered glass of water will immediately boil away even when the temperature is far below zero.

Which it is most of the time. Mars is a cold world. At midsummer noon on the Martian equator, the ground temperature might get as high as seventy degrees Fahrenheit. But at the height of a person's nose the temperature would be zero, and that night it would plunge to a hundred below or even colder. The thin Martian atmosphere retains almost none of the Sun's heat: it reradiates back into space, even at noon on the equator.

There is water on Mars, however. The polar caps that can be seen from Earth even with an amateur telescope contain frozen water, usually overlain with frozen carbon dioxide: dry ice. Explorers found layers of permafrost—frozen water—beneath the surface, enough underground water to make an ocean or at least a sizable sea.

There is abundant evidence that water once flowed across the surface of Mars. The entire northern hemisphere of the planet may once have been an ocean basin. Mars was once considerably warmer and wetter than it is now.

But today the surface of Mars is a barren desert of highly oxidized iron sands that give Mars its rusty red coloration. Those sands are loaded with superoxides; the planetwide desert of Mars is more like powdered bleach than soil in which plants could grow.

Yet there is life on Mars. The First Expedition discovered lichen-like organisms living inside cracks in the rocks littering the floor of the Grand Canyon of Mars. The Second Expedition found bacteria living deep underground, extremophiles that metabolize solid rock and water leached from the permafrost.

And the human explorers discovered an ancient cliff dwelling built into a niche high up the north wall of the Valles Marineris. There were once intelligent Martians, but they were wiped out in a cataclysm that scrubbed the entire planet clean of almost all life.

Curious explorers from Earth sought to understand those

long-vanished Martians. But others of Earth preferred to ignore them, to pretend that they had never existed. In an irony that stretched across two worlds, the greatest discovery made on Mars led directly to the determined effort to put an end to the exploration of the red planet.

TITHONIUM BASE: MORNING

■

Carter Carleton woke from a troubled sleep. The vague memory of a dream faded in his mind even as he tried to recall it more clearly. Something about the university and the board of regents' kangaroo court, back on Earth. Better forgotten, he told himself as he pulled the thin blanket off his legs. Better in the deep bosom of the ocean buried, like Shakespeare said.

As he sat up on his narrow bed the aroma of brewing coffee wafted into his cubicle. With it came the nasal twanging of some country-and-western song. "Damned cowboys and their recordings," he muttered, planting his feet on the floor. Then he grinned inwardly. Those cowboys have doctorates in geology and biochemistry, he reminded himself.

Officially, the base was named in memory of the late Darryl C. Trumball, the Boston financier who had donated a considerable share of his personal fortune to the exploration of Mars. But everyone called it Tithonium Base, situated on the floor of the Tithonium Chasma section of the four-thousand-kilometer-long Valles Marineris, the immense Grand Canyon of Mars.

The floor was radiant-heated but still it felt cold to Carleton's bare feet. Not as cold as outside, he thought. A glance at the weather readout on the digital clock by his bedside showed the outside temperature hadn't quite reached ninety below zero yet.

Morning on Mars. Carter Carleton still felt thoroughly out of place among the scientists and technicians who made up the personnel of the Tithonium Chasma base. He was older than any of them, gray-haired and getting pudgy despite his daily toil at the dig. The only anthropologist at the base. The only anthropologist on Mars. The only anthropologist within some hundred million kilometers, for that matter.

Another day, he said to himself, grabbing his towel and toiletries. No, another *sol*, he corrected. Here on Mars they're called sols, not days.

"Whatever," he muttered as he trudged barefoot across his cubicle to the door of the common lavatory.

THE VILLAGE

■

In his condo in Albuquerque, Jamie Waterman dreamed also. He knew it was a dream, yet the Navaho side of him also knew that dreams reveal truths hidden during the waking day.

The village stood before him, sturdy dried-brick dwellings three and even four stories high. The street was unpaved, of course: nothing more than hard-packed dirt. The sunlight felt warm and good on his shoulders, and Jamie realized that he was wearing nothing more than an old checkered shirt, faded denims, and his well-scuffed boots. No space suit.

The villagers looked strange, very different from Jamie. Why not? he asked himself. After all, they're Martians.

Jamie walked among the Martian villagers unnoticed, unseen. They paid no attention to him as they scurried on their daily tasks. I'm just a ghost to them, he realized. I'm invisible. Unseen.

Then he recognized his grandfather Al striding along the bare dusty street toward him, wearing his best black leather vest and his broad-brimmed hat with the silver band circling its crown.

"Ya'aa'tey!" Grandfather Al called out the old Navaho greeting.

"Grandfather!" Jamie called to him, astonished. "But you're dead!"

Al grinned widely at him. "Naw, that was a mistake. I been right here, waitin' for you."

Jamie laid a hand on his grandfather's shoulder. He was as

solid as the stone bear fetish Al had given his grandson so many years ago. Jamie still carried it with him wherever he went.

"You're really here?" Jamie felt tears welling in his eyes.

"Long as you want me to be," said Al.

"And this village? This is the way it was?"

"Naw," Al said. "This is the way it's gonna be." Then he added, "Go with beauty, grandson."

TITHONIUM BASE: THE CAFETERIA

∎

By the time Carter Carleton had dressed and come out into the open central area of the base's main dome, bright sunlight was streaming through the dome's curving walls. Overnight, a polarizing electric current turned the plastic walls opaque, to keep the base's interior heat from escaping into the frigid Martian night. By day, the current was turned off and the walls became transparent to allow warming sunshine in.

Sunshine always made Carleton feel better. That's one advantage that Mars has, he said to himself as he headed for the cafeteria, off on the far side of the open area. There hasn't been a cloudy day here in millions of years. Except for the dust storms.

The cafeteria was completely self-service. If you wanted eggs for breakfast you cracked open a plastic package of powdered eggs and fried them yourself on one of the hand-sized skillets hanging over the grill. Staff members took turns cleaning up after each meal. It was perfectly ordinary to see a tenured professor of microbiology loading the dishwasher or sponging down the tables.

This early in the morning the scrubbing robots were still scouring the tile floor. One of the squat, round little turtles was buzzing down the edge of the cafeteria counter; it stopped ten centimeters before Carleton's loafer-clad feet. It beeped impatiently.

"Go around me, stupid," Carleton muttered.

The robot dutifully maneuvered around his feet and resumed its route along the counter's edge.

The grill still bore the same CLOSED FOR MAINTENANCE sign that had been there the day before. This place is going to seed, Carleton grumbled to himself. The bakery odor of fresh toast tempted him, but instead he chose a bowl of cold cereal and poured reconstituted milk into it. As he was reaching for the fresh raspberries, grown in the greenhouse in the adjoining dome, he heard:

"Dr. Carleton?"

Turning, he saw it was one of the junior technicians. The name tag on her shirt read MCMANUS. She was the base's only nanotechnician.

"Doreen," he replied, smiling the way he used to in his classrooms.

She had lovely, thickly curled auburn hair, but it was cropped close in a strictly utilitarian style. Her face was oval, with the large shy eyes of a waif. She was almost Carleton's height, but so thin and bony that Carleton wondered if she were bulimic. Instead of standard-issue coveralls she wore a mannish long-sleeved shirt and creaseless slacks of pearl gray.

"Do you mind if I join you?" she asked, unsmiling. Her voice was low but sweet; Carleton imagined she was probably a good singer. Mezzo-soprano, most likely. He saw that she was carrying a tray that held only a mug of fruit juice and a slice of toast. Nothing more. The toast looked burnt, at that.

"I'd be glad of the company."

It was still early enough that only a few of the tables were occupied. Voices murmured; the intercom speakers purred soft rock music. Carleton picked an empty table and put his bowl of cereal down.

Once she was settled in the chair on his right, Doreen McManus asked, "Are you going outside again today?"

Carleton groused, "Are you going to twist my arm again?"

Her expression grew even more serious. "Dr. Carleton, you simply—"

"Call me Carter, please. When you call me 'Dr. Carleton' it makes me feel a hundred and fifty years old."

"Carter, then," she said, with the beginning of a smile.

"And you are going to twist my arm again, aren't you?"

"That hard-shell suit of yours is awfully old."

"It works fine. No complaints."

"But the nanofabric suits are so much easier to work in."

He picked up his spoon, hesitated, then put it down on the table again with a tiny clink.

"Everybody else uses the nanosuits," she said earnestly.

"I'm sorry. I just don't trust them."

"But—"

"That doesn't mean I don't trust you, Doreen. I just feel safer inside an old, reliable hard-shell suit."

She looked at him with her big puppy eyes for a long, silent moment. Carleton realized her eyes were an exotic grayish green color. It reminded him of a jewelry stone. What was it called? Tourmaline, he remembered. With an effort, he looked down and started spooning up his cereal.

"Would you mind if I went with you this morning?" she asked.

"In a nanosuit?"

"Yes, that's what I'd be wearing."

He grinned at her. "Trying to shame the old man?"

"You're not old."

"Old enough," he said, with a practiced sigh.

"Would it be all right?"

"To come out this morning? Sure. The work's pretty boring, though. Except for the explosions."

"I don't mind."

"Okay, then."

"Doreen, good morning!" Carleton looked up to see a dark-haired, thickset younger man approaching them. With a glance at Carleton, he plunked his tray on the table as he asked, "All right to sit here, Dr. Carleton?"

Kalman Torok, Carleton saw: one of the biologists. There

were only two hundred and some people at Tithonium Base and Carleton—with his long years of memorizing students' names—knew most of them on a first-name basis. Name tags helped, of course.

Behind him came an older woman whom Carleton recognized as Nari Quintana, the base's chief medical officer, a diminutive, spare older woman with a bony, hard-edged face and mousy dull brown hair. She sat down without asking permission and began unloading her tray onto the table.

As he picked up his steaming mug of coffee Torok asked gloomily, "Have you heard the latest? They say they're going to shut us down and ship us back to Earth." He spoke in British English with a decided Middle European accent.

"Who says that?" Carleton snapped.

Torok raised his heavy black brows. "It's the buzz. Everybody's talking about it."

He talks with his eyebrows, Carleton said to himself. They're more expressive than his whiny voice.

"I don't believe it," said Doreen. "They're closing the base over in Hellas, but not here."

"Here," said Torok, as if he had superior knowledge.

"They can't shut us down," Carleton said. "That would be stupid."

"Criminal," Quintana agreed. "I'd have to return to Caracas."

"Not to CalTech?" Doreen asked. "I thought you were on the medical staff there."

She shook her head sadly. "I gave up my position at CalTech to come to Mars."

"And what happens to your work?" Carleton asked Torok.

The biologist sighed. "It would be the end of my experiment on growing plants in the indigenous soil. I would write a paper on it when I got back to Budapest, I suppose."

"Couldn't you bring soil samples back to Budapest?" Doreen asked.

"What good would that do?" Torok countered, those thick

dark brows knitting. "I'd have to start all over again and the university would never pay to build a simulation chamber large enough to be useful."

He fell into a morose silence. Quintana picked listlessly at her plate of eggs and soymeat bacon while Torok took a sip from his mug.

"God, what I'd give for a decent cup of coffee," the Hungarian groused, thumping the mug onto the tabletop. "Instead of this crap."

"It has to be decaffeinated," Quintana replied sharply. "Caffeine denatures vitamin C. You know that."

"Yes, I know. Still—"

"Do you want to come down with scurvy, like they did on the First Expedition? You're on Mars! Keep that in the front of your mind every day, every minute."

Torok started to glare at the harsh-tongued physician, but shrugged instead and muttered, "I won't be on Mars for much longer. Neither will you."

Trying to make it sound bright, Doreen said, "Well, if we're sent home you'll be back with your wife and kids again, Kal."

Torok's face grew even more somber. "She prefers to have me here."

"Oh?"

Carleton asked, "What about you, Doreen?"

"If we have to leave I'll go back to Selene and work in the nanolab."

"On the Moon?"

"You can't do nanotech work anywhere on Earth," she replied. "Not legally."

"And you, Professor?" Torok asked. "Where will you go?"

Carleton still winced inwardly when anyone addressed him by the title that had been stripped from him.

"I'm staying right here," he said firmly. "And so are all of you. They can't shut us down. Waterman won't let that happen."

SAN SIMEON, CALIFORNIA: BOARD OF EDUCATION

■

"Meeting will come to order," said chairperson Lisa Good-fellow. The four other men and women sitting around the oval table stopped their conversations and turned their attention to the chairperson.

Seated at the opposite end of the table from the chairperson was Oliver Maxwell. While the board members were dressed in California casual clothes—open-neck shirts and relaxed, comfortable jeans—Maxwell wore a sky blue sports jacket over his shirt and tie.

"In deference to Mr. Maxwell, who has a plane to catch, I propose we consider his item on the agenda before anything else. Any objections?"

No one said a word. The chairperson smiled at Maxwell. "The floor is all yours, sir."

Maxwell remained in his chair, smiling back at the board members. He was a stocky man in his late forties, with crinkles around his deep-set eyes.

"This won't take long. I represent the Mars Foundation, as most of you already know. The Foundation wants to make its package of learning materials available to the schools of your district." Almost as an afterthought, he added, "For free, of course."

"A package of learning materials?" asked one of the board members.

"About Mars. About the exploration work going on there,"

Maxwell said. "The life forms that they've found. The cliff dwellings. The ancient volcanoes. The kids'll love it."

"About Mars," said the chairperson, almost in a whisper.

"Videos, texts, pictures . . . the kids'll love it," Maxwell repeated.

One of the two male board members, tanned and sun-blond as a beachcomber, knit his brows. "This is science stuff, isn't it?"

Nodding, Maxwell replied, "The exploration's being done by scientists, yes. But it's exciting. It's an adventure in discovery!"

The beachcomber shook his head. Turning to the chairperson, he complained, "Look, they tried to ram Darwin down our throats years ago. These scientists are always trying to sneak their ideas into the school curriculum. It's our duty to protect our children from their secularist propaganda."

"But it's not propaganda!" Maxwell cried, sounding genuinely hurt. "It's real. They're actually searching for the remains of a village that intelligent Martians lived in millions of years ago!"

"Yeah. And I'm descended from a monkey."

"There's no proof that intelligent people lived on Mars," said the woman across the table. "It's all unproven theories."

"But—"

The chairperson smiled sweetly at Maxwell once more. "We thank you for the Foundation's very generous offer. The board will take it under consideration."

"But—"

"I know you have a plane to catch. We'll get in touch with you once we've come to a decision."

Reluctantly Maxwell got to his feet and shuffled out of the meeting room. He knew what the board's decision would be. And he didn't look forward to the next stop on his itinerary: Salt Lake City.

ALBUQUERQUE: DURAN CONDOMINIUMS

∎

Jamie Waterman awoke slowly from his dream about the Martian village. For long moments he lay unstirring in his bed, looking up at the soft eggshell white of the ceiling, his eyes focused on the past.

Al's been dead more than twenty years, he said to himself, and still I dream about him.

Turning his head, he saw his wife sleeping beside him. Vijay's beautiful dark face looked relaxed, untroubled. Jamie wished he could feel that way.

I was there when Al died, when the Sky Dancers took him away, Jamie remembered. Not like when Jimmy died. Vijay was alone then. I was a hundred million kilometers away. She had to deal with our son's death by herself.

Slowly he blinked away the memory of his dream, the memories of the dead, and slipped quietly out of bed. Vijay stirred slightly but didn't wake up, her long dark hair tousled, her lustrous eyes softly closed. I'll never leave you again, Jamie promised silently. Not for anything.

He padded to the bathroom and shut the door as quietly as he could.

Another day, Jamie thought as he looked into the shaving mirror. Just like yesterday and the day before. Just like tomorrow will be. Going through the motions. The excitement's gone. Now we're just trying to hold on, trying to keep them from shutting us down.

Why bother? he asked himself. Why not let the bastards

close down the program and bring everybody home? Why fight the inevitable?

His unhappy face stared back at him: broad cheeks, coppery skin, dark brooding eyes. Strands of gray flecked his close-cropped jet black hair. His mouth turned downward unhappily. He saw his father's Navaho face; his mother's golden hair and pink skin were inside him, didn't show.

Jamie showered, then shaved even though he felt he didn't really need to. When he slowly opened the door to the bedroom, Vijay hadn't stirred in their bed.

If the shower and the shaver didn't wake her she must be really out. Good, he thought. She deserves her rest. Putting up with me isn't easy.

He dressed as quietly as he could in his newest jeans and a crisply starched white shirt. Rummaging carefully through his dresser drawer, he pulled out his best bolo, the silver and onyx one that he usually reserved for formal receptions at the university. Softly, softly he filled his pockets with change and keys and facial tissues. And the bear fetish with the wispy white eagle's feather that Al had lovingly tied to it just before Jamie left for Mars the first time.

The feather's looking pretty shoddy, he thought. Worn down by the years. Just like me.

Vijay slept on. Sleep is the best healer, Jamie said to himself. She says she's okay; she smiles and acts normal and pretends she's over it. For me. She puts on the good face for my sake. But Jimmy's death still haunts us. We should've done what real Navahos do: we should've left this condo and moved someplace else, someplace far away from all these memories.

With his boots in one hand he tiptoed to the edge of the bed. So beautiful, he thought as he gazed down at her. It shouldn't have happened to her like this. She deserves better.

Help her find her path through this, he prayed silently to gods he didn't really believe in. With a grimace he added, And while you're at it, I could use some help myself.

TITHONIUM CHASMA: THE RIFT VALLEY

■

It's hard to think of this as a valley," said Doreen.

Carleton heard her in the earphones built into his suit's glassteel helmet. "A rift valley," he said.

She made a little frown. "I've had some geology classes, Professor."

"Please call me Carter."

"Sure."

Her nanosuit was transparent. It looked to Carleton as if she were wearing nothing over her coveralls more than a plastic rain suit with an inflated bubble over her head. Even the life support pack on her back looked too small to do its job, flimsy. Yet she was standing out on the surface of Mars in the morning sunlight, snug and apparently perfectly safe.

Carleton felt like a shambling Neanderthal beside her. His spacesuit was a heavy, cumbersome shell of cermet with flexible joints at the elbows, knees and waist. Semiflexible, he corrected himself. I'll know what arthritis feels like when it hits me, trying to move around in this outfit. He pictured himself like Falstaff, clanking unwillingly into battle inside his heavy suit of armor.

Doreen had volunteered to help him lug his equipment out to the digging site, so he had allowed her to carry the spades and tongs and brushes while he pushed the cart that was loaded with the explosives and detonators.

She's right, he thought as he looked past her at the cliffs looming over them. It doesn't look like a valley. The cliffs on

Carleton's left were more than three kilometers high. The valley was so wide that he couldn't see its other wall: it was over the horizon.

They call Mars the red planet, he mused as they trudged along to the site. Yes, most of its surface is rust red dust. Iron oxides. A red desert, from pole to pole. But look at that cliff face: bands of ochre and pale yellow and light brown along with the iron red. You can't stand here for ten minutes without wanting to be a geologist.

Several klicks along the cliff face was the sloping ramp of dirt and rocks that Jamie Waterman had used for the first transit down to the floor of Tithonium, back during the First Expedition, more than twenty years ago. The original Mars base had been up on the plateau in those early days. But it was down here on the valley floor that the Martian lichen had been discovered, struggling to stay alive through frigid nights and dust storms that smothered everything in their path.

And in that notch high up in the cliff wall Waterman had found the ruins of buildings: brick structures erected by intelligent Martians more than sixty million years ago. Intelligent Martians who were wiped out by an extinction-level meteor strike, just as the dinosaurs on Earth had been driven into extinction by a killer meteor impact.

There were three buckyball cables running along the cliff face now, to carry people and equipment from the base on the valley floor to Waterman's village up in the cleft in the rocks. Only, it wasn't a village. Carleton was convinced of that. Some sort of shrine, more likely. Or a fortress. The village was down here, on the valley floor. Had to be. If only I could find it, he thought. If the damned lichen are smart enough to live down here, where it's warmer and there's some moisture from the frost that forms overnight, then the Martians must've been smart enough to do the same.

Except that he hadn't found any village. Not yet, he told himself. It's here, you just haven't gone deep enough yet.

"Is that the site?" Doreen asked, pointing with a spade toward the edge of the pit a few dozen meters ahead.

"That's it," Carleton said.

"And you think there's a village buried here?" Doreen put down the spade and the bag of brushes.

They stopped at the edge of the pit. It was fifty meters across and about twenty meters deep, almost square in shape. Its bottom looked freshly swept, cleaned of all debris and dust, nothing but bare jagged rock. To one side of where they were standing rested the tables bearing mesh grids for sifting rubble and the hoist that Carleton used to lower himself into the pit.

As he carefully took his packages from the cart and lowered them to the ground in his stiff-jointed suit, Carleton said, "Ground-penetrating radar showed indications of a gridwork about thirty meters below the surface. Nature doesn't produce grids; intelligence does."

"But you haven't found anything," Doreen said, not accusingly, he thought. If anything, she sounded sympathetic.

"Haven't gone deep enough yet. The village is underneath sixty-some million years of compacted dust." If it's here at all, he added silently.

"And you excavate with explosives?"

"Beats digging."

"But doesn't that blow up the fossils you're looking for?"

"I'm not down deep enough for fossils yet. When I find something I'll start digging by hand."

"Sounds weird, blasting away like that."

He chuckled at her. "There's precedent for it. Dart or Broom or one of those paleontologists in South Africa a century or more ago, they used dynamite to excavate fossil sites."

"It still sounds weird," Doreen insisted gently.

"Don't sweat it," he said. "I sift through the rubble after each blast, to see if there's anything in it. So far, nothing. It takes a long time, but digging by hand would be really tedious."

He could see Doreen's face clearly through the nanofabric bubble of her helmet. She looked intrigued, but he thought he saw doubt in her big doe's eyes, as well.

"You're doing this work all by yourself?"

"Nobody's willing to help me. I'm something of a pariah, you know."

"I've heard about that," Doreen said. "Some sort of scandal? You had to resign your professorship at Penn?"

"I was set up. The fundamentalists took control of the board of regents and they didn't like what I had to say about Darwin, so they set me up with a Mata Hari."

"Mata Hari?" Doreen clearly had never heard of her.

"A spy. A seducer. A whore."

She looked at him, and he was glad that all she could see in the reflective gold coating of his helmet visor was a mirror image of herself. Good, he thought, feeling his cheeks burning with unrepressed fury at his memories.

At last she said, "I'll help you."

"Help me?"

"With your work here. I've got nothing much else to do. The nanosuits work fine and they don't need any maintenance to speak of. I'll help you dig."

He was surprised at her offer, but he heard himself reply immediately, "No. You'll just make difficulties for yourself."

"They can't make trouble for me," she said. "I don't live on Earth, remember? I'm a citizen of Selene. I'm free."

■

The paperless office is still nothing more than a distant day-dream, Jamie said to himself. No matter how hard he tried to keep his office neat and tidy, the clutter always crept in to drown him. His office was no bigger than any of the others along the corridor of the Planetary Sciences Department building. Its door bore a modest sign:

J. WATERMAN
SCIENTIFIC DIRECTOR
MARS PROGRAM

Inside, the office had space only for a regular university-issue desk of genetically engineered faux maple, littered with papers, a bookcase stuffed with reports and folders, and a single plastic chair for visitors. The room had a window that looked out at the elevated interstate highway that ran through the heart of Albuquerque. This early in the morning, the rush-hour traffic was just beginning to build up.

Jamie had come in early to try to get some work done before his conference call was scheduled. He squeezed around his desk and slid into the swivel chair, booted up his desktop computer. He shook his head at the litter that threatened to engulf him. Got to clean this place up, he thought as the computer ran through its self-check and then announced with a sharp beep that it was ready for work.

Scanning the morning's schedule, he saw that he had more

than two hours before the conference call would come through. He started to review the latest reports from the teams on Mars.

It's been nearly two years, he realized. Two years since I left Mars. Two years since Jimmy died. Skydiving. Of all the stupid things a teenager could do, he had to get his kicks by jumping out of an airplane. Why? Because his father had, years before. But I did it because I had to: it was part of my training for the Mars mission. I didn't do it for fun. The Russians wouldn't okay me for the mission if I didn't jump. I wasn't there to guide Jimmy, to make him understand, to protect him. I wasn't there for my son. Or for Vijay.

I know it's hit her hard. She tries to put a good face on it, pretends she's gotten over it. For my sake. She doesn't want me to see how she's hurting. But I know the pain is there. I feel it. Mothers get sick when their sons die. They wither away. They get cancer.

He shook his head, trying to clear away the past. Focus on today, he told himself. This morning.

The exploration of Mars was proceeding slowly. Not like those breathtaking heady weeks when they had first landed, when every day seemed to bring an exciting new discovery. Now the exploration went more slowly. That's the way science works, Jamie told himself. You break through into a new area, new ideas, and it's mind-blowing. But then you get bogged down digging out the details, searching for the clues, building up the evidence.

It takes time, exploring a whole world.

The original Mars base had been at the edge of the Tharsis highlands, but once they discovered the lichen clinging precariously to life at the floor of Tithonium Chasma, and Jamie discovered the ancient ruins notched into a cleft in the cliffs there, they moved the base to the canyon floor and enlarged it. A smaller base had been established almost halfway across the planet in the enormous impact crater called the Hellas Basin, but Jamie knew that they couldn't afford to keep it going.

Nearly three hundred men and women were working on Mars, resupplied regularly by flights from Earth and the lunar nation of Selene. That's about a hundred more than we can maintain on our current funding, he admitted silently.

Yet we don't know much more about the Martians than we did twenty years ago, Jamie grumbled to himself, when I first glimpsed the remains of their cliff dwellings. Just that they're gone, wiped out in the same cataclysm that killed off the dinosaurs here on Earth sixty-five million years ago.

An intelligent species, destroyed by the impersonal, implacable crash of a meteor big enough to blow away Mars's atmosphere and wipe out all life more complex than those hardy little lichen.

They never knew what hit them, Jamie thought. Then he corrected himself. They knew. They realized that death had come screaming out of the sky. They were intelligent enough to understand. But they didn't have the level of technology to do anything about it. All they could do was die.

"Christ," he muttered, "I'm getting morose in my old age. Death and dying is all I think about anymore."

At least we've got those big telescopes watching for asteroids heading toward Earth. We can spot them years in advance. We can send rockets out to them, divert them away from a collision course. We won't be wiped out the same way the dinosaurs were. The way the Martians were.

With a shake of his head he turned his attention to the morning's reports. There was a lengthy analysis of the lichen that lived in the rocks strewn along the valley floor. Jamie scanned the abstract, frowning, then studied the graphs that summarized the authors' findings. The lichen are dying off, he saw. Slowly, slowly, but there's less and less water vapor in the atmosphere, less water to keep them alive.

Mars is dying. The whole planet is dying. Jamie leaned back in his chair and rubbed his aching eyes. Who isn't dying? he asked himself.

His phone buzzed. Startled, Jamie glanced at his desktop

clock and saw that more than two hours had passed since he'd arrived at his office. I've just pissed away two hours, he scolded himself.

The phone buzzed again.

Thoroughly disgusted with the news about the lichen and his own failing, Jamie tapped the phone's keypad. The face of the president of the Navaho Nation appeared on the flat screen mounted on the wall to his right. She was older than Jamie, her hair dead white, pulled back off her face and tied into a long queue that draped over her shoulder. She was wearing a plain blouse of light tan, with turquoise and coral beads sewn along the edge of the collar. Her face was wrinkled, as weathered as the mesas of the Navaho land where she lived, but her dark eyes sparkled with warmth and lively intellect. She had the same broad cheekbones and stocky build as Jamie.

He glanced again at the digital clock and grinned, despite himself. She's right on time. Unusual for a Navaho.

"Ya'aa'tey," Jamie said, dipping his chin slightly.

"Ya'aa'tey," she replied. It is good.

"Our friend in Boston is late."

The president smiled. "He must be learning Navaho ways." They both laughed.

"Everything goes well for you?" Jamie asked.

"Almost everything."

"Almost?"

With a shrug, she replied, "The Anglos are trying to buy more of the reservation's land. They say they need it for the people who were driven from their homes by the big floods. If we don't sell they say they'll go to court and take the land anyway."

"Refugees." Jamie knew that the greenhouse warming that had flooded coastal cities and driven out millions of now-homeless refugees was also bringing rains to the lands of the Navaho people, turning stark brown desert into inviting green pastures. White politicians and real estate developers coveted those newly green acres. The pressure to open the reservation to settlement by the refugees was growing every day, every hour.

"There's plenty of open land in other places," the president said, "but they're putting a lot of pressure on—"

The phone buzzed once more, interrupting her. Jamie touched the keypad and his wall screen split into two images. The new one showed C. Dexter Trumball, in his office high up in one of Boston's financial district towers.

"Morning," Dex said curtly.

Each time Jamie saw Dex he was struck all over again by how much the former geologist had grown to resemble his late father. Dex Trumball still had all his hair, but his handsome face had thinned over the years since he and Jamie had worked together on the Second Mars Expedition. And those blue green eyes of his seemed sharper, more penetrating, as if he knew things that no one else knew. His father's eyes, scheming and demanding.

"How's the weather in Boston?" Jamie could see a briskly clear blue sky through the window at Dex's back.

"You haven't seen the news?" Dex asked. "This morning's news from Washington?"

"No," said Jamie.

"The president's zeroed out the Mars program."

Jamie felt it like a sharp blow to his heart. "She zeroed out . . . ?"

"What does that mean?" asked the Navaho president.

"It means the U.S. government will stop funding us when the new fiscal year starts."

"She can't do that!" Jamie protested.

"She's done it."

"Congress won't let her get away with it," he insisted, but he knew he was clutching at straws.

Dex's expression was halfway between a sneer and a scowl of disgust.

The Navaho president said, "Other nations help to fund the program, too. Maybe—"

"America puts in the lion's share," Dex said. "Once Washington pulls out the others will do the same."

"But—"

"We're sunk," Dex growled. "Screwed. Dead in the water."

Not while I breathe, Jamie said to himself. Not while there's a beat left in my heart.

TITHONIUM CHASMA: THE DIG

■

Carleton would not allow Doreen to handle the explosives. Not that they were actually dangerous, but he would not take any chances. She might be just what she says she is, he told himself, a nanotech engineer with nothing better to do while she's here on Mars. But she *might* be another plant by those psalm-singing sonsofbitches, he fumed inwardly as he planted the strips of plastique in a careful pattern across the bottom of his excavation. Who knows? She might be one of those fanatics who'd be willing to blow herself up just to destroy me. Like the old suicide bombers back in the Middle East, years ago.

Still, he was glad of her company. He talked to her as he put down the strips of plastic explosive, absently chatting away as if they were strolling along a campus path back on Earth.

"Everything we know in biology supports Darwin's concept of evolution through natural selection," he was saying. "Hell, biologists have even watched populations of fishes splitting into separate species, in lakes in Africa."

"But so many people are against Darwin," Doreen said, more to keep him talking than out of conviction, he thought. She was sitting up on the lip of the pit, her nanosuited legs dangling into the excavation.

"Know-nothing fundamentalists," he grumbled as he worked. It was impossible to bend far enough inside the hard-shell suit to lay down the doughy strips. Carleton had to get down on his knees. As he worked he crawled along the rough base of the pit like an oversized infant encased inside a robot.

"I think they see Darwin as a challenge to their beliefs," Doreen said.

"I think they don't think at all," he groused. "They just follow orders from their know-nothing ministers."

"Now be fair," Doreen countered. "If Darwin's right and we humans are just another kind of animal, it destroys their belief that we're special, that we were created by God separate and apart from all the animals."

"Yeah, and given dominion over the Earth so we can slaughter all the other animals and chop down all the trees and just generally screw up the environment."

"It destroys their belief that God sent his only son to redeem our souls," Doreen said firmly. "It hits them where it hurts the most."

"You don't understand," he said. "It's not about religion. It's about politics. It's about power. Their leaders use religion to keep their followers in line. When you're told you're doing God's work you're willing to do just about anything they tell you to."

"But they really believe their religion."

"Of course they do. That's what makes them so ruthless. They think they're on God's side."

"Doesn't everybody?"

He looked up at her, from his kneeling position. "Is that what you believe?"

"It's what they believe, Professor."

"And you? What about you?"

She hesitated a long moment before answering, "I'm not certain of what I believe. I know that I don't have all the answers, that's for sure."

"But you're a Christian."

"A Quaker."

Surprised, he blurted, "A Quaker?"

"Society of Friends," Doreen said.

"I never met a Quaker before," Carleton admitted.

"There aren't that many of us. We've only got four regulars at Selene."

A Quaker, Carleton mused silently. William Penn was a Quaker. Philadelphia was founded by the Quakers. The University of Pennsylvania, too, if I remember right. But the university isn't run by Quakers anymore. Hasn't been for a long time.

He felt the old anger simmering inside him again. Squatting on the floor of the excavation, he craned his neck to see Doreen up on the lip of the pit. A Quaker. Could a Quaker be a Mata Hari? he asked himself. Not very likely, he answered. Or are you just thinking with your testicles again?

Finally he finished laying out the explosive strips and planting the thumb-sized detonators in them. Carleton laboriously slipped the climbing rig's harness over the shoulders of his hard suit, then pressed the button on it that activated the winch. Through the thin Martian air the winch's motor sounded like the faint whine of a mosquito.

Once he reached the lip of the excavation Doreen came over to help him out of the harness. Then he took her gloved hand and led her fifty paces from the rim of the pit.

"You're going to set it off?" she asked.

"Got to call control, back at the base," he said, pecking at the suit radio's keypad on his left wrist. "The geologists want to know when I blast, so they don't get their seismometer records screwed up."

She watched him as he called the base and told the excursion director he was ready to fire the explosives.

"Hold on while I check with the rock jocks," the controller's cheerful young voice came through his helmet earphones.

Doreen started to ask, "Do they ever stop you from—"

"Dr. Carleton? You're cleared to detonate at 11:15 precisely. It's now 11:06:33."

"Eleven-oh-six-thirty-three," Carleton repeated, his eyes on the digital clock set into the wrist pad. "Check. I'll blow at 11:15, on the tick."

The explosion, when it came, disappointed Doreen. It wasn't a ground-shaking blast: just a little *whump* followed by a cloud of dust that slowly wafted away from the pit.

She walked beside Carleton to the edge of the excavation. Its floor was covered now with broken, shattered bits of rock.

"Now we start the day's real work," he said to her.

IT TOOK HOURS TO spade up the rubble, pack it into containers, and hoist it up to the surface. Carleton was impressed with Doreen's willingness to work. And the fact that she could move so much more easily in her nanosuit than he could in his unwieldy hard shell. The strangely small sun climbed higher in the saffron sky. Temperature's getting up to twenty below, Carleton surmised as they hauled rock shards to the sifter.

He felt perspiration trickling along his ribs and saw Doreen absently try to wipe her brow, only to bump her gloved hand against the spongy bubble of her inflated helmet.

"You should've worn a head band," he told her. "Keeps the sweat out of your eyes."

Blinking hard, she said, "I didn't think I'd be sweating when it's so cold."

"The suits keep your body heat in."

"Now you tell me."

The sifter rattled away. Carleton stopped it to study the contents of the tray beneath it, running his gloved fingers through the dust, finding nothing more than grains of rusty sand. Then he and Doreen poured still another load of shattered rock and started the machine rattling again. Even in the gentle gravity of Mars his arms were starting to ache.

"So much of science is manual labor," he said as they strained to lift another carton of rubble onto the sifter's grid. "Just plain donkey work. Hours of it. Years of it. All for the chance of making a discovery."

"It's a lot easier in the nanolab back at Selene," Doreen

said, puffing slightly from exertion. "Nanomachines are teensy little things."

He laughed. "And the Moon's gravity is even lighter than Mars's."

"We should be using nanomachines here," she said.

"Here? For what?"

"They could build bigger domes for us, pull out atoms of iron and other metals from the ground and build really strong domes, big as you want."

Carleton felt impressed. "You could do that?"

"Sure," she replied, her voice eager. "Back at Selene they build spacecraft out of carbon soot. Nanomachines turn the carbon into pure diamond, stronger and lighter than steel."

"So you think we could build a bigger, safer base with nanobugs."

She nodded brightly inside her helmet. She's really good-looking, he thought. Not much of a figure but her face is pretty, with those big soulful gray-green eyes. Carleton smoothed the rubble over the grid and reached for the switch that would start the sifter working again.

"That's a funny-looking piece of rock," Doreen said, pointing to one of the shards on the grid.

Carleton grunted and picked up the odd-shaped rock in his gloved hand. It rested in his palm easily. He held it for a moment, then turned it over and brought it up almost touching his visor so he could look at it more closely.

He goggled at it. He actually felt his eyes bugging out, felt the breath gush out of him.

"Dr. Carleton?" Doreen said. "Carter? Are you okay?"

It took several tries before he could say, "It's a funny-looking piece of rock, all right. It's a vertebra! I'll eat camel dung if it's not a goddamned mother-loving vertebra!"

ALBUQUERQUE: UNIVERSITY OF NEW MEXICO

■

Let's put this in perspective," Jamie said to Dex and the Navaho president. "It doesn't have to mean the end of everything."

"The hell it doesn't," Dex muttered.

"Most of our funding comes from the Foundation," said the Navaho president. "The government's contribution is important, I know, but we get most of our money from private donors, don't we?"

Dex answered, "Private contributions have been tailing off. It's harder and harder to get major donations; the big money people have been backing away from us, and now, with the goddamned feds pulling out of the program, it'll be tougher than ever to get them to come through."

The president said, "I know we're not supposed to make a profit out of Mars, but my Council people have been making noises."

"Noises?" Jamie asked.

"You know, questions. They're wondering why we can't get something out of the program."

Dex started to say, "You're running the world's biggest conservation effort, and—"

"The biggest in two worlds," the president corrected, with a sly smile.

"Three," Dex immediately countered. "Don't leave out the Moon."

Jamie listened to them arguing mildly back and forth,

remembering how Dex had originally come to Mars on the Second Expedition, bubbling with plans to make a tourist center of the red planet. Ostensibly a geologist, C. Dexter Trumball had insisted that if private donors such as his father were expected to finance the exploration of Mars they had to be allowed to make a profit out of it. He had his father's vision of using Mars to make money. But once he saw the ancient cliff dwellings, once he realized that this seemingly barren planet had sustained intelligent life, Dex defied his father and helped Jamie turn legal stewardship of Mars to the Navaho nation.

A friendship had grown between the two men, a friendship that held strong even after Dex returned to Earth to face his furious father.

It was a supreme irony, granting control of the red planet to the red-skinned Navaho, who regarded the guardianship of Mars as a sacred trust and would allow only scientific exploration. The news media trumpeted the story while financial backers such as Darryl C. Trumball howled about betrayal and turned to their lawyers. The International Astronautical Authority upheld the Navaho claim, and so did the World Court—as long as at least one member of the Navaho nation actually lived on Mars. International law prohibited any nation or corporate entity from claiming ownership of a planet or even a pebble-sized asteroid, but anyone could claim exclusive *use* of a body in space if they were actually working on that body.

So the Navaho nation controlled Mars as long as one Navaho lived and worked on the planet. The scheme had succeeded for nearly twenty years. Mars was being explored by international teams of scientists. Tourism was limited to virtual reality simulations, where paying customers could experience a visit to Mars without leaving their living rooms on Earth, without disturbing the frigid desert sands of the red planet.

With a conscious effort, Jamie returned his attention to the meeting and the problems of the day.

"The VR tours are bringing in a steady income," the

Navaho president was saying, "especially when we open up a new territory to walk through."

"So what's the problem?" Jamie asked.

"The Council's hoping for more income," she replied, her normally stolid face frowning slightly. "Maybe a bigger percentage of the gross."

"Christ, you're already getting everything above our operating costs," Dex Trumball snapped.

"Your operating costs include a pretty fat fee," said the president.

"My Foundation people can't work for free!"

The president sighed. "It's just like the casinos: you're making more money out of the VR tours than we are."

"But you're not doing anything," Dex insisted. "You don't have any costs at all. It's all pure profit for you."

Jamie jumped in before the president could reply. "Dex, listen: no matter how much money the VR tours bring in, the Diné will always need more."

"And my Foundation's supposed to be an endless source of bucks?"

"We have a lot of legal fees coming up," the president pointed out. "Washington is making claims on reservation land. Squatters are moving in on us."

Dex's youthful face broke into a wicked grin. "We could offer the refugees land on Mars. Like the old Homestead Act, let 'em settle—"

"No!" Jamie shouted.

Laughing, Dex replied, "I was wondering how long it'd take you to yell."

"You're not serious," the Navaho president said.

"Not really," Dex admitted. Then his expression turned crafty. "Although I bet we could build big domes, pump air into them, bake the oxides out of the soil and start growing crops."

Scowling, Jamie said, "Don't even joke about that, Dex."

But Dex went on, "With the new fusion torch ships the transportation costs wouldn't be so bad, I bet."

"Dex—"

"Y'know, it's just crazy enough for some politicians in Washington to go for it. Send the refugees to Mars! A trillion-dollar boondoggle."

"It's not funny," Jamie insisted.

"Yeah," Dex admitted. "I guess not. Wouldn't work anyway. Even with the fusion rockets it's too damned expensive to ship millions of people off-planet."

"So can we get a better break on the revenue income?" the president asked, returning to her point.

"I don't see how," Dex replied immediately. "Besides, we've got a bigger problem now."

"Bigger?" asked Jamie.

"With Washington backing out of the program, the Foundation's going to have to carry the funding load pretty much alone."

"But there's the Europeans, the Chinese—"

"And the Russians, I know. They'll all back away, you wait and see. Besides, what they're putting into the pot now isn't enough to take up the slack."

"So it's up to the Foundation," Jamie said.

"Yeah, but the donations are getting harder to come by. The big money's going into reconstruction, restoring the electric power grid, new housing for the refugees. Everybody and his brother has their hands out. It's endless."

"And Mars is a luxury," the Navaho president murmured.

"Worse than that," said Dex. "The religious nuts want to close us down. They don't want us finding anything else about the Martians. They don't even want to think that there was another intelligent race on Mars."

"The New Morality?"

"And the Holy Disciples in Europe and all the rest of them. They don't like us finding anything that conflicts with their twelfth-century view of the world. They want to forget about Mars. They want everybody else to forget about Mars, as well."

Jamie sank back in his desk chair. "So they're putting pressure on you."

"Not just me. On our donors, our backers. Spend your money here on Earth, they say. Help your fellow human beings instead of poking around on Mars."

"That's a strong argument," said the Navaho president.

Searching for a ray of hope, Jamie said, "But the universities want to continue the exploration."

"The universities are under pressure, too," said Dex, with a shake of his head. "And now that the White House has skunked us, it's going to be tougher than ever to raise new funds."

INTERVIEW

∎

So how can you possibly keep your team on Mars now that the government has canceled its funding for the program?"

Jamie stared at the interviewer. He had spent most of the day answering questions from reporters. He had appeared on four different network news shows, skipping lunch to sit before their cameras and answer the same questions over and over again.

Normally Jamie enjoyed interviews. He got a kick out of the cut-and-thrust, where the interviewer was trying to dig out something sensational and he was doing his best to get across the points he wanted to make despite the interviewer's loaded questions. But now, after this long day of interrogation, Jamie felt tired and irritable.

They're ready to bury us, he realized. Half of them don't even know that most of our funding comes from private sources, and has for nearly twenty years. Washington pulls out and they think we're dead.

This interview in the studio of a local Albuquerque affiliate of a major network was being aired live across the nation. Jamie had postponed his dinner to appear in the studio. He had phoned Vijay at home twice to tell her he'd be late and twice gotten the answering machine's bland response. Has she heard the news? he wondered.

His interviewer of the moment was in Los Angeles, speaking with Jamie over a closed video circuit. Rhonda Samuels was a crafty middle-aged woman with a practiced smile and a cobra's eyes. Her ash blond hair was so carefully coiffed that Jamie thought it could have been a helmet. Her beige suit fit her trim figure without the slightest wrinkle. Jamie felt distinctly grungy in the shirt and jeans he'd been in since early morning. He was glad he'd worn the onyx bolo.

How can we keep exploring Mars without money from Washington? Jamie fingered the bear fetish in his pocket as he framed his answer.

He remembered how his grandfather Al would sit in silence for long moments while he was dickering with one of the artisans who produced the jewelry and hand-painted pottery that Al sold in his shop on the Plaza in Santa Fe. Al was never in a hurry when he spoke to his fellow Native Americans. "Take some time, Jamie," he would advise his grandson. "Size up the person you're talkin' to. Get the feel of the situation before you open your mouth."

But this was television, where five seconds is an eternity.

Rhonda Samuels interrupted his silence.

"I mean," she said, her voice low but hard-edged, "without government funding you won't be able to keep the exploration team on Mars, will you?"

"Actually, Ms. Samuels," Jamie said, trying to make it bright despite his inner weariness, "the government was only contributing about a tenth of our total funding. Most of our support comes from private sources."

Her brows shot up. "Private sources?"

"The Mars Foundation, which is based here in New Mexico," Jamie explained. "One of our major backers is the Trumball Trust, in Boston. Then there's—"

"But without the government's contribution, can you afford to keep those men and women on Mars?"

"I think so. We're doing the math. And we're looking for additional donors."

"Additional donors?" she asked.

"People or institutions that want to help us carry on the exploration of Mars."

"But in the meantime, if your budget is strained by Washington's decision, won't that have repercussions for your exploration team?"

"Repercussions?"

"On their safety," Rhonda Samuels said. "If you have to cut your budget, won't that affect the safety of the explorers on Mars?"

Jamie forced a strained smile. "Safety is always uppermost in our minds."

"Ahead of everything else?"

"Yes, of course."

"Were you thinking safety first when you were on Mars and you pushed your superiors to allow you to make the first excursion into the Grand Canyon?"

"Nobody died," Jamie said tightly.

"But there certainly were dangers involved."

"There are dangers involved in all exploration. You learn to deal with them. We have an excellent safety record."

"But what if someone was seriously injured, or came down with an illness you're not equipped to deal with on Mars. What would happen, with the nearest hospital a hundred million miles away?"

Jamie smiled gently. "We'd send a fusion torch ship to take the patient back to Earth. It's not like the old days, when it took months to travel to Mars. Fusion torch ships can make the trip in less than a week."

Sharply, she asked, "Why aren't you on Mars, then?"

Jamie cursed himself for not expecting that one. He lifted his chin a notch and replied, "Personal reasons. Family reasons."

"Your son's death."

Nodding, he said, "He died on Earth, not Mars."

Shifting slightly in her chair, Samuels asked, "How old are the members of the exploration team? What's their average age?"

She must think I keep all the personnel files in my head, Jamie said to himself. Aloud, he replied "Mostly pretty young.

Postdocs in their late twenties, thirties, for the most part. I guess the oldest person on the team right now is Carter Carleton."

Her eyes widened. "Carter Carleton? The maverick anthropologist? He's on Mars?"

"He has been for nearly a year," Jamie said. "And he's no more of a maverick than you are."

Samuels hesitated for the barest fraction of a second, then turned to face straight into the camera. "We'll be back in a moment. But first this."

The overhead lights dimmed slightly and the muted monitor screen suddenly showed a housewife staring into a sink full of dirty dishes.

From the larger flat panel that linked to Los Angeles Rhonda Samuels said to Jamie, "You're doing fine." A younger woman rushed to her side with a brush in one hand and a spray can in the other.

"I just want you to understand," Jamie replied slowly, "that we'll never knowingly endanger our people on Mars."

She nodded while her assistant fussed with her perfect hair. Jamie thought of Edie Elgin, the TV newswoman he'd lived with when he was in Houston training for the First Expedition. Beautiful, bright, gutsy Edith. She was married now and living in Selene, the underground city on the Moon. Married to Douglas Stavenger, no less, Selene's founder and de facto leader.

"One thing, though, Dr. Waterman. Call me Rhonda. Not Ms. Samuels. Got it?"

"Got it," Jamie said, nodding.

"In one!" called the floor director, a hand on the intercom plug tucked into his ear.

Jamie sat up a little straighter and tried to clear his mind as the hairdresser scampered out of view.

The floor director pointed at Jamie and the interviewer turned on her brittle smile again. "Dr. Waterman, let me ask you a different question."

"Fine, Rhonda," said Jamie.

"What are we getting out of the exploration of Mars? What have you discovered that's worth the billions of dollars that have been spent on your program?"

Jamie felt his cheeks flare with sudden anger and hoped the cameras didn't pick it up. Forcing himself to take a calming breath before speaking, he answered, "That's sort of like asking how high is up."

"What have you found?" Samuels insisted. "After all, you've spent billions—"

"Life," Jamie said sharply. "We've found the most important thing that's ever been discovered, Rhonda. We've found that ours is not the only world on which life exists. More than that, we've found *intelligent* life. Intelligence arose on Mars, just as it has on Earth."

"But it's gone extinct."

"That's not the important point," Jamie said. "The important point is that intelligence is not rare in the universe. We've explored two planets—Earth and Mars—and found intelligence on both of them. Two for two. There's probably all sorts of intelligent species on other worlds."

"Really?" Rhonda Samuels's carefully painted face looked almost fearful.

"Really," said Jamie.

She hesitated, cocked her head slightly to one side. Getting instructions through her earplug from her director, Jamie guessed.

At last she said, "Dr. Waterman, you've made the point that you would never knowingly endanger the men and women now on Mars."

"That's right."

"But how can you be sure of that? Aren't they in danger every day they're on Mars, every moment?"

Jamie rocked back slightly. "I don't think they're in such terrible danger."

"You don't? Aren't you being naïve about that? After all, they can't breathe the air, can't walk in the open without wearing spacesuits. Do you have adequate medical facilities on Mars? Can you evacuate someone if a medical emergency comes up?"

"We've never had that kind of a problem."

"The people have a right to know just how much danger your team on Mars is in."

"We know how to deal with the conditions on Mars. We do it every day."

"Every day," Samuels repeated, as if it was an accusation.

Then she turned from Jamie to look squarely into the camera again. "I think we owe it to the courage of those fine men and women struggling to survive on Mars to bring them home, now that the budget for exploring Mars has been cut to a dangerously low level."

Jamie sat there with his mouth hanging open while the floor director shouted, "Okay! We're out!"

ALBUQUERQUE: DURAN CONDOMINIUMS

■

It was dark by the time Jamie parked his Nissan hybrid in his assigned space next to Vijay's convertible. It was late summer, monsoon season: his wife hadn't put the top down on her car in weeks.

There were puddles on the parking lot and lightning flickering beyond the Sandia Mountains, flashing against the clouds in the dark brooding sky. That's something we never have to worry about on Mars, Jamie told himself. Hasn't rained there in sixty million years, at least.

When he opened the door to his home Vijay was sitting on the deep leather sofa watching the television news.

"You're a popular bloke today," she said, smiling as she got to her feet. Born of Hindu parents in Melbourne, she had never overcome her Aussie accent.

Jamie kissed her lightly. "The White House's gift to me."

"It's a shame, what they did," Vijay said. "A crime."

"Yeah."

"You look tired."

"I've been on the grill all day, just about."

She picked up the remote from the coffee table and clicked off the TV.

"How about you?" he asked. "How do you feel?"

Her bright smile lit up her dark face. "Fine. Worried about you, though."

"You want to go out for dinner? Roberto's maybe. Or that new sushi place?"

"I don't really feel up to it, Jamie. I'm sure you'd rather kick off your boots and stay home, woul'n't you?"

He shrugged.

"There's hot dogs in the fridge. And I think we still have a few bottles of beer."

Jamie slipped his arms around her waist and pulled her close, her rich voluptuous body pressing against his. "Fine," he said. "Hot dogs and beer. Typical American meal."

She laughed. It was an old joke between them: typical Americans, he a half-Navaho and she a Hindu from Australia.

DEX TRUMBALL WAS NOT laughing. He had flown to New York to discuss a tax audit of the Trumball Trust with the director of the Internal Revenue Service's northeastern regional office. After that grim afternoon he went with his latest trophy wife to sit through a long and boring dinner at the Metropolitan Club in Manhattan, and then endured an even longer and more boring speech by an architect who showed digital images of the new city she was building in the mountains of Colorado. With millions of people driven from their homes by the greenhouse flooding, the federal government was spending hundreds of billions on erecting new cities.

The speech had ended with a plea for donations, of course. The audience was wealthy: most of them were getting even wealthier on government contracts to build housing and roads and all the infrastructure that was needed to shelter the refugees and start them on new lives.

Now Dex sat in the plush quiet bar, nursing a scotch and water, listening to the architect drone on and on. His wife had excused herself and hurried off to their hotel. Thinking of her in bed watching TV as she waited for him, Dex wondered why he was going through the motions of being polite to this bore.

"We've learned quite a lot from the life-support systems they've developed on the Moon," she was saying, emphasizing each word with the clicking tap of a manicured finger on the polished mahogany of the bar. She was rail thin and her voice had an irritating nasal twang to it. "We'll be recycling the water and all the waste systems, turning garbage into electricity."

Dex nodded absently, wondering how he could escape her determined enthusiasm without being boorish about it. The architect was swiveling slightly on the stool to one side of him; on the other was an old friend of his late father's, a dimwitted old coot who thought that anyone under the age of eighty was a flighty kid who needed firm direction from his elders.

"You still involved in this Mars business?" the old man asked. Dex thought that a century ago he would have been a poster boy for communist propaganda about bloated capitalists: the man was bald and corpulent, several chins lapping over the black tie of his tuxedo. His eyes were narrow, squinting, piggish.

Nodding, Dex said, "The Trust funds the Mars Foundation."

"Damn luxury we can't afford anymore," the old man said, his voice grating, harsh. "Cut your losses, Dexter, and turn your attention back here to Earth, where it's needed."

Dex bit back his first impulse to tell the old fart to go to hell. Instead, he replied mildly, "Mr. Younger, you could afford to fund the entire Mars operation out of your own pocket, you know that?"

"What? Me?"

"The team we're supporting on Mars costs a lot less than one of the cities Ms. Battista here wants to build."

"But people *need* my cities!" cried the architect.

"Sure they do," Dex said. "And we need to continue exploring Mars, too."

He wished he believed his own words.

IT WASN'T UNTIL HE and Vijay were sitting together on the sofa and the dishwasher was chugging away in the kitchen that Jamie said, "Pressure's building to shut down the program."

"Close it? You mean bring everybody home?"

He nodded, tight-lipped. "We've already had to shut down the new base at Hellas."

Varuna Jarita Shektar had been the physician on the Second Expedition. She and Jamie had met in training, traveled to Mars together, and slowly but irrevocably fallen in love. The two of them stayed alone on the red planet for four months after the rest of the team had left for Earth and before the replacement team had arrived, Adam and Eve in a barren, frigid new world that was to them a Garden of Eden.

"But they can't shut down the entire operation," Vijay said, her luminous dark eyes blazing with indignation. "They simply can't. They mustn't!"

Jamie wished he could work up such righteous wrath so easily. But he couldn't. It was all bottled up inside him. Everything. Including Jimmy's death. Especially Jimmy's death.

"Vee . . ." he started to say. But the words caught in his throat.

She was still incensed. "How can they even *think* about shutting down the program? After all you've done, all you've discovered."

"Vijay," he said, grasping her by the shoulders. "If I hadn't been on Mars . . . if I'd been here with you . . . and Jimmy . . ."

She stared at him, her eyes wide with sudden understanding. "Jamie, no."

"If I'd been here, the way a father should've been, he wouldn't have—"

"No!" she snapped. "Don't say it. Don't even think it!"

"But—"

"It's not going to bring him back."

"I know. But still . . . I feel responsible. It's my fault."

It had taken him nearly two years to say those words.

"It's not your fault any more than it's mine," Vijay said.

"Yours? How could it be your fault?"

"I was here. I should've kept a better watch on Jimmy. I should've . . ." Her voice faltered and tears misted her eyes.

He pulled her close, heard her sobbing softly, her head on his shoulder.

"Vee, we'll get through this. Together. The two of us."

"That's all that's left, isn't it? The two of us."

"I don't want to lose you, Vijay."

"You'll never lose me, love. We're one person, the two of us. Together always."

"You're all I have in the whole world."

She pulled away from him slightly, blinking tears away as she smiled sadly and said, "No, Jamie. That's not true. You have Mars, don't you, love?"

He couldn't reply to that. But inwardly he thought, I might not have Mars much longer. They're going to take that away from me, too.

TITHONIUM BASE: THE FOSSIL

■

Nearly everyone in the base crowded around the big stereo table. Ordinarily used to show three-dimensional views of Martian terrain, now it was a blank, unlit white—with the palm-sized fossil vertebra resting in front of Carter Carleton. It was light gray, the color of ashes; bits of dirt still clung to it here and there.

Carleton surveyed their eager faces as they pressed close, felt the heat of their bodies, the scent of their excitement. Directly across the table from him stood Chang Laodong, the mission director, bald and dour in his dumpy-looking blue coveralls with their mandarin collar, looking, as usual, as if he'd been sucking on a lemon.

Trying to suppress the supreme delight of this moment, Carleton spread his hands and, smiling, said, "Well, it's a vertebra. No doubt of it."

Chang forced a pale smile. "We must obtain verification of your identification from qualified paleontologists."

Nodding, Carleton replied, "I've already sent stereo images of the fossil to half a dozen of the top universities."

"And to program headquarters in New Mexico?"

"Of course," Carleton replied. In his excitement he hadn't initially thought about Waterman, back in Albuquerque, but then Doreen had reminded him of the mission protocol.

Chang stared hard at the fossil, as if he could force it to give information by sheer willpower.

"It certainly looks like a vertebra," said Kalman Torok, running a hand through his thick mop of hair. "See the ridges?"

"And the central cavity where the spinal cord runs through," added one of the other biologists.

"What kind of an animal is it from?" someone asked.

"Who the hell knows? This is all brand-new territory!"

"From what I know of physiology," Carleton said slowly, deliberately working to keep his voice calm, "this looks like it came from a quadruped. Bipedal vertebrae don't have such thick walls."

"Then it's not from a Martian. One of the intelligent species, I mean."

"How do you know?"

"If it's not bipedal—"

"Intelligent species don't have to be bipedal."

"I always thought Martians had six limbs."

"And they were green!"

Everyone laughed, except Chang.

Looking unconvinced, the mission director repeated, "We must get verification from experts."

Carleton grinned at him. "With all due respect, Dr. Chang, there are no experts."

"No?"

"This is a Martian fossil. The first fossil to be discovered on Mars. As Petersen said, we're entering new territory here, totally new territory."

"Now wait," Torok said, his heavy brows knitting. "It's got distinct similarities to terrestrial vertebra. That's how you identified it in the first place, isn't it?"

"Well, yes," Carleton admitted. "But—"

Edging along the table toward Carleton, forcing the others to step back to let him by, Torok mused, "This brings up a fascinating conundrum. Do Martian fauna have structural plans that are similar to our own? Does form follow function, as the architects say?"

"That is not for us to decide," Chang said firmly. He was a

geologist, and had been put in charge of the base because his days of useful scientific work had ended years earlier, Carleton was certain.

"You already expressed the opinion that it's not from a biped, did you not?" Torok said to Carleton.

"Yes, but that's just an educated guess."

To the entire crowd, Torok said, "We have the opportunity to learn how much of our own form and structure is unique to Earth and how much is part of a general biological plan. There are Nobels waiting for us!"

Everyone whooped and cheered enthusiastically. Even Chang managed a pained smile. But when Torok reached for the fossil Carleton grabbed his thick wrist.

"What?" the biologist demanded. "No one can touch it but you?"

"Let me make a cast of it first," Carleton replied tightly.

Torok smiled at him. "You're being very proprietary."

Smiling back, Carleton said, "Wouldn't you be?"

Torok shrugged good-naturedly and stepped away from the fossil.

"I presume," said Chang, "that you will no longer be using explosives?"

"Right. From now on we dig in the pit the old-fashioned way, with hand picks and wire brushes."

"We?"

"I'm going to need a gang of volunteers to help excavate the site," Carleton said, looking directly at Chang.

"Impossible," the director said flatly. "The schedule is fully committed. No one is available."

"I'll help you," said one of the biologists.

"Me, too," a woman technician called out.

"And me."

"None of you is excused from your regular duties!" Chang shouted. "The schedule must be maintained."

"We'll do it in our spare time," the woman said. Half a dozen others nodded agreement.

"I'll set up a schedule," said Doreen McManus. "I'll need you all to tell me when you'd be free to help."

Grinning, Carleton ignored the mission director, scooped up his fossil, and started toward the laboratory he had taken for himself on the other side of the dome, where he could make a plaster cast of the vertebra. Almost half the assembled staff followed after him, chattering among themselves, laughing, eyes alight with the thrill of discovery.

This is like old times, Carleton said to himself. Like back at the university. It's good to have an entourage!

Chang planted his plump fists on his hips and glared at them all. He saw the power of his position eroding, his authority melting away like snow in the springtime sunshine. But there was nothing he could do about it. Not at this particular moment.

ALBUQUERQUE: DURAN CONDOMINIUMS

■

With the first ring of the phone Jamie's eyes snapped wide awake. That's the emergency line! he told himself. The apartment had a direct phone link with the program's headquarters on the university campus. Jamie always thought of it as the emergency line. No one used it unless something urgent had happened.

He sat up in bed and grabbed the handset before the phone could ring again. Glancing over his bare shoulder at Vijay, stirring slightly in her sleep, he half-whispered, "Waterman."

"Dr. Waterman?" Jamie recognized the young man's voice: he was one of the grad students who worked the night shift at the headquarters monitoring consoles.

"Yes."

"This is Oscar Samosa, sir."

"What's happened?" Jamie felt his insides knotting.

"We just got a transmission from Tithonium—"

"What's happened?" Jamie hissed angrily.

"They think they've found a fossil, sir. Dr. Carleton says—"

"Carleton? A fossil?"

Vijay rubbed her eyes, muttering, "What's the matter?"

"Dr. Carleton sent stereo images," Samosa was saying, his voice trembling slightly with excitement. "He's also sent them to a shitload of universities."

"Can you pipe the imagery to my computer?"

"Sure. No sweat."

Vijay leaned her bare body against him, pressing her ear to the side of his head, trying to hear what was being said.

"Okay, good," Jamie said into the phone. "Thanks for calling me."

"Sorry about the hour," Samosa apologized. "I thought you'd want to know."

"You did the right thing."

He hung up the phone, turned and kissed Vijay so hard on the lips that she gasped, then leaped out of bed and shouted a heartfelt "Yahoo!"

"What on Earth is it?"

"It's not on Earth, it's on Mars!" Jamie said, almost breathless with excitement. "A fossil! Some sort of bone that Carleton's dug up."

"A fossil?"

"He's done it!" Jamie pranced naked to the bureau and started pulling out shirts, socks, underwear. "He's found the remains of the village, I'm willing to bet!"

"You think so?"

"It's got to be." He rushed to the closet and pulled out his well-traveled roll-on suitcase.

"Where are you going?"

"Boston," Jamie said, stuffing clothes into the bag. "I've got to get together with Dex about this."

Vijay smiled at him despite her bruised lip.

BOSTON: TRUMBALL TRUST BOARD ROOM

■

Sorry I'm late," Jamie said as he entered the board room. "My flight was delayed."

Dex Trumball got up from his high-backed chair at the head of the long, polished conference table, looking more like his own father than ever in a dark three-piece suit and narrow tie. "Should've taken a Clippership, Jamie. Get you here in twenty minutes."

Jamie was wearing a suede sports jacket over his open-necked shirt and jeans. "They don't have Clippership service in Albuquerque," he said as he took his seat halfway down the table and nodded greetings to the other board members. "I'd have to go down to the spaceport in Alamogordo."

The table was only half filled, he saw. A lot of absentees for this hastily called special meeting of the board.

"You wouldn't get me on one of those rockets," grumbled the white-haired man on his left. "Shoot off into the sky like that. I don't care how fast they go."

Jamie made a slow smile. "I've ridden on lots of rockets, Mel. They're safer than airplanes, really."

"Maybe," the white-haired man muttered. "Maybe."

Dex tapped on the table with a jeweled pen. "Well, now that our science director is here we have a quorum. So I'll call this special meeting of the Trumball Trust board of directors to order."

The board room was elegantly paneled in light walnut. One entire wall was windowed: Jamie saw the towers of Boston's financial district clustered out there, and beyond them the choppy waters of the harbor. Sailboats coasted between the islets, colorful billowing sails against the foaming whitecaps and sparkling blue water. Jamie always felt slightly uneasy at the sight of so much water. Even as a child, a day at the beach scared him. So much water. The ocean he looked at now stretched to the horizon and beyond, all the way to Britain and Europe, he knew. It almost made him shudder.

He listened perfunctorily as the board members agreed to skip the reading of the last meeting's minutes. Then Dex nodded toward the grossly overweight woman sitting at his right.

"Treasurer's report," he announced.

"Here comes the bad news," someone said in a stage whisper.

No one laughed. No one even smiled.

The treasurer was an obese middle-aged brunette wearing a dark gray business suit over a ruffled white blouse. It made her look ridiculous, Jamie thought. Hair poufed out in the latest style. But her report was crisp, pointed.

"In summary," she concluded, "unless we find significant new sources of funding to make up the shortfall from the government's withdrawal, we will be forced to curtail operations on the surface of Mars."

A dreary silence fell across the room.

"Any questions?" Dex asked.

Jamie said, "I know it's listed under new business, but maybe I should tell you now about what Carter Carleton's discovered."

"That's the reason why I called this special meeting," said Dex. Glancing swiftly around the table he continued, "I presume there's no objection to going directly to Jamie's news."

No one objected.

Jamie took in a breath, then started, "You know about the cliff dwellings. Carleton's an anthropologist and he believes that the structure tucked up in the cliff weren't dwellings at all."

"What were they, then?"

"We still don't know. Maybe a religious shrine. Maybe a storehouse. But there's no sign of permanent habitation in those buildings."

Dex said, "So Carleton's been digging down on the canyon floor."

Nodding, Jamie explained, "Penetrating radar from our orbiting satellites indicated a gridwork pattern buried beneath some thirty meters of ground. Carleton thinks it's the site of a village where the Martians actually lived."

"Carleton's some sort of an oddball, isn't he?" asked one of the board members. "I seem to remember that he got into trouble at Penn."

"He was accused of rape," said the woman across the table from Jamie, her tone hard, cold.

"They never convicted him."

"They didn't acquit him either," she countered. "He resigned his professorship and left the university."

"He's found a fossil," Jamie blurted, trying to get them back on the subject.

"A fossil? You mean a bone or something?"

"It looks like a vertebra," Jamie said, pulling his pocket phone from his shirt pocket. He tapped a few keys and an image of the fossilized bone appeared on the wall screen at the end of the room.

"A vertebra," said the old man who had grumbled about rockets.

"From the spine of a Martian animal," Jamie added. "Carleton is right. There's a village on the valley floor, all right, buried under sixty million years of accumulated dust and debris."

"A village," someone breathed.

"We'll find skeletons of the Martians," one of the younger board members said.

"Not if we don't bring in new funding," Dex pointed out. "We can't even maintain our current level of activity on Mars at the rate we're going now. We need more money."

"This discovery will help," Jamie said. "Every paleontologist on Earth will want to go to Mars. Every anthropologist, too."

"They'll have to pay their own way," Dex said. "The goddamned government isn't going to fund their transportation anymore."

"Maybe we can talk the White House into reconsidering," said Jamie.

Dex cocked a brow at him, as if to say that Jamie was talking nonsense. But he remained silent.

"What I want to know," said one of the younger men farther down the table, "is why have so many of our regular donors dropped out?" His hair was still dark, though thinning. "I mean," he went on, "they agreed to long-term commitments and now they've broken their word."

"What do you want to do, sue them?" groused one of the women.

"I want to know why they're backing away from us," the young man answered. "It's not just the government's dropping out, they were reneging on us before the White House's announcement."

"It's the greenhouse flooding," said the man on Jamie's right. "Everybody's under tremendous pressure to help the refugees."

"It's a good thing the state of Massachusetts built the weirs across the Charles River," one of the other board members said. "Otherwise Boston would be under water too."

"The federal government put in half the money, didn't they?"

"Washington did, yes. How do you think the damned weirs are holding up so well? The local contractors had to satisfy federal inspectors."

"Not so easy to bribe them, eh?"

With a shrug, "Maybe it just takes too much money to buy them off."

An uneasy laugh went around the table.

"We're getting off the subject," Dex said mildly.

"Which is . . . ?"

"Finances," said the treasurer firmly. "We're staring at a disaster curve. We can't possibly house an influx of people at Tithonium Base. Once we close the base at Hellas, Tithonium will be overcrowded until we can start bringing people back home."

"I've got another piece of bad news," Dex said.

"More bad news?"

"Public Broadcasting won't be airing our monthly programs."

"That's our major publicity outlet!"

"They can't pull the plug on us!"

Dex said, "They can and they will, starting next month. No more educational shows from Mars."

Jamie said confidently, "They'll change their minds once they hear about the fossil. They'll want to send a crew to Tithonium to cover Carleton's work."

"Maybe," said Dex, guardedly. "But they claim that the public's lost interest in Mars. Our audience numbers have been going down steadily."

"But I thought we had millions of viewers," exclaimed the treasurer.

"We do," Dex replied. "But not enough to satisfy the network decision-makers."

"It doesn't cost them a penny to air our shows," one of the board members grumbled.

"It's part of a concerted effort in Washington to dump all support for Mars," said Dex. "I've heard that their next step will be to have the IRS remove the Mars program from its list of approved charities."

"You mean they won't allow a tax deduction for contributions to the Foundation?"

Dex nodded somberly.

"That will kill us!"

"That's exactly what they're trying to do," said Dex. "I've talked with both Massachusetts senators and several others on key Senate committees. The knives are out. The White House wants to end all support for the Mars program. Period."

Jamie sank back in his padded chair. Before he could frame a response in his mind, the oldest woman at the table said, "It's the greenhouse floods. Washington's got to devote every possible resource to helping the refugees and rebuilding. Mars is a luxury."

Dex looked at her and for the flash of an instant Jamie thought he saw anger flare in the younger man's eyes. But Dex sucked in a deep breath, then replied, "The flooding's just an excuse. The conservatives running the government have always been against the exploration of Mars. What we've found goes against their religious beliefs."

"I can't accept that," the white-haired woman said. "I'm a Believer and I see nothing wrong with what we're doing on Mars."

Dex made an impatient gesture. "Look. No matter what our personal beliefs, the facts are that the New Morality and its associated fundamentalist groups are in control of the government now. And the government is doing its damnedest to shut us down."

"What recourse do we have?" asked one of the older men.

Dex gave him a lopsided grin. "Wish I knew, friend. The Europeans don't put enough into the pot to keep us going for a month. Japan's been hit by greenhouse floods worse than we have—"

"They've had some pretty bad earthquakes, too," another board member interjected.

"And tsunamis."

"China's concentrating on its lunar development program; they never had much interest in Mars. India's fighting a war with Pakistan and the Islamic world doesn't give a crap about anything that isn't mentioned in the Quran."

"Latin America?" asked one of the board members. "Brazil or maybe Argentina . . . ?"

Another board member snorted derisively.

"So where are we?"

"Broke, pretty damned near," Dex confessed. "Unless we find a new influx of money we're up shit's creek without a paddle."

"You mean we're going to have to shut down the entire operation?"

"That's how it looks," Dex admitted.

"No!" Jamie snapped. "We've worked too hard. We've discovered too much. We can't stop now! We can't just fold up and leave!"

"What else can we do?" Dex asked, his voice almost pleading.

Jamie answered immediately, "I'll go to Washington. I'll take this news of the fossil right into the Oval Office. I'll splash it all over the news media. I'll make them see that they *have to* continue funding us."

"If you could do that . . ." Dex mused, the beginnings of a grin flickering on his face.

"Then the private donors will come back in," Jamie said. "Won't they?"

"They might. Some of them, at least."

"And we'll find new ones." Jamie's eyes swept the other board members seated along the table. "We've discovered a fossil! We're going to uncover a village that's been buried for sixty million years! The great discoveries are just starting!"

Dex laughed and said, "Go get 'em, tiger."

But inwardly Dex thought that Jamie's hopes were doomed to fail. I know how to bring in the money, Dex said to himself. But Jamie would be against doing it my way. He'd hate it. Absolutely hate it.

■

Jamie, you can't just barge into the Oval Office," said Francisco Delgado, the president's science advisor. "Hell, I haven't seen her myself in three weeks."

Delgado was a compactly built man with the physique of a former athlete who had gone soft. His brown-skinned face was starting to show jowls, although his hair was still dark and thick, as was his heavy brush of a moustache. He wore a dark gray business suit with a lighter gray sweater beneath its jacket. Jamie had known him since Delgado had been a biology professor from the University of California at Santa Cruz, and a consultant to the crew selection committee for the Second Mars Expedition.

Dressed in stiffly new jeans and a pullover under an old, thin blue windbreaker, Jamie was walking with the science advisor along the Reflecting Pool between the phallic spire of the Washington Monument and the Athenian harmony of the Lincoln Memorial. When Jamie had phoned from Boston to ask to see him, Delgado had suggested a breakfast meeting. Jamie was surprised that breakfast turned out to be a sweet bun and a plastic cup of coffee purchased from a street vendor.

It was a chilly morning, gray, with a hint of rain in the humid air. Only a few tourists were meandering by this early in the day, many of them pushing baby carriages, looking cold and unhappy with the weather.

Delgado walked briskly, paper-wrapped bun in one hand, coffee cup in the other. Jamie kept pace with him and within a few minutes he no longer felt chilled: in fact, Jamie wished he had a hand free to unzip his windbreaker.

"I need to talk to her," he said. "This new discovery changes everything."

The science advisor shook his head as he munched on his breakfast bun. "It doesn't really change a damned thing, Jamie. They're already talking about reducing the budget for the National Science Foundation."

"But that's where most of the university grants come from!"

"Don't I know it."

"Cut off the NSF funds and the universities won't be able to support their work on Mars."

"Well, that's where the battle line is now. That's what I'm fighting to protect."

Jamie looked into Delgado's troubled eyes and realized this man was on his side, but struggling against tremendous forces.

"What can I do to help?" he asked.

"Not a hell of a lot, Jamie. They're not interested in Mars."

"Let me talk to the president," Jamie begged. "Maybe I can make her see the situation more clearly. Maybe I—"

"She won't see you," Delgado snapped, his tone hardening. "She can't afford to be seen with you."

"Can't afford . . . ?"

"Look: she was elected by a paper-thin majority and now she's facing the off-year elections with everybody blaming her for the greenhouse floods and anything else that's happened during her first two years. Those Bible-thumping New Morality zealots already control the House of Representatives. By November they'll have the majority in the Senate!"

"So she can't afford to antagonize them, is that it?" Jamie asked.

Delgado turned on his heel and strode away. Crumpling the empty wrapper in one hand while he gulped the last of his coffee, he walked up to a trash receptacle and dumped both. Jamie followed him and did the same.

Over his shoulder, Delgado said, "Come with me, Jamie. There's something I want to show you. Something you need to see."

Ignoring the line of taxicabs parked along Constitution Avenue, Delgado hurried up toward the Ellipse. At first Jamie thought they were going to the White House after all, but Delgado veered off at Seventeenth Street and marched Jamie into a glass-walled office building. There was no plaque on the entrance, no sign announcing what the building was or which government agency might be housed in it.

Puffing slightly from the pace the science advisor set, Jamie followed Delgado through the inevitable security checkpoint in the quiet, nearly empty lobby. After they went through the metal detector a sullen-looking overweight guard in a blue National Security Agency uniform handed them identification badges. Jamie eyed the heavy black pistol holstered on the guard's hip as he clipped his badge onto the front of his windbreaker. Delgado led Jamie into a waiting elevator.

"What is this place?" Jamie asked as the elevator doors closed. To his surprise, it went down, not up.

"It's a new climatology facility," the science advisor answered.

"Why—"

"There's something you've got to see. Something that just might put things into the proper perspective for you."

The elevator went down four levels, then stopped with a lurch. The doors slid open.

There were more people in the corridor down at this level than there had been in the lobby. Still, the men and women seemed to Jamie to be moving at a leisurely pace. Government employees, Jamie thought.

The smooth cream-colored paneling of the corridor was set with a series of doors, all of them blank except for five-digit numbers stenciled on them. Mounted beside each door was a small keypad. Delgado walked Jamie to the end of the corridor and tapped out a security code on the pad next to its double doors. They slid open noiselessly.

Jamie followed the science advisor into a darkened room, lit only by the giant display screens that filled three of the walls. People sat at what looked to Jamie like electronics consoles. The place reminded him of a NASA mission control center, except that the usual crackle of tense excitement was missing.

The wall displays were electronic maps, Jamie saw. He recognized satellite views of the continental United States, Europe, Latin America.

Delgado walked him through the consoles to the display of the United States.

"Take a good look," said the science advisor. "This is a real-time display, with the cloud cover removed."

Jamie recognized the image, although as he stared at it he realized it looked slightly wrong, subtly different from the maps he was accustomed to.

Pointing with an outstretched arm, Delgado said, "We're holding our own along the East Coast, pretty much, although the dams and flood control systems have cost us so much the federal budget'll be in the red for generations to come."

That's why Washington isn't under water, Jamie realized.

Delgado went on, "But take a look at the Gulf of Mexico. Look at Florida. See how the sea level is moving in."

Jamie could see that the coastline he was familiar with was no longer there. The Gulf of Mexico was encroaching from Texas to the tip of Florida. He couldn't find Galveston. Miami was an island, surrounded by the Atlantic.

"That's the way it is today," Delgado said, his voice grim. "Now see what happens in five years."

The image shifted. Most of Florida disappeared under water. The Mississippi River swelled into a connected series of lakes that swallowed entire cities. The Gulf of Mexico grew noticeably larger and covered most of Louisiana.

"That's what we're up against, Jamie. And it's not going to stop. The Arctic is melting down! So's the Antarctic. Fresh water runoff from Greenland will interrupt the Gulf

Stream in another couple of decades. Maybe sooner. When the Stream shuts down, Europe goes into the deep freeze."

In the greenish light from the wall displays Delgado's face looked splotched, ghastly. Jamie heard the bitterness in his voice, the anger.

"We're facing major flooding of the country's heartland. People in the Pentagon are talking about marching into Canada to take their wheat belt, for god's sakes! And maybe a new Ice Age to top it all off!"

Jamie stared at him in silence.

"And you want to spend money on frigging Mars? You expect the president to give you a Christmas present, all wrapped up in a bow? Forget it!"

With a silent shake of his head Jamie turned away and started for the door. I won't forget it, he said to himself. I can't.

TITHONIUM BASE: CONFLICT

■

Chang Laodong looked distinctly uncomfortable as he sat behind his desk facing Carter Carleton. The mission director's office was small but three of its four walls were covered with smart screens that displayed treasures of Chinese art: silk paintings of misty mountain scenes, statues of powerful arch-necked horses, the inevitable portraits of Buddha and Mao. Otherwise the office was strictly utilitarian, with only Chang's desk, the chair before it, and a sofa and low table along one wall, flanked by two more small chairs.

As always, Chang was wearing high-collared blue coveralls. He had summoned Carleton to his office to discuss the anthropologist's demand for field workers to help excavate the village site. In his mind's eye, the mission director saw all his carefully prepared work schedules being torn apart, his meticulous plans being thrown into chaos.

Two hundred and forty-two men and women were based here at Tithonium, he knew. Biologists studying endolithic lichen and underground bacteria. Geologists studying satellite data of south polar cap melting. Atmospheric physicists investigating decline of moisture in atmosphere. Paleontologists searching for more rock dwellings along the walls of Grand Canyon. And the geysers: spurts of liquid water bursting out of ground. What is the heat source that liquefies permafrost? That is important!

All my responsibility, Chang told himself. All on my shoulders. Their work depends on my leadership, my ability to organize them properly, to bring their work into smooth, harmonious totality.

And this one stubborn anthropologist who's made a lucky discovery. He sits there smiling, handsome as a video star. What does he care how he upsets my plans? He thinks he has the upper hand over me.

Chang forced a smile. "There is great excitement Earthside over your discovery," he began.

"Yes," said Carleton, his own smile broadening. "I've received several dozen messages from all over the world. Even China."

Chang closed his eyes slowly, a tactic he used when he did not want to reveal his inner thoughts. He felt a surge of anger at this upstart who was wrecking his schedules, who was threatening to wrest control of this operation from his hands.

Carleton thought of a lizard basking on a sunny rock as he waited for Chang to open his eyes again. And his mouth.

"Waterman urges me to provide you with all the assistance you may require," Chang said at last, his eyes still closed.

"I'm glad to hear it."

Snapping his eyes open, Chang added, "He also tells me that the United States government is canceling all its funding for our operation. We may be forced to abandon our work here and return to Earth."

Carleton's head flicked back as if he'd been slapped. Good! Chang thought. Let him understand the consequences.

"We can't stop the work here!" the anthropologist said. "Hell, we've just started."

"I agree with your sentiment," said Chang. "But if the Foundation cannot raise enough money to replace funds that the American government is withdrawing, we will be forced to go home."

"Waterman won't let that happen. He'll figure out a way."

"Let us hope so. In meantime, there is the question of how to adequately assist you in your work."

"I've got plenty of volunteers."

Chang shook his head slowly. "I cannot allow staff

personnel to work for you on a volunteer basis. They are already working eight to twelve hours a day on their assigned duties. More, in many cases."

"But if they want to—"

"Their eagerness to help you outweighs their common sense. They cannot help you with your digging for several hours each day and still work effectively at their regular tasks. Productivity will decline. People will fall asleep on their jobs. There will be accidents, dangerous accidents."

Carleton started to reply, hesitated, then offered, "What about the team coming back from Hellas Base? They're supposed to be shipped back to Earth. What if some of them volunteered to work with me full time?"

"Highly trained geologists and biologists, slaving like coolies in that pit of yours?"

His smile turning almost into a smirk, Carleton replied, "Dr. Chang, may I remind you that I'm a highly trained anthropologist and I've been slaving like a coolie for months. By myself. Now I need help, and your superiors Earthside agree that you should provide it to me."

Chang's self-discipline snapped. "May I remind you that you are a fugitive from very serious criminal charges on Earth!"

Carleton's smile evaporated. "Those charges are baseless and you know it."

"I know that the charges have never been settled. We took you into our program and allowed you to come to Mars despite them."

Grimly, Carleton said, "That's got nothing to do with the question at hand. Will you allow me to use some of the people returning from the Hellas base?"

Chang closed his eyes again, thinking, It is a good stratagem. People returning from Hellas are due to be shipped home. A few of them can stay here at Tithonium and work with him. Waterman is urging me to help him. This is how to do that without wrecking all our other work.

"Well?" Carleton demanded.

Opening his eyes, Chang said mildly, "You may ask personnel returning from Hellas. If any of them volunteer to remain here instead of returning to Earth, let it be so."

Carleton took in a deep breath, as if he'd just accomplished an incredibly difficult feat. "Thank you, Dr. Chang," he said, his voice low.

"How many hands will you need?" Chang asked.

"Six, for now. More than that and we'll just get in each other's way. But later on, as things progress . . ."

"Six," Chang repeated. "We can accommodate six additional people here without straining our resources."

"Five, actually," said Carleton. "Ms. McManus has already volunteered to work with me."

"The nanotechnologist? She has her regular duties."

"She says she can spend at least half her days working on the excavation."

Chang couldn't help asking, "And where will she spend her nights?"

Carleton's face froze. After several heartbeats he replied tightly, "That's her business, not yours."

SOUTHWEST AIRLINES FLIGHT 799

■

As he rode the jet airliner back toward Albuquerque Jamie desperately tried to think of some way, some method of raising support for the Mars program. I'll have to see New Mexico's senators, he told himself. Maybe get the people running the spaceport down in Alamogordo to put pressure on the politicians.

I can go to the media, he added. Get Dex to put together a TV special out of all the virtual reality tours we've done on Mars. Do a VR show on the fossil Carleton's discovered! That ought to bring in public support. Maybe we can start a public drive for funds, get ordinary people to contribute to keeping the Mars program going.

He leaned his head against the seat back, planning, thinking, hoping. Out of the corner of his eye he saw the land sliding past, endless miles of dry brittle brown where once there had been green fields of grain as far as the eye could see. The greenhouse warming had cruelly brought both drought and flooding to America's heartland. The nation's breadbasket was withering away.

Jamie closed his eyes, feeling overwhelmed by what was happening to the world, to two worlds, to him and everything he cared about. He closed his eyes and immediately found himself on Mars.

In his mind he stood at the edge of the tranquil sea, beneath a clear sky of perfect turquoise blue, while the Sun's warmth baked into his bare shoulders. The gentle waves lapped at his feet and the water stretched to the horizon and far beyond. Strangely, Jamie felt no misgivings at seeing so much water on Mars. It's not very deep, he told himself; nowhere near as deep as the ocean basins on the blue world. Then it struck him: Mars was once a blue world, too!

Turning, he looked back across the land. It was not a frigid red desert. The land was golden with grain that waved gracefully in the gentle breeze. Far in the distance mountains rose dramatically, bluish green almost up to their bare granite summits.

Water means life, Jamie knew. Mars is young and alive. He looked up into the cloudless sky, squinting against the Sun's brightness. But Coyote will send monsters to destroy all this, he knew. This will end. Soon.

"This is First Officer De La Hoya speaking," a woman's voice came through the cabin speakers. "We're approaching the Albuquerque area."

Jamie blinked and rubbed his eyes, his vision of ancient Mars fading away. Outside the airliner's window he saw a familiar yet strange landscape sliding by. Rugged mesas and tortuous arroyos—covered with green. The abrupt climate change had bizarrely brought plentiful rain to the stark scrublands of the desert Southwest. The Gulf of California was invading the Colorado River basin. Yuma was already flooded and there were dark jokes about Albuquerque itself becoming a seaside resort town. The lands of the Navahos and other Native Americans farther north were green and burgeoning.

The Navaho side of Jamie's mind remembered grimly that the Anglos were already making inroads on reservation land. Refugees driven from the flooded coastal cities formed a pressure bloc that was trying to drive The People from their own territory.

"To our left in just about a minute you'll be able to see a Clippership launch from the New Mexico spaceport near Alamogordo," the plane's first officer continued.

Passengers on the right side of the cabin got up from their seats and crowded over the shoulders of those in the left-hand seats for a view of the rocket's liftoff. Jamie, on an aisle seat, leaned forward and peered through the plane's oval window.

"There it is!" somebody shouted.

Jamie saw a pillar of white smoke rising fast beyond the distant mountains, up, up into the crystalline blue sky. He knew that the Clippership was a squat cone of gleaming composite plastic carrying up to a hundred passengers across the Pacific in half an hour. Or maybe this flight was going to one of the space stations in orbit around the Earth. He remembered the thunder of the rocket engines on his flights, the bone-rattling vibration of all that power, the press of three times normal gravity squeezing you down into your acceleration couch. And then it all cut off, all at once, and you were weightless, held down on your couch only by the restraining straps, your stomach dropping away inside you.

If you've got to fly, he thought with an inward smile, that's the way to do it.

The jet airliner circled around the Sandia Mountains as the Clippership's distant exhaust trail slowly dissolved and disappeared. By the time the plane landed there was no trace of it in the sky.

Jamie was surprised to see Vijay waiting for him in the baggage claim area, dressed in slacks that hugged her round hips deliciously and a bright orange blouse with a vivid red scarf knotted around her waist in place of a belt. She stood out in the crowd like a Technicolor goddess in the midst of drab black-and-white mortals.

She ran to him, all smiles, and kissed him as though they hadn't seen each other in months. Jamie dropped his travel bag and clung to her. Other passengers stared and grinned at them. Somebody whistled appreciatively.

"What're you doing here?" he asked, once they came up for air.

"Thought I'd surprise you."

He laughed. "I'm surprised, all right."

"Want to take me to dinner and tell me about your trip?"

That brought Jamie back to bleak reality. Bending down to pick up his travel bag, he said, "It looks pretty bad."

Vijay nodded. "I thought as much. Dex was rather evasive."

As he started toward the luggage carousel to pick up his roll-on, Jamie asked, "You talked with Dex?"

"I phoned when I got your message that you were going to Washington. I was trying to get you but you were already on the plane, I guess."

Jamie hadn't had the heart to phone his wife after his meeting with Delgado. On the flight back to Albuquerque he'd spent most of his time wrestling with the decisions he would have to make. He knew what he was going to do, what he had to do, but he didn't know how to tell her.

Once he'd retrieved his roll-on, they walked past the rumbling carousels and the car rental desks, out into the warm air of early evening. The Sun had set and a cool breeze was sweeping down from the mountains, silhouetted in flaming red against the darkening twilight sky. Jamie saw that they were getting glances from other people. Still the same old prejudices, he thought. Even in a sports jacket and a short haircut they see me as a Navaho. Then he thought that maybe they were looking at Vijay's dark, beautiful face, her long black hair, her stunning figure. With her voluptuous shape, even in the casual blouse and slacks she was wearing she could stop traffic.

"We'll take my car," Vijay said. "I sent yours back home."

Jamie's Nissan was equipped with an autopilot and global positioning system that could guide the car without a human driver. He had programmed it to find its way back to his assigned parking slot at the condominium's parking lot, but he didn't fully trust the electronics.

"I hope it's there when we get home," he muttered. "In one piece."

Vijay giggled at him. "For a bloke who's been to Mars several times you have no faith in modern technology."

"Maybe not," he admitted soberly.

The top was down on her convertible. Jamie carefully deposited his bags in the trunk while Vijay started the engine. As he got into the seat beside her, she said, "How's P.F. Chang's sound to you? They're celebrating their fiftieth anniversary or something."

He nodded absently. "Fine."

As they drove out onto the interstate, Vijay asked, "So how bad is it?"

Jamie watched the traffic zooming past as he tried to think of what to say, how to tell her. Vijay was a good driver, he knew, but she paid no attention to speed limits. Too aggressive, he thought.

"Really bad," he said at last, almost shouting over the rush of the wind. "We might have to shut down everything and bring everybody back home."

Vijay glanced at him out of the corner of her eye. "But you won't let them do that, will you?"

"Not if I can help it."

She pulled smoothly off the highway and wound around the confusing roadways of the huge shopping mall in which the restaurant was located. In silence. No more questions, not for a while. Jamie studied her face as Vijay maneuvered the convertible into a parking space and turned off its engine.

How can I tell her that I'm going back? Jamie asked himself. That I've got to go back?

He looked up at the darkening sky. Through the glare of the shopping mall's garish lights it was hard to see more than a few of the brightest stars. One big bright one hung low over the mountains to the west. Venus, he guessed. He turned in his seat and searched, but he couldn't find Mars.

Vijay opened her door and started to get out of the car.

"Going to leave the top down?" he asked.

"No rain in the forecast, love. Monsoon season's finished, they claim."

"Still . . ."

With a laugh, she swung her legs back into the car, closed

the door, and pressed the button that started the fabric top rising. The electric motor whined until the top locked itself in place with a pair of firm clicks.

"Feel better?" Vijay asked.

"Yep."

She started to open the car door again but he reached for her. "Vijay . . ."

She melted into his arms, leaning over the transmission stick in the console between them.

"You're really wonderful," he said.

"I'm glad you noticed."

"Are you trying to cheer me up?"

She shook her head. "Why would I have to do that?"

"Then how come . . . ?"

"You've made up your mind, haven't you, Jamie? You're going back."

There it was, out in the open.

"I didn't know myself until halfway back to Albuquerque. But you knew before I did, didn't you?"

"Once Dex told me how bad things are I knew what your reaction would be."

In the shadows of the car's interior he could still see the anticipation on her face, the glow in her eyes.

"Jamie, you've been moping around for more'n two years now," Vijay said softly, "blaming yourself for what happened to Jimmy. Now they've hit you with this and—"

"And I've got to go back to Mars. I can't let them close down the program."

"Do you think your being on Mars will make any difference?"

"I don't know. But I've got to go."

"Of course," she said. "And you do want me to go with you, don't you?"

"You're willing to go?"

He could hear the smile in her voice. "Hey, mate, we lived all alone on Mars for four months, di'n't we? Time for a second honeymoon, don't you think?"

"Are you sure?"

"Sure as taxes, love."

For a long moment he couldn't say a word. Then, "Do you think we can put Jimmy's death behind us?"

"No," she replied, her voice dropping lower. "We'll never put Jimmy out of our minds. But we'll move on, Jamie. We'll move on."

"To Mars."

"To Mars," she agreed.

In the shadows of the car he tried to look into those fathomless jet black eyes of hers; he felt all the wonder that always astonished him whenever he realized that this incredible woman actually loved him as much as he loved her.

"Okay," he said. "On to Mars."

"Fine," said Vijay. "But right now let's get to the restaurant. I'm starved."

TITHONIUM BASE: CELEBRATION

■

They held an impromptu celebration—of sorts—the night that the personnel from Hellas Base returned to Tithonium. No one planned it, no one was really in a celebratory mood. It took three trips in one of the broad-winged rocketplanes to bring all twenty-three of the men and women with their personal effects back to Tithonium. They were downcast, subdued, dejected at the realization that they had to abruptly leave their work, cut short the studies they'd been undertaking at the vast impact crater of Hellas.

As soon as their leader, Yvonne Lorenz, set foot inside the base's main dome, Chang bustled her into his office and closed the door firmly.

Seeing the dispirited expressions on the new arrivals, Kalman Torok said loudly, "What's the matter? You don't want to go back home?"

A few of them shot annoyed glances at the biologist.

"Like packing up and leaving in the middle of a program is a good career move?" one of the women snapped.

Torok shrugged good-naturedly. "Come on and have a drink," he said. "I'm buying."

Officially there was nothing stronger on the base than fruit juice, but most of the men and women kept private stashes of some sort. One thing led to another, and soon most of the people in the base had gathered in the cafeteria section of the dome. Several had brought bottles or flasks from their private quarters and splashed the various liquors into the plastic cups of juice—with one eye on Chang's closed door. The mission director enforced the rules with iron rigidity. Or tried to.

Carleton, in his makeshift workshop, heard the growing chatter and laughter across the dome. He looked up from the plaster cast he had lovingly made of the fossil vertebra.

"Sounds like a party," he said to Doreen McManus, who was watching him work.

She got up from the spindly stool she'd been sitting on and slid the door open a crack.

"It is a party," she said. "Looks like everybody who isn't on duty is in the cafeteria."

"Want to join them?" Carleton asked.

"Are you finished?"

He lifted the white plaster cast from the work table. "Isn't she a beauty? A lot better than those stereo images the computer generates."

He held it out to her and Doreen took it in her hands. "It is a beauty," she agreed, with an approving smile.

"The first of many," said Carleton as he took the actual ash-gray fossil and tucked it into a plastic specimen case he'd appropriated from the biology storeroom shelves. He closed its lid with a firm snap.

"Let's show it off," Doreen suggested.

Carleton grinned at her. "Why not?"

Soon the gathering that was spilling beyond the cafeteria's neatly arranged rows of tables was toasting Carleton and his discovery. The crowd's mood had lifted considerably since the drinking had started.

One of the astronauts who had ferried the team in from Hellas loudly insisted on calling the fossil "Carleton's clavicle," even when several of the others pointed out that it was actually a vertebra.

"Clavicle," the buzz-cut astronaut shouted, in a voice that drowned out everyone else. "It rhymes better."

Basking in the warmth of their approval, Carleton shook his head and laughed. He saw tall, gangling Saleem Hasdrubal stumbling through a tango with one of the women technicians. How can someone get drunk on fruit juice? he wondered. Sal's a Muslim, he doesn't drink liquor. Maybe Black Muslims don't abstain from alcohol. Or maybe fruit juice is enough to set him off.

Downing the last of the drink in his hand, he realized that Doreen was no longer at his side. Looking around, Carleton saw that she was chatting with a tall, lean young man who was wearing a denim shirt and chinos. The Navaho kid, Carleton remembered, brows knitting: Billy Graycloud. A computer geek.

Suddenly seething with anger, the liquor's warmth fueling him, Carleton marched through the crowd toward them.

"Goodbye, Raincloud," he growled.

Doreen looked startled, the Navaho more so.

"Uh, it's Graycloud, Dr. Carleton. Billy Graycloud, sir."

"Whatever." Carleton grasped Doreen's wrist. "The A team has arrived. Go back to your tepee."

And he towed Doreen away from the youngster. Graycloud stood there dumbfounded, his coppery cheeks flaming deep red.

"That was cruel," Doreen said, barely loud enough over the noise of the ongoing party for him to hear it.

"Fuck him," Carleton snapped.

"Is that what you were afraid I'd do?"

He turned on her angrily. "Now look, if you think—"

Just then Chang's office door slid open and the mission director stepped out, with Yvonne Lorenz behind him. Carleton stopped in midsentence. All the laughter snapped off as if a switch had been clicked. Everyone froze where they stood. In the abrupt silence Carleton could hear the soft footfalls of Chang's slippersocks against the plastic flooring.

Furtively trying to hide their liquor bottles and flasks, the crowd in the cafeteria melted away before him as Chang strode into their midst, arms stiffly at his sides, hands balled into round little fists.

"Carter Carleton, I too wish to congratulate you," Chang said. "You have made an important discovery. You will be honored for it."

Blinking with surprise, Carleton said, "Why, thank you, Dr. Chang. Er . . . would you like some juice?"

With the slightest dip of his pudgy chin, Chang said, "Yes. I want to offer a toast."

Doreen, standing at Carleton's side, picked up an empty cup and poured a splash of the nearest fruit juice into it, then wordlessly handed it to the mission director.

Chang raised his cup and proclaimed, "To Dr. Carleton. May your discovery be the first of many. May we uncover a village of ancient Martians and learn much about them."

Somebody shouted, "Hear! Hear!" But Chang impatiently waved them all to silence.

"I am not finished," he said.

Turning to Yvonne Lorenz, Chang went on, "To you who have been forced to abandon your work at Hellas site I offer my thanks for your toil and my regret that your effort has been terminated. I have added my highest recommendations to each of your personnel files."

They murmured thanks.

Chang half-turned and gestured to Dr. Lorenz. She was a short, slim Provençal with dark hair that was streaked with gray, a lean face that ended in a pointy chin, and eyes the color of a polar sea. Like almost everyone else, she wore coveralls, but hers were carefully tailored to her petite figure.

In a low but firm voice she said, "I believe we should all thank Dr. Chang for his generous recommendation. I realize most of you are disappointed to be sent home. I know that I myself am."

"I won't miss living in that damned camper," said one of the astronauts. No one laughed.

Lorenz said, "I must admit that our living accommodations were . . . eh, what is the word?"

"Rugged."

"Crowded."

"Piss poor—especially when the toilets broke down."

That brought a chuckle. But Lorenz said, "No, the word I wanted is 'Spartan.' Our living conditions were Spartan."

"You can say that again."

"She already did."

"Please," Lorenz said, making a silencing motion with both her tiny hands. "Hear me out. Dr. Carleton has asked for five volunteers to help him excavate the village. Five of us may remain here if we are willing to assist Dr. Carleton."

For a moment no one spoke. Then one of the men asked, "What kind of work would this be?"

"Manual labor," Carleton answered, raising his voice so that they could all hear him clearly. "For the most part it'll be digging and hauling a lot of dirt and rock. Not glamorous. Hard physical labor."

They looked at one another. Carleton knew exactly what was on their minds: How will this look on my résumé?

He added, "Of course, we'll also be sifting through the digging to look for fossils. Even artifacts, eventually."

No one said another word. They shifted uneasily on their feet, thinking, weighing, pondering.

"If any of you wants to talk to me individually," Carleton said, "I'll be happy to go into as much detail as you like."

Lorenz said, "Five of you will be able to stay on Mars. Your work will not be the same as you have been doing, but you may have an opportunity to help uncover great discoveries."

Chang added, "You have five days to make your decisions. In five days rocket from Earth will take up orbit above us. By then you must decide if you wish to remain to assist Dr. Carleton or return home."

"Can we get credits in anthropology out of this?" one of the younger men asked.

Carleton smiled at him. "If you like I'll give colloquia on anthropology."

Doreen piped up, "I might be able to arrange for Selene University to give course credits for working on the dig."

"Very good," said Chang. "Five days to make a decision." He put his cup down on the corner of the nearest table and glanced at his wristwatch. "It is late. Past ten o'clock. We all have much work to do tomorrow."

With that, the mission director turned and walked back through the crowd, heading for his private quarters.

"He is right," said Yvonne Lorenz. "We shall have to unload the plane and prepare for departure in five days."

The crowd started to break up and drift toward their individual cubicles. Doreen stood uncertainly beside Carleton. He could see the doubt in her eyes.

Drawing in a breath, he said, "I'm sorry about my boorish behavior. I just didn't like the way that kid was looking at you."

She smiled a little. "You were awfully gruff with him."

"Maybe," he acknowledged.

"Possessive."

"The word you're looking for is *dominant.*"

She didn't reply, but she allowed Carleton to lead her across the floor of the dome to the flimsy accordion-fold door of his compartment. All the others were entering their own spaces, most singly, although there were several couples. Doreen scanned the area for Graycloud but didn't see him. The others pointedly ignored Carleton and Doreen McManus as he stood in front of his door, gazing steadily into her wide, gray green eyes.

"They're all going to know about this," he said to her, almost solemnly.

She made a little shrug. "Everybody knows about everybody here. It's okay."

"I'm an accused rapist, back Earthside."

"That's a hundred million kilometers away," Doreen said.

He said, "Eighty-three million, two hundred thousand klicks, as of this morning. I checked."

Doreen smiled up at him. "You want to, don't you?"

He smiled at her. "When love speaks," he quoted, "the voice of all the Gods makes heaven drowsy with the harmony."

Holding her arm gently, he slid open the door of his cubicle with his other hand, glad that he had put clean sheets on his bunk that morning.

ALBUQUERQUE: UNIVERSITY OF NEW MEXICO

■

The day after Jamie returned from Washington the terrorist attack struck the campus.

He was in his office, on the phone with Dex Trumball, trying to make arrangements for his flight to Mars.

"You want to go back?" Dex asked, his image on the wall screen showing the disapproval that he tried to keep out of his voice.

"I have to," said Jamie.

"Why? To preside over the funeral?"

"To try to keep the program alive. There isn't going to be any funeral, not if I can help it."

Dex shook his head. "It doesn't make sense, Jamie. There's nothing you can do there that you can't do here."

"I've got to go."

"Don't get mystical on me. And don't—"

Three explosions rocked the building, so close together they sounded like the beats of an enormous ceremonial drum. The window of Jamie's office cracked, the room shook as if struck by a sudden earthquake. Books slid off the shelves.

"What the hell was that?" Dex hollered.

Jamie saw black smoke billowing above the campus buildings outside his window, then heard the wail of sirens. Footsteps pounded by in the corridor outside his door.

"Jamie, are you okay?"

"Yeah," Jamie answered shakily, staring at the rising smoke. "I'll call you back, Dex."

He rushed to his door and yanked it open. The corridor was empty now. Hurrying downstairs, Jamie saw that the lobby of his building was a blackened, smoking ruin, windows shattered, doors punched in, ceiling tiles dangling precariously. In a few minutes, firefighters and campus police officers were hauling bodies outside, where ambulances were pulling up. People were screaming, crying, bleeding.

Jamie helped lift the bloodied, mangled bodies of students and staff people out into the sunshine. A crowd was growing outside the yellow tapes the campus police were stringing across the parking lot. City police were arriving. A SWAT team van squealed to a stop.

"Goddamn towel-heads," one of the campus cops muttered as they tenderly laid the dead body of a young female student on the concrete. Her legs had been blown off. Jamie fought down the urge to throw up.

It seemed like hours, but Jamie's wristwatch told him that hardly thirty minutes had passed since the explosions. Television vans were pulling up. Helicopters thuttered overhead. The lobby of the Planetary Sciences building was a twisted, shattered mess.

His pocket phone jangled. Straightening up, he fumbled in his jeans pocket for it, flipped it open.

"Are you all right?" Even in the phone's minuscule screen he could see the wide-eyed fright on Vijay's dark face.

"I'm fine, honey," he said, wiping at his sweaty brow.

"You're not hurt?"

"No. They bombed the lobby. I was in my office."

"They said on TV that four people were killed."

Jamie glanced at the bodies laid out in a row. "It's more than that."

"But you're okay?"

Nodding, he replied, "Yes, I'm fine."

"Your face looks bruised."

He almost smiled at her. "Dirt, more likely. I've been helping get the bodies out of the lobby area."

"Come home, Jamie. That's where I'm heading, right now."

"The police'll probably want to ask me some questions. I'll get home soon's I can."

"I love you, dear," said Vijay.

"Same here, love."

He clicked the phone shut, returned it to his pocket. And felt the bear fetish that Grandfather Al had given him all those years ago. It didn't make him feel any better, any safer.

One of the paramedics came up to him, pulling off his latex gloves. "That's the last of the bodies. Thanks for your help."

He took the man's proffered hand, then walked off a ways, feeling stunned, numb. Who would do this? he asked himself. Why?

A city policeman stopped him to take his name and phone number. "The investigators'll wanna talk to you. You're not plannin' on leavin' town, are you?"

Jamie couldn't help a wry grin. "Only to Mars," he murmured.

"Huh?"

"No," he said, more distinctly. "I won't be leaving town in the next couple of weeks."

"Okay, good," said the police officer.

"Any idea of who did this?"

The policeman shook his head. "Hasn't been anything like this since the troubles in the Middle East, back when I was in the Army."

"Was this the only building hit?"

"They got the astronomy building, too. Over on the other side of the campus. And one other. Three, altogether."

And then Jamie realized who had set off the bombs. Oh my god, he repeated silently as he walked stiff-legged alone around the Planetary Sciences building to a side entrance. Oh my god. It wasn't Islamic fundamentalists. We have our own fanatics right here at home.

He picked his way through the litter in the hallways and entered his own office. It was messier than usual, but otherwise undamaged except for the obvious crack that ran the length of his window. I'm on the far side of the building, Jamie told himself as he sank slowly into his swivel chair. The blast didn't carry this far.

A knock on his door made him look up. The president of the university stepped in, looking grim.

Minor T. Halberson had been a star football player for the University of New Mexico's Lobos. Now he was a bishop of the New Morality movement and president of the university. He was a big man, still trim and tanned despite the distinguished gray flecking his temples. He was handsome, in a rugged, athletic way. He knew how to raise money, which was the primary qualification for a university president.

"You're not hurt?" Halberson asked, without any preliminaries.

"No, I'm okay," said Jamie.

"You look kind of grimy, if you'll pardon my saying so."

Jamie said, "I'll wash up when I get home."

"May I?" Halberson gestured toward the chair in front of Jamie's desk.

"Sure."

"This is terrible," said Halberson as he eased his bulk onto the squeaking plastic chair. "I never thought I'd see the day when terrorists would strike here."

"Neither did I."

"Car bombs." Halberson's normally smiling face was grave, ashen.

"The police told me they hit the astronomy building, too."

"And bio."

"All science buildings."

"Twenty-two killed, altogether."

"In the name of god."

Halberson looked sharply at Jamie. "You know I'm a Believer, Jamie, but this . . . this has nothing to do with God."

"The people who set off the bombs think it does. They think they're doing God's work."

"That's a perversion of everything that Christianity stands for."

"Tell them."

Halberson drew in a deep breath. "I don't blame you for being angry, Jamie. This has been . . . soul-shattering."

Jamie nodded, tight-lipped. Don't blame him for this, he warned himself. He's just as shook up about it as you are.

"It seems clear," Halberson said slowly, "that these attacks were aimed at the scientific work being done here on campus."

"But why?" Jamie wondered. "Why are they so set against exploring Mars?"

"Because you threaten their faith," Halbserson answered.

"We found the remains of another intelligent race and that threatens their faith?"

"Their narrow definition of it, yes. I think this news about finding a fossil tipped them into violence."

Jamie shook his head wearily. "I don't get it. We're uncovering facts on Mars. You can't make facts go away. You can't blast facts out of existence."

"They think they can," Halberson said. "Believe me, Jamie, I've had to deal with these fundamentalists in the church. They want everyone to forget that you've found intelligent life. They want to erase all traces of your discovery and return to where we were before you ever went to Mars."

"That's stupid! It's impossible!"

"They don't believe so. And they're willing to die in order to destroy you and everything you've learned."

Jamie fell speechless.

"It's obvious that they want to pressure the university into dropping our Mars program."

"Obvious," Jamie agreed.

"You yourself might be a target, Jamie."

Jamie felt a jolt of surprise. "Me?"

"You're the scientific leader of the program. If these terrorists want to stop the Mars program, what better way than to assassinate its chief?"

Or murder his wife, Jamie immediately thought.

"I'm ordering a security detail for you," Bishop Halberson said.

"And for my wife, too?"

"Yes, if you want it."

"I do."

"Is there anything else I can do? Just name it, Jamie. I know we don't agree on religious faith, but I'm just as infuriated by this barbarism as you are."

He's sincere, Jamie realized. Looking into Halberson's sorrowful eyes, Jamie believed that he could trust this man.

"It's all right," he said gently. "You won't need to protect me for very long. I'm going back to Mars as soon as I can make the arrangements."

"And your wife?"

"She's going with me. It's safer on Mars than it is here."

■

Thirteen-year-old Bucky Winters stared disconsolately at the tabletop model he had spent so many hours constructing.

"But . . . zero?" he asked. "No credit at all?"

"I'm afraid not," said Mr. Zachary.

Andrew Zachary was not only Bucky's art class teacher, he was head of the Longstreet Middle School's Arts and Achievement Department. Known to the students as an easy marker, Zachary was in his midforties, his face round and pleasant, his dark brown hair just starting to recede from his forehead. The students liked him; he tried to come across as their friend while still teaching them how to value their self-respect through using their hands to create art works.

Bucky was small and skinny, his face all bones and big blue green eyes with dark rings beneath them from the allergies that racked his existence. Like all the students, he wore the school uniform: a white tee shirt bearing the school's emblem of an extinct Florida panther, and a pair of shorts that sagged below his knees.

The teacher and his student were standing on opposite sides of the big display table in the middle of the arts room. On the table was a model of the Tithonium Base on Mars: three removable papier-mâché domes set on a large photo image of the Martian red, barren ground. Inside the domes

Bucky had painstakingly drawn the outlines of the base's laboratories, living quarters, offices, cafeteria and airlocks. He had even drawn in the beds and other furniture of the individual living units.

"But you said we could do anything we wanted to get special credit," Bucky reminded his teacher.

Zachary sighed. "The Mars project is not on the school's curriculum, Bucky. You don't study Mars in your science class, do you?"

"No. But I thought . . ." Bucky's voice trailed off into a hurt silence.

Zachary came around the table to stand beside Bucky. He almost put a comforting hand on the boy's shoulder, but realized that such contact could be considered sexual harassment if his student reported it.

"It's good work, Bucky. It really is. But it's not in an area that we can consider for class credit."

Bucky wanted to spit. He'd spent long hours at his computer at home to get all the details of the Mars base right. He'd thought he'd get an A-plus for his work.

"What's wrong with Mars?" he asked, almost in desperation.

Zachary spread his hands in a gesture of futility. "The school board decided that Mars shouldn't be part of the curriculum."

"How come?"

"Well . . . the scientists on Mars claim they've discovered the remains of intelligent Martians who lived millions and millions of years ago."

"So? That's great, isn't it?"

"Well, not really. You see, Bucky, there's no real proof that there were actual living people on Mars. It's just one of the scientists' theories, really."

"If they found buildings, isn't that proof?"

Zachary wrung his hands unhappily. "The school board feels that if we start teaching about Mars, then we'll have to get into Darwin and evolution and all that other controversial material. It's much easier to skip the entire business and stick with the curriculum as the school board has approved it."

"Darwin?" Bucky asked, puzzled. "What's Darwin?"

CLIPPERSHIP ROBERT TRUAX

■

Jamie felt distinctly uncomfortable as he and Vijay stepped from the access tunnel into the passenger compartment of the Clippership. The thought of riding the squat, conical rocket craft into orbit didn't bother him at all: it was the destination, not the journey, that made him jittery.

A young male attendant in a snappy royal blue and silver uniform showed them to their seats in the circular compartment. There were no windows in the curved bulkhead; thick insulation seemed to smother all sounds. It reminded Jamie of walking into a hushed planetarium chamber. He noted that fewer than half of the fifty seats were occupied.

"First class," Vijay murmured as they clicked their shoulder harnesses into place.

"Dex paid for the tickets out of his personal pocket," Jamie said. "He claims the Foundation can't afford any luxuries."

"That was nice of him."

Jamie grinned at her. They both knew that Clipperships had two passenger decks but only one class of accommodations. Everybody rode first class. Someday, Jamie thought, when Clippership travel becomes more popular, they'll start squeezing in more seats and cutting down on the services. Enjoy the first-class treatment while you can.

Each seat had its own foldout display screen that could show entertainment videos, educational documentaries, or real-time views from the cameras mounted on the ship's exterior. Vijay opted for the outside view of the servicing trucks scurrying around the Clippership's launch pad. Jamie leaned back in his plush reclinable chair and closed his eyes.

This is going to be tricky, he told himself for the thousandth time.

Douglas Stavenger was the acknowledged leader of the lunar nation of Selene. He had the influence—if he chose to wield it—to convince Selene's governing council to take over the task of providing the Mars explorers with the supplies they would need to keep going in spite of the cutoff of funding from the U.S. government.

Jamie had never met Stavenger. To get to him, Jamie had turned to Stavenger's wife, Edith Elgin. Edith and Jamie had lived together in Houston nearly thirty years earlier, when Jamie was in training for the First Expedition. He had left for Mars and never saw her again; she had climbed up to a top position in the broadcast news industry, covered Selene's brief war of independence, and stayed on the Moon to marry Stavenger.

Edith had agreed easily enough to setting up a meeting with her husband when Jamie had called her from Albuquerque. He didn't know whether he should feel surprised, pleased, or alarmed. So instead he worried.

"This is your captain speaking." The confident male voice coming through the intercom speakers startled Jamie out of his anxiety.

"We're cleared for liftoff in ninety seconds. You'll experience eight minutes of acceleration forces; two and a half gees. Then we'll coast into orbit and rendezvous with Space Station *Wilson*. IAA regulations require that you remain in your seats at all times with your safety harness buckled. You can play around in zero gee once you're inside the station. For now, please lower your seats back to the full reclining position. Thank you."

"Too bad we won't be spending an overnight at the station," Vijay teased as they cranked their seats down.

Jamie knew she was referring to making love in zero gravity. There was even talk of building a "honeymoon hotel" in orbit.

"On the way back," he told her. "I'll change our tickets."

"We'll have to wait that long?" She put on a pout.

"Business before pleasure."

"Five seconds," the ship's computer-synthesized voice called out. "Four . . . three . . ."

Jamie gripped Vijay's hand. The rocket engines roared with the hot breath of a thousand dragons but inside the cabin their bellowing was muted, distant. The heavy hand of acceleration squeezed Jamie down into the cushions of his couch. He could see on Vijay's display screen the ground hurtling away, then the view was obscured by the smoky exhaust of the rocket engines.

The compartment quivered, but it was nothing like the bone-rattling vibration he remembered from flights into orbit in the older-style rocket boosters. They've improved the ride, Jamie said to himself. Too bad there aren't more paying passengers to enjoy it.

The noise dwindled and then the pressure cut off abruptly. Jamie's arms floated up off the seatrests, as did Vijay's. He heard passengers cooing and sighing with delight as all sensation of weight dropped away. They raised their seatbacks and looked around. Then somebody coughed and gagged. There's always one, Jamie thought as he reached for the air blower control and dialed it to maximum. Sure enough, someone behind them was throwing up noisily. Hope she made it to the retch bag, he said to himself. One vomiting passenger started a chain reaction; soon several of them were heaving loudly and Jamie started to feel nauseous himself.

One of the uniformed flight attendants hurried down the aisle past them as Vijay patted Jamie's hand and said, "Put in the earplugs. It's better if you can't hear 'em."

It'd be better if I couldn't smell them, Jamie thought. He grabbed the plastic bag containing earplugs from the pocket built into the chair's armrest while bile burned up into his throat.

BY THE TIME THE Clippership made its rendezvous with the space station fifty-four minutes later, the passengers had calmed down and the stench of vomit had been cleared from the cabin's air. A female flight attendant ran a short video that advised the debarking passengers not to try any acrobatics in zero gee.

"You will feel a stuffiness in your sinuses as your body fluids adjust to the lack of gravity," said the cheerful white-smocked woman on the screens. "This is perfectly normal. Your body is adapting to the microgravity environment."

Vijay and Jamie didn't see much of the space station. The terminal where the Clippership docked was designed to accommodate arrivals who were not accustomed to the nearly zero gravity of the orbiting station. Passageways were thickly carpeted and narrow enough for passengers to grip the handrails set on both sides of the bulkheads so that they could proceed cautiously, hand by hand, to the reception area.

Jamie's head felt stuffy as he shuffled along in the slowly moving line. Vijay was just ahead of him, apparently handling the microgee with no trouble at all. A young man several places up the line, wearing the gray coveralls of a technician, laughingly allowed himself to float off the floor and rise until his crewcut hair bumped gently against the overhead.

Several of the older passengers groaned at the sight.

"Please don't attempt any gymnastics in this confined space," called the female attendant from the head of the line.

"Get down, Grabowski," a rougher voice demanded. "Don't start with your wiseass crap."

Jamie laughed softly. The temptation to show off was irresistible in some men. Especially if they were young and there were young women present to show off for.

Moving carefully, Jamie and Vijay left the other arrivals and followed the illuminated arrows along the bulkheads that led them to the docking port where the lunar shuttlecraft would depart for Selene. A pair of smiling attendants were at the port and guided them through the open hatch of the shuttlecraft.

The shuttlecraft's passenger compartment was less than half the size of the Clippership's, and much more utilitarian. Jamie and Vijay found their seats and strapped in.

"Whew!" Vijay gusted, her expression halfway between a grin and a grimace. "I'd forgotten how snarky zero gee can be when you're not used to it."

Keeping a straight face, Jamie replied, "You're not reneging on our overnight stay on the way back, are you?"

She started to shake her head, but thought better of it. "I don't know about you, love, but I'm out of training."

Very seriously, Jamie said, "Might take a few nights to get our sea legs back."

Vijay smiled impishly. "Well, if you've got the time . . ."

"We'll see," he said. "Depends on how things go with Stavenger."

SELENE

■

Jamie and Vijay never saw the outside of the lunar shuttle-craft. The passenger compartment was small, only a dozen seats, but every one of them was filled. They looked like business people, Jamie thought as he surveyed the other Moon-bound passengers. Suits, mostly dark in color although there were a couple of bright sports coats in the lot. Not scientists or techies: no jeans or pullovers, except for his own.

The shuttlecraft accelerated at nearly a full g halfway to the Moon, then turned around and decelerated the rest of the way to the surface of the huge crater Alphonsus. The g force was enough to keep everyone's stomach reasonably in place for the five-hour-long trip. They even had a meal in transit with no more difficulty than sipping the wine from covered containers. An animated video showed the passengers the details of the shuttlecraft's trajectory and its highly efficient plasma propulsion system.

"It took the Apollo astronauts more than three days to make the trip from Earth to Moon," explained the video's voice track. "Today it takes only a few hours to travel the same distance."

The thrust was enough to banish the woozy feeling of zero gee. Jamie felt almost normal by the time the shuttlecraft settled down on the dusty concrete landing pad at Armstrong Spaceport.

"Here on the Moon you are now in one-sixth of normal terrestrial gravity," the safety video warned. "Please use extreme caution when walking or moving about. Weighted boots are available at the visitors' center for a nominal rental fee."

Neither Jamie nor Vijay bothered with the boots. They headed out of the shuttlecraft in the slow shuffling strides they both remembered from earlier visits to the Moon. Other passengers stumbled and staggered in the low gravity.

They rode the automated electric bus through the long tunnel that connected the spaceport to the city proper. It looked like an oversized golf cart, roofless, with ten rows of double seats. Jamie used his pocket phone to pull up a map of Selene and locate the hotel.

"This place has grown, even in the few years since I was here," he said, showing Vijay the labyrinth of tunnels that made up the underground community.

"People come up here to retire," she said. "The low gravity and all that."

All that meant escaping from Earth's problems, Jamie knew: from the crime and poverty and the disastrous flooding and climate changes that racked the world.

"Pretty expensive retirement," he muttered.

"The rich always run away," Vijay said. "They use their money to insulate them from troubles."

Is that what we're doing? Jamie asked himself silently as the bus rolled smoothly, quietly through the shadowy tunnel. Running away to Mars? No, he immediately answered. We're exploring a new world, we're searching for new knowledge. Which is why the fundamentalists hate us.

"I don't know if I could live in these tunnels," Vijay said. "Not full time."

"Aussies do," Jamie said. "In Coober Pedy."

"The opal mines," she murmured. Then she added, "But they can go up on the surface any time they want."

Jamie said, "There's the Grand Plaza, under the dome. Plenty of trees and greenery up there. They even have a swimming pool."

Nodding, Vijay murmured, "Still . . ."

By the time they reached their hotel room, guided by the

electronic maps on the corridor walls, their two travel bags were already on the king-sized bed.

Jamie glanced at his wristwatch. "Hungry? It's just about dinnertime."

"Let's unpack first," she suggested.

It didn't take long. Soon they were walking up the gently sloping ramp that led to the hotel's restaurant. There were no stairs in Selene: too tricky for newcomers to the low lunar gravity.

"This is lovely," Vijay said once they were seated at a small table. The restaurant was almost full, but the patrons' conversations were quiet, muted. Soft music purred from the speakers set into the ceiling, something classical that sounded vaguely familiar to Jamie. Human waiters in dark jackets moved among the tables, together with flat-topped little robots that carried the food and drinks.

"Big day tomorrow." Vijay smiled brightly, trying to make it sound cheerful.

"Right," Jamie agreed. Inwardly he wondered what it was going to be like seeing Edith again.

Once they had ordered and the human waiter was walking away from their table, Jamie started to say, "Um, Vijay, you know that Edith and I . . ."

"I know," she said, her dark eyes on him. "You told me years ago."

"I haven't seen her since then," he muttered. "I wonder what she's like now."

"We'll soon find out, won't we, love?"

SELENE: STAVENGER RESIDENCE

■

Like almost all of Selene, the home of Douglas Stavenger was in one of the underground corridors that made up most of the city. Up on the airless surface of the Moon, temperatures could swing from two hundred degrees above zero in sunlight to nearly two hundred below in shadow. Hard radiation from deep space bathed the barren lunar surface, and a constant infall of micrometeoroids peppered the ground, sandpapering the mountains over eons of time into tired, rounded humps.

Underground was safer, the deeper the better.

"I couldn't live here," Vijay said, frowning slightly as she and Jamie walked along the corridor, following the path mapped out on his pocket phone.

"You said that before," Jamie reminded her.

"Yes, but now I'm certain of it."

"You lived on Mars," he said.

"But there we had a dome, we could move around, we could look outside. We could work outside—"

"In spacesuits. Or in an enclosed tractor."

"But it wasn't like this. . . . This is like being a mole or a wombat, living in tunnels." She shuddered with distaste.

Eying a trio of coverall-clad people coming up the corridor toward them, Jamie half-whispered, "Better not let them know how much you don't like it here."

Vijay smiled at them as they approached. They noted Jamie's western-cut shirt and jeans, the colorful scarf Vijay wore knotted at her throat over her poppy red blouse.

"Can we help you?" one of the men asked.

Jamie said, "I think we're in the right corridor. Level four, corridor A?"

The man nodded, smiling. "Looking for Doug Stavenger's place? It's right down the corridor." He pointed.

Jamie thanked them and they went their separate ways.

Vijay shook her head. "I don't understand how they can live like this. It's so completely . . . artificial."

"Maybe we ought to ask Dex how he does it."

"Dex lives in Boston."

"He spends a lot of time in New York. That's a completely artificial environment, too."

"At least you can walk out in the open."

"If you're carrying a weapon," Jamie countered.

At last they came to a plain door, no different from the others spaced along the corridor, except that it was marked STAVENGER.

"This is it," Jamie said, taking in a breath. Edith's in there, he thought. I wonder—

The door opened before he could find a buzzer to push. A solidly built young-looking man smiled at them. His face was handsome, his skin darker than Jamie's, lighter than Vijay's. Jamie realized that he was taller and wider of shoulder than himself, but his compact physique disguised his true size. He was wearing a soft velour pullover of deep blue and comfortable light gray slacks.

He smiled and put out his hand. "Welcome. I'm Douglas Stavenger."

His grip was warm, strong without being overpowering.

"Jamie Waterman," he introduced himself. "This is my wife, Vijay."

"Come on in," said Stavenger, with an ushering swoop of his arm.

They stepped into an unpretentious living room tastefully furnished with a pair of sofas facing each other, an oval metal coffee table between them. A pair of cushioned armchairs were placed on either end of the low table. The floor was carpeted, grass green. The pictures on the wall looked like actual paintings, not flat-screen images, mostly landscapes from Earth.

"Make yourselves comfortable," Stavenger said, gesturing to the nearer sofa. "My wife will be—"

At that moment Edith entered from an open doorway on the far side of the living room. She seemed to light up the place, radiantly blond and smiling bright as a Dallas cheerleader, big wide eyes the color of Texas bluebonnets, wearing a short-skirted sleeveless frock of white patterned with golden yellow flowers.

Jamie felt suddenly tongue-tied.

"Hello, Jamie," she said, striding straight to him.

"Edith," he managed.

She kissed him on the cheek, then turned to Vijay. "You must be Varuna Jarita."

"Vijay, please. It's easier."

"Vijay," Edith acknowledged, taking both Vijay's hands in her own. Dark and light, Jamie thought. They couldn't look more different if they came from different worlds.

Then he realized, "My god, Edith, you haven't changed a bit. You look as if you haven't aged at all."

Edith flicked a glance at her husband. "We're aging, but a lot slower than most folks."

"Nanomachines," Vijay guessed.

"Yes."

"You, too?" Jamie asked.

Edith smiled, almost demurely. "Me, too. Doug wants to keep me just as young as he is."

"It's a bit incredible, i'n't it?" said Vijay.

"It certainly is."

Stavenger gestured again to the twin sofas. "Sit. Relax. Would you like something to drink? Wine? Rocket juice?"

Jamie laughed. "No rocket juice, thanks. I've heard about that."

"Some wine, then?" Edith suggested. "It's new and kind of thin."

"Our first vintage," Stavenger explained.

Jamie and Vijay sat on one of the sofas, Edith on the facing one, while Stavenger ducked behind the counter that separated the living room from the kitchen.

"How do you like living here?" Vijay asked.

"It's fine," said Edith.

"Doesn't it bother you to be underground all the time?"

"You didn't grow up in west Texas, honey. This is a whole lot better, believe me. 'Sides, we've got the Grand Plaza any time you want to see trees and some flowers."

Jamie listened to them chatter and realized the two women were communicating on a level far beyond his male power of understanding. They're sizing each other up, he thought; getting to know each other in some subliminal way.

Stavenger carried in a metal tray bearing a frosted bottle of wine and four stemmed glasses.

"We make these in our glass factory," he said as he poured for them. "Bricks for construction, too."

Jamie sipped at the wine. It was thin and slightly tart. They do a lot better in New Mexico, he said to himself.

"So," Stavenger said, setting his glass down on the coffee table, "Edith tells me you need to talk to me."

Jamie nodded. "We need your help."

" 'We' being the Mars program?"

"That's right. You've heard about Washington zeroing Mars out of the federal budget."

"That's a blow, isn't it?" Stavenger said softly.

"It's not just Washington's cutoff. It's becoming increasingly hard to get private donors. Several of our biggest contributors have backed away from us."

Vijay interjected, "They're all under pressure to help alleviate the problems from the climate shift."

"Those are serious problems," Stavenger murmured.

"I know," said Jamie. "But we mustn't let them stop the exploration of Mars."

"Why not?" Stavenger asked, with a smile.

"Why not?" Jamie snapped.

Raising his hands almost defensively, Stavenger said, "I'm playing devil's advocate for the moment. Why shouldn't the exploration of Mars be stopped? Aren't the greenhouse disasters on Earth more important?"

Jamie glanced at Vijay, who nodded encouragement to him. If you want help from this man, he thought, you've got to be honest with him. You've got to bare your soul to him.

Taking a deep breath, Jamie began, "First, I don't see it as an either-or situation. We can work on the greenhouse problems and explore Mars, too. They're not mutually exclusive."

"Everyone else seems to think they are," said Stavenger.

Shaking his head, Jamie went on, "The greenhouse crisis is being used as an excuse to kill the Mars program."

"Used as an excuse?" Edith asked, her blue eyes widening. "Who by?"

"The fundamentalists. The New Morality and their people in government. They don't want us to learn more about the Martians. They want to bury everything we've discovered, forget about it forever. They've got control of the government, they're scaring the big money into lining up with them. Everywhere I turn to, there's this big invisible enemy all around me, stifling me, pushing me down. I feel like I'm drowning."

Stavenger looked at his wife for a moment, then turned back to Jamie. "So you're asking Selene to take up the funding burden for you?"

"I don't think of it as a burden."

"A poor choice of words. But you need financial help, don't you?"

Jamie hesitated, then admitted, "Yes. It boils down to funding."

"Always does," Edith murmured.

Stavenger reached up and scratched at his dark brown hair. The gesture made him look suddenly boyish.

"Look," he said. "Selene isn't prosperous enough to spend billions on something that won't bring us any return."

"It won't cost billions," Jamie said.

"No?"

"Basically, what we need is help with transportation. I plan to ask the men and women on Mars to stretch out their stays an extra year, so we can cut our transportation costs just about in half."

"Except for life-support supplies," Vijay interjected.

Jamie suppressed an urge to scowl at her. "Supplies are a major part of it, yes."

Stavenger asked, "How much of your life-support requirements do you generate from Mars itself?"

"We take oxygen and nitrogen from the atmosphere to make breathable air," Jamie replied. "Water from the permafrost. We grow some of our own food hydroponically."

Nodding, Stavenger said, "But you need protein, medical supplies, that sort of thing."

Impressed with Stavenger's understanding, Jamie said, "Right."

"We've been there. We've worked damned hard to make Selene as self-sufficient as possible. We use aquaculture to raise protein: fish, shellfish, frogs."

"Gives us a lot more protein for the energy inputs than a herd of cattle would," Edith added.

"Or even rabbits and smaller land animals," said Stavenger.

"You understand what we're up against, then," Jamie said.

"Yes," Stavenger replied, "but the question that needs to be answered is still, what's in it for Selene? We can't afford to be philanthropic."

"We're talking about exploring a new world!" Jamie said, trying to keep his tone even, reasonable. "A world that once bore intelligent life."

"I know that. But that exploration costs money. That's why you're here."

"Yes," Jamie admitted.

"I'm willing to do whatever I can to help you," Stavenger said. "But I've got to bring something reasonable to our governing council."

"Reasonable," Jamie muttered darkly.

"If there was some hope of a payback, some kind of return on our investment—"

"Exploring Mars isn't a profit-making operation," Jamie snapped. "Science doesn't give you a payback, not right away."

"I know that, but still—"

"But still, you're going to sit on your backside and let them close down the Mars program. The same people who tried to take over Moonbase, the same know-nothings and power brokers who've banned nanotechnology, who sat there for fuck-ing *decades* and let this greenhouse disaster roll over them, you're going to let them shut down the exploration of a new world without lifting a finger to help us!"

Jamie realized he was on his feet, standing in front of Stavenger, glowering down at him, while Vijay pulled at his sleeve.

I've got to apologize, Jamie told himself. I lost my temper. I shouldn't antagonize this man. I shouldn't be yelling at him.

But before Jamie could force a word past his lips, Stavenger smiled up at him.

"That's what I needed to see," Stavenger said, his voice mild, pleased. "I needed to see some passion. You're entirely right: this isn't a matter of profits and money. It's part of the struggle between knowledge and ignorance, between those who want to push back the frontier and those who want to control people."

Jamie stammered, "I didn't mean to . . ."

Vijay tugged harder at his sleeve and Jamie sat down on the sofa beside her with a thump.

Edith was smiling too. "I told you it was in his blood," she said to her husband.

"So I see," Stavenger murmured. Looking across the low table at Jamie, he said, "The frontier is where new knowledge comes from, whether it's the intellectual frontier of a labora-tory or the physical frontier of an unexplored territory. Selene is a frontier nation."

"So you'll help us?" Jamie asked.

"Let's see just how much I can coax out of the governing council."

Jamie stared at him, openmouthed.

"Thank you," Vijay said for him.

Stavenger's smile thinned a little. "Just don't expect a lot. Don't hope for miracles."

■

This is stupid, Dex Trumball said to himself. I'm acting like some asshole sneak thief.

It was past midnight. The offices of the Trumball Trust, on the top floor of the Trumball Tower in Boston's financial district, were empty and dark. Even the cleaning crew and their busy little robots had gone for the night. Everything was dark and quiet, except for Dex's office.

His office was unlit except for the big smart screen on the wall opposite the drapery-covered windows. The screen showed an image of the Grand Canyon in Arizona.

Sitting in the shadows behind his desk, Dex muttered to the silent image, "You're nothing but a little scratch in the ground, pal. Put you on Mars and you'd be just a minor alleyway compared to the *real* Grand Canyon."

But there was a complex of buildings on the rim of the Arizona canyon, and a spidery bridge arching across the chasm. People paid good money to visit and goggle at the canyon and drive across that bridge. They paid for rides on muleback down to the canyon's bottom. Good, steady money.

The desk phone said, "Mr. Kinnear on line one, sir."

Dex realized he was biting his lips. He opened his mouth, hesitated a heartbeat, then said, "On screen two, please."

Roland Kinnear's round, pleasantly smiling face appeared on the wall next to the picture of the Grand Canyon. He looked youthful, but Dex knew that was from cosmetic therapies. His hair was still light blond, and seemed a bit thicker than Dex remembered from their last meeting. A pencil-thin moustache adorned his upper lip.

"Hello, Dex," said Kinnear amiably. "It's been a long time."

Dex smiled back at the screen. "Hi, Rollie. Going on seven years, according to my files."

Kinnear laughed. "Still writing everything down, are you?"

"I guess," said Dex, trying to look relaxed. He had known Kinnear since they had attended Harvard Business School together, decades earlier.

"Must be past midnight in Boston," said Kinnear.

"Twelve twenty-two."

"We're just getting ready for our sunset cocktail here."

Kinnear was at his home on Hawaii's Big Island, Dex knew. Relaxed. Easygoing. But Rollie had a steel-sharp mind for business underneath his smiles and pleasantries.

Looking past Kinnear's image to the breeze-tossed palm trees and the surf rolling up on the beach, Dex said, "So, are you really retired or is this just a smoke screen?"

Laughing, Kinnear said, "I'm no more retired than you are, Dex. You and your Mars Foundation."

"Glad to hear it."

"Oh?"

"I want to run an idea past you. Do you mind?"

Without an instant's hesitation, Kinnear said, "Go right ahead."

"I was thinking about that tourist operation you run in Arizona."

"The Grand Canyon operation? It's a money-loser. The Parks people won't let me expand the facility. Took *years* to get them to okay the bridge, and we still get protesters now'n then. Some day the bastards'll blow up the bridge, you wait and see."

"How'd you like to work with the Navaho Nation instead of the feds?"

"What're you planning to do, build housing on their reservation land?"

"No, no. Tourism."

"Tourism?"

"On Mars."

For the first time Dex could remember, Kinnear went absolutely speechless.

Dex went on, "We've got a Grand Canyon on Mars, you know. A hundred times bigger than yours."

"On Mars?" Kinnear echoed.

"Transportation's easy," Dex said, stretching the truth. "The new fusion ships get you there in a few days. You're not in zero gee at all, hardly: it feels like regular Earth gravity most of the way."

"Dex, have you dipped into the cooking sherry? On flickin' *Mars*? Who the hell's going to pay the kind of money that'd take?"

Be careful with him, Dex warned himself. Don't let him know how desperate you are.

"Listen," he said lightly. "When space tourism started, people paid twenty million bucks, American, to spend a few days on a space station in Earth orbit."

"How many people?" Rollie asked. "Five? Six?"

"More than that. But within a couple of years guys like Branson were selling tickets for rides into orbit for twenty thousand bucks apiece. He made millions on it."

"And now people go for vacations on the Moon," Kinnear murmured.

Dex realized his old friend had done some homework, after all. Good. Now reel him in slowly.

"How much do you think people would pay for a two-week vacation on Mars?" he asked.

"Anybody can make a virtual reality visit to Mars for a few dollars, Dex. You sell 'em, remember?"

"How much would you pay for a *real* visit to Mars?" Dex asked, dangling the bait. "Walk through the buildings in the cleft in the valley wall. See the remains of the village that they're digging up. Plant your footprints where no human being has ever stepped before."

Kinnear looked thoughtful. "It'd be strictly a high-end operation. Very expensive. Only a small market."

"But a highly profitable market. Big ticket price."

"The scientists will allow it? I thought they're keeping Mars off-limits to tourism."

"I'll handle the scientists," Dex said.

"And the Native Americans?"

He *has* done his homework, Dex realized. He replied, "They want to make money out of Mars just as much as we do. They'll go for it, if we control the operation carefully."

"Visit Mars," Kinnear mused. Then he broke into a beaming grin. "Could be the big prestige item among the glitterati, couldn't it?"

"We could invite some big shot politicians," Dex suggested.

"Go for stars instead. Better publicity. Might get lucky with some of those big-busted twits." Kinnear laughed.

Same old Rollie, Dex said to himself. He hasn't changed.

Then he thought: But neither has Jamie.

BOOK II
VISITORS

*The Old Ones knew that The People had come to the blue
world after a long struggle. Once they had lived on the
red world, but Coyote—the Trickster—led them to their
downfall and then brought on a devastating flood that drove
them away.*

*First Man and First Woman emerged into the blue world
and carried all the memories of The People with them.
But in time the memories faded and the younger generations
began to doubt that they were anything more than dreams
and visions.*

*What they forgot was that dreams and visions show a reality
that is as strong and certain as the greatest tree or the
highest mountain.*

*What they forgot was that without dreams and visions
The People wither into mere husks.*

CRATER MALZBERG

■

W ell, y'know, a watched pot never boils."
"Oh lord, spare me your stupid clichés."

Itzak Rosenberg and Saleem Hasdrubal were unlikely part-
ners. Izzy was an Oxford-educated Londoner, small and soft-
looking, with the frizzy reddish blond hair of his distant
ancestors from Poland and Belarus. Sal was from Chicago,
tall and lanky enough to have made his way through school
playing basketball.

They argued about everything, from international politics
to ethnic cuisines. They even argued about the importance of
geology versus biology. Izzy, a geologist, had been blown
away when he was nine years old by his first visit to the chalk
cliffs of Dover; the secret history that they contained in their
layered striations set him on his life's course. Sal had been
equally thrilled with his first visit to the dinosaur reconstructions at Chicago's Field Museum, on a class trip when he was
in the seventh grade. He won a basketball scholarship to Pur-
due, then went on to the University of Chicago for an eventual
doctorate in cellular biology.

Now they stood glumly in their nanosuits on the surface
of Mars, near the minor crater Malzberg, disappointed that
the geyser they were hoping for had so far refused to erupt.

They had been living at the crater's edge for more than a
week in one of the campers, a bullet-shaped vehicle with a
big, bulging windshield that looked like an insect's eyes; it
rode on a set of eight springy metal wheels. It looked to

Sal's city-raised eyes like an urban bus, although he'd never seen a bus so coated and smeared with reddish dust.

All around them stretched the barren rusty plain, cold and silent except for the faint whisper of a thin breeze. The Sun hung high in the cloudless butterscotch sky, but the thermometer on the wrist of Izzy's nanofabric suit read thirty-six below zero. Summer weather, he thought wryly.

Dr. Chang, the mission director, was stretching the safety regulations to allow these two scientists to go out on this excursion without an astronaut to drive the camper. But there were only nine astronauts at Tithonium Base and they were committed to other, larger excursions along the floor of the rift valley and out to the huge volcanoes of the Tharsis highlands.

Originally, Chang had sent an automated rover to the Malzberg crater, a small six-wheeled robot that was supposed to go into the crater and deploy a set of sensors that would monitor the heat flow and other conditions at the site. But the doughty little rover had broken down inside the crater. Rosenberg and Hasdrubal had been sent to repair it, but the machinery was too old, too worn, too clogged with years of Martian dust, for them to get it working again. Despite the detailed advice from technicians back at the base, they could not bring the rover back to life.

So now they stood at the edge of the crater waiting like expectant fathers for a geyser that had so far failed to materialize. They had come out as repairmen but had urged Chang to let them stay and observe as scientists. Chang had reluctantly allowed it; not all that reluctantly, actually: he wanted to capture a geyser as much as they did.

The crater was slightly less than two hundred meters across, oval in shape, about thirty meters deep. Its rim of rubble was new and fresh looking. There were no smaller craters inside it, an indication that it was quite young. Two dozen metal boxes and pole-like instruments were arrayed along its slopes and bottom: seismometers, heat-flow probes, digital cameras, even miniaturized spectrometers in case the geyser actually blew and there was some erupting gas to analyze. A half-dozen shallow trenches showed where they had scooped up soil samples to analyze back at the base for the dim chance of finding microbial life.

"Everything's right," Sal Hasdrubal said, to no one in particular. "It's a young crater. The heat flow measurements peak at its bottom. The permafrost layer is only a dozen meters down from the surface. Why doesn't it blow?"

"It will, sooner or later," said Rosenberg.

"Later might be a thousand years from now."

"Or this afternoon."

Hasdrubal shook his head inside his transparent helmet. "Nah. The fucker's gonna blow soon's as we pack up and leave."

"Which will be tomorrow," said Izzy. "We'll have to lift the rover into the cargo bay, if we can."

Sal shifted his gaze to the inert rover, sitting squat and silent alongside their camper. Dumb little fucker, he said to himself. Then he shrugged inwardly. Shouldn't complain. I guess after ten years of work you're entitled to a breakdown.

"We'll get it in," he said to Izzy. "Only weighs one-third of what it would on Earth."

Rosenberg gave him a doubtful look. "We'll have to use the winch."

"Yeah," Hasdrubal agreed. Then, drawing in a deep breath, he said, "Come on, let's get back into the camper. This friggin' suit's startin' to smell like a garbage can."

"You have a lovely way with words, Sal."

They began trudging back to the waiting camper, two nanosuited figures completely alone as far as the eye could see.

"How come they don't name craters after Muslims?" Hasdrubal abruptly asked.

"They're named after scientists, mostly," said Rosenberg. "Newton, Kuiper, Agassiz . . ."

"Plenty named after Jews. Why not Muslims?"

Rosenberg sighed heavily. "Perhaps it's because there are so few Muslim scientists?"

They had reached the camper's airlock hatch. As he pecked at the keypad to open it, Sal countered, "Oh yeah? What about Abdus Salam? He won the Nobel Prize, for chrissake. What about Alhazen or Avicenna or Omar Khayyam? He was a great astronomer, you know."

"Oh, spare me," Rosenberg muttered.

"It's anti-Islamic prejudice," Sal said as he climbed up into the coffin-sized airlock and sealed the hatch, leaving Rosenberg standing outside by the silent robotic rover.

"By the well-known Jewish cabal," Rosenberg retorted, his voice sounding close to exasperation in Sal's clip-on earphone.

"You said that, I didn't."

Once they had wormed out of their suits and vacuumed most of the dust off them, they went up to the camper's front end and sat at the padded seats. The faint pungent tang of ozone penetrated even up to the cockpit, baked out of the superoxides in the dust by the heat of the camper's interior.

Hasdrubal sat in the driver's seat, Rosenberg beside him. Through the curving windshield they could see the crater, as inert and uncooperative as ever. Both men were unshaven: Rosenberg's once-neat little goatee looked decidedly ragged, Hasdrubal's jaw was covered in dark fuzz.

As they checked the instruments, Sal muttered, "The heat flow's there, goddammit. Why don't she blow?"

"Not enough heat to melt the permafrost, obviously," said Rosenberg.

"Oughtta be. Look at the numbers."

Rosenberg sighed again. "Science, my friend, is the difference between what you think ought to be and what actually is."

Sal nodded reluctant agreement. "It's a perverse universe."

"It is indeed." Rosenberg started out of his seat. "Let's get some lunch. I'm famished."

Hasdrubal watched him head back to the minuscule galley built into the camper's curving bulkhead, then turned back to stare out the windshield again. Come on, goddammit, he urged silently. I know you're gonna blow, why not do it while I'm watchin'? Why not let me see what you can do?

But the crater remained silent, inactive.

Sonofabitch, Sal cursed fervently.

Suddenly a bright streak arched across the sky. A sonic boom pinged weakly in the thin Martian air.

"Hey, there's a ship comin' in," Hasdrubal called back to the galley.

Rosenberg barely looked up from the sandwiches he was making. "It must be the flight that's bringing Waterman in," he said.

TITHONIUM BASE: ARRIVAL

■

Vijay could see Jamie's spirits rising as the landing craft screeched through the cloudless atmosphere of Mars toward the Tithonium Base site.

"There's the domes," he said, pointing at the display screen set into the bulkhead of the windowless passenger compartment. She saw three pinkish white circular structures huddled close together, connected by short hump-topped passageways.

He's happier here, she thought. He's in his element. He's home.

The flight from Earth orbit to an orbit around Mars had taken only four days in the new-smelling torch ship. Powered by nuclear fusion, the vessel accelerated at almost one full g halfway to its destination, then decelerated at a slightly lower rate until it was orbiting around the red planet. Vijay remembered her first flight to Mars, nearly twenty years earlier, in an old-style ballistic rocket. It had taken more than six months, on a graceful, gradual elliptical trajectory that arced between the two worlds. With the fusion torch, their trajectory was almost a straight line.

Tithonium Base had sent the spindly-legged L/AV, a landing/ascent vehicle, to mate with the torch ship and take them aboard, together with several tons of supplies. Now the fragile-looking lander was descending to the surface of Mars like a spider gliding down an invisible silken thread to the ground.

His hand clutching hers, Jamie stared at the screen that

displayed the outside camera views, eager as a little boy watching for Santa's sleigh. Leaning close to him, Vijay couldn't help feeling a tremble of trepidation as she watched the craggy cliffs of the valley sliding past. They seemed terribly near.

The lander's retro rockets screeched once, twice in the thin air and kicked up a cloud of rust-colored dust that blotted out their view. They felt a gentle bump as the noise died away.

"We're down," Jamie whispered, still staring at the screen, still gripping Vijay's hand.

"We're on the ground," announced the pilot astronaut, from up in the cockpit. "You can unbuckle your safety harnesses now."

But the two of them still peered at the screen as the reddish dust wafted away on the gentle breeze. Vijay realized that the domes were much larger than the one she and Jamie had lived in, some twenty years ago. This close, she saw that their white tops were rusty looking, caked with years of Martian dust, although closer to the ground they were transparent. She could see vague figures of people moving around inside the dome closest to them. The farther dome's insides looked lushly green: the hydroponics greenhouse, she knew. On the other side of the main dome stood the maintenance center and its garage where the big camper vehicles were housed.

Slowly they got to their feet, a little cautious in the light gravity. Jamie's hair almost brushed the low overhead of the cramped compartment. The cockpit hatch opened and the pilot ducked through, smiling.

"Made it," he said. "Piece of cake."

"Good landing," said Jamie.

"It'll take a minute for the access tube to connect. Be careful of the low gravity."

"The downside of getting here so fast," Jamie said. But he was grinning about it.

Vijay had been to Mars twice before. Each time, the months-long flight had given her and the other passengers plenty of time to adapt to Mars's gravity. Their big wheel-shaped spacecraft had started out spinning at a rate that gave a feeling of regular Earth gravity, then gradually slowed its spin until the wheel was simulating the one-third g of Mars. By the time they landed on the red planet they were fully acclimated to the lower gravity.

They stepped to the L/AV's main hatch and peered through its tiny window, heads touching. The access tube was inching across the dusty ground like a giant segmented caterpillar, one end connected to the main airlock in Tithonium Base's dome, the other blindly groping for the lander's hatch. It too was coated with a fine powdering of red dust.

The lander's hatch was part of the vessel's own airlock, Vijay knew, but they could walk through the access tube in their shirtsleeves from the hatch into the dome. No need for airlocks or spacesuits.

"Just like getting off a plane back on Earth," Vijay murmured.

Jamie nodded. "Almost."

He went back to their seats and took their travel bags from the webbed overhead bin. Vijay reached for her bag, but Jamie grinned at her. "I can handle them both; they're much lighter here."

The access tube connected at last and the astronaut, after ducking quickly back into the cockpit to check his instrument readouts, came back and unlocked the hatch.

"Pressure's in the green," he said, pushing the hatch open and making a sweeping gesture. "Welcome back to Mars, folks."

Jamie took Vijay's wrist with his free hand and together they stepped through the slightly springy plastic tube toward the open hatch of Tithonium Base's main dome.

There was a crowd on the other side of the hatch. Vijay saw the surprise on her husband's face, then the slow, pleased, warm smile that spread across his features. The dome's high ceiling was lost in shadows, but clear Martian sunshine poured through the transparent windows that circled the lower section. Beyond the heads of the people clustering around them she could see partitions for workshops, laboratories, and people's living quarters. There was a large open space across the way with tables arranged in orderly rows: the cafeteria, she guessed.

A stone-faced Chinese gentleman in high-collared blue coveralls stepped forward and put out a chubby hand. Jamie had to let go of Vijay to take it in his own.

"Welcome to our humble abode," said Chang Laodong.

"Thank you," Jamie said. "It's good to see you again, Dr. Chang." He raised his voice and said to the crowd, "Thank you all."

They applauded. They actually clapped their hands together in spontaneous applause. Vijay saw her husband's coppery cheeks flush slightly with embarrassment. And pleasure. The crowd—scientists, engineers, astronauts, technicians— gathered around Jamie to shake his hand, pat his back, smile and tell him how glad they were to have him here among them.

Vijay stepped aside and let Jamie have his moment. Then she saw that Dr. Chang had also been shunted aside by the crowd's press. He did not look happy at all.

"MAY I ASK," SAID Dr. Chang, with exaggerated politeness, "why you have chosen to come here at this time?"

The mission director had invited Jamie and Vijay into his office for tea and a few moments of private conversation. Chang had apparently converted one of the sleeping rooms into an office, Jamie realized once he saw that the compartment had walls topped by a ceiling, rather than the usual two-meter-high partitions. He noticed a bookcase filled with precisely spaced specimens of rock behind the mission director's metal desk. Jamie recognized samples of the Martian "blueberries" first discovered by an early robotic camper, and a slab of the layered sedimentary rock from the Condor Chasma region.

The three of them sat around a low lacquered table where a beautifully enameled teapot and tiny sipping cups had been arranged in careful symmetry. Off to one side of the table stood an incongruous, strictly utilitarian ceramic thermos of scalding hot water.

Jamie hesitated before answering. The old Navaho way, Vijay understood. Jamie seldom spoke without thinking first, even in casual conversation. She realized that this particular conversation was anything but casual. Although he was trying hard to conceal it, Chang seemed as tense as a drawn bowstring.

"We're facing a crisis," Jamie said at last.

Chang nodded solemnly and muttered, "The American government's withdrawal of funds."

"It's more than that," said Jamie. "There is a concerted effort to force us to shut down our work here. To force us to abandon Mars altogether."

Chang lifted his pudgy chin a notch. "So I understand. But surely you could counter such a threat better on Earth than here."

"Perhaps," Jamie admitted.

"Then . . . ?"

Vijay understood the conflicts simmering beneath Jamie's impassive expression. She waited for her husband to find the right words.

"I need to know how the men and women here feel about their situation," he began slowly. "I need to know how *you* feel about all this, what steps you are prepared to take. You personally, not merely as director of the program here."

Now it was Chang who fell silent before replying. Vijay suppressed an urge to giggle. Between them they could be monuments on Mount Rushmore, she thought. Two great stone faces.

"I personally? I do not understand."

"Dr. Chang, would you be willing to spend another year here? After your regular term is finished?"

"Stay an additional year?"

"Yes."

"Without returning home?"

Jamie nodded. "If we can get a significant number of people to agree to extend their stays on Mars, we could cut our transportation costs almost in half."

"Transporting personnel is one thing. Transporting supplies is another matter altogether. Supplies will still be needed, no matter how long the staff agrees to stay without replacement."

"I understand," said Jamie. "I need to talk with the life-support team. I want to see if we can grow more of our food here, in situ. That would cut down on the resupply flights we need."

Chang rocked back in his chair.

Before the mission director could say anything, Jamie added, "I want to determine how close to self-sufficiency we can make this base."

"Self-sufficiency," Chang echoed, in a near whisper.

"Selene is willing to lend us technical expertise," Jamie added. Vijay felt her brows go up. That was a stretch. Stavenger hadn't promised anything so definite.

"This is an extremely difficult matter," said Chang, picking his words carefully. "It will require much thought, much investigation."

"That's why I'm here," Jamie said, with a slow smile.

"I see. I understand."

Shifting in his chair slightly, Jamie shifted the subject. "I'd also like to meet Dr. Carleton. He is here at the base, isn't he?"

Chang nodded. "He was not among those who greeted you on your arrival."

"No, he wasn't."

"He is most likely at his digging site. He spends much time there."

"Of course."

"He will undoubtedly want to meet you this evening, when he returns from his digging."

"Good," said Jamie.

But Vijay thought there was something beneath Chang's bland words, something unspoken about Dr. Carter Carleton. She wondered what it might be.

TITHONIUM BASE: INTRODUCTIONS

■

Carter Carleton was not at his excavation site. He was in bed with Doreen McManus, propping himself on one elbow as he gazed down at her lean naked body, glistening with perspiration. A line from an ancient motion picture popped into his mind: *Not much meat on her, but what there is is choice.*

Doreen smiled up at him. "This is much more fun than digging in that pit."

He grinned back. "We've got two professors of geology, a biochemist and an astronaut working the dig, if I remember the schedule correctly."

She nodded. "They ought to be finishing their shift right about now."

Carleton made an exaggerated sigh. "I guess I'll have to get dressed and see them when they come in."

"And Dr. Waterman is due to arrive this afternoon. I think he's already here."

"Really?" Carleton got up from the bed and picked up his paper-thin bathrobe.

"Didn't you hear the applause a little while ago?"

"Applause? No." With a grin, "I was busy."

Doreen's face grew serious. "You really didn't hear it?"

"You did?"

"You mean you were so completely absorbed by lovemaking that you didn't pay attention to anything else?"

He sat on the edge of the bed and began to stroke her hip.

"This is the very ecstasy of love," he quoted, "Whose violent property leads the will to desperate undertaking."

"No more desperate undertakings," Doreen said, putting a finger to his lips. "You'd better—"

The intercom phone buzzed. Carleton had the answering recording on. They heard his voice say, "I'm either not in or busy. Please leave your name and I'll get back to you." Doreen smiled at the word *busy*.

"Dr. Carleton," said a man's voice, "this is Jamie Waterman. I've just arrived at the base and I'd like to see you at your earliest convenience. Thanks."

Carleton slowly got to his feet. "Duty calls."

The living quarters at Tithonium Base were nothing more than single rooms shaped like wedges of a pie, in sets of ten built in a circle around a common lavatory. Carleton flung his robe over his bare shoulder and opened the lavatory door a crack. It was empty, so he stepped in.

Sitting up in bed, Doreen heard the door click shut. She sat there unmoving, thinking that the only time Carter ever mentioned the word "love" to her was in one of his silly quotations from Shakespeare. Still—it was better than nothing.

She got out of bed and padded to the lavatory. Carleton was in the shower stall, singing off-key in the billowing steam. He looked surprised when Doreen squeezed in. The stall was so narrow their bodies pressed together.

"That's what I like about you," Carleton said, grinning. "A dirty mind in a clean body."

After several slithering moments, Doreen said, "I'd like to meet Dr. Waterman."

"Sure," he said absently, his soapy hands slithering along her buttocks.

"I think he'd be interested in using nanotechnology to enlarge—"

"No."

She flinched at the sharpness of his rejection.

"Why not?"

"I don't want you making an ass of yourself in front of Waterman or anybody else."

"But I can show him how to enlarge the base! We could turn the whole rift valley into a completely Earthlike environment! It's called terraforming."

Carleton scowled at her. "It's called contamination. Mention that to Waterman and he'll send you packing on the next flight out of here. He's dead set against altering the native environment."

"But the base, this dome, isn't that altering the native environment?"

"We've got to do that. Waterman won't stand for anything more than the bare minimum we need to survive here."

"But Carter—"

"No," he said again, even more firmly. "Not a word of it. That's final."

She bit back a reply, but to herself Doreen said, It's not final, you chauvinist old fart.

CHANG SHOWED JAMIE AND Vijay to one of the larger cubicles and left them to unpack.

"This is bigger than what we had before," Vijay said, looking around the spare little space. "Two bunks, even."

"The dome's much bigger," said Jamie. "And stronger. Did you notice the ribs supporting it? Not like the pressurized plastic bubbles we used back when. This dome's built to last."

Tossing their bags onto the nearer of the two beds, Jamie said, "We'll have to push them together."

Vijay nodded as Jamie went to the phone and placed a call to Dr. Carleton. By the time they had hung their clothes in the slim closet and arranged their toiletries on the bureau nearest the lavatory door, Carleton had called back and invited Jamie to meet him at his laboratory.

"You go ahead," Vijay told him. "I've got to talk with the medical staff, see where I can fit in."

Carleton had appropriated one of the dome's smaller laboratory spaces for himself and turned it into a combination workshop, office and conference room. Jamie rapped on the shaky accordion-fold door; after a couple of moments Carter Carleton slid the door open.

"Dr. Waterman," Carleton said, smiling handsomely. "This is a pleasure."

Taking Carleton's proffered hand in his own, Jamie said, "Please call me Jamie."

"And I'm Carter."

Stepping into the laboratory, Jamie saw that it was crammed with a worktable along the far partition, a miniature desk with a swivel chair made of bungee cords, bookshelves that were mostly empty, two spindly-looking stools and a small chair of molded plastic. Blank roll-up smart screens were taped onto two of the room's two-meter-high partitions.

"It's not much," Carleton said, still smiling as he gestured to the plastic chair, "but it's home."

Jamie saw the fossil sitting squarely in the middle of the otherwise empty desktop.

"That's it?" he asked.

"That's a cast," said Carleton, crossing the room in three swift strides to pull a plastic container from the bookshelf. Popping its lid open, he held it out for Jamie. "This is the real thing."

Jamie peered into the container. The fossil was gray, ridged; it looked hard and durable.

"Go ahead and take it out," Carleton urged. "It's okay."

Jamie turned it over in his hands. "I don't know much about anatomy, but it sure looks like a vertebra to me."

"The best paleontologists Earthside agree. It's a vertebra, all right. Probably of an animal that walked on four legs, not upright."

"Then it's not from one of the intelligent Martians."

"Who knows?" Carleton said. "Maybe they scuttled around on four legs. Or six. Or a dozen!"

"Have you found anything else?" Jamie asked.

"Not yet. We're digging by hand now, going much slower."

"I understand."

Carleton took the fossil back from Jamie and placed it lovingly in the plastic container. He put the container back on the bookshelf, then perched himself on a corner of his desk.

"The talk around here is that you've come to tell us we're going to shut down," he said.

Jamie shook his head. "Just the opposite. I'm here to find out how we can stretch what funding we have to allow us to stay as long as we can."

"Good."

"I'd like you to talk with Dex Trumball and some of his Foundation people. We should be setting up a video program to show your fossil and explain what you're doing here."

"Fine by me," said Carleton.

Jamie eyed the anthropologist for a silent moment, framing his thoughts. Then he asked, "How would you feel about staying here for another year or so? Without going home."

Carleton broke into a dazzling smile. "I wouldn't leave here under any circumstances. The only way they'll get me back to Earth is in a coffin."

MANHATTAN: WORLDWIDE NEWS NETWORK

■

Orlando Ventura sat at the foot of the small conference table, but he knew all the others depended on him for the crucial decisions. Well, almost all the others: the "consultant" from the New Morality depended on no one except his own inner certainties—reinforced by orders from Atlanta.

Ventura was a compact type, prone to paunchiness, but he kept his figure reasonably trim with daily workout sessions and ruthless, no-mercy games of tennis on the rooftop courts of the Worldwide News building. He had touched up his long, wavy hair with subtle dabs of gray at his temples; it made him look more mature, he thought, more serious and reliable.

"So what's our approach on this Martian fossil?" asked the bureau chief, sitting at the head of the table. The chief was rake thin, all nerves and twitches, totally bald except for a ridiculous fringe of darkish hair that he kept long enough to tickle his collar.

Everyone turned to Ventura, but before he could reply the New Morality consultant said softly, "Alleged fossil. No one has proved its age or even proved that it came from a Martian creature. It might be simply a strangely shaped piece of rock."

"It makes for more audience interest if we call it a fossil," said Ventura, strongly enough to be firm, not so intense as to sound confrontive.

Ventura thought of the consultant, who sat at the bureau chief's right hand, as a censor. No one in the network hierarchy would admit it, but they didn't want the New Morality causing trouble for them. The rival network Global News had nearly gone bankrupt when the New Morality arranged an international boycott of their broadcasts—and the products that they advertised.

The consultant's name was Shelby Ivers. He was a minister from the New Morality's headquarters in Atlanta. He looked like a chubby, pink-faced, well-scrubbed young man with short dark hair combed forward to hide a receding hairline. Instead of the usual ministerial garb of funereal black he wore a cheerful checkered sports jacket and a tie of royal blue. Beneath his white shirt, Ventura was certain, a silver crucifix hung around his neck, its size determined by the man's estimation of the cleanliness of his soul.

"The scientists themselves haven't agreed that it's a fossil," sniffed the consultant, frowning down the table toward Ventura.

Lena Pickering, a sharp-eyed blond producer, said with her usual annoying nasality, "The scientists never really agree on anything, do they?"

Score one for Lena, Ventura thought, knowing that she was ambitious and wanted a spot on his staff.

"Look," said the bureau chief, squirming in his chair, "everybody's calling it a fossil. We'd look pretty dumb if we just called it a rock, wouldn't we?"

"Call it an alleged fossil, then," insisted the consultant.

"A probable fossil?" suggested Ventura's director, sitting halfway down the table.

"A possible fossil," said the woman across the table from him.

"A fossil," Ventura insisted.

"But—"

"We can put in a disclaimer at the beginning of the show," Ventura said, raising his voice enough to cut off all the others. "Say that the scientists believe it's a fossil and until proven otherwise that's what we're going to call it."

Everyone fell silent as the consultant drummed his fingers

on the conference tabletop for a few moments. At last he shrugged. "I'll write the disclaimer for you," he said.

"Fine," said Ventura.

"All right," the bureau chief said, trying to smile, "that's settled. Now, I've got an idea for you to consider. How about having a cohost on this show with you, Lannie?"

Ventura winced at the nickname, but shuddered inwardly at the thought of sharing the spotlight. "A cohost?" he asked, in a deathly soft voice. "On *my* show?"

"Edie Elgin. She was a media star back during the First Mars Expedition," the bureau chief said.

"She's retired. Lives on the Moon now," said Ventura's top researcher, a meek-looking younger guy whose bland exterior hid a fervent ambition.

"She was shacked up with one of the scientists who went to Mars," Ventura said thinly.

"Right. James Waterman. He's chief scientist of the whole Mars program now."

The consultant spoke up. "She'd be prejudiced in his favor then, wouldn't she?"

Nodding in the consultant's direction, Ventura said, "There is that."

"Or maybe she's pissed at him for dumping her," said one of the women.

"She dumped him, more likely. She's married to Douglas Stavenger now."

"The man whose body is filled with nanomachines?" the consultant blurted, frowning with distaste. "She'll be even more biased. We can't have that kind of imbalance."

The bureau chief steepled his fingers in front of his chin. "Maybe not, then," he muttered. "It was just a suggestion."

Ventura shot a silent glance of thanks toward the consultant, thinking that he owed the guy one. He also realized for the first time that the bureau chief was out to get him.

"So who's going to be on your panel, Lannie?" the chief asked, as if he'd never suggested a cohost.

"We'll need a scientist, of course."

"More than one," said Ventura's own producer, sitting on his left.

Lena Pickering said with a grin, "You put on two scientists, they'll start arguing with one another."

"You put on three and you'll get six different opinions," muttered one of the men halfway down the table.

"Well, that's good, isn't it?" said the bureau chief. "Controversy builds audience interest."

Ventura shook his head. "When scientists start arguing they go into their own specialized language. It's all incomprehensible gobbledygook. The audience can't follow them."

"It's a real turnoff, chief."

The bureau chief scratched at his bald pate. "Okay, okay. One scientist, then. Who else?"

"A Believer," said the consultant. "We've got to have a Believer on the panel."

"You volunteering?" Ventura asked. He meant it to sound like an invitation, but despite his intentions it came out more like a challenge.

The consultant stared at him for a moment. "Me? Heavens, no! I'm not a public persona."

No, Ventura replied silently. You never show your face to the public. You do your work behind their backs.

"How about Penny Quinn?" one of the women suggested. "She's always interesting."

"She's off the wall."

"Is she a Believer?"

"I'm pretty sure she is. And she's a woman. You don't want this panel to be all male."

"Why not?"

"Neanderthal!"

The consultant folded his hands on the tabletop and said earnestly, "We must have a Believer. If we have a scientist, then we must have a Believer, in the interests of fairness and balance."

Where do you get this "we" stuff, Ventura asked silently. But he owed the guy a favor, so he said nothing.

Half a dozen names were suggested, all of them shot down by one or another of the people around the table.

"Why not get the Pope?" someone grumbled.

Ventura brightened. "That's not a bad idea."

The bureau chief scowled down the table at him.

"No, I don't mean the Pope himself," Ventura explained. "But there's that priest at the Vatican, the one that was supposed to go on the First Expedition but got sick and had to be replaced."

"Yeah, I remember. He got appendicitis, didn't he?"

"Gall bladder."

"Anyway, why not him?" Ventura asked. "He's a scientist *and* a priest, for god's sake. He advises the Pope about scientific matters, if I remember right."

"What's his name?"

"Di something-or-other."

"DiNardo," said Ventura.

The consultant looked less than pleased. "He's a geologist, isn't he? A scientist."

"But he's a priest, as well."

"But he's a scientist."

The argument went around the table for more than half an hour. In the end, while the bureau chief swallowed a handful of pills without water, they decided that the panel would consist of a British paleontologist who was spending a year at Yale; an evangelist minister whose TV shows always pulled in a huge audience; an actress who was starring in a docudrama series about the Salem witch trials; an author who'd written several books debunking the notion that intelligent life had ever existed on Mars; and two university students, one majoring in planetary sciences and the other in theology. Plus the Rev. Dr. Fulvio A. DiNardo, S.J.

Ventura nodded, satisfied that he had gotten what he needed for an exciting, informative show. And no goddamned cohost.

TITHONIUM BASE: THE DIG

■

Jamie and Vijay were finishing their breakfasts in the nearly empty cafeteria.

"They start early here," Vijay said, between sips of tea.

Jamie started to reply, but saw a lanky young man walking slowly toward their table. Like almost everyone else at the base, he wore plain grayish blue coveralls, unadorned except for the nametag pinned above the left breast pocket.

"Dr. Waterman?" the youngster asked, in a voice so soft Jamie had to strain to hear it. "I'm supposed to guide you around the dig this morning."

The young man stopped a respectful two meters from Jamie's chair. As he got to his feet, Jamie saw that he was quite tall, well over six feet, but youthfully slim, not yet grown into his adult weight. He wore his jet black hair in a long ponytail, and his face was lean, with high cheekbones and the coppery skin of a fellow Native American.

"You're Billy Graycloud?" Jamie asked, putting out his hand.

"Yessir. The resident Navaho. Until you arrived, of course." He smiled shyly.

"Have a seat. We were just finishing. This is my wife, Vijay."

The kid dipped his chin. "Billy Graycloud," he said to Vijay as he sat down.

"I'm pleased to meet you, Billy," she said, with a smile.

Jamie said, "Dr. Chang tells me you're a computer analyst."

Graycloud looked down at his boots. "I will be, I guess, once I get my doctorate."

"From UNM?"

"Uh, nosir. Arizona. In Tucson."

Jamie knew that Graycloud had been picked to maintain the Navaho presence on Mars. No nation was allowed to claim Mars or any other body in the solar system as its sovereign territory. But corporations or other legally recognized "entities" could claim exclusive use of an asteroid or part of a planet, as long as they maintained a physical presence on-site. By international agreement, the Navaho Nation had been granted control of the utilization of the red planet—as long as at least one Navaho actually resided on Mars. The Navaho Council regarded this grant as a sacred trust and, under Jamie Waterman's direction, kept Mars off limits to everyone except the scientists who were exploring Mars and their support staff.

As Vijay gently teased out Graycloud's life history from the awkward, insecure student, Jamie realized with a jolt of surprise that if they had to abandon their work on Mars and return everyone home, the planet would be wide open to any other group that wanted to exploit it. Just like the whites did to the red men in America, he thought. The fact that his mother was a descendant of the *Mayflower* pilgrims didn't alleviate Jamie's fears one whit.

"Well, anyway," Graycloud was saying to Vijay, "Dr. Chang told me to escort you out to the dig. . . . Not that you need escorting, I know. You've been on Mars a lot more'n I have."

Jamie smiled at him. "I'm glad of your help, Mr. Graycloud."

"Uh, Billy. Call me Billy, sir."

"Okay, Billy. And you'll have to call me Jamie."

Graycloud blinked at Jamie. "I . . . I don't know if I can do that, sir."

"You'll have to. When you call me sir it makes me feel a thousand years old."

Graycloud smiled uneasily.

The three of them got up from the table and left the cafeteria. Vijay gave Jamie a peck on the cheek and headed off for the infirmary. Graycloud led Jamie to the main airlock area.

"You ever use a nanosuit before, si . . . uh, Dr. Waterman?"

Jamie shook his head. He saw a row of transparent suits hanging limply along a partition. They looked like plastic raincoats, almost.

"They're a lot better than the old hard-shells," Graycloud said. "Easier to put on. Quicker, too."

Picking up the drooping arm of the nearest suit, Jamie asked, "Do they give you as much protection against radiation?"

"Supposed to. We've got a nanotech expert from Selene here at the base and she checks radiation dosages all the time. No problems so far."

"So far," Jamie echoed.

Graycloud's brows knit. "If you'd feel more comfortable in a hard-shell—"

"No," Jamie said gently. "I'll go with your recommendation, Billy."

Graycloud swallowed visibly, then nodded. "Okay, let's find you a size medium."

JAMIE FELT SLIGHTLY NERVOUS as he and Graycloud stepped through the main airlock's outer hatch and onto the ruddy sand of Mars. The nanosuit seemed terribly flimsy; it was like wearing nothing more than a plastic slicker.

Then it struck him. I'm on the surface of Mars! Not inside one of those stiff old hard suits, clomping around like a two-legged turtle. I'm practically in my shirtsleeves!

The reddish ground was littered with rocks, some as small as pebbles, many as large as a man's head. Jamie looked up, and through the transparent bubble that enclosed his head he saw the cables running up the seamed, rugged cliff face to the niche in the rocks where the Martian buildings were.

"You okay, Dr. W?" Graycloud's voice sounded concerned in the headphone Jamie had clipped to his ear.

"I'm fine, Billy."

"No problems with the suit?"

"None." Jamie almost laughed. "I was thinking about the first time Dex Trumball and I rappelled down the cliff face from up top on the plateau. The first time we walked into the buildings and actually touched them."

"Must've been a helluva moment," Graycloud said.

"It sure was."

"Uh, if you want to see the dig, it's over this way."

Jamie followed the student across the rock-strewn floor of the canyon. He noticed several areas along the cliff's base that were taped off, like a crime scene. The endolithic lichen, he realized. The biologists don't want anybody near them.

They walked toward a small group of people who were clustered around a hole in the ground. Most of them wore nanosuits, although a couple were in the bulkier hard-shells.

"Which one is Dr. Carleton?" he asked Graycloud.

The younger man pointed. "Over there, in the hard suit with the orange sleeve stripes, by the sifter. That's Doreen McManus with him. She's the nanotech specialist I told you about."

The figure in the hard-shell suit turned slowly, awkwardly, like a medieval knight in a rusted suit of armor.

"Waterman!" Carleton called. "Over here."

Jamie stepped carefully around the scattered rocks toward Carleton, Graycloud beside him. The anthropologist's face was hidden behind the reflecting coating of his helmet visor but his voice in Jamie's headphone was brimming with enthusiasm.

"Take a look at these." He gestured with a gloved hand to a half dozen plastic containers arranged in a neat row along the table by the sifter. Each one had an odd-shaped rock in it. "We just pulled them up this morning."

None of the rocks was larger than palm-sized. They all looked gray and undistinguished to Jamie. His geologist's eye noticed that one of them had a darker band in its middle.

Reaching for it, Jamie asked, "May I?"

Carleton said, "Gently. Be careful with it. I think that darker streak might be pigment."

"Pigment?"

"Might be a shard from pottery."

Using two hands, Jamie picked up the irregularly shaped piece out of its plastic container. The gloves of his nanosuit were so delicate that he could feel the rough edges of the shard. It was thinner than his little finger, slightly curved. By god, Jamie thought, this really could have been part of a bowl once.

He looked up at Carleton. "You'll have to have this analyzed."

"Damned right."

Jamie handed the piece back to the anthropologist. "Do you have the equipment you need?"

"Some. I can do a spectral analysis of the pigment."

"If that's what it is."

Carleton's voice dropped a tone, went darker. "Yes, if that's what it is."

"The geology team can do a thorium/lead dating measurement," Jamie mused, "to tell how old it is."

"Not potassium/argon?"

Remembering earlier attempts at fixing the dates of Martian rocks, Jamie replied, "The argon tends to outgas over time; throws the measurement off."

"I'll want a carbon-14 run, too. Then we can see if the pigment's a different age from the rest of the shard," Carleton said as he carefully deposited the piece back in its container.

Jamie shook his head. "This stuff probably dates back sixty million years. C-14 won't be any good for that kind of time."

Carleton chuckled. "You're right. I was thinking of human artifacts, on Earth. We're a lot younger, aren't we?"

"Yes, we are," said Jamie. Silently he added, And we're still here. Not extinct.

Jamie looked again at the other rocks in their little boxes. "And what about these?"

"Don't know yet. I'm collecting anything that looks even faintly interesting. For example, this one," he pointed to a slim fragment, "just might be a piece of bone."

Jamie saw that it had a slight indentation running its length, but otherwise there was nothing that looked bonelike to his eyes.

"You'll have to do an MNA test on it."

"Martian nucleic acids, right." Carleton hesitated, then said, "The bio people tell me they need more sensitive equipment. The stuff they have here is pretty primitive compared to what's available back on Earth."

Jamie remembered that biologists on Earth had teased molecules of DNA from sixty-million-year-old fossils of dinosaurs. There was even talk of recreating a *Tyannosaurus rex* a few years ago, before the fundamentalists took control of the Congress. What would the New Morality think about us recreating a Martian? Jamie wondered. They'd blow up this base and everybody in it, he thought.

He asked Carleton, "You've already talked to the biologists here at the base?"

"About my vertebra. I asked them to do an MNA run on it."

"I see."

"Their equipment isn't sensitive enough. If there's any organic material left on the vertebra it's so minuscule that their reading is down in the noise."

"We'll need better equipment, then," Jamie muttered. Then he added, "Or we'll have to send the fossil back to a lab on Earth."

"Oh no!" Carleton said sharply. "That's *my* discovery. That fossil doesn't leave my sight."

"We could ship you back home with it."

"I'm staying here. And so are whatever finds we make. I'm not letting any Earthside lab steal my credit."

Jamie started to reply, but pulled in a deep breath instead. No sense starting a fight here, he told himself. The man's had his troubles with university bureaucracies in the past. I can't blame him for being possessive. He wants the mountain to come to Mohammed. Trouble is, resupply missions cost money. Money that we haven't got.

Then he thought, But on the other hand, if the biologists want so badly to test his fossil for nucleic acids, maybe they'll have enough clout to fund a mission here. That would be helpful.

"I'll see what I can do," Jamie said.

"Good," said Carleton. "And while you're at it, I could use a few trained paleontologists, too."

Jamie smiled at him and suppressed an urge to ask if he wanted anything else.

ROME: THE VATICAN

∎

Monsignor Fulvio A. DiNardo, S.J., scurried along the garden pathway from the television studio toward the stately building that housed the Pontifical Academy of Sciences, where his office was.

He walked fast, short arms pumping, short legs scampering beneath his black, knee-length surplice, which he wore over his workaday clerical suit. He looked more like an overaged wrestler than a priest. Although he was not tall, his build was burly, with a barrel-shaped body and thick limbs heavy with muscle. He kept his scalp shaved but there was always a dark stubble over his jaw no matter how closely he shaved. Despite his fierce appearance, Monsignor DiNardo was a truly gentle man, a dedicated Jesuit, a confidant of the Pope and the cardinals who advised the pontiff. He was also a world-class geologist.

He nodded perfunctorily to the priests and nuns and friars strolling much more leisurely along the walk. They seemed almost like statues compared to his heart-pumping pace. DiNardo had always been a man on the go. Once he had tried using a bicycle to get across the Vatican grounds faster, but Cardinal Castiglione had nearly had a heart attack over the incident and forbade DiNardo from resorting to such infamous tactics. DiNardo obeyed, of course, although he tried to point out to his apoplectic superior that he had considered a motorbike but rejected the idea as too noisy, too disruptive.

So now he hurried toward his office on foot, looking like a black-garbed badger trotting on its hind legs.

DiNardo had actually been selected to be the lead geologist on the First Martian Expedition, but was struck down by a gall bladder attack mere days before he was to leave Earth. Jamie Waterman replaced him and went on to discover the ruins of Martian buildings in the cliffs of Tithonium Chasma.

I might have made that discovery, he had often thought. And just as often he'd told himself that God, in His infinite wisdom, had given that glory to the Navaho. DiNardo couldn't see how that furthered God's plan for the universe, but he accepted the situation with a good heart—or tried to.

Now DiNardo mopped his shaved scalp with a blood red handkerchief as he neared the Academy building.

The television broadcast had been a farce, he thought angrily. That slimy moderator, Ventura, had no interest in discussing the discovery of a fossil bone on Mars. He was out for sensation, not science. Moderator! DiNardo silently spat the word. The man is an immoderate egomaniac.

Ventura: "So is this odd-shaped piece of rock really the remains of a living creature?"

DiNardo: "I believe it probably is. It appears—"

Ventura: "Probably?"

DiNardo: "Very likely."

Evangelist: "It's all a matter of what the Lord expects us to believe: either His word as revealed in the Bible or the doubtful guesses of scientists all the way out on Mars."

Ventura: "What do you think, Becky? Is it a fossil or just a funny-shaped rock?"

Actress: "It's hard to tell, isn't it?"

Author: "Look, I proved in my book, *The Mars Hoax*, that all this baloney about intelligent Martians is just hype by scientists trying to increase their funding."

DiNardo: "Then how do you explain the buildings? The cliff dwellings?"

Author: "Built by some of the Navahos that that guy Waterman brought to Mars."

DiNardo: "That is nonsense! Preposterous!"

Ventura: "You heard it here, folks. But remember, Mr. Quentin's opinions are his own, and not necessarily the view of Worldwide News."

Author: "You can read the truth in my latest book, *The Mars Hoax Revisited.*"

And so it went, for a solid hour. DiNardo was glad that he had been in Rome, in the Vatican's TV studio, and not in New York or wherever Ventura's show originated. The temptation to throttle that idiot author would have overpowered his self-control.

He almost smiled as he rushed up the marble stairs to his office. That would have made a spectacular television moment: Jesuit priest strangles popular author. I wonder what penance Cardinal Castiglione would have given me for that?

DiNardo's smile faded as he stepped into his cramped little office and dropped his bulk into his desk chair. The parts of the Vatican that tourists saw were adorned with frescoes by Titian, Raphael and other Renaissance masters. Vatican wallpaper, some wags called it. But here at the Academy of Sciences the walls were plain, bland eggshell white: economical and not distracting.

I must word this memorandum carefully, DiNardo told himself as he stared at his blank computer screen. It must be logical and convincing. Yet although he placed his fingers on the grubby keyboard, smudged with years worth of his banging on it, no words came to him. And his mind drifted, turned without his conscious volition to the problem that had become the central focus of his existence.

How could a just and merciful God have created a race of intelligent creatures and then snuffed them out in the flicker of a moment? All right, it was longer than a moment, but geologically speaking the Martians perished virtually overnight. How could God allow that?

An intelligent race, knowledgeable enough to build structures, to erect cliff dwellings high up in the walls of Mars's Grand Canyon. Intelligent enough to worship God, undoubtedly. Perhaps their vision of God was different from ours; certainly it must have been. But they were intelligent! God gave them the brains to build a civilization, just as He did for us.

DiNardo's breath caught in his throat. God sent the Flood to us. He destroyed all of humankind except for Noah and his family. Or is that merely a metaphor, a faint remembrance of an ecological disaster that caused widespread devastation?

It was no metaphor on Mars, he knew. A giant meteor came crashing down out of the sky and blasted the poor Martians into extinction. Dead, every last one of them. Killed.

Why? DiNardo cried silently. Why did God permit this to happen? Why did He *make* it happen?

As a lesson to us? Could a loving God be so cruel as to extinguish an entire race, just to teach us to fear Him?

Could the fundamentalists be right? Is this greenhouse warming we're suffering now a retribution from a God grown angry at our evil ways? Did He create the Martians merely to show us what He can do when we displease Him?

No. DiNardo shook his head. That I cannot accept, cannot believe.

But why, then? Dear Lord, why did You wipe them out?

He realized with a sudden flash of inspiration that there was only one way for him to find the answer to that question. The answer lay millions of kilometers away, buried beneath the red sands of Mars. I've got to go there! he told himself. I've got to find out for myself what happened to those creatures, why they perished.

You had your chance, more than twenty years ago. God sent Waterman to Mars instead of you. Looking up at the plain wooden crucifix above his office door, DiNardo asked fervently, Lord, may I have another chance? May I get to Mars at last? Is it Your will that I reach Mars and seek out the truth of what happened to those souls?

I'm nearly ten years older than Jamie Waterman, he thought. But if Carter Carleton is young enough to go to Mars, then why not me? I'm in presentable physical condition. My blood pressure is under control as long as I take my medications. The fusion ships travel there in a matter of mere days. It's no more difficult than flying from Rome to Los Angeles, really.

Monsignor DiNardo began pecking at his keyboard, his passionate yearning to go to Mars burning all other thoughts out of his mind, even the tightness of breath he felt as he bent over the keyboard and poured out his soul.

I've *got* to get to Mars, he told himself. I've got to!

TITHONIUM BASE: NUMBER CRUNCHING

■

Jamie sat at the desk in the cubicle that Dr. Chang had given him to use as an office. It was a minuscule enclosure, barely big enough for a couple of bungee-cord chairs and a fold-up writing table that served as a makeshift desk. Like all the other cubicles in the dome, its walls were two-meter-high plastic partitions. Only the pie-slice personal quarters and Dr. Chang's office had real walls that extended to a real ceiling.

Jamie had spent the morning out at the dig, actually helping the team patiently excavate Carleton's pit, using modified laser drills to break up the rock floor and then old-fashioned whisk brushes to carefully, tenderly clean eons of dust from the fragments. Most of the pieces they uncovered were meaningless lumps of stone, as far as Jamie could see, but every once in a while Carleton would exclaim:

"This could be a knee joint!"

Or: "Looks like the end of a handle to me."

The anthropologist was amassing a small but growing collection of what could be fossils and ancient artifacts. The geologists dated them all to between sixty-seven and sixty-three million years old, the right approximate age for the time when the meteor bombardment had wiped out almost all life on Mars. Jamie wondered if the dating was accurate. Sometimes even the most unbiased of scientists saw what they wanted to see, instead of what was before their eyes.

He thought of Percival Lowell, the wealthy Bostonian who built an observatory in the clear mountain air of Flagstaff,

Arizona, and spent the rest of his life studying Mars. Lowell saw canals on Mars and wrote popular books about the possibility—the *certainty*, as far as he was concerned—that Mars was inhabited by intelligent engineers who built a planetary system of canals to save their cities from global drought. Lowell's canals turned out to be mostly eyestrain, and his own zealous desire to prove that intelligent Martians existed.

They did exist, Jamie thought wryly, sixty-some million years before Lowell's time. But they weren't clever enough to build a global network of canals. It wouldn't have helped them, anyway. The catastrophe that wiped them out would have buried their canals along with their villages and every trace of them, except for the cliff dwellings.

Yet Lowell was right in one sense, Jamie knew. Mars is dying. A long, slow, agonizing death. The hardy little lichen that have made an ecological niche for themselves inside the rocks strewn across the valley floor are dying away. The atmosphere's faint trace of moisture is dwindling. Unless we step in and intervene, the lichen will go extinct, just like all the other life on the cold, dry surface of Mars.

But long before that we'll be gone, Jamie thought. Our funding is petering out. We'll have to leave Mars. Leave the planet and let it die.

Trying to shake off his feelings of impending doom, Jamie left his cubbyhole and went to the infirmary to take Vijay to lunch. Afterward he repaired to his shoebox of an office and pulled up the latest messages from Selene. The distance between Mars and the Earth/Moon region made two-way communication impossibly awkward. Even traveling at nearly three hundred thousand kilometers per second, it took light about four minutes to span the distance when Mars was closest to Earth. At the moment, the one-way lag in transmission was almost nine minutes, which meant eighteen minutes between hearing "Hello" and the next words sent from the Earth or the Moon.

So one side talked while the other side listened. Then they

reversed roles. At the moment, Jamie was listening to Douglas Stavenger.

"We have a good deal of experience in developing life support facilities out of local resources," Stavenger was saying. His handsome, smoky-skinned face was smiling genially. "The key to Selene's success has been building a self-sufficient community out of what's available here on the Moon."

Jamie nodded to himself. During its war for independence, Selene was cut off from all imports from Earth. The embargo was brief, but it taught the lunar inhabitants a crucial lesson: they had to survive on their own resources.

"From what my engineer friends tell me, you've got an easier situation on Mars than we do here on the Moon. You've got an atmosphere, and it's got some oxygen and nitrogen in it. All we've got is vacuum: we have to bake oxygen out of the soil—er, I mean the regolith." Stavenger's smile turned slightly embarrassed. "The tech guys would pound me if they heard me call it soil."

Soil contains living creatures, Jamie knew. The powdery crust of the Moon was absolutely lifeless. And waterless, except for reservoirs of ice in deep craters near the poles where comets had crashed eons ago.

"Anyway, I've asked a few friends to put together a study on how you can make your base self-sufficient—or as close to self-sufficiency as possible. They're mostly retired engineers and geologists, so it won't cost you much. They're glad of an interesting project to occupy their minds."

And I'm glad it won't be expensive, Jamie thought.

"They'll be pestering you with questions," Stavenger went on. "In time, one or two of them might actually want to come to your base and see the conditions there for themselves. I presume that will be okay with you. That's all I've got for you at the moment. I'll wait for your answer."

Jamie activated his computer's microphone and replied, "I'm delighted that you can help us, and I'll be willing to field any questions your people send. I'll get our most competent people to provide any information you need. One thing: remember that the, um, regolith here on Mars is loaded with superoxides. We can get plenty of oxygen from it, but we also have to bake the superoxides out of the soil if we want to try growing plants in it."

He talked for another ten minutes while the computer typed out his words on its display screen. Jamie read the message, made a few corrections, then finally tapped the TRANSMIT key.

It's all in the numbers, he told himself. Whether we leave or stay, whether we live or die, it's all a matter of numbers.

But then the Navaho side of his mind corrected, It's a matter of spirit, as well. Who will have the courage to stay on this red world? Who will dare to stand against Coyote and his devilish tricks?

TITHONIUM CHASMA: THE VILLAGE

■

"This is what we've got so far," Carleton said, bending slightly over the display that lit up the big, square stereo table.

It was late afternoon. Carleton's digging crew was still out at the excavation site. The rest of the dome's personnel were in their labs or workshops, except for a team of scientists and astronauts on their way back from an excursion to the Tharsis volcanoes, and the inevitable few people lounging in the cafeteria, on the other side of the big dome.

Jamie looked down at the three-dimensional image of a gridwork of lines. Most of them were straight and intersected in neat right angles, although along one side of the image the lines meandered crookedly.

"This is the radar imagery?" Jamie asked.

"Deep radar, yes," said Carleton. Doreen McManus stood at his side, tall, lean, silent. The glow from the table's display underlit her sculptured, serious face.

Carleton was much more animated. Pointing to a small red rectangle at one corner of the display, he explained, "This is where we've been digging. We're already pulling up some blocks that might be bricks from the foundations of these buildings."

"Those are buildings?"

Nodding vigorously, Carleton replied, "Certainly looks that way. Foundations, at least. The buildings themselves must have collapsed under the weight of the millions of years of dust accumulating over them." Tracing the lines with a finger-tip, "These were streets. They laid out their village in a grid, very orderly."

"And here?" Jamie pointed to the lines that curved lazily.

"They must have been running along the edge of the river. That's where the stream flowed."

Jamie straightened up and focused on Carleton's face. The anthropologist was beaming happily.

"We've got a lot of work to do," Carleton said. "We've only just begun to peck at one corner of this village."

"Dr. Chang wants to send out teams to follow the ancient riverbed and scout for other sites," said Jamie. "The satellite imagery shows some interesting possibilities."

"Chang." Carleton almost spat the word. "He's a geologist. What does he know about excavating sites?"

"He's the mission director."

"And you're the science director for the whole program. You outrank him."

Glancing at McManus, Jamie saw that she was looking across the dome toward Chang's office cubicle. Its door was firmly closed.

"I don't want to get into a power struggle with Dr. Chang," he said quietly.

Carleton's jaw settled. "The man's belittled my work since day one. I honestly believe he doesn't understand the magnitude of what we've found."

Jamie took a slow breath. "I'll speak with him. He does have the responsibility for the whole team here, you know. You're not the only—"

"I know I'm not the only scientist working here," Carleton acknowledged. Then, with an impish grin, he added, "But I'm the most important one."

McManus spoke up. "Have you seen the bricks that we've uncovered? They're from the foundation of this building here." She pointed with a bright red lacquered fingernail.

"You're sure?" Jamie asked Carleton.

"Absolutely. It's from their village. They lived down here where the water was, where the river flowed."

"And the buildings up in the cliffs?"

Carleton shrugged. "Who knows? A ceremonial center, most likely. I don't think we'll ever know for sure."

"Maybe not," Jamie murmured.

"So you'll talk with Chang?" Carleton pressed. "We need to expand the dig. That means more people working on it. We need to uncover the entire village, the farms around it, everything."

Nodding, Jamie said, "I'll talk to him. But don't expect miracles. I don't want to go over his head."

"Somebody's got to," Carleton said darkly.

As IF HE KNEW what was transpiring, Chang remained closeted in his office the rest of the day. Jamie was reluctant to interrupt whatever the mission director was doing, even if it was nothing more than avoiding him. No confrontations, he told himself. This isn't going to be settled by power politics, not here, not among these people. We've got to find a path that we can all travel, a method we can all agree on.

So Jamie spent the rest of the afternoon catching up on reports from Dex and the research groups scattered around more than a dozen universities on Earth—and Selene University, on the Moon. In his mind's eye Jamie pictured a delicate web of thoughts and ideas as men and women in Asia, Europe, the Americas, Australia and even in the underground city of Selene, worked to puzzle out the history of Mars and its vanished people.

He couldn't help thinking of the extinct Martians as people, even though he knew consciously that they probably did not look at all like human beings. But they *thought* the way we do, Jamie realized. They loved and feared and hoped and died the way we do. Maybe that's what the Bible means when it says God created man in his image: it means intelligence, the moral knowledge of good and evil. It doesn't matter what the body form looks like. It's intelligence that makes us godlike.

Then he remembered the Navaho creation myth. The People had lived on a red world before coming to the blue world. A great flood had driven them out of the red world.

No, he told himself firmly. That is myth. The Martians didn't migrate to Earth. They died here, every last one of them.

JAMIE TRIED TO USE dinner as a social opportunity. Although he almost inevitably took his meal with Vijay, Jamie always attempted to invite one or two of the staff people to share their mealtime. It was easier to catch up on who was doing what over the dinner table. And the discussions weren't always limited to the scientific work going on.

This evening they dined with Itzak Rosenberg and Saleem Hasdrubal at a table for four in a corner of the busy, noisy cafeteria. The area smelled of sizzling cooking oil and a vague aroma of vinegar. Whoever selected the evening's music had picked Russian classics. Jamie thought he recognized the dark strains of Rachmaninoff over the clatter of dishware and hum of conversations.

Jamie wanted to ask the two of them about staying another year on Mars. But he wanted to approach the subject obliquely, carefully. Better to sound them out first, get to know them a little, before popping the big question.

Rosenberg seemed somewhat nervous at first, but Hasdrubal leaned back in his creaking plastic chair and, despite his stern, almost fierce appearance, joked about their disappointing stint at the crater Malzberg.

"It's all Izzy's fault," Hasdrubal said, draping a long, lean arm around his colleague's shoulders. "The crater wouldn't pop a geyser as long as he was watching."

Rosenberg looked uncomfortable, as if his partner's arm weighed too heavily on him. "We're accustomed to disappointments," he murmured.

"We?" asked Vijay.

"The Children of Israel," Hasdrubal answered immediately. "Their history has been full of disappointments and diasporas."

"That's not really funny, Sal," said Rosenberg.

Hasdrubal looked at Rosenberg for a long, silent moment. "No, I guess it's not, considering what happened to Israel."

Thinking of the nuclear holocaust that had devastated much of the Middle East, Jamie glanced at his wife, then poked at the soymeat steak on his plate. Vijay's a shade darker than Hasdrubal, he realized.

Trying to change the subject, Vijay asked, "What kind of a name is Hasdrubal?"

"Carthaginian," said the biologist. Before anyone could ask more, he explained, "My great-grandfather was one of the original Black Muslims. When he changed his name from Jefferson he wanted something elegant, so he picked Hasdrubal."

"He was a brother of Hannibal, wasn't he?" Jamie asked.

Nodding, Hasdrubal added, "And my great-grandad was a reader of ancient history. Damned near took the name Caesar, but my great-grandmam talked him out of it."

"Are you planning to go back to the crater?" Vijay asked.

Rosenberg answered, "No. We have it fully instrumented. If and when it blows we'll get it all on record: imagery, heat flow, seismic data, the works."

"I've analyzed the dirt for biological activity," said Hasdrubal.

"And?" asked Vijay.

"Nada. Zip. Dirt's loaded with superoxides. Not enough organic material in it to support a bacterium."

"How deep does the superoxide layer go?" Jamie asked.

"It varies," said Hasdrubal, waggling a long-fingered hand in the air.

"It's more than twenty meters down at the Malzberg site," said Rosenberg.

"That's awfully deep, i'n't it?" asked Vijay.

Hasdrubal nodded. "In some places it's only a couple of meters down. Depends on where you are."

"So what are you going to do now?" Jamie asked.

Hasdrubal took a swig of his fruit juice, then answered, "Carleton wants us to volunteer for his dig." He broke into a toothy grin as he put his mug down. "But we have other plans."

"We're going to take a camper out and follow the path of the old river," said Rosenberg.

"See if we can find other villages buried underground," Hasdrubal put in.

"Dr. Chang has approved that?"

"Approved it?" Hasdrubal echoed, his grin going even wider. "He just about insisted on it. 'Specially when we told him Carleton had approached us."

Rosenberg leaned his elbows on either side of his dish and dropped his voice several decibels. "If Carleton's for it, Chang's against it. They don't like each other. Not at all."

Jamie studied the geologist's round, bland face with its mop of tightly curled strawberry hair and the silly-looking little tuft of a goatee. The man was grinning, as if he found the conflict amusing.

"That troubles me," Jamie said.

Rosenberg made an elaborate shrug. "Not much you can do about it, actually."

Hasdrubal interjected, "Unless you wanna get in the middle of it."

TITHONIUM CHASMA: THE CLIFF DWELLINGS

■

Jamie's heart was thumping as he rode the cable lift up the sheer face of the cliff. He was excited, not afraid. Sealed inside a nanofabric suit, he felt almost as if he were in his shirtsleeves riding past layer after layer of Mars's geologic history. Bands of red rock, then gray, then an almost golden tan. Cracked, seamed, striated. The history of a world sliding past his eyes as he dangled in the climbing harness that hauled him up to the cleft where the buildings stood.

He remembered the First Expedition, their third morning on Mars, the jolt of sheer exhilaration he'd gotten when he'd spotted a rock that bore a streak of green. He'd been certain, rationally, that the green was an inclusion of copper. But still, green in the middle of the planetwide desert of rusty red! It turned out to be copper, as Jamie had suspected, but the excitement that it might have been life—that was a moment he'd never forget.

And then he'd discovered the cliff dwellings. At first no one believed him. He had seen the niche from a distance; even the camera imagery he had brought back to their base was hazy, indistinct. A Navaho imagining things that remind him of home, they all said. It wasn't until the Second Expedition when he and Dex had driven purposefully out to the edge of the canyon and rappelled nearly a full kilometer down to the cleft in the worn old cliffs that they saw beyond a doubt that the buildings actually were there.

That was more than a thrill. Even inside the cumbersome

old hard-shell suit he wore his knees had gone weak on him.

Chang had recited safety protocols at him when Jamie told the mission director he wanted to go to the cliff buildings. Jamie had quietly insisted on going alone.

"I don't want to take anyone from their work," he'd said.

Scowling, Chang said, "Take your fellow Navaho."

"Graycloud? He's got his own tasks to do, doesn't he?"

It took some discussion, but Chang had finally agreed to allow Jamie to ride up to the buildings alone. Jamie got the impression that the mission director was just as glad that he didn't have to take anyone away from their assigned jobs to escort him.

Now he pressed the control stud on the front of his climbing harness and the cable drive decelerated. Jamie rose slowly past the lip of the cleft and stopped the cable altogether, his feet dangling in midair, his body twisting slightly in the harness. His throat went dry. There they were, six buildings made of sun-dried brick, bleached white with age, silent, empty, waiting for him.

It's better to do this alone, he told himself. Just these ancient buildings and me. No one else. No distractions.

He swung his legs and planted his booted feet on the edge of the cleft, unhooked the harness, then walked a dozen steps toward the buildings. The solid rock overhead formed a shield against the elements, not that it had rained or snowed on Mars for eons. There was frost from time to time, Jamie knew, pitifully thin coatings of rime that condensed on the rocks overnight and evaporated with the morning sun. The endolithic lichen living inside the rocks on the valley floor depended on that meager source of moisture.

Stepping to the face of the nearest building, Jamie wondered why the seasonal frosts hadn't eroded the brickwork more. It's had sixty-some million seasons to do its damage, he told himself. Yet, as he touched the bleached white wall with his nanogloved fingers, he saw that its surface was scarcely pitted. Archeologists had studied these buildings, he knew. He'd read their reports. No one could explain how the structures had remained relatively undamaged over all those millions of years. These bricks must be more than adobe, he reasoned. Maybe the Martians could teach us something about construction materials.

Another one of Mars's mysteries, Jamie said to himself. And he smiled. Someday we'll figure out the answers to all the mysteries. And Mars will be a lot less interesting.

Or will it? The answer to one mystery usually leads to still more unknowns.

Morning sunlight was slanting into the cleft as Jamie ducked through the low doorway of the building and stepped inside. Whoever built these structures wasn't very tall. He remembered how he and Dex Trumball had to get down on all fours, inside their bulky hard-shell suits, and crawl through the entrance. In the flexible nanosuit he could walk through if he hunched over.

Twenty years worth of curious, two-legged explorers from Earth had swept away all the dust that had accumulated in the buildings. The rooms inside were bare, their stone-covered floors cleared and somehow sterile looking. Archeologists had come and gone, cleaning, searching, sifting the dust, seeking artifacts, fossils, some hint of who built these cliff structures, some clue about their purpose in the lives of their vanished builders.

Over the span of more than twenty years they had found precious little. Practically nothing, Jamie knew. The rooms had been empty. No furniture, no altars, not a scrap or a shard to indicate why the structures had been built up here in this inaccessible site, or what they had been used for. The Martians had taken their secrets with them.

Except for the drawings.

Jamie clambered up the aluminum ladder that had been placed for access to the next floor. The drawings were on a wall on the uppermost floor. One wall out of the entire complex of buildings. Was this your shrine? Jamie asked the vanished Martians. Your school?

A battery of full-spectrum lamps faced the wall, connected to a thermionic nuclear power pack, pointing at the drawings like an execution squad. The lamps were off, but there was enough sunlight coming in through the light well in the ceiling that Jamie could make out the etched figures clearly.

Archeologists had sprayed the wall with a monomolecular coating of clear hard plastic, so that no one could damage the lines of finely etched figures. Jamie shook his head at their precaution. Sixty million years of time hadn't erased the drawings. But maybe a handful of thoughtless assholes could mess them up, he admitted to himself.

At first the scientists thought the figures had been writing: line after line of delicate curves and swirls etched into the rock facing of the wall. Gradually the teams of archeologists and philologists who had come to Mars to study the figures came to the conclusion that they were pictographs: a form of writing, to be sure, but one that used pictorial symbols rather than arbitrary shapes to form words.

Jamie reached out with a gloved hand, barely able to suppress the very human urge to touch the symbols. He saw a circle with rays coming out of its perimeter, so much like the sun symbols of the southwest Native Americans that his breath still caught in his throat whenever he looked at it. Other symbols vaguely reminded him of snakes, triangles, even a few that sort of looked like trees.

Line after line of carefully wrought pictographs. They had eyes like ours, Jamie told himself. And hands, fingers. They had minds like ours.

The lines of precise, regularly spaced figures ended about a meter above the cleanly swept floor. Then came ragged, lopsided symbols, obviously scrawled in desperate haste compared to the orderly pictographs above them. The methodical lines of symbols had been inscribed deeply into the stone by chisels or similar instruments. The childlike scribbles had been scratched out quickly, roughly, as if the person who scraped them onto the rock had been looking over his shoulder, staring death in the face.

It's their history, Jamie was certain. They were telling the story of their people, their way of life, their beliefs, their dreams. And then it happened. That giant meteor hit like the fist of devastation. The skies went dark. Their crops died. It became winter forever.

Jamie stared at the symbols as if he could make them speak to him by sheer willpower. But they remained mute, lifeless.

Are they prayers? Jamie asked himself. Was this collection of buildings placed up here in this inaccessible cleft in the rocks as some sort of temple? Will we ever know?

Jamie stood there, as silent and unmoving as the stones themselves, until the sunlight began to fade.

"Dr. Waterman." The excursion monitor's voice in his earplug sounded foreign, alien. "You're at the limit. Temperature's starting to go down."

It took him two tries to make his voice work. "Right. I'm starting back."

With enormous reluctance he turned away from the carvings and made his way back down to the lowest level of the building. It was late afternoon. He'd been in the building almost the whole day.

Time to get back to the base, he told himself. Before it starts to get really cold.

As he slipped his arms into the climbing harness and clicked its lock on his chest, Jamie took one more look at the bleached white buildings. And he realized what he had to do.

∎

H ey, geek boy!"
     Bucky Winters looked up. He'd been sitting on the
bench by the batting cage, tying up the laces of the cleated
baseball shoes he'd borrowed, hoping to get a tryout for the
school's team. But Lon Sanchez and a couple of the other
older boys had descended on him.

"Whatcha doin'?" Sanchez asked, grinning. His two pals
were just as big as he was, twice Bucky's size.

"Trying out for the team," said Bucky. He'd taken a double dose of allergy pills so he could get through this tryout
with clear sinuses and dry eyes.

"No you ain't."

"Yes I am," said Bucky, getting to his feet.

Sanchez bent down slightly so that his red, angry face was
hardly an inch in front of Bucky's. His two cohorts came up
on either side; Bucky was surrounded.

"We don't want any geek boys screwin' up our team."

"I know how to play!" Bucky insisted. "I'm better at short-
stop than Ricky is."

"The hell you are."

"Give me a chance at a tryout and I'll prove it."

"No way, geek. Take off your cleats and go home."

"Go back to Mars," said the oaf on his left.

"Yeah, we don't want any Mars boys on our team."

"We heard about your big project."

"Yeah. It's a shame somebody mashed it flat," Sanchez said, smirking.

Bucky's temper flared. "You're the one who busted up my model!"

Sanchez grabbed Bucky by the front of his shirt. "That's right, Mars boy. And if you don't get the fuck outta here we're gonna bust you up, too."

Bucky kicked Sanchez in the shins as hard as he could, making him yowl with pain, then punched him squarely in the nose. Blood spurted. The other two were stunned with surprise for a moment, but before Bucky could get away, they grabbed him and helped Sanchez beat him into unconsciousness.

When all four of them were brought before the school's principal, Sanchez pointed to his bandaged nose and claimed that Bucky started the fight. Bucky's head was bandaged, his ribs were encased in a plastic cast, his face was lumpy with bruises.

"You struck the first blow?" the principal demanded of Bucky.

Through swollen lips Bucky admitted, "Yes, ma'am."

The principal shook her gray head. "First this Mars business and now you've started a brawl. You'd better be very careful, young man. You're in a downward spiral."

BOSTON: TRUMBALL TRUST HEADQUARTERS

■

Dex Trumball tried to hide the mistrust he felt. Why has this priest flown here all the way from Rome? he wondered silently. What does he want?

Monsignor DiNardo was smiling patiently at him as he sat in the bottle green leather armchair before Dex's wide, curved desk of Danish teak and brushed aluminum. The priest wore a plain black business suit, with his clerical collar and its touch of purple. DiNardo looked burly, with bulging shoulders and a barrel chest, his scalp shaved but the dark shadow of a beard stubbling his jaw, yet he still seemed somewhat dwarfed in the capacious armchair. Dex resisted the urge to get up and see if the priest's feet reached the carpeted floor.

"It was good of you to see me on such short notice," DiNardo said in English, a hint of soft Italian vowels at the ends of his words.

Dex made a hospitable smile. "Not at all, Fa . . . uh, Monsignor. Would you like something to drink? Coffee? Something stronger?"

DiNardo shook his head. "Thank you, no. The rocket flight brought me here in half an hour, but my insides are still on Vatican time."

"I see."

An uneasy hush fell over them. DiNardo seemed to be fishing for the words he wanted while Dex fiddled impatiently with his fingers, waiting for the priest to start talking. Does he know about my negotiations with Kinnear? Dex wondered nervously. No, he can't. Rollie can keep his mouth shut. I haven't even mentioned it to the Navaho president yet.

At last Dex broke the silence. "I saw the video show you did with Orlando Ventura."

"That abomination!" DiNardo spat.

"You held up your end pretty well," said Dex.

"They had no interest in the importance of the Martian fossil. They belittled the greatest find since Lucy."

"They're not interested in science, that's for sure."

"No, they want to deny it all."

Dex nodded agreement. Then, "We're working to put together a documentary about the fossil. A *real* documentary, not a circus."

"I would be glad to participate in it, if you feel I could be of help."

"Certainly. Will the Vatican . . . ?"

DiNardo caught Dex's implication. "The Holy See will have no objection. Not everyone who believes in God is blindly anti-science."

"I'm glad to hear that. We're up to our eyeballs in fundamentalists."

"There are factions within the Vatican, to be sure," DiNardo admitted easily. "But they have not affected the Pontifical Academy of Sciences, I assure you."

Not yet, Dex thought. Aloud, he mused, "You could be a very important voice in our documentary. You could show that there's no real conflict between science and religion."

DiNardo hesitated, then said merely, "I will be glad to do what I can."

"Great. I'll tell the people producing the show to count you in."

"*Buono*," said DiNardo. Then he went on, "Now, I must ask a favor of you."

Here it comes, Dex said to himself. "A favor?"

"I wish to go to Mars."

Dex blinked at the priest. "Go to Mars? You?"

With a self-deprecating little smile, DiNardo said, "I am a

trained geologist. I was selected to be the lead geologist on the First Expedition, if you remember."

"I know. But that was more than twenty years ago."

"I am not quite an invalid. In fact, I am in very good health."

"But you're . . . what, fifty-five, sixty?"

"Fifty-seven. Jamie Waterman is almost fifty. Carter Carleton is sixty-three. I won't be the oldest fossil on Mars."

Dex acknowledged the priest's little joke with a forced smile.

"I will undergo the most rigorous physical examinations your program can subject me to," DiNaro said before Dex could think of anything to say. "Of course, with the fusion torch ships the trip to Mars is much easier than it was twenty-some years ago."

"Yes, but why . . . ?"

DiNardo lifted his round chin and let out a sigh. "I want to help. I believe that having a priest go to Mars might help to counter the voices speaking against the program."

"You know that we might have to shut down the whole shebang and bring everybody home."

"I am aware of that. I believe that my going to Mars could help you gain more donors to keep the program funded."

Dex couldn't help grinning. "You want to be the Mars poster boy?"

Perfectly serious, DiNardo replied, "If it will help."

TITHONIUM BASE: JAMIE'S OFFICE

■

Jamie's little cubicle was crowded with both Carleton and Chang in it. Jamie could feel the tension crackling between the two men. Not good, he told himself. These two have to work together if we're going to get anywhere.

Dr. Chang sat in the stiff plastic chair in front of Jamie's fold-up desk. Carleton had dragged in a rolling chair made of bungee cords from the adjoining cubicle. It filled the entrance to Jamie's office; there was no room to get it farther into the cramped workspace.

"I have considered your request of staying past my regular term of service," Chang was saying, his stubby arms crossed on his chest, his back to Carleton.

Jamie waited for the other shoe.

"I will remain here as long as necessary, as mission director."

Carleton said, "I thought you had family that you wanted to get back to."

"I have a wife and son in Beijing," Chang replied, without turning to look at the anthropologist. "However, my duty is plainly here."

"I'm glad you've decided," Jamie said, with a slow smile. "I know Dr. Carleton intends to remain, too."

"Damned right," said Carleton.

"I will remain mission director," Chang repeated. It was a demand, not a question.

"Yes, certainly," answered Jamie. "Your experience will be very valuable to all of us."

Carleton said nothing.

"I've talked with almost everyone here," Jamie said. "Most of them are willing to extend their stays."

"Several wish to leave," Chang said.

Nodding, Jamie replied, "That's all right. We need some interchange of personnel. We can't expect to freeze everyone in their places."

"We need geologists," Chang said. "We should send an excursion team to the south pole—"

"We won't be able to do that," Jamie interrupted. "We just don't have the resources."

Undeterred, Chang went on, "The south pole is a conundrum. It is shrinking. Millions of tons of frozen carbon dioxide go into gaseous state each year. Gaseous carbon dioxide produces a greenhouse effect in atmosphere."

Carleton grunted. "Some greenhouse. Temperatures are still below freezing."

"But getting warmer," Chang countered. "Yet humidity in the atmosphere is decreasing. Warmer atmosphere should support higher humidity level, not lower. A conundrum."

"I agree it's an important problem," Jamie said. "But we just don't have the resources to send a team to the south pole."

"Then there is an ancient riverbed in the valley here," Chang said. "Mapping the course of the riverbed is important."

"The satellites are doing that with deep radar," said Carleton. "What we really need are more grunts to help excavate the village."

Chang insisted, "There must be other villages along the course of the riverbed."

Carleton smiled easily and rolled his chair slightly to Chang's right, so he could see the mission director's face.

"Isn't there an old Chinese proverb to the effect that a bird in the hand is worth two in the bush?"

Chang inched away from him.

Carleton went on, "We have a village to excavate. As I understand it, the Foundation people in Boston are putting together a video documentary about it, which they hope to use to raise more funds for us. I think all our efforts should be put into digging out this village."

Chang tried to hide his scowl, failed. "There is more to be done than your one village."

Before Carleton could reply, Jamie jumped in. "You're both right. There's an enormous number of things that we've got to do. But the village *is* very important. The question we have to settle is how much of our resources we should put into the village, and how much elsewhere."

"Tracing the riverbed course," said Chang. "Studying water geysers and underground heat flow. Melting at the south pole—"

"My village will bring new money into our program," Carleton insisted. "You'll never get to the south pole without an influx of new funding."

"The village is important," Chang conceded. "But it is not the only thing we must consider."

"Right," Jamie agreed. "Personally, I'd like to see more effort put into decoding the writing up in the cliff dwellings."

"They weren't dwellings," Carleton said. "A religious center, more likely."

"I'd still like to know what those symbols mean."

With a shake of his head, Carleton argued, "Forget about it."

"Forget it?"

"It's a forlorn hope, Jamie. The best philologists in the world have cracked their skulls on those symbols. It's useless."

"But—"

"I know, I know. People have deciphered ancient languages: Sumerian, Cretan linear B, Sanskrit."

"Proto-Chinese," Chang added.

"Yes, but in every case they found a Rosetta Stone of one kind or another, a relic where the unknown language was written down side by side with a known one, so the philologists could translate from the known language to the unknown."

Chang nodded reluctantly.

"There's no Rosetta Stone on Mars. The Martian writings are completely alien. There's no known language that we can translate from. We'll never understand their writing."

"Never is a long time," Jamie muttered.

"Don't waste time or effort on it," Carleton insisted. "Don't waste the limited resources we have on bringing more philologists here. They can study the imagery back in their offices on Earth."

"I suppose so," said Jamie.

"We'll never understand their writing, I'm afraid. It's just not possible."

A sly smile crept slowly across Chang's fleshy face. "August Comte," he murmured.

"Ohgoost what?" Jamie asked.

"Comte," said Chang. "Nineteenth-century French philosopher. Founder of positivism."

"What's he got to do with Martian writing?" Carleton wondered.

"Comte said it would forever be impossible to learn the chemical composition of stars. Yet within a few years astronomers started to use spectroscopy to do precisely that."

Jamie grinned. "With spectral analysis you can determine the chemical composition of anything that glows. And a lot more."

Chang finally turned in his chair to face the anthropologist. "There is another old Chinese proverb, Dr. Carleton: Never say never."

LONDON: ROCK RATS MUSIC, INC.

∎

Rafael Goodbar was not his real name, of course, but then music producers seldom used their true names anymore. The Reverend Caleb Mordecai hadn't used his baptismal name in many years either: Willie Barcum just sounded too wimpy for a man who was rising in the eyes of the Lord.

Names aside, Rev. Mordecai had a mission to accomplish here, and Rafael Goodbar wasn't making it easy for him.

Goodbar was obviously Jewish, thought Reverend Mordecai. He had the heavy-featured, fleshy face and hooded eyes of a Son of Israel. He was wearing a luridly flashy short-sleeved shirt that exposed his flabby, hairy forearms. Mordecai half expected to see tattoos, but none were evident.

"Let me understand you," said Goodbar, smiling. Rev. Mordecai thought the smile looked forced, oily, devious. "You want to put me out of business."

"Not at all," the minister replied. "We merely request— request, mind you—that you allow our editorial board to review the lyrics of your songs before they are recorded."

"Editorial board," Goodbar said heavily. "You mean, censors."

"Heavens no!" Mordecai exclaimed. "We do not censor. That would be illegal, or so the secular courts have maintained."

"So what does your editorial board do?"

"We make suggestions. Recommendations, actually. When we find lyrics in a song that are offensive, we recommend that they be altered."

"And if I don't make the alterations?"

"We suggest to the Faithful that they boycott the song."

"Just the one song?"

It was Mordecai's turn to smile. "That would be impractical, at best. No, we recommend that our followers boycott everything that the producing company puts on the market."

"Which would put the producer out of business."

Mordecai glanced heavenward, then leveled his mild blue eyes at Goodbar. "If you are disseminating lyrics that harm impressionable young listeners, you are doing the devil's work, Mr. Goodbar. You don't deserve to remain in business."

Goodbar countered, "But this is all a matter of opinion, isn't it? What you think is harmful, other people enjoy listening to."

"They enjoyed marijuana and other drugs before we put a stop to the narcotics traffic!" Mordecai snapped.

"Oh, the drug business has been stopped? I hadn't noticed."

The man is an unrepentant sinner, Mordecai said to himself.

Leaning his hairy forearms on his desktop, Goodbar added, "You're trying to censor songwriters, which would never hold up in the courts and you know it. We still have a few rights remaining, Reverend."

Icily, Mordecai replied, "And the godfearing people of this nation have the right to boycott the kinds of unmitigated trash that you and your kind spew into the ears of impressionable young people!"

Goodbar spread his hands in a gesture that Mordecai found distinctly and repulsively Semitic. "Look," said the producer, "you know and I know that this isn't about religion or morality. You just don't want the kids to hear anything that challenges their authority figures. You don't want anything that doesn't toe your line."

"We will not tolerate any challenges to the Word of the Lord."

"Bloody nonsense," Goodbar said amiably.

Mordecai flinched.

"So go ahead and boycott," Goodbar said. "See how much good it does you. The kids'll just want to hear the songs even more once they know the Holy Disciples is against them. It'll be good publicity for me."

"You think so? We'll see." Mordecai rose to his feet. Goodbar remained seated behind his desk.

The minister went to the office door, hesitated, then turned back toward the producer.

"You're either on God's side or you're doing the work of the devil," Mordecai warned.

"You can go to hell," Goodbar said cheerfully.

"No," Mordecai retorted. "Hell is where you're heading. And soon."

Rafael Goodbar—whose birth name was Raymond Herschfield—was shot to death at a Dog Dirt concert three months later. His killer surrendered easily to the police, smilingly explaining that he was doing God's work.

TITHONIUM CHASMA: EXCURSION TEAM.

■

Hasdrubal and Rosenberg were arguing again as they drove in the springy-wheeled camper along the floor of the Tithonium valley.

"I say she's a lesbian," Hasdrubal insisted.

"So what if she is? Shirley's a virgin, I'm rather certain, but she's as heterosexual as you or I."

Hasdrubal looked down at his partner, sitting in the cockpit seat beside him. The seat's pseudoleather padding was worn smooth, cracked in places, he noticed. Rosenberg was driving, both hands gripping the little steering wheel, his eyes focused on the bumpy, rock-strewn landscape before them. Rugged red cliffs towered over them on their left.

"She's always hanging out with other women," Hasdrubal said, ticking points off on his long, slim fingers. "Far's I know she hasn't come on to any of the guys—"

"You mean she hasn't come on to you."

Raising a third finger, "And when a guy gets near her she runs in the other direction."

Rosenberg broke into a grin. "Aha! She ran away from you. Can't blame her, actually: you must have frightened her."

"Me?"

"You can appear rather fearsome, you know. Like some Watusi warrior in coveralls."

"Bullshit," Hasdrubal grumbled.

Still smiling, Rosenberg murmured, "When at a loss for *le mot juste*, lapse into profanity."

"Double bullshit," Hasdrubal said. He slid out of the right-hand seat and got to his feet like a jointed ladder unfolding, stooping to keep his head clear of the bulbous glassteel canopy that curved above. He used both hands to steady himself against the folded-up bunks as the camper swayed and jounced over the rough ground.

"Extraordinary," Rosenberg muttered as the biologist headed back toward the lavatory. Shirley's no lesbian, he told himself. At least she didn't indicate it on her personnel file. The personnel files were strictly confidential, of course, but any member of the exploration team who had even a limited knowledge of computer hacking could sneak a peek at them. Rosenberg ran a hand through his tightly curled thatch of strawberry hair. Perhaps Shirley's clever enough to know that the files aren't actually all that secure, he thought. Perhaps she put herself down as hetero because she doesn't want anyone to know her true orientation.

The camper rocked sharply as it trundled across a shallow crater.

"Hey, watch it!" Hasdrubal's voice boomed from the lavatory.

Rosenberg quickly put his free hand back on the steering wheel.

Hasdrubal came back past the bunks and bent over Rosenberg's seat. "You need a break?" he asked.

Glancing at the digital clock on the control panel, Rosenberg said, "In another fifteen minutes."

"We'll be there by then."

"Right. We can stop and have a bite of lunch before we go outside."

"Good enough," Hasdrubal muttered, sliding back into the right-hand seat. "Just try to avoid the major potholes, will ya?"

Rosenberg frowned at his partner.

Ground truth, Hasdrubal said to himself. That's why Chang's sent us out this time, to determine if the deep radar imagery from the satellites has really spotted the outlines of another buried ancient village. The sensors can provide us with all sorts of data, but until somebody digs up hard, palpable evidence, the kind you can hold in your hand, the sensor data is suspect. It's not enough, never enough. You need ground truth before you can actually believe it.

Well, it's okay with me. Gives me an excuse to dig up soil samples from another spot. Might find some bugs if we bore down deeper than the damned superoxide layer covering the surface.

He tapped the map display on the control panel. "Coming up on the coordinates."

"So I see," said Rosenberg. "Why don't we set up camp by that large boulder there, at two o'clock."

Hasdrubal glanced at the house-sized boulder, then looked down at the map display again. "Okay. That's damn near spang on top of the village."

"If it's actually there."

"It's there," Hasdrubal said firmly. "The big job is to prove it."

"Rather." Rosenberg braked the camper slowly to a full stop. "But let's have a spot of lunch first."

Two hours later the two of them stood panting with exertion beside the probe they had set up where the radar imagery indicated the village's gridwork pattern of streets was laid out thirty-some meters below the valley floor. Their nanosuits were spattered with red dust up to their knees; their gloves and forearms were also coated with rust.

The probe stood vertically, one end stuck into the ground, the other pointing skyward, a flimsy-looking quartet of slanting legs supporting it. Rosenberg thought it looked like a minimalist's model of the Eiffel Tower. A thick power cable ran back to the external outlets on the curving side of the camper.

"How deep is it now?" Hasdrubal asked, straightening up from his kneeling position. Placing both hands on his hips, he arched backward slightly, trying to ease the strain on his spine.

Rosenberg read from the meter on the probe's cluster of instruments. "Seventeen meters. We still have quite a ways to go."

"Ready to pop the laser again?"

"One tick." Rosenberg ran a gloved finger down the indicator lights on the miniaturized box of the instrument panel. "All right. The laser's recharged and primed to go."

Stepping back from the probe, Hasdrubal said, "Okay, hit it."

A puff of gritty, grayish gas spurted out of the hole and wafted away slowly in the calm air.

"Down another two meters," said Rosenberg.

"Good. But we're not going to be deep enough before the sun sets."

"No. We'll finish tomorrow."

"Why don't we knock off now," Hasdrubal said. It was more than a suggestion. "My back's killing me."

Rosenberg nodded inside the inflated bubble of his helmet. "I'm with you. Too bad someone can't develop nanomachines to do the digging for us."

Hasdrubal grinned at his partner. "Too expensive. We're a lot cheaper."

"Slave labor."

"Damned near."

They shut down the probe for the night and trudged wearily back toward the camper, two thoroughly tired men alone in the rocky cold wilderness of Mars. The massive cliffs loomed over them, glowing russet and pink in the slanting light of the setting sun. Their camper sat like a fat metal caterpillar, sunlight glinting off its curved bug-eye canopy.

Hasdrubal reached the airlock hatch and popped it open. "Well, tomorrow we'll have to guide the supply rocket down."

Rosenberg grunted. "I don't really trust those automated hoppers. Some of them have been in service for nearly twenty years."

"That's why we take over their final guidance," Hasdrubal said, climbing into the airlock.

Rosenberg looked unconvinced.

"Don't worry. I'll put 'er down nice and easy. No sweat."

Rosenberg still looked unconvinced.

TITHONIUM BASE: INFIRMARY

■

In the few days she had been at the base, Vijay had come to recognize that Nari Quintana ruled the infirmary with a stainless steel fist. The daughter of a Venezuelan oil millionaire and his Japanese wife, Dr. Quintana was serving her second term of duty on Mars. Small, spare, with straight dull hair, she reminded Vijay of a little brown sparrow hopping from bed to bed, making her morning rounds. But everyone warned that this little sparrow had the ferocity of an eagle whenever anyone stirred her wrath.

"Her first name means thunderclap in Japanese," one of the medical technicians had told Vijay when she'd first come into the infirmary, uninvited, to see what she could do to help. "It's very appropriate."

So far, Vijay and the formidable Dr. Quintana had gotten along tolerably well. Quintana was obviously suspicious that the wife of Jamie Waterman would try to usurp her authority. But Vijay smiled as she explained that she only wanted to help in any way she could.

Now she sat before Dr. Quintana's desk. The woman's office wasn't much larger than a phone booth, Vijay thought, and it was as austere and undecorated as Quintana herself.

"I'd like to make more of a contribution than I have so far," Vijay said, as sweetly as she could manage. "I mean, there must be something more that I could do, besides checking the supply stocks for hitchhiking insects and running routine physicals on the staff."

Quintana's sharp eyes flickered. "You've had enough of the nitpicking, eh?"

Smiling, Vijay replied, "I know someone has to make certain that the packages in storage don't harbor bugs, but I do have a degree in psychology, if that could be of use to you."

"Yes, I know," was as much as Quintana would unbend.

For several moments, Quintana said nothing. Then, abruptly, she stood up.

"Come with me," she said peremptorily as she headed for the door of her office.

Vijay jumped to her feet and followed the doctor.

"Morning rounds," Quintana said over her shoulder as she led Vijay to the infirmary's row of eight beds. Four of them were empty. Vijay understood that most of Quintana's patients were suffering from rather minor accidents rather than disease. The exploration team were mostly young and never left Earth until their health had been thoroughly checked. And Martian microbes were enough different from terrestrial biology that there was nothing on Mars that could infect humans. At least, that's what the biologists concluded.

This morning, though, a young maintenance technician was lying asleep in one of the beds, an intravenous drip tube in his arm.

"Gastric ulcer," Quintana said, eying the computer display screen over the head of the bed.

"He seems awfully young to have an ulcer," Vijay said, also peering at the display screen.

"Allergic to aspirin. He took aspirin every morning to protect his heart," Quintana explained to Vijay. "But it attacked his stomach, instead."

"Some people are allergic to aspirin and don't know it," Vijay murmured as they moved to the next bed, a woman who had twisted her ankle when she slipped on a wet tile in the cafeteria.

"Until a stomach ulcer explodes and they lose half their blood supply in a few minutes."

Vijay said, "An allergy like that wouldn't show up on a routine screening, either."

"Yes, true. Everyone here has been thoroughly screened before being accepted for the Mars program, but the screening can't possibly catch everything." Quintana spoke in flat midwestern American English.

Physical screening is easier than psychological, Vijay thought, remembering Trudy Hall. She had been thoroughly screened for the Second Expedition, yet she had cracked up emotionally and nearly killed the entire team. Psychological testing could only go so deep, she knew. Mars tests each of us in its own way.

"They seem a healthy enough lot," Vijay replied as she walked along the row of beds beside Quintana. "Of course, they're mostly pretty young. That helps, doesn't it?"

Quintana almost smiled. "Chang, Carleton and your husband are the oldest here."

"And me," Vijay pointed out. "I'm forty-two."

The chief physician actually did smile. "I am thirty-nine."

"Are you married?" Vijay asked.

"Divorced."

"Oh. I'm so sorry."

"Twice."

Vijay had the sense to shut her mouth.

The three accident cases were minor injuries, except for one of Carleton's digging crew who had jumped into the excavation pit thinking that Mars's light gravity would make the thirty-meter drop easy. He had broken both his ankles, and learned that although weight is only one-third of normal on Mars, mass—the amount of matter in a body—doesn't change because of the lower gravity. His bones had broken just as they would have on Earth.

"The major causes of human pain and suffering," Quintana pronounced as they left the man's bed: "pride and stupidity. They often go together."

Vijay thought that maybe the young man—who was a meteorologist who'd volunteered to help Carleton—was trying to show off for some of the women at the dig. Testosterone is the most dangerous drug of all, she thought.

"What are you doing for him?" Vijay asked.

Quintana glanced back at the young man lying in his bed. "We've harvested stem cells from his bone marrow and now we're cultivating them. In a few days we can reinject them and rebuild the bones good as new."

Vijay nodded. Stem cell therapy was once considered miraculous; now it was routine.

"He doesn't deserve it," Quintana added. "Stupidity like his needs a stronger lesson."

Tough love, Vijay thought. Quintana's a hard case, all right.

As they started back toward Quintana's office, Vijay asked, "Would it be possible for me to set up shop as the resident psychologist? Would that be helpful to you?"

"We do psych tests regularly," Quintana said quickly. "The program office beams questionnaires up from Earth. Everyone is required to participate."

"I see," Vijay said. "I just thought I might offer a kind of counseling service . . . if anyone needs it."

Quintana said nothing until they reached her office again. Sliding its door shut, she went around her desk and sat once more in the wobbly little chair behind it. Vijay took the only other chair.

"I am the chief physician here," Quintana began. "I am also the only physician here. That is, until you arrived."

"There are the medical technicians, though," said Vijay.

"Of course. Five of them. Usually they outnumber our patients."

"What you're saying is that you don't need me."

Quintana shook her head hard enough to make her mousy hair flutter. "You are here because you are Jamie Waterman's wife and you want to be with your husband. You are also a trained physician with a background in psychology. It would be foolish not to use your talents in some manner."

"Yes, but how?"

Pursing her lips, Quintana said, "You tell me. You've seen the infirmary and the kinds of cases we get here. What can you do to help?"

Vijay hesitated, thinking, She's batted the ball back into my side of the court.

"I don't require an answer this minute," Quintana said. "Take your time. Think about it."

"I know what I'd like to do," Vijay said.

"Yes?"

"I'd like to run a psych profile on the people here. Not the kind of multiple-choice tests they beam up from Earth, but real, personal, in-depth interviews with as many of the personnel as will sit down with me."

"You plan to write a paper for a psychology journal?"

Nodding, Vijay said, "That would be appropriate, don't you think? A psychological profile of the men and women on Mars. You and I could be coauthors."

"I am not a psychologist."

"No, but you're the chief physician here. Your input and insights would be very important to the study. Either way, I'll be available to help you with your patients in any way I can, whenever you need me."

Quintana tapped her desk top absently. Vijay noted that her fingernails were unpolished and clipped very short. Yet the nails on her right hand were longer and well-shaped.

"You play the guitar?" she asked.

Quintana blinked with surprise. "My father taught me when I was a little girl. I brought two of them to Mars with me."

"How wonderful. I can play piano a little."

"No piano here." Quintana's suspicion and anxiety eased somewhat. "But I can teach you the guitar, if you like."

TITHONIUM CHASMA: EXCURSION TEAM

∎

I have good news and bad news," said Izzy Rosenberg.

Puffing from exertion, Hasdrubal looked up from the tubular probe sticking out of the rust-colored sand. "Is this a joke?"

Rosenberg was inside the camper, checking the data from the miniature sensors down at the business end of the probe.

"I wish it were," he said. His voice sounded worried in Hasdrubal's headphone.

Looking toward the camper, parked twenty-some meters from the probe, Hasdrubal said guardedly, "Tell me the good news first, then."

"The GC/MS has picked up a whiff of carbon."

"Carbon?" Hasdrubal stood up straighter. He could *feel* his eyes go wide. The gas chromatograph/mass spectrometer analyzed the gases boiled out of the rock by the laser pulses.

"Where? How deep?"

"At the thirty-meter level, rather where the foundations of the village should be."

"Carbon?" Hasdrubal repeated. "Like, from something organic?"

"It could be," said Rosenberg, his voice curiously flat, unexcited. "Fossilized wood, perhaps. Construction material."

"Or the remains of a body!"

"Whatever. It's definitely not the rock we've been drilling through above that level. It must be part of the village. Building foundations, perhaps."

"Yow!" Hasdrubal leaped into the air and flung his arms over his head joyfully.

"You haven't heard the bad news, Sal."

"Bad news?"

"The laser's drained our battery power almost completely."

"That's not so bad. We'll recharge 'em from the solar cells."

"Not enough sunlight left in the day. Besides, the resupply hopper is due in fifteen minutes. By the time we set it down and transfer the supplies to the camper the sun will be on the horizon."

"Recharge 'em tomorrow, then, first light." Hasdrubal started walking toward the camper.

"Yes, I suppose so."

"The fuel cells're okay, aren't they?"

"So far."

Frowning inside his collapsible bubble helmet, Hasdrubal snapped, "What th'hell's that supposed to mean?"

Rosenberg answered, "I don't like going through the night without the batteries to back up the fuel cells."

Yanking open the airlock's outer hatch, Hasdrubal smiled as he said, "Don't be chicken, Izzy. We got plenty of power."

"I suppose so."

"You're a worrywart, Izzy," said Hasdrubal, climbing into the coffin-sized airlock. He sealed the outer hatch and touched the keypad that started the pumps chugging. "You oughtta relax, enjoy life, like me."

"Extraordinary." In Hasdrubal's headset, Rosenberg's voice sounded halfway between astonishment and disgust. "We're two days' ride from the safety of the base, alone out here in a glorified omnibus without a working backup power system, the temperature outside is already twenty-nine below zero, and there's nothing between us and this near-vacuum that's pretending to be an atmosphere except a few millimeters of metal, and you say I should relax. Extraordinary. Simply extraordinary."

The airlock panel cycled from red light through amber and

into green. Hasdrubal chuckled as he popped the inner hatch. Izzy's twitchy today. Wonder what's really bothering him?

He pulled his nanofabric bubble helmet off his head and unsealed the torso of the suit.

"What's itchin' you, buddy? Your shorts twisted or something?"

From up in the cockpit Rosenberg answered, "The supply rocket's due in eleven minutes. I just got a confirmation from the base."

"Okay," said Hasdrubal as he stepped past the folded-up bunks and slipped into the cockpit's right-hand seat. "I'll bring her in, no sweat."

Rosenberg wasn't perspiring, but he looked decidedly edgy.

"Relax, pal." Hasdrubal tapped at the control panel's keyboard, changing the touchscreen displays from their usual configuration to the setup for guiding the resupply hopper down to a soft landing.

"Base says the hopper's oxygen tank pressure is low."

Hasdrubal peered at the displays that sprang up on the panel. "Yeah, so I see. A smidge. Nothing to worry about."

"It's dropping," Rosenberg said, pointing to the graph curves with a shaky finger.

"Yeah, yeah. Still plenty good enough. Damn tank's prob'ly sprung a pinhole leak. We'll have to fix it once she's down."

"In the dark?"

"Tomorrow. Stop worrying."

Rosenberg got up from the driver's seat and headed back toward the lavatory. Hasdrubal studied the displays. Everything nominal except for the oxy tank pressure, and that wasn't anything to really worry about.

By the time Rosenberg returned to the cockpit the hopper's radio beacon was sending a strong beeping signal. Hasdrubal leaned back in his seat.

"She's comin' right down the pipe," he said to Rosenberg, as Izzy slipped into the left-hand seat. "I won't even hafta touch a button."

Still, he reached for the tiny T-shaped joystick that was tucked into a slot on the control panel and balanced it on his left knee.

"There it is!" Rosenberg shouted, rising halfway out of his seat.

They saw a black dot against the darkening saffron of the Martian sky. As the two men watched, the dot grew and took form: a boxy, octagonal shape with four spindly legs jutting out from corners of its structure and a rocket nozzle hanging from its underside. Adapted from the lander/ascent vehicles of the first Mars missions, the hoppers were now used to ferry supplies and equipment from Tithonium Base to teams in the field.

His eyes flicking from the descending hopper to the displays on the control panel, Hasdrubal touched the joystick with a fingertip.

"Just a smidge closer . . ."

The rocket nozzle flared bright hot gas for a flash of a second. From inside the camper's cockpit they heard it as a thin shriek. The hopper seemed to hesitate in midair, then slowly descended, like an old man settling into an invisible chair. Smaller methane gas jets puffed from around the edges of the octagon and then the hopper touched down, its insect-thin legs bending slightly.

"There y'are," said Hasdrubal grandly as he shut down the controls. "Easy as pie."

Rosenberg grinned weakly at his partner.

"I told you—"

The hopper blew up in a bright explosion of white-hot flame billowing into the thin air. The shock wave rocked the camper.

"Holy shit!" yelled Hasdrubal.

Rosenberg closed his gaping mouth with an audible click, then tried to speak, but found his throat was too parched and constricted to get out any words.

TITHONIUM BASE: THE GARDEN

■

Jamie was in the greenhouse dome with Kalman Torok, kneeling in the reddish sandy strip between rows of string bean and pea plants. Most of the dome was devoted to long hydroponics trays, where soybeans, cereal grains and fruits were being grown without soil. But this little patch of a garden was Torok's work. Sunlight poured through the transparent wall of the dome; it felt pleasantly warm inside.

"You should have seen the look on Chang's face when I asked him for a shipment of beetle grubs and earthworms," Torok was saying, his round face split into a happy grin. "The old sourpuss looked as if I'd suddenly grown horns."

Jamie smiled back. "But it's worked. You've turned this sterile ground into productive soil."

Digging his fingers into the faintly pinkish dirt, Torok corrected, "It wasn't sterile, not completely. Damned little organic material in it, but there was some. We had to bake all the oxides out, of course."

He held a palmful of dirt up to Jamie's face. "Smell it. Go ahead, take a whiff."

Jamie sniffed. "It . . . it almost smells like dirt back home."

"Almost," said Torok, still smiling. "It's taken two years of work, but we've almost got a plot of terrestrial soil here on Mars."

Jerking with surprise, Jamie saw a tiny black beetle push its way out of the dirt and crawl feebly across the clump in Torok's hand.

The biologist laughed. "One of my assistants."

Jamie grinned back at him as Torok gently deposited the handful of dirt back on the ground and patted it smooth. Both men straightened to their feet.

"The next resupply mission will include a shipment of genetically engineered bacteria that can fix nitrogen for cereal grains," Torok said. "If that works we'll be able to grow our own wheat!"

Looking over the tiny garden, Jamie asked, "Do you think you could grow enough food to feed the whole team here?"

Torok's smile faded. "It's not worth the effort. The hydroponics system is cheaper."

"Really? I thought—"

"Hydroponics takes a lot of water and nutrients, yes. But we recycle the water, and to turn Martian ground into productive soil you'd need to start by baking the oxides out, then bring in earthworms and beetles and such to aerate the dirt, and pump in nutrients by the ton to make up for the lack of organics, and—"

"We can build solar energy farms to provide electricity for baking out the oxides," Jamie interrupted. "And power the lamps, as well," he added, glancing up at the rows of full-spectrum lights hanging from the dome's superstructure. "That's what they do at Selene."

"You'd also have to seal the entire area, lay a concrete slab under it with a bioguard sheet to prevent back contamination into the Martian environment, surround it with more concrete and bioshields."

"That adds to the expense."

"And how," Torok said. "In time, though, I suppose you could make a garden big enough to be self-sufficient, recycling organic wastes the way they grow crops at Selene."

"So what's the problem?"

Raising his heavy dark eyebrows, Torok said, "Well, as I said, the big problem is back contamination. You don't want terrestrial organisms getting loose out in the Martian environment."

Jamie looked through the dome's transparent wall at the frigid, barren desert outside. "Earth plants couldn't survive for five minutes out there."

"Plants, no," said Torok. "But the microorganisms that live on them and in them—maybe yes. Those microbes are tough, and a lot of them are anaerobic. They don't need oxygen to survive."

Jamie nodded. "You're afraid they'd infect the Martian environment."

"It's a long shot, I admit. But we've got to protect the local environment against back contamination. Remember, it wasn't gunpowder and cavalry that destroyed the Native Americans; it was the microbes the Europeans brought with them that killed off men, beasts and plants."

Jamie nodded, thinking, We're aliens here. Visitors. We're not Martians and we never will be, no matter how much we want to be. If we're not careful we could wipe out what's left of Mars's native species, just like the whites decimated the Native Americans.

"But if we could protect the environment from contamination?" Jamie asked. "What then?"

With a shrug, Torok replied, "Building farms big enough to feed the whole crew here will take a lot of time. And money. In the beginning you'll have to bring in the nutrients and aerators and every gram of everything else you need from Earth. That's expensive."

"It's a project worth doing, if we're going to stay on Mars."

Torok's smile returned, but it was melancholy now. "If, Dr. Waterman. If."

"Can you do it?" Jamie asked.

"It can be done, I suppose. But I won't be here to carry it through."

"You're leaving?"

"My term ended two months ago. I've told Chang I'll leave on the next resupply flight."

Jamie stared at the biologist for a silent moment, then spread his arms. "But all this . . . you'd leave this behind you?"

With a dejected shake of his head, Torok replied, "My wife is suing for divorce back in Budapest. If I don't get back she'll win custody of my children."

"Oh," was all that Jamie could think to say. But then he heard himself suggesting, "Maybe she could come here to be with you. . . ."

"Two sons, ages four and six. And she won't leave Hungary, let alone travel to Mars."

"But what about this farm? What's going to happen to your work?"

Torok's brows contracted almost into a solid line. "I've asked several of my colleagues to look after it. That black giant, the American with the odd name, he showed some interest."

"Hasdrubal," Jamie said.

"Yes, Hasdrubal. He said he'd tend my garden—when he's not busy with other responsibilities."

Jamie realized there was nothing he could do. Torok was leaving, and his experiment would die of neglect without him.

His pocket phone buzzed. Jamie was glad of the interruption.

"Dr. Waterman, you have an incoming message from Mr. Trumball in Boston."

Looking at Torok's glum face, Jamie said, "I've got to get back to my office."

He hurried to the tube that connected the greenhouse dome to the main structure of the base.

Dex Trumball was excited, Jamie could see even on the small wall screen.

"It's a coup," he was saying, grinning happily. "A gift. From the Vatican, no less."

Jamie leaned back in his little chair and watched Dex pacing across his office, gesturing with both hands as he spoke. The distance between Mars and Earth defeated any chance of holding a true conversation. Dex talked and Jamie listened.

"He's a priest, Jamie. A Jesuit! We can get plenty of media time with him before he goes. He can counter those pious sonsofbitches who're trying to slit our throats. He can tell the people what we're doing, show them that there's no conflict between religion and science. It's a godsend, I tell you!"

As Jamie listened to Dex chattering on enthusiastically for almost half an hour, he was thinking, DiNardo's older than I am. He must be older than Carleton, even. Will it be safe for him to come here? The fusion ships make the flight fast and easy, but how will DiNardo handle the low gravity here? The whole environment? What will Chang think of having DiNardo here? Will he think I'm trying to subvert his authority? First Carleton horns in on the operation here, then I pop in, and now the priest who was originally picked to lead the geology team on the First Expedition. Chang's a geologist, for god's sake. He's not going to like this.

DEX WAS ACTUALLY FEELING slightly out of breath when he finally wound down and ran out of words. He was on his feet, in the corner of his office where the big windows met. Out there it was a sparkling blue New England afternoon. He could see planes landing and taking off at Logan Aerospaceport and sailboats cutting through the whitecaps of the bay and even the masts of Old Ironsides at its pier in Charlestown, across the harbor.

It'll take Jamie at least fifteen-twenty minutes to get back to me, Dex thought, even if he picked up my message as soon as it arrived at Mars. I ought to get back to work.

He returned to his desk and sat down, but couldn't concentrate on the tasks before him. Wheedling contributions out of increasingly reluctant donors. Dealing with half a dozen government agencies that want to stick their fat asses into our program so they can slow us down even more. Budgeting. That was the most depressing thing of all. How to stretch the funding they had without endangering the people working on Mars. Dex leaned back in his customized leather chair and stared at the ceiling.

But if I can swing the Navaho president onto this tourist idea, and start quietly soliciting funding from a couple of friendly bankers, then maybe . . . just maybe, we can put this program on a sound financial basis. Maybe even make a few bucks of profit. The Navahos would like that.

But how to get Jamie to agree to it? He's as stubborn as a jackass. Thinks Mars is his private preserve. No, worse. Jamie thinks it's his sacred duty to protect Mars. Keep it pristine. No visitors, except for scientists.

The chime of his phone broke into Dex's thoughts. "Dr. Waterman, from Tithonium Base," said the synthesized voice of his second wife.

Dex snapped to an upright posture and said crisply, "Open message."

Jamie looked wary. Not suspicious or unreceptive, really: just guarded, cautious. He was smiling, but it was the smile that Dex knew he used when he was trying to cover his true feelings.

"Dex, that's great news about Father DiNardo," Jamie began.

Monsignor DiNardo, Dex corrected silently.

"But I'm worried about a couple of things. First, he's kind of old for Mars, don't you think? What kind of physical condition is he in? And what's made him decide to come out here all of a sudden? If we take him, we'll have to make sure he's checked out very carefully. We'll need the best doctors we can find to give him a very thorough physical."

"No problem," Dex muttered, knowing that Jamie couldn't hear him.

"Second, if he comes here it'll probably disturb Dr. Chang. I mean, he's the mission director and a geologist. DiNardo's a geologist, too, and he's older and he was originally picked to head the geology team for the First Expedition. Chang's going to feel like DiNardo's breathing down his neck. That wouldn't be fair to him."

Jamie's smile turned warmer. "On the other hand, I agree that having a priest from the Vatican join us here could be a great public relations move. The fundamentalists have been working against us, and Father DiNardo can show that a deeply religious person can still be a scientist who wants to learn about Mars and the Martians."

Dex found himself nodding vigorously.

"So let's proceed carefully," Jamie went on. "It would certainly be great to have Father DiNardo here. I like the man and he's a good geologist. His presence here will create problems with Chang, but I'll try to smooth that out. Above all else, though, we've got to make sure that DiNardo's in top physical condition. So don't start beating the publicity drums until he's passed all the exams. Okay?"

"Okay," Dex replied immediately. "I'll have him checked out sixteen ways from Tuesday. And then we'll have something to stuff under the noses of those psalm-singing bastards!"

TITHONIUM CHASMA: EXCURSION TEAM

∎

Itzak Rosenberg stared at the fireball billowing up from the hopper. It quickly dissipated into the thin Martian atmosphere. He felt as if all the air had been sucked out of his lungs.

"Our supplies," he said weakly.

"Blown to hell," Hasdrubal muttered.

"What could have caused it?"

Hasdrubal was already on the comm link. "Base, this is Excursion Three. We got troubles."

The excursion controller was one of the astronauts. Her slim face, framed with short dark hair, looked puzzled. "The readouts here look screwy," she said.

"Damned hopper blew up!" Hasdrubal snapped.

"Blew up?"

"Exploded! There's nothin' left out there except some smokin' wreckage."

"That's why the readouts cut off," said the controller. In the tiny screen on the control panel she looked almost relieved.

"What the hell happened?" Hasdrubal demanded.

"Are you two okay?"

"Yeah. No damage to the camper."

"None that we can see from inside the cockpit," Rosenberg corrected.

Hasdrubal shot a glare at him.

"You'll have to go outside and look your vehicle over for possible damage," the controller instructed.

Nodding, Hasdrubal muttered, "Guess so."

"It's going to be dark in another hour," said Rosenberg.

The controller nodded back. "Then you'll have to make your damage inspection right away."

"Okay, we'll go out right away. But what the hell happened? Why'd that bird blow up?"

"We'll have to go over the diagnostics and get back to you on that. Meanwhile, you check out all your systems and do the exterior inspection."

"Right," Hasdrubal agreed.

"Keep this link open," said Rosenberg, with some urgency.

"Will do," promised the controller.

Rosenberg blurted, "Did the seismometers record the blast?" It was an idiotic question and he knew it but it just popped out of his mouth.

"I'll ask the monitors," the controller said. "Call me back when you complete your inspection."

"Don't shut down this link," Rosenberg repeated.

"Right. I'll keep it open."

Hasdrubal got up from his seat and headed back toward the airlock. Over his shoulder he called, "C'mon, get into your suit."

"I'm staying inside," Rosenberg said, his voice quavering slightly. "I'll check all our systems while you do a visual inspection outside."

Hasdrubal stopped at the narrow closet where their nanosuits hung. For a moment he said nothing. Then, "Go faster if the two of us look her over."

"I . . . I'll stay inside," Rosenberg said. "I need to, Sal." He felt as if he were glued to the cockpit seat. He thought he couldn't get up even if he wanted to. His legs were too weak to support him. He couldn't even turn around to look at his partner.

"Okay," Hasdrubal said, his voice sounding strange, suspicious, almost accusing. "You stay in."

* * *

JAMIE WAS PORING OVER the latest communications from Selene, reports on their underground farms and the amount of electrical power they needed to keep the crops growing. We'll have to devote a lot of acreage to solar panels, he thought. The maintenance is going to be tough, keeping them clean of dust. Maybe we can automate that, something like windshield wipers. Then he thought about the monstrous dust storms that swept across the planet. He remembered the storm that nearly buried the camper on his first excursion to Tithonium Chasma. With a shake of his head Jamie realized that maintaining a solar-energy farm was going to be a lot more difficult on Mars than on the airless, weatherless Moon.

"Uh, Dr. Waterman?" A soft voice interrupted his musing.

Looking up, Jamie saw that it was Billy Graycloud standing at the entrance to his cubbyhole of an office.

"Come in, Billy," he said.

The youngster didn't move. "There's been an accident."

"Accident?" Jamie shot up from his chair.

"Nobody hurt," Graycloud said quickly. "It's the excursion team, you know, the two guys tracing the old riverbed. Their resupply rocket blew up."

Jamie could see a small crowd gathered around the entrance to the communications center halfway across the dome.

"They're okay?" he asked, coming around his makeshift desk.

"Seem to be," Graycloud replied. Then he added, "So far."

HASDRUBAL WAS HOLDING A blackened chunk of metal in his hands as he sank his lanky frame into the padded cockpit seat. Rosenberg stared at it.

"Found this in the ground about a meter and a half from our left front wheels."

"What is it?"

Turning the scorched fragment in his hands, Hasdrubal answered, "What it *was* was a piece of a storage container. I think. Hard to tell."

"A meter and a half?"

"Give or take a skosh."

"If it had hit us . . ."

"Would've gone through the skin of this bus like an anti-tank missile."

Rosenberg shuddered visibly.

"Everything okay in here?" Hasdrubal asked.

"All the systems are on line. No internal damage."

"Are *you* okay?" Hasdrubal stared at his partner.

Rosenberg took a deep, deliberate breath. "I'm . . . rather shaken, you know."

"I can see that."

"Control says the hopper's oxygen line must have been leaking. It touched off the methane. That's what caused the explosion."

"They think."

"That's what the diagnostics indicate." Rosenberg felt somewhat better, stronger, as he talked about the impersonal data from the controller's monitoring systems. Yet he still saw in his mind's eye that white-hot explosion. We could have been killed, his inner voice kept repeating. We came within a meter and a half of death.

"Dripped oxy on the hot methane pump, prob'ly," Hasdrubal was saying.

Rosenberg nodded. "Yes, that's their explanation."

"How old was that hopper? Some of 'em date back to the first expeditions, don't they?"

"I believe so."

Holding the fragment of debris in one hand, Hasdrubal pointed to the comm screen, which was a blank gray. "Comm link still open?"

"It should be."

"Okay. I'll show this to the geniuses back at base. You go back and heat up some dinner."

Rosenberg hesitated. "Why don't we start back to the base?"

"Now? It'll be dark in another few minutes." The biologist jerked a thumb toward the scenery outside. The pale shrunken sun was almost touching the jagged horizon. The sky was already turning deep violet.

"I know, but . . . we'll have to head back before we run out of supplies."

"Tomorrow, after the sun comes up."

"We can run at night."

"And run down the fuel cells? No way. We're not goin' anyplace until the sun comes up," Hasdrubal insisted. "That's final."

TITHONIUM CHASMA: NIGHT

■

Hasdrubal and Rosenberg ate a warmed-up prepackaged meal in tense silence, broken only by the controller calling from the base to ask about their condition.

Rosenberg went to the cockpit and spoke to the controller. The thermal shutters covered the bug-eye windows up there, preventing the camper's internal warmth from leaking out into the bitter Martian night. When Rosenberg returned he slid into the folded-out bunk that now served as a bench. Across the narrow table sat Hasdrubal, his dark face watching Rosenberg thoughtfully.

"You're scared, huh?"

"It's . . . I'm not frightened, really."

"Not much."

"It's just that . . . it's unsettling. Hoppers shouldn't blow up. We shouldn't be stranded out here without supplies. It's not right!"

A slow, patient smile eased across Hasdrubal's face. "Now look, Izzy. We're not stranded. We got plenty of food and water for the trip back to base. We'll be fine."

"The batteries are down."

"We'll recharge 'em tomorrow soon's the sun comes up."

"Hurry sunrise," Rosenberg muttered.

They finished their meal, scraped the crumbs into the recycler and placed their plates and cups into the microwave for cleaning. Hasdrubal put a fingertip on the power button, then thought better of it. Save it for daytime, he told himself.

Rosenberg folded the table and slid it into its place beneath his bunk.

"I'll hit the john," Hasdrubal said.

"If you don't mind . . ." Rosenberg pushed past him and hurried into the lavatory.

Poor bastard's scared shitless, Hasdrubal thought. Then he amended, But his bladder's full.

Once they had peeled down to their skivvies and arranged the blankets over their bunks, Rosenberg said, "I've never liked the cold. That's what's bothering me, actually. The night and the dark and cold."

"We'll get through it."

They climbed into their bunks and clicked off the lights. The camper's interior was completely dark except for the faint ghostly greenish glow from the instrument panel up in the cockpit.

Rosenberg murmured into the darkness, "When I was a child in Cambridge, once my sister was born I had to sleep up in the attic. It was always cold up there. Even in the summertime. And drafty. I could feel the wind coming through chinks in the window frames. I could never get warm up there. Never."

"Hey, you wanna talk about cold, you oughtta live in Chicago. Wind that can knock you off your friggin' feet. And cold! Freeze your balls off."

Rosenberg said nothing.

Chuckling, Hasdrubal said, "I remember one winter we had so much snow the whole friggin' city stopped. Nothin' was moving. Took two days before the damn snowplows cleared the streets in our neighborhood. Left snowbanks higher'n my head."

"Higher than your head? Really?"

"I was just a kid then. A lot shorter."

"Oh."

"We'll be okay. Get some sleep. You'll feel better when the sun comes up."

"Yes, I suppose so," Rosenberg said. He closed his eyes.

And heard the thin moan of the wind outside. He touched the curving skin of the camper. It felt ice cold. Just a few millimeters of metal between us and death, he thought. It's down to a hundred below zero out there.

He shuddered beneath his two blankets.

JAMIE HEARD THE WIND sighing, too. He lay next to Vijay, warm and sweaty after making love. She seemed to be drowsing now, but Jamie wasn't ready for sleep yet. He listened to the wind and remembered his first night on Mars, when the soft wind seemed to be stroking the dome they had just erected, touching it with questioning fingers, wondering at this alien construct on the lonely plains of the red world.

Mars is a gentle world, he told himself, listening to the wind. It means us no harm. They'll be all right buttoned up in their camper. There's nothing to worry about, really.

Yet he thought of the two men more than a hundred kilometers from the safety of the base. And he heard Dr. Chang's flat refusal ringing in his memory.

"No. I will not permit it," Chang had said.

Jamie had rushed to the mission director's office as soon as he'd heard of the hopper's explosion and volunteered to drive a camper out to the excursion team.

Chang sat stubbornly behind his desk, his face set in a determined scowl.

"I could carry supplies to them," Jamie had said, "so they could continue their excursion instead of coming back here."

"No," Chang repeated.

"But—"

Chang seemed to puff up, like a toad that feels threatened. "Dr. Waterman," he said slowly, stiffly. "You are the scientific director of the program. I am the mission director. My authority rules over everyone on this base. You may remove me, send me back to China, but you cannot overrule my decisions here. Is that understood?"

Jamie replied softly, "I only wanted to be of help."

"The excursion team does not need your help. Or anyone else's. There are protocols in place, procedures to follow. They will return to the base tomorrow under their own power. They do not need to be rescued."

Jamie started to answer back, thought better of it and merely nodded.

Holding up one stubby finger, Chang went on, "Your presence here creates some difficulties in lines of authority. Many personnel here look to you for leadership and not to me."

That's what this is all about, Jamie said to himself. I should have been sensitive to it.

Chang added, "Everyone is well aware how you took control of First Expedition from Dr. Li Chengdu when you were nothing more than a substitute geologist."

"I'm not trying to take control of this operation from you, Dr. Chang," Jamie said, with real conviction. "I'm only trying to help you."

As if he hadn't heard a word Jamie said, Chang closed his eyes and murmured, "If you desire to take command I will offer my resignation at once."

"That's not necessary. Not at all."

Chang's dark eyes slowly opened. Jamie saw that they were bloodshot. "Very well. Please do not interfere with my responsibilities."

"I'm sorry," Jamie said, getting to his feet. "Please excuse me."

Chang made a single, curt nod.

Now Jamie lay awake in his bed, wondering what he could do without setting off Chang's sensitivities, how to tell him that DiNardo was coming to the base. The man's planted a minefield around himself, Jamie realized. Sooner or later something's going to explode.

BOSTON: LAHEY CLINIC

■

"Your priest's in fine condition, Dex. No physical reason why he can't make the flight to Mars."

Dr. Paul Nickerson was walking with Dex Trumball along the crowded corridor that ran from the CAT scan laboratory back to the Lahey Clinic's suites of offices for senior medical staff.

"He's okay to go, then," Dex said.

"Physically, there's no problem," said Nickerson. He was slightly shorter than Dex, lean and loose-limbed. Even in his white lab coat he coasted along like an ice skater. Nickerson's face was thin and long-jawed, his walnut brown hair cropped so close to his scalp it looked like fuzz.

Dex was in his usual dark blue three-piece suit. "That's the second time you said 'physically,' Paul. Is there a mental problem? Emotional, I mean."

Nickerson didn't reply for several paces. Patients shuffled past, many of them in the pathetic bile-green paper gowns that the staff made them wear. Just to humiliate them, Dex had always thought. A hefty black nurse hurried past, looking stern and determined.

"Well?" Dex prodded.

Nickerson opened a door and gestured. "Come on in here, Dex."

It was a small conference room, Dex saw. Oval table, eight padded chairs, smart screens on the walls, all of them blank gray.

"So?" he asked as Nickerson shut the door and leaned against it.

Raising his brows, the physician replied, "This might be my prejudice more than anything else, but . . . well, haven't you wondered why a man pushing sixty would want to travel out to Mars?"

Dex sat one hip on the edge of the mahogany table and relaxed, grinning. "He's a geologist. He was selected for the First Expedition but had a gall bladder attack."

"And he's waited twenty-some years to get what he lost?"

"He wants to help us. He's going to do a video documentary for us to counter all that New Morality crap about the Martians being a fake."

Nickerson shook his head. "I think there's an emotional problem here."

"You're wrong. He's passed all the psych exams with no sweat."

"Still . . ."

"Look, Paul, I've been to Mars. I wouldn't want to go back but I know what's going through DiNardo's mind. He's a scientist, for chrissake! Mars is like a golden carrot. He wants to get there before he dies."

Nickerson aimed a finger at Dex like a pistol. "Ahah! Before he dies."

Frowning, Dex said, "You want him to take more psych exams?"

"It wouldn't hurt. We have some very good people here at the clinic. At the very least, they should have a few conversations with him."

Dex grumbled, "You're just trying to run up the bill."

MONSIGNOR DINARDO LISTENED TO Dex's halting explanation in the examination room as he put on his street clothes.

"They want me to undergo a mental examination?" he asked, his voice soft as always, but with a hint of genuine displeasure behind it.

"He's a flatlander," Dex said, waggling one hand horizontally. "He thinks anybody who wants to go into space must be nuts."

DiNardo chuckled appreciatively as he pulled on his trousers. "Sometimes I myself wonder."

"He just wants you to talk to one of their staff psychiatrists."

"You know," the priest said, "one could make the case that all scientists are slightly insane. Monomaniacal."

"Come on, now . . ."

"No. Really," DiNardo said. "Most scientists could make much more money in other professions. But they are fixated on science, on learning, on discovering." He shook his head in wonderment.

Dex asked impatiently, "Will you talk to the shrink? We've got to put this thing to bed."

"Of course," said DiNardo. He wormed his arms into his black jacket, then felt for the bottle of pills in the left pocket. Still there. No one had disturbed them. No one knew about them. The medication had not shown up in the blood tests the doctors had performed. Good.

■

The executive committee of The New Morality, Inc. had just convened an emergency meeting. At the head of the long glossy conference table sat the newly ordained Archbishop Overmire, the signet ring on his right index finger symbolizing his accession to the leadership of the movement and presidency of the corporation.

Overmire glowed with success. Twenty-five years younger than the recently deceased archbishop, he looked tanned and energetic, broad shouldered and barrel chested, his midsection taut beneath his custom-fitted dark clerical jacket. The archbishop's face was youthful, his cool brown eyes bright, his sandy hair long enough to just touch his collar. His smile seemed genuine.

"I must admit with all humility," he said to the other corporate officers and ministers arrayed around the long table, "that I'm somewhat nervous chairing this meeting for the first time. Please forgive me if I make any errors."

A murmur of assurances went around the table. Eighteen men were seated there, half of them in clerical garb, the others in business suits that were almost as dark. Four women were among them, all in conservatively cut skirted suits except for the one female minister, placed at the bishop's left hand.

Down at the foot of the table sat Shelby Ivers, who had flown to Atlanta from New York for this special meeting. He stared up the length of the table at Archbishop Overmire, trying to tell himself that what he felt was admiration, not envy. Still, Ivers couldn't help thinking that one day he himself might rise to the leadership of the New Morality. If he prayed and worked hard. If he played his cards right. If Overmire didn't live as long as the previous archbishop. At least, he thought with a sigh, Overmire's on record as rejecting rejuvenation treatments. But so did the old archbishop, until he needed a replacement heart.

Looking back down the long table at Ivers, Archbishop Overmire shrank his smile a little and said, "I'm sure you have all been informed about the problem that Reverend Ivers has uncovered."

Nods and murmurs of agreement from the others.

The archbishop went on, "Despite the Vatican's assurances that the Roman Church will work with us in all respects, this priest is preparing to fly to Mars."

"He's some sort of scientist, isn't he?" asked one of the businessmen halfway down the table.

"A geologist," said the woman minister, almost hissing the words.

"How can a priest be a scientist?"

Archbishop Overmire's smile turned charitable. "No man can serve two masters," he murmured.

Ivers spoke up, "He not only is preparing to join the other scientists on Mars, he's working with the Mars Foundation to produce a video documentary."

"About Mars?"

Nodding vigorously, Ivers answered, "And the alleged Martians."

"We can't allow that!"

"We'll organize a boycott—"

Overmire silenced the committee members by raising his hands, palms outward, in a gesture of calm.

"This is not the time for an outward show of power," he said mildly.

The others exchanged puzzled glances.

"We have worked long and hard," the archbishop explained, "to attain our rightful influence over the government.

We control many individual states. We have a majority in the House of Representatives. In November we will drive the secularists out of the United States Senate and two years from now we will put our chosen man into the White House."

"Then why shouldn't we—"

"This is not the time to make a public issue over the secularists on Mars. Things are flowing our way; we don't want to do anything that might interrupt that flow."

"But with all respect, Archbishop," said one of the businessmen, "we can't allow this priest to confuse the public with his blasphemous claims."

"Up until now," Overmire said, softly, "we have treated the Mars exploration with what one might call benign neglect. We have not actively refuted them—"

"There's plenty of conspiracy theorists claiming it's all a hoax," muttered one of the older men.

"Yes, true enough," said the archbishop. "But our policy has been merely to work behind the scenes and discourage the media from giving undue publicity to the scientists on Mars. Isn't that so, Reverend Ivers?"

"That's been our policy, yes, Archbishop."

"I think that policy has worked well enough. Our polls show that the general population's interest in Mars ranks quite low in their priorities. Climate change and the associated economic and family displacements are at the top of the list, along with crime and child abuse, followed by personal fulfillment and health issues."

"If I may interrupt, Archbishop," Ivers said, in an attempt to impress the committee without alienating its chairman, "this Father DiNardo could be a serious challenge to our policy."

"How so?" the archbishop asked, his smile turning brittle.

"He is ostensibly a man of God: a Catholic priest who serves in the Vatican. He is also a scientist, a geologist of international reputation. That flies in the face of our position that secularists cannot be good Christians."

"And he is preparing to star in a video documentary," the archbishop added.

"I've tried to discourage the networks, but they're actually bidding for the rights to broadcast the documentary! They want to air it! They think it will gain a significant audience."

The archbishop folded his hands on the tabletop. "We can deal with the networks at the highest level."

One of the women murmured, "Can you be sure . . . ?"

Overmire gave her his saintly smile. "True power doesn't need to show itself. The networks respect our power, believe me. A few words in the right places and none of them will air the documentary, I promise you."

Ivers objected, "But then the Mars Foundation will simply post the documentary on the Internet. Anyone will be able to see it."

"There's nothing we can do about that," said one of the businessmen.

"Isn't there?" the archbishop said, one brow cocked slightly.

"What do you suggest?"

"The success of an Internet posting depends on the publicity it generates. There are millions of postings every day. The size of one posting's audience depends critically on publicity, on the 'buzz' that the posting generates."

Everyone nodded, even Ivers, impressed with the archbishop's depth of knowledge.

"We can see to it that publicity for this Mars show is minimal. We have enough clout with the media to bury the Mars posting."

Ivers started to object, thought better of it, then said merely, "But once the documentary is on the Net, word of mouth might generate a big audience. It could grow and grow."

"It could," the archbishop admitted. "But it won't. We have almost every church in the land on our side. We'll arrange a . . . ah, a studied neglect. Not an openly announced boycott, something more subtle. No big announcements, no fanfare. No fuss. Not enough noise to make people curious. We'll simply have our people delete the documentary from their files. Pastors will quietly ask their flocks to see to it that their children do not watch the documentary. Schools will be similarly enlightened. After all, the documentary is all secularist heresies, isn't it?"

"But the Catholics . . ."

His smile warming, Archbishop Overmire said, "The Catholics will stand at our side over this issue. We'll make the parallel with Galileo."

"Galileo? That was five centuries ago!"

"And the Church formally admitted they were wrong about him, eventually," one of the clerics said.

With a pitying little shake of his head Archbishop Overmire pointed out, "There are still people high in the Roman church's councils who disapprove of the Papal admission of error."

"But they *were* wrong," Ivers blurted. "They forced Galileo to admit that the Sun goes around the Earth. That isn't the way it is."

Overmire replied, "No, the Church was not wrong. Galileo was put on trial not for his astronomical discoveries, as the secularist scientists would have you think. He was put on trial for disobeying the authority of the Church. And he was manifestly guilty of that, I assure you."

Ivers fell speechless.

The archbishop went on, "We will not try to stop this renegade priest from spewing his heresy. We will simply make certain that his views are ignored by the public."

Everyone around the gleaming table nodded agreement.

"True power," said the archbishop, "can accomplish wonders. In two years' time, when we have put our own man into the White House, then we can take off the gloves, so to speak. Then we can show everyone how much power we have to wield. Everyone, including the secularist scientists."

TITHONIUM CHASMA: MORNING

∎

From up in the cockpit Hasdrubal heard water running in the lavatory. Turning, he saw Rosenberg shuffling through the narrow gap between their two bunks.

"Lookin' kinda bleary this morning," he said cheerfully.

Still in his skivvies, Rosenberg plopped into the right-hand cockpit seat. And winced. "It's cold," he said.

"Put on your coveralls, you'll warm up."

Rosenberg nodded glumly. "Had breakfast?"

"Nope. I been waitin' for you."

"I'll boil some water." Rosenberg got up from the seat, the bare skin of his legs making a soft sucking sound against the pseudoleather.

"The solar cells are recharging the batteries," Hasdrubal called back to the galley.

"Good," said Rosenberg.

"Thought you'd wanna know. Make you feel better."

"Thanks."

While Rosenberg dressed, Hasdrubal checked in with the controller back at base. Once he started smelling the instant coffee, Hasdrubal ended his call and, turning, saw that Rosenberg had pulled up the table between their bunks. He got up and went to his bunk as Rosenberg put down two bowls of boiled oatmeal and a pair of steaming mugs of coffee.

"When do we start back?" Rosenberg asked, sliding onto his bunk.

"Base wants us to bring back some of the hopper's wreckage."

"For diagnosis."

"Yeah."

Looking forward through the camper's cockpit windows, Rosenberg said, "There isn't that much to retrieve."

"Accident investigation people back Earthside want as much as we can show 'em. Help them nail down the cause of the explosion."

"But we already know that, don't we?"

"Not officially."

Rosenberg frowned and muttered something too low for Hasdrubal to hear.

"I'll do it," the biologist said. "You don't have to go out."

"I'll go with you."

"You don't have to if you don't want to."

"I want to. I shouldn't let this get to me the way it did last night."

"Hey, we all get the spooks, one time or another."

"You didn't."

"I got my troubles, man."

"Such as?"

Hasdrubal grimaced. "Don't tell anybody."

Rosenberg looked up at him. "Of course not."

"Promise?"

"Yes, certainly. What is it?"

"I'm scared of spiders."

"Spiders?"

"Saw some dumb-ass video when I was a kid, about giant spiders eatin' people. Scared the shit out of me. Still does."

Rosenberg broke into a gentle smile. "Well, in that case, my friend, I suggest you stay on Mars. The nearest spider is millions of kilometers away."

CARTER CARLETON FELT NERVOUS in the flimsy nanosuit. He had to admit that it was lighter and much more flexible than the hard-shell he usually wore to go outside the dome, but still—there was nothing between him and the near-vacuum of the Martian atmosphere except a layer of nanofabric no more than a few molecules thick. He knew it was his imagination, but he could *feel* the hard radiation from deep space slashing through the transparent fabric and tearing apart the DNA in his body's cells.

Walking beside him, Doreen McManus asked, "Isn't this better than that clunky old hard suit?"

"I suppose," Carleton said, without his heart in it. The things a man will do just to get laid, he told himself. Not that Doreen's made an issue of it. She's damned persistent, though.

They had spent the day at the dig, as usual, Carleton wearing his hard suit. But once they came back inside at the end of the long hours and vacuumed off the dust they'd picked up, Doreen had quickly peeled off her nanosuit and started to help Carleton with his more cumbersome outfit.

"It's like a knight's armor," Doreen said as she helped Carleton lift the torso up over his head.

"That's one of the things I like about these old suits," Carleton rejoined. "The romance of it all."

She laughed. "You're just a fuddy-duddy."

"I'm glad you didn't say an *old* fuddy-duddy."

Once they had tucked the various pieces of his suit into its locker, Carleton started toward the cafeteria.

But Doreen reached for his arm. "Carter, wait."

"You're not hungry?"

"No. Not now."

"I'm starving. How can you spend all day out in the field and not work up an appetite?"

Suddenly she looked pained. "Carter . . . we've got to talk."

A twitch of alarm flashed through him.

"Talk?" That means trouble, he knew. Always.

Doreen said, "Let's go outside."

"Outside? Again? We just got back—"

"Please. Just for a few minutes. You can wear a nanosuit; it won't take you more than a minute or two to get into it."

"I don't understand."

"For me, Carter. Please?"

He stood there gazing into her big gray-green eyes. They were troubled, he saw, even though she was trying to smile for him.

"All right," he said, wondering if this was just a ploy to get him to try the damned nanosuit.

Now they stood a dozen paces outside the main airlock, Carleton feeling decidedly edgy in the flimsy suit, with the ridiculous inflated balloon of a helmet over his head. Doreen stood in moody silence beside him. It was nearly sunset. Temperature must be down to fifty below, Carleton groused to himself. Still, he had to admit, it's comfortable enough inside this glorified raincoat. Except for the radiation. The thought made his skin crawl.

To their left rose the towering cliffs of the canyon, the slanting rays of the setting sun casting shadows that brought out every seam and wrinkle in the ancient rocks. The glowing disk of the sun hung above the horizon on their right, small and wan, reminding Carleton that they were a long, *long* way from home.

"All right," he said, with a cheerfulness he didn't really feel, "I'm wearing the suit. Are you satisfied?"

"Carter, we have to talk."

That again.

Doreen reached into the pouch on her right thigh and pulled out a hair-thin wire. Plugging it into a hardly visible socket on the collar ring of her suit, she held the other end out to Carleton. He stepped closer and let her plug the wire into his suit's receptacle.

"There, now we can talk without using the radios."

So no one can overhear us, Carleton realized. Her voice sounded different over the wire, edgier, brittle.

Trying to hide his growing irritation, Carleton asked, "What's this all about, Dorrie?"

"There's going to be a resupply mission arriving in another six weeks," she said.

"Yes. It's supposed to bring that priest from the Vatican with it."

"And take a dozen people who want to leave Mars."

At last he understood. "You're not leaving?"

"Yes I am, Carter." Her voice was so low he barely could hear it.

"But why? Where are you going?"

"Back to Selene," said Doreen. "That's my home. It's time for me to go back."

"But why?" he repeated, thoroughly astonished. "I thought you and I—"

"Carter, it's been good between us. For a while there I thought I really loved you."

"You thought . . . ?" He felt bewildered, betrayed.

For long moments Doreen didn't answer. Finally she said, "You don't love me, Carter. I'm just a convenience for you, a body to warm your bed and stroke your ego."

"That's nonsense," he snapped. "What's your real reason? Is it somebody else? That Indian kid?"

"Of course not!" she said, genuinely shocked. "It's you. You don't care about me, not really. You don't even care about my ideas, my work."

"That nanomachine business? You want to terraform Mars with nanomachines?"

"Part of it, yes. So people can come here and live and work safely—in comfort."

"Nanocrap," he snarled. "It's nonsense and you know it."

Her face deadly serious, Doreen replied, "I'm not going to argue with you about it. I'm leaving when the resupply flight comes in."

"And what about me?"

"What about you, Carter?" Her voice sounded almost sorrowful. "How do you feel about me? Do you feel anything at all except your own needs?"

Puzzled and slightly angry, he replied, "For god's sake, Doreen, we're living together aren't we? We share our lives, our work, our bodies, everything."

She fell silent again.

"Isn't that enough?" he demanded.

Very softly, she said, "You've never said you love me."

So that's it, he thought. The same old ploy. They always want to hear you plight your troth.

"Doreen, love is a big word. . . ."

"It's a four-letter word. The same as fuck."

Carleton shook his head inside the inflated helmet. I'll never understand them, he told himself. Never. Trying to control his growing irritation, he grasped Doreen by the wrist and started back to the airlock.

"You're not leaving, Doreen," he said, almost in a growl. "I want you here. I need you here."

She didn't reply as she let him lead her back to the dome. She simply pulled the wire from his suit collar and let it trail in the dust behind her.

And Carleton remembered a line from *Hamlet*: Where the offense is, let the great axe fall.

TITHONIUM BASE: SUNSET

■

As Jamie and Vijay stepped out of the airlock they saw another couple striding forcefully toward the hatch, one of them trailing a hair-thin wire from the collar rim of her suit. Once they got close enough to recognize their faces, Jamie said hello to Doreen McManus and Carter Carleton.

Neither of them replied. They walked past Jamie and Vijay without a word, without a nod.

Turning to his wife, Jamie said, "Carter looks pissed."

Vijay watched them step into the airlock and close its outer hatch. "You mean angry."

Jamie nodded.

"In Oz pissed means drunk."

"He's not drunk," Jamie said. "He's sore as a guy who fell into a clump of cactus."

Vijay snickered. "In Australia we'd say he's mad as a frilled lizard."

"Colloquialisms," said Jamie.

"That's a ten-dollar word," she said. "I'm impressed."

"Come on," he said, tugging at her wrist. "Let's see the sunset."

They walked hand in gloved hand away from the airlock hatch, out onto the rock-strewn floor of the valley. The sun was just touching the uneven horizon; the cloudless sky was a deep butterscotch color, although behind them it had already darkened so much that the first stars were visible.

"Dr. Waterman," Jamie heard in his headset, "please remember to stay within camera range."

Jamie nodded inside his inflated bubble helmet. "We're not going that far," he replied to the safety monitor.

Vijay looked down at the dusty ground, stamped with boot prints and the tracks of wheeled vehicles.

"Not like the old days anymore," she said. "I remember when you could actually step where no one had stood before."

Jamie replied, "You still can, but you've got to go a lot farther."

"We've never been to the other side of the valley, have we?" she asked.

"Not yet."

"D'you intend to go there?"

"Sooner or later," he said. "Right now we're concentrating on tracing the fossil river that ran along the valley floor."

"Think you'll find more villages?"

"That's the hope." Then Jamie added, "Chang wants to send a team to the south pole and study its melting firsthand."

"That's a long ways off," said Vijay.

Nodding, Jamie went on, "The ice cap has lots of frozen carbon dioxide in it. The cee-oh-two doesn't melt, it sublimes—goes straight from solid to gaseous carbon dioxide."

"Isn't that a greenhouse gas?"

"Right. Mars is undergoing global warming, just like Earth."

Vijay laughed. "Maybe the temperature'll get above freezing one of these days."

Looking across the broad, barren valley floor, Jamie said, "Maybe it'll get warm enough to melt the permafrost. Maybe this desert will bloom again, eventually."

"In a million years."

"More like ten million, I'd guess."

Vijay fell silent for a few moments as they walked slowly away from the dome. Then she asked, "Will we be able to stay? I mean, from what Dex says about finances . . ." Her voice trailed off.

"We'll have to stretch the available money. We certainly can't afford to send a team to the south pole. Or even the other side of the valley. We've got to make this base as self-sufficient as we can and cut down on the number of resupply trips."

"Will that be enough, Jamie?"

Grimly, he answered, "It'll have to be."

They walked a few paces farther, then Jamie stopped and slipped his arm around Vijay's waist. The sun was halfway down the horizon, the sky already a deep violet.

"Couldn't cuddle in the hard suits," Vijay murmured.

With a chuckle, Jamie replied, "True, but you could squeeze two people into one of the larger sizes."

"Really?"

"So I've been told."

Vijay thought about it for a moment. "Criminy, that'd be worse than doing it in an airliner's lavatory, woul'n't it."

"Romance at its most poetic."

"There goes the sun."

The last spot of brightness winked out. There was only a moment of twilight, then the sky turned inky dark, spattered with brilliant stars.

"And if we're lucky . . ." Jamie held his breath.

Vijay leaned closer to him as they watched the stars, bright, solemn, hardly twinkling at all.

"There it is!" she cried.

Jamie felt the breath gush out of him. Overhead the sky shimmered with delicate sheets of pale green, pink, ghostly white, curtains of the aurora that flickered like candlelight high above them.

"The Sky Dancers," Jamie whispered.

For several minutes the two of them stood transfixed on the arid, dusty floor of the tremendous valley, staring up at the aurora that weaved and coiled above them. Jamie knew that with almost every sunset on Mars the aurora flared as high-energy subatomic particles from the solar wind impinged on the inert neon, xenon and other noble gases in the Martian atmosphere. But the Navaho part of his mind recalled the Sky Dancers on Earth, in the desert scrubland of New Mexico, the night that Grandfather Al died. They're watching over us, he thought. We're not alone.

"It's fading," Vijay sighed.

"It only lasts while we're in darkness and the high atmosphere is still in sunlight," Jamie said, knowing that the Sky Dancers had other places to go, other eyes to delight, other omens to warn of.

"Look!"

A meteor trail streaked across the deep violet sky like a fiery finger tracing a path through the heavens.

"Wow!" Jamie managed to say before the meteor's blazing track winked out. "That was a big one."

"Should we make a wish?"

"Yeah. Wish that we don't get hit by a meteor shower," Jamie said, remembering the shower that peppered the dome of the First Expedition. One of the tiny stones had even hit his helmet. Remembering how close he'd come to death, Jamie suddenly felt very vulnerable in the flimsy nanosuit.

"We'd better get inside," he said to Vijay.

The safety monitor reinforced the notion. "Dr. Waterman, temperature's dropping rapidly."

"Right," he said crisply. "We're coming in."

As they trudged back toward the lights of the dome and the airlock hatch, Vijay said, "That was spectacular, Jamie."

He looked at her, but it was already too dark to make out her beautiful face. Smiling ruefully, Jamie said, "Mars is a beautiful world. But it can be dangerous."

"You don't want to leave, do you?"

"Hell no," said Jamie.

BOSTON: VIDEO STUDIO

■

Monsignor DiNardo sat in the barber's chair while the makeup specialist smoothed a creamy lotion over his stubborn shadow of a beard.

"Italians," the young woman muttered, more to herself than the priest. "All that testosterone."

She was blond and blowsy. It was hard for DiNardo to tell her age, what with the cosmetic and rejuvenation treatments available.

DiNardo looked at the big wall mirror in front of him. His chin and jaw looked baby pink, although his shaved scalp still showed a trace of stubble. "All my life my beard has given me difficulty," he said. "I'm sorry if it's making you work too hard."

"Oh, that's all right, Father," she said, suddenly embarrassed. "It's my job, after all."

"You are Catholic?"

"Born to it," she said, turning to the rows of bottles and jars on the counter.

"Irish?" he guessed.

"Nope. Italian, just like you."

"Ah! *Que paese?*"

"Huh?"

"What part of Italy do you come from?"

"Oh, my family's been here for a hundred years. More. I went to Italy once, though. To Rome and Florence."

"Did you enjoy it?"

She broke into a major grin. "I never had it so good. Guys were after me everywhere I went."

Of course. Blond and buxom, DiNardo thought.

"Boy, did I have impure thoughts on that trip!"

DiNardo laughed. "I could hear your confession, if you wish."

She laughed, too. "I go every week at my parish church, Father."

"Good."

She studied his face for several moments. "I think we're finished. You look fine."

Glancing into the mirror again, DiNardo thought he looked much as he always looked. His jaw was smooth and pinkish, but his eyes still drooped and had those bags beneath them.

He started to get out of the chair, but the makeup woman put a hand on his shoulder. "Father, could I ask you something?"

"Certainly," he said.

Her brows knit slightly. "I been watching them filming you in the studio. What you said about the Martians, is that real?"

"Of course."

"There really were living people on Mars, just like us?"

DiNardo nodded. "We don't know what they looked like, as yet. But they left buildings. They had a form of writing. They existed millions of years ago."

"But I saw this show on TV, the guy there says it's all a fake. He wrote a book about it and he said that the scientists have faked the whole thing just to get more money out of us."

"I am a scientist," he said gently.

The woman looked stricken. "Oh, I didn't mean you, Father! Those other scientists. The secular ones. The ones who're atheists and hate religion. They'd do anything to tear down our beliefs."

"I don't believe so," DiNardo said. "I know many of them and they are as honest as you and I."

"You really think so?"

"They are trying to understand how things work. On Mars, they are trying to puzzle out how the Martians lived. And how they died."

"But they're always changing their minds. They're always putting up some theory about this or that. And their theories always attack religion and God."

DiNardo forced a smile. "God isn't worried about what the scientists are doing. In reality, the scientists are trying to learn how God created the world and how He makes it run."

"You think?"

"They may not know it," DiNardo said, his smile becoming genuine, "but even the most stubborn atheist among them is working to uncover God's ways."

She looked unconvinced, but she murmured, "I never thought about it that way."

DiNardo got up from the chair and thanked her. He half expected her to ask him for his blessing, but she simply smiled, her fleshy face dimpling prettily.

DiNardo headed for the studio, where they would be recording the final sequence on the documentary about Mars.

She didn't ask the difficult question, DiNardo said to himself as he stepped through the doorway into the big, barnlike studio. She didn't ask how a loving and merciful God could create those intelligent Martians and then callously wipe them out, kill them all, with just a flick of His celestial finger.

That was the question that haunted Monsignor DiNardo: How could God be so cruel?

BOOK III
EXILES

■

The English class was watching *The Return of Zorro* on the big flat screen up at the front of the room. Bucky Winters sat toward the rear with his own notebook open on his lap, where the teacher couldn't spot it. She was half dozing up at her desk anyway, Bucky saw.

If she catches me I'm toast, he told himself. But half the class was either daydreaming or furtively watching their own notebook screens. Only a handful of students were actually following the adventures of the masked swordsman up on the big flat screen. The sound track, in Spanish with English subtitles, was loud enough to rattle the classroom windows.

Bucky was watching a forbidden video on his notebook screen. He had the sound track muted because he dared not risk letting the teacher see him using the earplug. So he followed the documentary about Mars without the sound, using the Spanish subtitles that the program offered.

Some guy was holding a piece of bone in his hand. At least, it looked like a bone. Bucky's understanding of Spanish was limited to street talk and restaurant vocabulary, but the words scrolling along the bottom of the screen seemed to be saying that this was once the backbone of a Martian animal.

Bucky wondered why this video was banned. He had recited the pledge in church along with his family and everybody else, but he thought it was stupid to promise not to watch any videos from Mars. So he'd kept his fingers crossed while he solemnly swore that he would not watch any documentary produced by the Mars Foundation.

This stuff is interesting! Bucky realized. He was fascinated by the gigantic valley on Mars, the red cliffs and the rocks that had tiny creatures living inside them. And the buildings up in that niche in the cliffs. Did Martians really build them or were they built by the explorers just to fool people? Bucky knew that Native Americans built dwellings in cliffs like that somewhere out west.

Now the explorers claimed they had found a whole village where real Martians used to live. Bucky wondered what it would be like to go to Mars and explore a whole world.

The class ended before the movie was finished, so the teacher promised they would see the end of it tomorrow. She turned off the screen and the overhead lights brightened. Everybody closed their notebooks and shuffled out into the corridor, heading for the next class.

One of Bucky's friends, Jimmy Simmonds, sidled up beside him. "Know what I found on the Net?" he asked, grinning broadly. "Girls! Naked girls screwin' their butts off!"

"You would," said Marlene Chauncy, one of the brightest girls in the school. "I found a docudrama about Judy Garland."

"Who's she?"

"She was an actress," Marlene said, trying to make it sound dramatic. "She led a very tragic life."

"Never heard of her," said Jimmy.

"What about you, Bucky? You didn't watch that drippy *Zorro* show, did you?"

"No, I—"

"You don't have to ask him," Jimmy said, laughing. "Bucky went to Mars again, didn't you?"

Bucky nodded, while the other kids laughed.

"Mars boy."

Even Marlene laughed.

TITHONIUM BASE: THE MISSION DIRECTOR

■

For several days Jamie looked for a way to tell Dr. Chang that Monsignor DiNardo would soon be arriving at the base.

"Why not simply tell him?" Vijay suggested. They were eating dinner in the crowded cafeteria, heads bent close over the table so they could speak without raising their voices above the clatter and chatter around them.

Before Jamie could reply, Vijay went on, "You're the scientific director, love. You outrank him, don't you?"

"It's not a matter of organization charts," Jamie said. "I don't want this to be a confrontation. I've got to find a way to get Chang to accept this without feeling threatened or angry."

Vijay smiled lightly. "He prob'ly already knows about it. He'd be a pretty poor mission director if he di'n't."

"Even so, I've got to tell him. I can't let DiNardo just pop in here without telling Chang about it first."

"Well, mate, you'd better break it to him soon. The resupply flight's due to arrive in a few days, i'n't it?"

"Four days." Jamie nodded, tight-lipped.

Vijay looked past his shoulder. "There he goes now. Whyn't you grab the chance?"

Turning, Jamie saw Chang weaving his way through the cafeteria tables, holding a loaded dinner tray in both hands. He spoke to no one and no one tried to speak to him.

"Looks like he's heading for his office," said Vijay.

"He spends most of his time in there," Jamie said. "His fortress."

"Go get him," she urged. "I'll wait here."

Jamie took a deep breath, then got up from his chair and hurried after the mission director. He caught up with Chang halfway across the dome, well clear of the cafeteria tables.

"Dr. Chang?" he called. "Can I talk with you for a moment, please?"

Chang slowed his pace but did not stop. "Dr. Waterman? Is something wrong?"

"No, not really," Jamie said. "I just need to speak to you for a few minutes. In private."

Dipping his chin slightly, Chang said, "In my office, then."

Jamie walked alongside the mission director and even slid open his office door for him. Chang placed his dinner tray on the low table in the corner of his office, then wordlessly gestured to one of the chairs next to it.

Once they were both seated, Jamie looked for a way to open the conversation.

"This is about the priest, I presume," said Chang.

"Yes," Jamie said, grateful that the subject was broached. "I wanted to tell you personally about his coming."

"That is kind of you. DiNardo arrives on the resupply flight. I saw his name on the manifest that Boston sent."

"Our decision to allow him to come was based on a number of factors."

"He is rather old for such rigorous work. Almost as old as Dr. Carleton."

"He's been thoroughly examined. His health is fine."

Chang nodded.

Jamie went on, "I don't want you to feel that Monsignor DiNardo's presence here in any way impinges on your authority as mission director."

"He is a fine geologist. I know his reputation and have studied his curriculum vitae. I met him once, at a conference in Taipei."

"Good," said Jamie.

"He will make fine addition to our geology group."

"Yes, but the reason we decided to allow him to come here is that he can be a powerful voice against the fundamentalists who are opposed to our work on Mars."

"I understand. You are struggling against those who wish to stop our work here and force us to return home. A geologist who is also a priest can be useful against them."

"That's why we decided to let him come," Jamie said, thankful that Chang was being reasonable.

Chang's usually impassive face worked itself into the beginnings of a smile. "I welcome a fellow geologist," he said, as if he actually meant it. "There is much work for him to do here."

"I'm delighted that you see it this way."

"How else would I feel?"

Jamie hesitated, then plunged, "I was afraid you'd be upset, unhappy perhaps, because we didn't include you in the decision-making loop."

Chang shook his head slowly. "It was not my decision to make. You are the scientific director. I am the mission director. Once Dr. DiNardo is here, he will report to me."

"Yes, of course."

"That is as it should be. I will ask Dr. DiNardo to participate in heat-flow studies. He can coordinate measurements of satellites and ground instruments. He need not leave this base."

"That will be fine," Jamie said gratefully.

"He will *not*," Chang went on, emphasizing the negative, "work with Dr. Carleton. Not at all."

And Jamie suddenly realized why Chang was being so cooperative. He wants to use DiNardo as a counterbalance to Carleton, Jamie told himself. He's a pretty crafty politician, underneath it all.

TITHONIUM BASE: THE RESUPPLY FLIGHT

■

Jamie could barely concentrate on the map displayed on the lighted stereo table. He kept glancing at his wristwatch, mentally counting the minutes until the resupply flight was due to establish itself in orbit around Mars.

Billy Graycloud stood beside him at the edge of the table, tall and gangling, his silent face focused on absorbing every word that Dr. Chang was uttering. Carter Carleton was on the other side of the table, beside Chang, looking almost amused as the mission director pointed out features on the map with his stubby fingers.

"We have traced the course of the ancient river bed up to this point," Chang was saying, indicating the spot where Rosenberg and Hasdrubal had reached weeks earlier. There was no mark on the map display to show where the hopper had exploded.

Sweeping his hand down the winding track of the buried river bed, Chang went on, "Detailed imagery of cliffs along this part of the valley shows no additional structures in the cliff face." The mission director looked squarely at Jamie. Almost accusingly, Jamie thought.

"The imagery doesn't show any large niches in the cliffs, does it?" Jamie asked, trying to make his voice sound conversational, not confrontive.

"Small niches," Chang answered, still bending over the table. "None as big as here, where the buildings are."

Carleton nodded and said, "I'm willing to bet we'll find other dwellings in the cliffs farther up the river."

"You told us they were not dwellings," Chang said.

With a grin, Carleton said, "Touché. I misspoke, for lack of a better word."

"Dwellings or not," said Jamie, "it seems clear that the Martians lived in villages along the banks of the river."

"Agreed," Chang said, straightening up and squaring his shoulders. "Question: should we put more resources into tracing the buried riverbed farther along valley, or concentrate on excavating the village here, by our base?"

Jamie glanced at Carleton, then said, "I wish we had the resources to do both."

"We do not."

Tapping the lighted map display with a forefinger, Carleton said, "I say we put everything we have into excavating the village here."

Chang did not turn toward the anthropologist. Still focusing on Jamie, he said, "Dr. Waterman, you are the scientific director. This decision you must make."

Jamie remained silent for several moments, even though he had known this question was coming and knew what his answer had to be. Yet he hesitated, hoping to mollify Chang at least a little.

"As I said," he began at last, "I wish we had the resources to do both. But we don't, as you pointed out, Dr. Chang."

"So?"

"So I believe we should use our available manpower to excavate as much of the village as we can, and continue mapping the riverbed and seeking evidence for other villages with the deep radar imagery from the satellites."

Chang seemed almost to be standing at attention, eyes still riveted on Jamie.

"Very well," he said. "That will be done."

The mission director pivoted and strode back toward his office, hands at his sides clenched into fists.

Carleton let out a low chuckle. "He didn't like that, let me tell you."

"Neither did I," said Jamie. "Neither did I."

JAMIE STARTED BACK TOWARD his own cubbyhole of an office, checking his wristwatch as he went. Graycloud walked beside him, slouching slightly.

The public address speakers set up in the dome's rafters announced, "RESUPPLY FLIGHT OH-EIGHT-ONE HAS ESTAB-LISHED MARS ORBIT."

A ragged, halfhearted round of cheers went up across the dome. Whoever was in charge of the PA system put on the "Going Home" movement from Dvorak's *New World* symphony.

Jamie grimaced as he stepped into his narrow cubicle. Graycloud was right behind him.

"I guess some of the guys are happy about leaving," the younger man said as Jamie slid around his improvised desk and sat down.

"I guess so," Jamie replied absently, thinking about Di-Nardo's arrival and the departure of twenty-six needed men and women. There would be four new people arriving with the priest: two from Selene and two from Earth. Twenty-six leaving, four coming in. We're shrinking, he said to himself.

Graycloud shifted from one foot to the other by the door-less entrance, looking uneasy.

"Don't tell me you want to go back, too, Billy."

"No, not me!" The youngster looked genuinely alarmed. "I'll stay as long as you want me to, Dr. W."

"That's good, Billy. Good." Jamie turned his attention to his desktop screen and called up the logistics program. Graycloud didn't leave, though, he simply stood by the en-trance, fidgeting silently.

Jamie glanced up at him.

"It's just that . . ." Graycloud's voice tailed off, but the ex-pression on his face looked urgent.

"What?"

"The writing. Those pictographs on the wall of the building. Would it be all right if I took a crack at translating them?"

Taken completely by surprise, Jamie suppressed his impulse to say, "You?" Instead, he merely leaned back in his springy little chair and waited for Graycloud to go on.

"I could do a computer analysis of the frequency of each symbol, then assign arbitrary meanings to each of the symbols and see if any sense comes out of it."

The kid's totally serious, Jamie realized. I'm trying to hold this operation together and he wants to tackle a problem that's stumped the best experts in the world.

"Hasn't anybody already done that?" he asked softly.

Graycloud shook his head. "I've read everything in the literature. A couple guys at Carnegie Mellon took a crack at it, but they didn't even try to guess at what the individual symbols mean. They just did a statistical analysis of the frequency of each symbol."

Despite himself, Jamie felt a glow of interest. "But how can you know what the symbols stand for? I mean, that's the whole point of the exercise, isn't it, trying to determine what they represent?"

"I'll just guess," Graycloud said, pulling up the only other chair in the cubicle and folding his lanky body into it. "The computers can rattle through thousands of guesses per second, y'know. If I guess wrong, we won't get any sense out of it. But if I guess right . . ."

Unconvinced, Jamie said, "That's a brute force way of going at it."

"Right! Exactly! But with enough computer power the brute force way might give us something!"

Jamie could see the enthusiasm shining out of the youngster's eyes. "How much computer power do you have access to?" he asked.

Graycloud actually glanced over his shoulder before answering. Hunching closer to Jamie, he lowered his voice as he replied, "At night I can put most of the units in the base together in parallel. We've got two supermodels and dozens of office and lab stand-alones. I can program them together. That's more teraflops than a whole university department!"

"You have your regular duties, Billy. When would you sleep?"

"That's the beauty part! Once I slave them all together they can chug along all night long on their own. All I have to do is check their results each morning."

"This wouldn't interfere with anyone's regular work? You wouldn't want to screw up anyone's computer."

"Nobody even needs to know about it," Graycloud said, practically twitching with eagerness.

Jamie shook his head. "No, I don't want you sneaking behind anybody's back on this."

Graycloud nodded, but without much enthusiasm.

"Write out a program plan, just a page or so will do."

"And try to get Chang to approve it?"

"He'll approve it," Jamie said. "I'll see to that."

"Really?"

"Really. As long as you can absolutely promise us that this won't foul up any of the work the computers are already programmed to do."

"No sweat! I guarantee it, Dr. W!" Graycloud shot to his feet.

Grinning at the lad's enthusiasm, Jamie got up from his chair and took Graycloud's hand in his own.

"Go write that program plan," he said.

"Yessir! Right away!"

As the youngster stumbled through the cubicle's entryway, awkward in his haste, Jamie heard himself lapse into the old Navaho saying, "Go in beauty, son."

He stood there for a moment, wondering if Graycloud heard that. Then, with a shrug, he went back to the logistics program. The kid wants to run with his idea, Jamie said to himself. As long as it doesn't bother anybody—

The PA system announced, "THE L/AV HAS MADE REN-
DEZVOUS WITH RESUPPLY OH-EIGHT-ONE. L/AV LANDING IS
EXPECTED IN TWO HOURS, GIVE OR TAKE A FEW MINUTES
FOR THE CARGO LOADING."

MARS ORBIT: TRANSFER

∎

Monsignor DiNardo was in the midst of his morning breviary when the command pilot called him over the ship's intercom, "Father DiNardo, we're ready to transfer you to the L/AV."

DiNardo's compartment was as small as a monk's cell, but more comfortably furnished with a soft bed and modern plumbing.

He put his rosary beads down on the metal dresser that was built into the curving bulkhead and touched the intercom keyboard.

"I am ready," he said. Ready to go down to Mars, he thought, his heart thumping.

He had already packed his meager belongings in his single black travel bag. Stuffing the beads into one pocket of his gray coveralls and his prayer book into another, he reached for his travel bag. And thought of a colleague in the seminary, ages ago, who would skim through his breviary by saying, "All the saints on this page, pray for me," over and over as he flicked through the pages.

DiNardo smiled to himself at the memory as he slung the bag over his husky shoulder and slid open the door of his compartment. The bag felt featherlight. Of course, he thought: the ship is spinning at only one-third normal gravity now. I weigh only thirty-some kilos. The best diet I've ever been on!

He headed along the narrow passageway toward the main

airlock, careful to grip the safety bars on both sides as he adjusted his stride to the lighter Martian gravity. During the four days of the flight from Earth the wheel-shaped torch ship had spun at a rate that produced a feeling of almost normal gravity. Now that they were in orbit around Mars, the spin rate had been cut down to one-third of a *g*.

The command pilot was still on the bridge, overseeing the transfer of the last of several tons of cargo to the landing/ascent vehicle. One of the other astronauts, a gangly, long-legged African-American woman with a lantern jaw and dark hair cut so short it looked almost like a skullcap, was waiting for him at the airlock hatch.

"You're almost there, Padre," she said, in a west Texas twang.

"Yes," DiNardo replied softly, his voice almost choking in his throat. "Thank you for a very pleasurable flight."

The astronaut chuckled. "You call sittin' in that bitty li'l compartment for four days and eatin' what passes for food on this bucket pleasurable?"

"It has brought me to Mars."

She sobered. "Oh. Yep, that it has. Good luck, Padre."

"God bless you, my child."

The airlock was connected to the L/AV's airlock, so there was no need to cycle it. DiNardo simply stepped from the torch ship into the tubular segment that linked it with the landing/ascent vehicle, much as an airliner passenger would go from the airport terminal gate through an access tunnel and into the airplane.

No windows, no view of the red planet outside. Another astronaut—male, short and wiry—greeted DiNardo inside the L/AV, showed him to a bucket seat. The seat's thin padding looked threadbare, worn. Four others were already buckled in: one woman and three men, fresh and fuzzy-cheeked as teenagers in DiNardo's eyes.

"We'll be on the ground in about half an hour," the astronaut said. "The ride ought to be pretty easy, but you'll have to stay strapped in until we touch down."

DiNardo nodded and started to pull his prayer book from his coveralls pocket, to resume his morning devotions.

"Would you like to go up to the cockpit?" the astronaut asked. "Just for a minute or so, but you can see outside from there."

DiNardo jumped out of his chair so quickly that he stumbled into the astronaut in the light gravity. Laughing, the man led him past the empty seats, up a short ladderway and through a hatch.

And there was Mars.

DiNardo's breath caught in his throat. He had seen thousands of images of Mars, pictures taken from orbit and from the surface. But this was no photograph. Through the curving window of the L/AV's cockpit he could see the red planet gliding past his goggling eyes. That's Olympus Mons! DiNardo realized. The largest mountain in the solar system, its massive flanks sheened with ice, its gaping caldera dark and mysterious. Close enough almost to touch! And that mass bulking up on the horizon must be Pavonis Mons.

He was gasping, he realized. And the pain had returned to his chest.

"You okay, Father?" asked the astronaut, his face suddenly taut with concern.

The other astronaut, seated at the craft's controls, turned to look up at him. "Don't sweat it, Reverend, this creaky old bird'll get you down on the ground all right."

"I'm fine," DiNardo lied. "Fine. It's . . . the excitement. I've waited . . . twenty-three years . . . for this."

The astronaut's expression eased and he showed DiNardo back to his passenger's seat and helped him strap in. Once the astronaut climbed back up to the cockpit, DiNardo dug the bottle of pills from his pocket and swallowed one of them dry. He had lots of experience doing that, furtively taking the heart pills so that no one knew he needed them.

After several minutes the astronaut called from the cockpit, "Separation in three minutes, folks. We'll be on the ground in fifteen."

On the ground, DiNardo thought. On Mars.

The pain in his chest eased, and DiNardo tried to resume his breviary prayers. But he closed the well-thumbed little book as soon as he felt the gentle surge of thrust that meant that the landing vehicle had separated from the torch ship.

I'm on my way, he told himself. *Deo gratias*. Thanks be to God for allowing me to reach Mars. The pain of the heart is a trifling price to pay for such a privilege. Glory be to God.

His chest constricted again and he reached for the bottle of pills once more.

"L/AV LANDING IN TEN MINUTES," the public address speakers blared.

Jamie looked through the opening in the partitions that formed his office and saw that a couple of dozen people were milling about the open area of the dome, waiting to leave Mars when the L/AV departed again. Their luggage was piled in a disorderly heap near the main airlock.

He knew he shouldn't feel this way but he couldn't help thinking of the departing men and women as traitors, turncoats, cowards who were running away from Mars rather than staying here to push the exploration further.

You're supposed to be scientists, Jamie berated them silently. You're supposed to seek out new knowledge, new understandings. Instead you're running away. When the going gets tough, you run away.

But then the Navaho part of his mind spoke: They have to find their own paths, seek their own goals. Look at that Hungarian, Torok: his marriage is falling apart and he has to go back to salvage what he can. No two lives follow the same course, no two lives arrive at the same destiny. You'll have to explore Mars without them. In time, there will be others to help you.

In time, Jamie thought. In time we could be shut down completely. The exploration of Mars could come to an end.

"Not while I live," Jamie whispered to himself. "Not while there's breath in my lungs or a beat in my heart."

He thought he could hear Coyote laughing, out on the frigid, bleak red desert of Mars. Laughing at him.

"L/AV LANDING IN FIVE MINUTES." The PA system broke into his thoughts.

Almost reluctantly Jamie got up from his chair and walked toward the small crowd shifting restlessly near the main airlock. What can I say to them? he asked himself. Nothing, he realized. They've made their choice. They're running away.

He spotted Kalman Torok among the others, looking edgy, running a hand through his dark hair.

Walking up to him, Jamie put on a smile and stuck out his hand. "Good luck in Budapest," he said softly.

Torok looked mildly surprised. "Thank you, Dr. Waterman. I hope I can come back here after I get this legal tangle straightened out."

Jamie nodded, not trusting himself to say more. He went from one person to another, shaking hands, smiling tightly, holding back the urge to plead with them to stay. We couldn't afford to keep them all, he knew. We couldn't feed them or pay their salaries.

Still, he felt betrayed. It's not their fault, he told himself as he went through the little group. It's mine. I should have paid more attention to the funding problems. I should have worked closer with Dex and the board in Boston. I've been sleepwalking the past few years while the program's been strangled.

He saw Carter Carleton in the crowd, standing beside Doreen McManus. They both looked grim, almost angry.

CARLETON'S MORNING HAD BEGUN badly and went downhill from there.

When he awoke, Doreen was already up and dressed in a freshly cleaned set of coral pink coveralls.

"Your flight suit?" he asked, putting as much sarcasm into the words as he could.

She frowned at him. "I'm leaving, Carter. Let's not make our last morning together a battle."

"No," he said, swinging his legs off the bed. "Of course not."

Once he was finished in the lavatory and came back into the bedroom she was gone. He dressed swiftly and strode out toward the cafeteria, looking for her. Good tactics, he thought. Get out in public where we won't make a scene. She's a smart little bitch.

But she was sitting alone at a table for two, off in a far corner of the cafeteria. Only about half the tables were occupied; most people had already taken their breakfasts. Carleton poured himself a mug of coffee from the one urn that was working, then went and sat across the table from her.

"You're really going through with this?" He wanted to sound firm, accusatory. It sounded almost pleading.

She put down her spoon and looked at him squarely. "I've got to go, Carter."

"But why? I still don't understand why."

"That's the problem, isn't it?"

Leaning closer to her, he whispered, "Is it because I haven't said I love you? All right, I love you. Does that make you feel better?"

"Not really." She turned her attention to her fruit salad again.

Carleton grasped her wrist hard enough to make her drop the spoon. "What the hell do you want from me?" he snarled.

"Nothing," she said. "Nothing at all."

"I need you, goddammit!"

Doreen took a breath. Then, "Carter, you don't need me. You just want some compliant woman to go to bed with you."

"No, it's more than that."

She dropped her eyes for a moment, then looked at him again. "Carter, I accessed the files of your hearing at the university."

"Those files were sealed!"

"You know better than that. It didn't take much to hack into them."

"That's private information," he growled.

"And you don't think enough of me to share it," said Doreen, almost sadly.

"It's . . . painful."

"They said you abused that girl. There are pictures of her bruised and battered."

"I didn't do it. You've got to believe that."

"I'd like to."

"So that's why you're leaving? You're afraid I'll batter you?"

Strangely, she smiled. "No, Carter. I'm not afraid of you."

"Then what?"

"Carter, you don't *care* about me. You don't care about my ideas, my work. You don't care about anything but yourself!"

"That's not true," he muttered.

"Yes, I'm afraid it is," she said. "Don't you understand? Can't you see it?"

He felt totally confused and more than a little angry. "You'll have to explain it to me," he said.

Doreen's eyes seemed to be searching him, seeking something that wasn't there.

At last she said, "Our relationship has been all one way, Carter. I give and you take. I know you're trying to protect yourself, that you've been terribly hurt and you're frightened of exposing yourself to more pain—"

"What do you think you're doing to me now?"

She reached across the table and put her slender hand on his. "I know it hurts. It hurts me, too. Did you ever think of that?"

He pulled away and got to his feet. "Come on," he said coldly. "I'll walk you to the airlock."

TITHONIUM BASE: ARRIVAL

■

The L/AV landed with a thump that almost chipped Monsignor DiNardo's clenched teeth.

"Sorry 'bout that," came the pilot's voice over the intercom speaker. "Damn retros hiccupped."

Somewhat shakily DiNardo unstrapped and got to his feet. The four other passengers also got out of their seats, grinning expectantly, chattering to one another. The other astronaut clambered down the ladder and strode past him, toward the hatch, muttering, "Any landing you can walk away from . . ." His grin looked slightly forced.

It took a few minutes for the access tube to connect to the L/AV's airlock. When the astronaut finally pushed the hatch open, he gestured DiNardo through. Age before beauty, the priest thought, with a glance at the four younger arrivals.

Jamie Waterman was standing in the tube, smiling warmly at DiNardo.

"Welcome to Mars," he said, extending his hand.

DiNardo felt his own face beaming back at Waterman. He took the proffered hand and squeezed it firmly. "I am happy to be here, at last."

There was a crowd at the other end of the access tube, just inside the dome's main airlock. For a moment DiNardo thought they were there to welcome him, then he quickly realized—with a flush of embarrassment—that they were the men and women who were departing, taking the L/AV back up to orbital rendezvous with the torch ship that would carry them back to Earth.

Jamie introduced DiNardo to Dr. Chang, who bowed stiffly and offered formal words of welcome to Tithonium Base to the new arrivals. They were silent now, a little awed as they looked around at the big dome that would be their home for the next year or more.

A pair of experienced hands took the newcomers in tow and led them toward their assigned quarters. But Chang pulled DiNardo away from them.

"I look forward to working with such a distinguished geologist," the mission director said, unsmiling, dead serious. "I assume you have a program of research in mind."

DiNardo glanced at Jamie, then made an Italian shrug. "I haven't had time to organize my plans, Dr. Chang. This has all happened so quickly. I would be glad to follow your direction and help in whatever way I can."

Chang's impassive face thawed a little. He dipped his chin slightly, then said, "We must discuss our ongoing operations, then. I will be most interested in your comments and suggestions."

"Thank you," said DiNardo, unconsciously bowing back to the mission director.

Jamie said, "Let's get you unpacked and settled in your quarters first."

"Of course," said Chang. "I will be in my office. Feel free to call me there when you are ready."

"Thank you," DiNardo said again.

DiNardo hefted his travel bag and let Jamie lead him across the emptying dome. "That's Carter Carleton over there," Jamie said. "You ought to meet him."

"Yes, certainly."

Jamie called to Carleton, but the anthropologist took no notice. He looked grim, absorbed in his own inner thoughts.

"Dr. Carleton," Jamie called again, louder. "Carter."

Carleton turned toward them, his face grim, scowling. "What?" he snapped.

Approaching him, Jamie said, "I'd like you to meet Monsignor DiNardo. He just arrived and—"

"Oh, yes, Dr. DiNardo." Carleton's expression softened a little. "Good to meet you." His hands remained at his sides.

"It is a pleasure to meet you," said DiNardo. "I congratulate you on your discovery."

"Yes. Thank you." Carleton turned and walked away, head bent forward.

DiNardo watched his retreating back. "There is a man with much on his mind."

"He and one of the women here have just broken up," Jamie said. "She's going back to Selene."

DiNardo nodded as they resumed walking toward his living quarters. "I wonder if it would be possible for me to say mass. There must be some Catholics here, and non-Catholics will of course be welcome."

Jamie seemed to think it over for a few paces before he said, "I don't see why not. Will you need anything special?"

Smiling, DiNardo replied, "Only some goodwill."

THAT EVENING JAMIE AND Vijay invited DiNardo to have dinner with them.

"The food's not bad," Vijay joked as they went through the cafeteria line. "Best on Mars, actually."

DiNardo smiled. The hot dishes were unidentifiable soy derivatives of one sort or another. The vegetables looked fresh, though, and there was a variety of fruit juices available. There was a tang of something spicy in the air; DiNardo reasoned that the cooks used spices liberally to disguise the lack of variety in the basic menu.

Once they were seated and had unloaded their trays onto the table, Vijay asked, "Is it proper to call you Monsignor DiNardo?"

Absently touching the purple on his clerical collar, DiNardo said, "Proper, but a bit pompous, I think. Why don't you simply call me Fulvio."

"I'm not sure I could do that," Vijay said.

"Please."

"Okay, I'll try. And I'm Vijay."

"And I'm Jamie."

"Very good," said DiNardo. He raised his glass of grape juice. "Here's to teamwork on Mars."

"On Mars," Jamie and Vijay echoed.

Once they started eating, Vijay asked, "If you don't mind me snooping, why'd you decide to come to Mars? I mean now, after all these years."

"I want to help," DiNardo answered.

"With the geology research?"

The priest shook his head. "Not merely that. I want to help show that science and religion are not enemies. I want to help you to continue the exploration of Mars."

Jamie sighed. "We can use all the help we can get, Fulvio."

NEW YORK: GRAND CENTRAL STATION

■

Dex Trumball shouldered his way through the crowd booming through the enormous terminal. Looking overhead he saw the magnificent mosaic set into the ceiling: the mythological beasts and gods and heroes of the starry constellations—all backwards, reversed left for right. Whoever did the tile work got it the wrong way round. But nobody noticed, nobody gave a damn. Dex saw that none of the scurrying commuters or gawking tourists even glanced up at the ceiling so far above them.

What caught their eyes were the huge animated advertisement screens mounted on the walls, hawking everything from cameras to salvation through Jesus. Wonder if we could put up scenes from Mars, Dex asked himself. Maybe clips from DiNardo's documentary. Probably too expensive; not cost effective.

With an inward shrug he pushed his way through the crowd and started up the short flight of marble steps toward the hotel that connected underground with the terminal. You could spend your whole life underground in Manhattan, Dex thought. Like living on the Moon. He himself hadn't been up at street level since he'd stepped aboard the maglev train at Boston's South Station.

The hotel lobby was quieter, less crowded. Dex glanced at his wristwatch and saw that he was running several minutes late. He looked around the lobby, peaceful and nearly empty at this time of the morning. There was Andersen standing in front of the men's shop window, looking at a display of Italian silk jackets.

Dex shook his head. Quentin Andersen didn't look like the sharpest publicist in New York. He was grossly overweight, his face florid and sheened with perspiration, his multiple chins lapping down over the wilted collar of his tailor-made shirt, his unbuttoned coat sagging around him like the flag of a defeated battalion. An Italian silk jacket won't do him any good, Dex thought. Rumor had it that Andersen was dying of cancer, but that rumor was at least ten years old and the man was still at the peak of his profession.

Walking up next to him, Dex muttered an apology for being late: "Train was held up coming out of Boston."

Andersen smirked. "Jesse James rides again?"

"No. A demonstration that blocked the tracks. Something about—"

"Protest against the church-and-state separation," said Andersen. "I heard about it."

He's got his ear to the ground, Dex said to himself. The lean, handsome mannequin wearing the silk jacket suddenly stirred to life, raising one hand and asking, "Would you like to try something on, sir?"

Dex was startled, but Andersen chuckled as he pointed. "Sensor set into the window alongside the speaker. You stop for more than thirty seconds and the program activates."

"We have an excellent selection of . . ."

Andersen turned and started walking away from the window. Dex followed him.

"Uses technology your people developed for Mars, I betcha," Andersen said, still laughing quietly at Dex's surprise. "Hasn't that gotten to Boston yet?"

"Don't know," said Dex. "I shop electronically. I haven't been inside a store in ages."

As they walked slowly across the hotel lobby Dex asked, "Speaking of Mars, what about our documentary? Will you manage the publicity campaign for it?"

"'Fraid not." Andersen lowered himself slowly into one

of the lobby's plush armchairs. To Dex it looked like a massive load of cargo being carefully deposited by an invisible crane.

Taking the chair next to him, Dex pressed, "You want more money?"

"Money's not an issue, Mr. Trumball."

Dex could feel his brows knitting. "Look, we need somebody who can stir up a buzz about our documentary. It's on the Internet but we're hardly getting any hits on it."

Andersen said nothing.

"We've got a priest from the Vatican talking about Mars, for chrissake! The controversy alone ought to be newsworthy but the goddamned networks won't touch it."

"Can't say I blame them."

"What's that supposed to mean?"

Andersen turned his fleshy face toward Dex. "Mr. Trumball, the word is out. Every mother-loving church in the country, just about, has told its congregation not to look at your documentary."

"That ought to make people run to see it," Dex said. "The kids, especially."

"You wish. The faithful go home from church and block your documentary so that their precious little darlings can't access it."

"But that's illegal! It's against the First Amendment."

Andersen pulled out a huge white handkerchief and ran it under his collar as he explained, "The First Amendment prohibits the *government* from restricting freedom of expression. It doesn't say diddley-squat about faithful God-fearing citizens doing it on their own volition."

"Their own volition," Dex snapped. "They're a bunch of brainless automatons. That mannequin in the store window has more intelligence than they do."

"The mannequin's not watching your show, either."

Feeling desperate, Dex urged, "That's why we need you! We need to create some buzz about the documentary, make noise about it, get people curious enough to look at it."

But Andersen shook his head, a slow ponderous back-and-forth wobbling of all that flesh. "You're flogging a dead horse, Mr. Trumball. The churches are against you. Even the Catholic parishes have told their people not to watch it. I'm not going to go against that kind of tide. It'd be suicide. I'd just be taking your money under false pretenses."

"You're just going to let the New Morality push our documentary into oblivion?"

"You got to know when to hold 'em, and know when to fold 'em." Andersen struggled to his feet. "Sorry you had to come down from Boston just to hear bad news, Mr. Trumball. But, believe me, I've looked at all the angles. Your documentary is a dead issue. Maybe some private schools will look at it, but don't expect a big audience."

Dex muttered a heartfelt, "Damn."

As he watched Andersen waddle off through the hotel lobby, Dex knew that his worst fears had been realized. The New Morality and their fellow fundamentalists were working hard to strangle the exploration of Mars.

He had only one card left to play. With a sigh, he pulled out his pocket phone and called for his limo. He wasn't looking forward to riding through the choking traffic all the way out to JFK airport. But Kinnear was in Hawaii, and if Dex was going to close a deal for bringing tourists to Mars he had to go to Kinnear.

I'll get it all signed and sealed, he told himself as he impatiently waited for the limo to show up. I won't breathe a word of this to Jamie until the money's on the table.

TITHONIUM CHASMA: THE CLIFF DWELLINGS

■

F ulvio, are you all right?" Jamie asked, alarmed. He could hear the priest's labored breathing in the headphone clipped to his ear.

"Yes," DiNardo answered, puffing. "I'm just . . . a little . . . out of breath."

They had ridden side by side up the cable lifts from the valley floor to the cleft where the ancient buildings stood. It had taken DiNardo three floundering tries to get his boots on the floor of the cleft. In the end, Jamie had to throw him a tether and reel him in.

Through the inflated helmet of DiNardo's nanofabric suit Jamie could see the priest's face was flushed, whether from exertion or embarrassment he couldn't tell.

"I have never been a mountaineer," DiNardo said, with an apologetic smile, as he unclipped the climbing harness.

"It's my fault," Jamie said. "We pushed you through without all the necessary training."

"I'm all right now. I simply needed to catch my breath."

Jamie nodded and held out one hand, as if to steady his companion.

DiNardo looked past him, and his mouth sagged open. "This is it," he whispered, eyes widening.

Jamie felt himself break into a broad smile. "This is it. The cliff dwellings."

The structures stood ghostly pale against the ruddy tones

of the overhanging rock, but straight and clean-lined, created by an intelligence that knew how to build for the ages.

As they began to walk toward the buildings, Jamie went on, "Carleton says they weren't dwellings. The Martians lived down on the valley floor. These buildings were some sort of temple, he believes, used for ceremonial purposes."

"They came here to worship?"

"Maybe."

They ducked through a low doorway and straightened up again inside the building. Sunlight filtered down from the light well that ran through the core of the structure.

"Do you think this was truly a place of worship?" DiNardo asked, his voice hardly above a whisper.

Heading for the ladder that led to the upper floors, Jamie said, "The Anasazi back in Arizona built storehouses for grain high up in rock clefts. They used the sites for protection against their enemies."

"Did these Martians have enemies among them?"

"Damned if I know."

DiNardo chuckled softly. "Be careful of the words you speak. I had a teacher, a stern old Irish Jesuit, who always warned us that we should not use such language. 'God might grant your wish and damn you for all eternity,' he would tell us."

"I can't believe that God would be so spiteful," said Jamie.

"Neither could I," said Monsignor DiNardo. Then, after a moment's hesitation, "Yet he did away with the Martians, did He not?"

Jamie looked at the priest. His face was etched with something beyond the kind of burning desire to know that drove Jamie. His eyes looked infinitely sad.

Vijay, meanwhile, was in the midst of a tutorial by Carter Carleton.

She had deliberately sought him out at lunch, and found him at a table with eight others. They made room for Vijay to sit across the table from Carleton, between a professor of geophysics and a postdoc cellular biologist. Carleton spent the mealtime discussing the work at the dig, although he did almost all the talking while the others listened and nodded.

He's handsome, Vijay thought. Handsome and basking in the attention everyone's giving him. Four of the eight others were women, three of them quite young. Vijay memorized their names from the tags on the coveralls and made a mental note to check their dossiers.

It's all part of my psych profiling, she told herself. I've got to know everyone's background as thoroughly as I can.

But it was Carleton who fascinated her. She had looked up his file as soon as she had gotten Nari Quintana's agreement for the psychology study. Carleton was by far the most interesting personality among the scientists and technicians. He had been chairman of the University of Pennsylvania's anthropology department, but had resigned under a cloud of accusations and recrimination. Vijay had pulled up news media reports of the scandal: a female student had accused him of sexual assault. The university's official records never mentioned the word *rape*, but the tabloids did, plentifully.

Fascinating, thought Vijay. Carleton came to Mars as a virtual refugee from the affair, claiming he'd been set up by religious fundamentalists because of his teaching about evolution. Now he was leading the effort to excavate the long-buried Martian village. And reveling in the attention it brought him.

He'd been shacked up with one of the younger women, Doreen McManus, Vijay had learned. But she'd gone back to Selene. If Carleton misses her, he certainly doesn't show it, she thought.

On the other hand, she mused, there's definitely tension between Carleton and Chang. Negative tension. Chang doesn't like the anthropologist, he sees Carleton as a challenge to his authority.

"Come on over to the stereo table," Carleton said to the group, "and I'll show you what I mean."

They dutifully left their half-finished lunches on the table and trooped across the dome. Halfway there Vijay realized that Carleton had come up alongside her.

"Are you really interested in this?" he asked, smiling at her. He was slightly taller than Jamie, she realized, and several centimeters taller than she. Slim, with a tight gut. On Earth he'd be deeply tanned from all his outdoors work. Here on Mars no one got sunburned, not inside the suits they had to wear.

"It's fascinating," Vijay replied. Carleton beamed, thinking that she referred to his work.

Carleton called up the three-dimensional display of the dig, then spent the rest of the lunch hour showing what they were uncovering.

"These along here are the foundations of what might most likely be living quarters."

"Houses?" asked one of the women students.

"Houses," Carleton said.

"Or not," said one of the older men. "Mustn't jump to conclusions."

Carleton nodded perfunctorily. "Yes, but look at the way they're grouped around what can only be a central plaza."

"Kind of small for a plaza."

"A miniplaza, then." Carleton's tone went harder. "I'm willing to bet that's where they had a communal fireplace. We've found traces of ash in a central stone-lined pit. That's where they cooked their food."

Another of the students, male, said, "They must have had fairly extensive fields of crops nearby."

Brightening, Carleton agreed. "We'll look for those once we've excavated the entire village. Croplands don't leave all that much for us to find, though. Seeds, maybe petrified parts of plants. Not like the foundations of these structures."

A tone chimed, echoing through the dome.

"Lunch hour's over," said Carleton. "Time to suit up and get back to work."

The group began to head for the main airlock, where their nanofabric suits hung waiting for them.

"Would you like to join us, Mrs. Waterman?"

Vijay was only half surprised by his question. "Me? I don't know anything about digging up old ruins."

"That's all right. I can show you what to do."

"Really?"

"If it interests you."

Thinking it over swiftly, Vijay said, "I have to check in at the infirmary. Would it be okay if I came out a little later?"

"Certainly. I'll look forward to it."

He gave her a brilliant smile, then turned and headed toward the airlock.

Vijay stood at the stereo table, thinking, A narcissist. He's definitely a narcissist. But is he also a rapist?

She thought not.

TITHONIUM CHASMA: THE DIG

It was midafternoon by the time Vijay finished her notes, suited up, and walked out to the dig. She recognized Carleton, standing in a bulky, grimy old hard suit by the big sifter on the edge of the pit with a pair of others in nanosuits flanking him on either side.

He recognized her, too.

"Mrs. Waterman!" she heard in her earphone. "Welcome!"

Vijay walked up to the anthropologist and they shook gloved hands. "Please call me Vijay," she said.

"Sure. Great. And you can call me Carter."

She peered over the edge of the excavation. "Those actually do look like the foundations of buildings."

"That's exactly what they are, Vijay."

For the next ten minutes Carleton pointed out to her the houses, the plaza, the street that ran straight toward the old riverbank, just as he had outlined them on the stereo display. Seeing the ancient remains in actuality, though, was different. Vijay felt an excitement that stirred her. Jamie was right. Real, actual people lived here, worked here, raised families here.

And died here, she realized. More than sixty million years ago.

"They were a lot shorter than we," Carleton was saying. "Built close to the ground."

"How can you tell?" she asked.

"We've made some measurements of the door frames. Reconstructions, actually, since the frames are all collapsed. But we have intact doorways up in the cliff structures."

"I see."

The setting sun was casting long shadows across the valley floor before Vijay realized that she had spent almost the entire afternoon with Carleton at the dig. The excavation was completely shaded now. The workers were climbing up out of the pit on the ramp that had been cut into one side of it.

"Another day older and deeper in debt," one of the postdocs wisecracked as he shut down the sifter's motor.

Carleton waggled a finger at him. "Wrong attitude, Lonzo. Another day finished and we're closer to having the whole village excavated."

"And what then?" Vijay asked.

He put a hand on her shoulder and turned her toward the dome. "By then we should know a lot more about the Martians than we do now. What they ate, how they lived—"

"What they looked like?"

He nodded inside the inflated bubble of his helmet. "Yes, I think we should even get a fairly good idea of what they looked like." Then, grinning, he added, "It would help if they left a few pictures around. Decorated their homes. Put up a sign or two."

"Do you think you'll find something like that?"

He shrugged inside the nanosuit. "Maybe they were iconoclasts. Maybe making images of themselves was forbidden."

"Like Muslims," Vijay murmured.

"Burial sites," Carleton said. "That's where we'll find out the most about them. We haven't found their cemetery, not yet."

Vijay wondered if the Martians buried their dead. Some cultures on Earth preferred cremation, she knew. Primitive peoples often left dead bodies out in the open to be consumed by scavengers.

"Can you have dinner with me?" Carleton asked.

Surprised, Vijay blurted, "I have meals with my husband."

"Bring him along. I'm broad-minded."

ONCE SHE HAD FINISHED vacuuming her nanosuit and hanging it on the rack by the main airlock, Vijay hurried across the dome to her quarters. Jamie wasn't there, so she walked to his office. He wasn't there, either.

Puzzled, almost worried, she stood outside the entrance of his cubicle and wondered if she should ask the excursion controller where her husband was. Then she saw him and Monsignor DiNardo walking slowly from the airlock, deep in conversation.

Feeling relieved, Vijay headed back toward their quarters. He'll come there before dinner, she told herself.

But Jamie spotted her from halfway across the dome and beckoned to her. She hurried to him.

"I didn't realize how late it was getting," Jamie said. "We spent the whole day up in the cliff structures."

"It is my fault," the priest said, with an apologetic smile. "I'm afraid I have taken your husband away from his duties."

Before Jamie could reply, Vijay said, "I went out to the dig. With Carter."

"Oh? I thought you were working with the medical staff."

"I played hooky this afternoon. Just like you."

DiNardo's brows knit. "Hooky?"

"Carter's asked us to have dinner with him," Vijay said to Jamie.

He turned to the priest. "I thought we'd eat with Monsignor DiNardo tonight. We have a lot to talk over, about the documentary that Dex made. We're going to add a segment from up in the cliff dwellings."

Vijay started to bite her lip, caught herself, then said, "Well, whyn't you two do what you need to, and I'll eat with Carter. Okay?"

Jamie glanced at DiNardo, then nodded. "Okay."

Vijay felt strangely disappointed.

■

Y ou're husband's a busy man," said Carleton, smiling across the small table at Vijay.

She made herself smile back as she glanced past Carleton's shoulder at Jamie and DiNardo sitting at the next table, huddled over their untouched dinners, talking intently. Jamie's back was to her.

"He's fighting to keep them from closing down our work here," Vijay said.

"Good for him," said Carleton. "But I suppose that doesn't leave him enough time for you."

Vijay marveled at the man's self-centeredness. *I was right,* she thought: *he's a complete narcissist.*

Misreading her silence, Carleton said, "I shouldn't be poking into your personal life, I suppose."

Vijay picked up her fork and surveyed the slices of soy-beef on her plate. "We all live in each other's pockets here, don't we?"

"I suppose we do."

They ate in silence for a few moments. Then Carleton said, "God, what I wouldn't give for a decent glass of wine!"

"It's a sacrifice we make for working here," she said.

"I suppose so. But still . . ."

Is he angling to see if I've got some booze stashed? Vijay wondered.

As if in answer, Careleton said, "I brought six bottles of single malt with me, but they're almost all gone now."

"Alcoholic beverages are forbidden by mission regulations."

He grinned at her. "Everybody brings something in their personal belongings. The bio boys cook up some interesting pharmaceuticals in their labs, you know. I'll bet even Chang has some rice wine stashed away somewhere."

Vijay chewed on the underdone soymeat, then asked, "You don't like Dr. Chang much, do you?"

With a shrug, Carleton replied, "As long as he doesn't get in my way he doesn't bother me."

"Does he get in your way?"

"He tries to, now and then. It doesn't do him any good."

She speared a leaf of lettuce from her salad. "He *is* the mission director, after all."

Carleton hmmphed. "He's a bureaucrat, not a scientist. He'd make a perfect mandarin bureaucrat for some Chinese emperor."

"Dr. Chang's a world-class geologist."

"Was. He hasn't done any geology in years. Decades."

Vijay fell silent, digesting Carleton's assessment. Sooner or later I'll have to get Chang's reading on Carleton, she told herself. That should be illuminating.

NEXT TO THEM, JAMIE and DiNardo were discussing the video broadcast they wanted to make from the cliff dwellings.

"If people could see the structures," Jamie was saying earnestly, "understand that they're real, that living, thinking creatures made them while dinosaurs were living on Earth, then . . ." His voice trailed off.

"Then you think that they would give more support to our work here," DiNardo finished for him.

"That's what I'm hoping."

Gently, DiNardo shook his head. "I hope so, too. But I do not expect it."

"You don't? Why?"

"Mars is not important to them. It is that simple."

"Not important?"

"As horrible as that may seem to you, I believe it to be the truth. Most of the people on Earth simply do not care about Mars. Their concerns are much closer to home."

"The greenhouse warming," said Jamie.

"And even more personal problems. Crime. War. Half the people of Earth don't have enough to eat. Food is a very real worry for them."

"I suppose so," Jamie admitted.

"It is an old, old problem," DiNardo said. "Galileo had trouble finding money to support his work. Leonardo da Vinci wrote job application letters to the rich and powerful."

Jamie made himself smile at the priest. "Today we write grant applications."

"But the problem is still serious. In democracies such as the U.S.A. the people are the ultimate decision makers. And I am afraid that the people think Mars is a luxury that only a small elite band of scientists cares about."

"But don't you find," Jamie asked, "that there's a concerted effort to downplay what we're doing? An organized campaign to belittle our work, to keep it out of the public's eye?"

"An organized campaign against us?"

"By the New Morality and other fundamentalist groups. Even some ultraconservatives in the Catholic Church."

Jamie feared he had gone too far, but DiNardo looked thoughtful for a moment, then replied, "There are ultraconservatives in the Curia, this I know. I have to deal with them."

"That's why you're so important," Jamie said, some urgency returning to his voice. "You can show the people that there's no basic conflict between religion and science. Show them that we're not a bunch of atheist monsters trying to destroy their religious faith."

DiNardo glanced down at his half-finished meal before replying, "I am not so certain of that, I'm afraid."

Jamie blinked at him.

"Mars is testing my faith," said DiNardo, looking suddenly bleak. "Testing it severely."

* * *

SLOWLY, PATIENTLY, VIJAY SWUNG their conversation to Carleton's relationship with Doreen McManus.

"I'm overwhelmed with what a rumor mill this place is," she said as they worked on their desserts: a fruit cup for her, a lemon tart for him.

Carleton said, "It's like a university campus, only worse. We're smaller. As you said, we're all living in each other's pockets."

"Or pants," she said, grinning to show she meant it to be humorous.

"There is that," Carleton agreed, smiling back at her.

"It's a pressure cooker in here, all right."

Carleton nodded.

Vijay plunged, "Doreen McManus went back to Selene, di'n't she."

Carleton's face went taut for an instant, but he quickly regained his composure. "Good for her."

"The word is that you two were a couple."

"She's just a kid. She got too emotional to stay here."

"Too bad."

Vijay waited for Carleton to say more, but he concentrated on mopping up his lemon tart.

She decided to push a bit. "Do you miss her?"

Carleton looked up and made a crooked little smile. "It was fun while it lasted. At least she didn't accuse me of rape."

Vijay asked, "Can I ask you—"

"No," he snapped. "I've talked enough about that. It's over and done with."

"I suppose so," she said weakly.

"A moment ago you called this place a pressure cooker," Carleton said, almost accusingly. "But it's worse than that. It's Coventry."

"Coventry?"

"A place of exile. A place where they send troublemakers to get rid of them."

She blinked with surprise. "That's how you think of Mars?"

"That's what this is. You, me, all of us here—we're exiles, outcasts. We don't belong here. We can't survive here without this dome. We can't even breathe the air outside or walk out in the open without spacesuits. We're aliens. Exiles."

"Most of the people here worked their bums off to get here," Vijay protested.

"And now that they're here," Carleton retorted darkly, "they all wish they were home."

"No!"

"Yes. They may not admit it, but there isn't anyone here who wouldn't prefer to be back on Earth."

"You, too?"

He folded his hands in front of his face, half hiding his expression. At last he admitted, "Me, too. But I can't go back. I'm really exiled."

Vijay thought it over swiftly. "I can think of one person who prefers it here."

"Your husband."

"Yes. Jamie *wants* to be on Mars. He's at home here."

"He's a madman, then," said Carleton.

Vijay started an angry reply, thought better of it, and said nothing. Carleton returned his attention to the remains of his dessert. A tense silence stretched between them.

She could see him struggling to regain control of himself. He's let his mask slip, Vijay thought, and now he wants to get it back in place.

At length, Carleton's smile returned. He pushed his chair back and got to his feet. "I still have some single malt back in my room. Care to have an after-dinner drink with me?"

Vijay automatically glanced at Jamie, sitting with his back to her.

"I'm not sure that—"

Something exploded out in the night. The dome shook, glasses and dishware rattled, Vijay's tea sloshed in its cup. People jumped to their feet, staring, looking around. Someone knocked his chair over with a crash.

"What the hell was that?"

Suddenly everyone remembered that they were on Mars, millions of kilometers from help, with the thin cold air outside keening like an alien beast.

Exiles, Vijay thought. He's right. We've exiled ourselves.

TITHONIAE FOSSE: HAMMER BLOW

■

Half the people in the cafeteria were on their feet. Everyone was staring, wide-eyed, fearful.

Chang bolted out of his office and looked up at the dome's structural support beams, lost in shadow.

"Something exploded!"

"I didn't see a flash."

"Nothing's on fire."

"Are you sure?"

Jamie headed for the monitoring center. Check the life-support consoles first, he told himself. He noted that the dome didn't seem to be punctured. There was no rush of air, not even the high-pitched whistling of a pinhole leak. My ears haven't popped, he said to himself. Air pressure's holding okay.

The monitoring center was the largest cubicle in the dome, packed with consoles that kept constant real-time watch over all the sensors and observation equipment on the ground and in orbit high above. Four people were sitting in the middle of all the screens, earphones clamped to their heads, eyes focused on their displays.

Before Jamie could ask, their chief, standing near the cubicle's entrance, said, "Got a satellite image of a big flash up on Tithoniae Fosse, 'bout a hundred, hundred-ten klicks from here."

"Up on the plain?" Jamie asked.

"Right."

Chang pushed past Jamie. "Life-support systems?" he asked sharply.

"All in the green," said the chief technician calmly. "No problems."

Chang gusted out a pent-up breath.

"Might be a meteor strike," Jamie said. "A fairly big one."

"Goddamn seismograph gave a big lurch," the chief technician said, pointing to one of the screens.

"Let me see," said Chang.

The nearly flat line of the seismograph record spiked sharply, Jamie saw. An impact. The technician monitoring the satellite sensors powered up a blank screen. Standing to Chang's side, Jamie saw a false-color infrared view of the plain spreading northward from the rim of the valley: Tithoniae Fosse.

Several others were crowding up at the cubicle's entrance.

"It's okay," Jamie said, raising his voice. "Seems to be a meteor strike up on the plain."

Izzy Rosenberg wormed his way through the gang at the entrance. "A meteor strike? Where? How far? How big?"

Chang pointed to the monitor screen in front of him. "Repeat it," he said to the technician.

The satellite imagery flared with a sudden burst of light that blanked out the screen. Christ! Jamie thought. If that had hit here, even if it only hit the greenhouse—we'd all be dead.

"It overpowered the camera's sensitivity," Rosenberg muttered.

"Must have been a big one," Jamie repeated.

Sal Hasdrubal's voice called out, "Let's go out and see it!" Turning, Jamie saw the tall man looming over the heads and shoulders of the crowd jammed at the entrance to the cubicle.

"It's night," someone objected.

"The rock hit up on the plain," someone else observed.

Undeterred, Hasdrubal said, "We can ride up on the cables; they go to the top."

"And what do you do then, walk a hundred kilometers?"

"In the dark?"

"There's two campers in the old dome up there," Hasdrubal said impatiently. "Power 'em up and let's go!"

"No," said Chang. He said it quietly but with the firmness of the Rock of Gibraltar. All the other voices stilled. "We send a rover, not people. Monitor the rover from here."

"But it would take half a day to program a rover," Rosenberg objected.

"And somebody'd have to carry it up the cliff to the plain," Hasdrubal added.

Jamie said, "Dr. Chang, I think sending a small team would be faster and more effective."

"Mission protocol does not allow excursions at night," Chang said, scowling. Jamie knew that he was right, almost. Camper missions had gone out for days, even weeks at a time. They weren't supposed to drive at night, but Jamie remembered Dex and Possum Craig and others who had bent that rule out of shape.

Rosenberg jabbed a finger at the mission director. "Dr. Chang, that strike was big enough to blast out a new crater! It must've heated the ground considerably, melted the permafrost! We've got to get to it before the area freezes over again!"

Chang remained unmoved. "No excursions at night. Besides, the campers stationed at the old dome cannot run at night. The batteries are flat and need sunlight to recharge."

"But we could get to the dome tonight," Jamie heard himself say, "and have the campers ready to run by sunrise."

Chang glared at Jamie, then seemed to relax. His shoulders slumped slightly. His expression lost a bit of its rigidity.

With the merest of bows, Chang said, "If the scientific director recommends such a procedure, I will ask for volunteers to assist him."

Jamie realized he'd just been appointed head of the excursion. Fingering the bear fetish in the pocket of his coveralls, he said to himself, All right. That's the path I'll have to take.

* * *

"NOW WE'LL SEE HOW well the nanosuits protect against the cold," Jamie said to Vijay, trying to sound unruffled and fearless.

They were back in the cafeteria, pulling together enough food to take care of the three men who had been picked for the excursion: Rosenberg, Hasdrubal and himself.

"I'll monitor your life-support sensors," Vijay said as she shoved shrink-wrapped sandwiches into the insulated case Jamie was carrying.

"Good," he said.

She gripped his arm, forcing him to turn and look at her. "If I tell you to stop and return to base, you stop and return. Understand?"

Nodding, "Sure. Right."

"I mean it, Jamie. I want you to promise me."

He was staring into her eyes. Then he broke into a slow, almost shy smile. "I promise, Vijay. I'll come back to you."

She made herself smile back at him even though she felt terribly worried about this sudden mission into the hundred-below-zero cold of the Martian night.

As they went to the airlock and the rack of nanosuits stored there, Vijay saw that half the dome's people were gathered there, milling, buzzing. She glanced at her wristwatch: barely half an hour had passed since the meteor had hit.

Then she saw Carter Carleton off to one side of the crowd, looking more amused than anything else.

Jamie was moving through the crowd, which made way for him like the Red Sea parting for Moses. He saw Hasdrubal already in the extra-large nanosuit that he used, medical sensors attached to its inner lining.

Reaching for one of the medium-sized suits, Jamie asked, "Where's Rosenberg?"

"Not coming," said Hasdrubal. "He's been replaced."

"Replaced? What do you mean?"

"Outranked by our senior geologist," said Hasdrubal, pointing.

Turning, Jamie saw Monsignor DiNardo pulling a nanosuit over his black coveralls.

"You're going out?" Jamie exclaimed, surprised.

DiNardo said, "This is what I came for."

"But . . ."

"You think I am too old for such an adventure?" DiNardo grinned at Jamie. "I am not so much older than you, Jamie."

Hasdrubal let out a grunt. "The geezer squad."

DiNardo waggled a finger at him. "I prefer to think that I will give our little excursion a closer link with God."

Jamie tried to smile. But he thought, Coyote will be waiting for us out there in the dark. Coyote the trickster, the destroyer. We'll need DiNardo's God. We'll need all the help we can get.

NIGHT

■

Vijay wanted to kiss Jamie before he left, but there were too many people crowded around the airlock and once Jamie pulled up the hood of his nanosuit and inflated it into a bubble helmet it was impossible anyway.

So she watched him and the priest and Hasdrubal trudge to the airlock hatch. Jamie waved to her before stepping through. She waved back, feeling suddenly alone and afraid.

The hatch closed. The telltale lights on its control panel cycled from green, through amber and to red.

They're outside now, she thought. They're walking to the cable lifts.

The crowd broke up. Dr. Chang walked briskly toward the monitoring center, hands at his sides, shoulders bunched forward.

"You look like a lady who could use a drink."

Carter Carleton was standing beside her, looking bemused. "I still have that single malt in my quarters," he said.

"No," Vijay said firmly. "I have work to do." She started toward the infirmary, where the medical monitors were.

"They'll be perfectly fine," Carleton said, walking beside her. "Those suits are good to nearly two hundred below."

"Are they?"

"They test them with liquid nitrogen, I'm told."

Vijay shuddered at the thought of stepping into a vat of liquid nitrogen, suit or no suit.

Carleton reached for her arm, but Vijay kept striding determinedly.

"Look," he coaxed, "they won't even get to the cable for another ten minutes. You have time for a quick drink. Just one."

"Not tonight, Carter," Vijay answered, thinking, Not ever. Not with a man who tries to move in when my husband's out risking his butt.

"When they come back then," Carleton said easily. "We'll have a celebratory drink together then."

Without another word, Vijay left him standing in the middle of the open dome as she headed for the infirmary. He doesn't give up easily, she said to herself. You've got to give him that.

JAMIE KNEW IT WAS only his imagination, but he felt cold in the nanosuit. Just a couple of molecules separate me from unbreathable air that's close to a hundred below zero, he kept thinking. Just a couple of molecules.

They walked along the well-trodden ground, three little pools of light from the lamps built into the shoulders of their suits bobbing in the enormous empty black night of Mars. Overhead hung the stars, silent and solemn, spread across the sky so thickly Jamie could barely make out the familiar shape of Orion. The Milky Way flowed leisurely across the heavens, and one bright blue star beckoned to him: Earth, the blue world.

Jamie couldn't reach into his coverall pocket to feel the bear fetish, but he knew it was there. Guide me, Grandfather, he prayed silently. Help me get through this.

"There's the cables." Hasdrubal's voice in Jamie's earphone sounded tense. He could hear DiNardo puffing, but the priest said nothing.

"We've reached the lift," Jamie reported on the radio frequency that linked to the excursion controller. He pictured in his mind the group clustered around the controller's console:

Chang, Rosenberg . . . would Vijay be there or in the infirmary?

As if in answer, Vijay's voice came through. "All your medical readouts are fine. No worries."

Jamie still shivered involuntarily as he helped DiNardo clip the climbing harness across his barrel chest, then checked Hasdrubal's harness.

"Hey, who checks you?" Hasdrubal asked.

Coyote, Jamie almost said aloud. Instead he answered, "I've been doing this since you were in diapers, friend."

The three of them rode up on the cables side by side in almost complete silence. Jamie had expected Hasdrubal to make some chatter, but the lanky biologist kept his thoughts to himself. He thought he heard DiNardo mumbling something, praying perhaps. They were facing the cliff, which whisked by in a blur of strange, almost menacing shadows in the weak light of their shoulder lamps while their booted feet dangled in empty air.

It took almost fifteen minutes to reach the top of the cliff. Thanking the nanosuits for their flexibility, Jamie swung over and planted his boots on the solid rimrock. Hasdrubal did the same, then the two of them helped DiNardo get himself set on the ground and out of his harness.

Jamie held up his left arm to peer at the greenish glow of the GPS readout among the instruments on the pad he wore on his wrist.

"The dome's this way," he said, starting off toward the horizon.

"We have you on the positioning system," came the voice of the excursion controller. "You're exactly five hundred and seventy-two meters from the dome."

The original dome from the First Expedition had been sited more than a hundred kilometers to the northwest, on the other side of the Noctis Labyrinthus badlands. When it became obvious that the main base for the explorers should be down on the floor of the rift valley, Jamie had approved the geologists' insistence that they keep a pair of campers up

on the plain for excursions to the Tharsis Bulge highlands
and their massive shield volcanoes.

Now we're going to examine an impact, Jamie said to himself as the rounded hump of the dome rose like a sharp-edged
black shadow against the starry sky. That's something different from the blue world, Jamie thought as they walked toward
the dome: there's hardly any haze on Mars, especially at night,
when the temperature's so cold. No foliage or buildings, either. You can see the stars right down to the horizon.

The dome was powered by a small nuclear reactor, buried
half a kilometer away. It had provided electrical power for
nearly twenty years; Jamie remembered that it would need
refueling in another five years or so.

The dome's airlock was big enough for all three of them to
squeeze in together. Its dim red lighting still seemed bright to
Jamie after spending nearly an hour out in the night.

Once they stepped through the airlock's inner hatch,
though, the dome lit up brilliantly. Jamie blinked and suppressed an urge to laugh out loud.

"Well, the lights work," said Hasdrubal. He stepped quickly
to the monitoring console that sat next to the airlock.

"The heat, too," DiNardo said. "*Gratia Dei.*"

Jamie realized he wasn't the only one who had felt cold
out in the night.

Hasdrubal scanned the console screens. "According to the
readouts, the air's okay. Kind of chilly in here, though, not
quite up to twenty degrees Celsius."

Jamie grinned. "That's better than outside."

"Amen," said Monsignor DiNardo.

The three of them pulled down the hoods of their suits as
they looked around the dome. It was a spare facility: one row
of cubicles for sleeping quarters, a compact galley that hadn't
been used in months, consoles that monitored the life-support
systems, a communications console, and across the open floor
sat the two campers.

Big enough to carry four persons in relative comfort, the
campers were cylindrical in shape with big bug-eye windows

up front. They rested on eight sets of springy wheels that always looked to Jamie as if they were too fragile to support the weight. But on Mars they were fine. Their once-gleaming aluminum skins were caked with red dust; it made them look rusty, hard used.

Glancing at his wristwatch, Jamie said, "Let's check out the campers, then get some sleep. Big day tomorrow."

"Dontcha think we should call base and let 'em know we're here?" Hasdrubal suggested.

Jamie knew it was strictly routine. Their monitors back at the base watched them every step of the way. Still, he called back to Dr. Chang. I'll call Vijay once I'm in one of the sleeping cubicles, he told himself.

LOS ANGELES: CAMPAIGN HEADQUARTERS

∎

I'm not going to kiss ass for those yahoos!"

Malcolm Fry wasn't angry, but he was upset as he paced across the room they had set up to be his private office. As a candidate for the U.S. Senate, Fry spent precious little time at his campaign headquarters. He was on the road constantly, crisscrossing the state by plane, bus, and his personal hydrogen-fueled minivan.

Fry was "black enough" to entice the minority vote, but not so liberal that he frightened the conservatives. He had made his money the old-fashioned way, in construction and real estate, and now was spending a considerable portion of it in this exhausting campaign.

He was a big man, his hands still calloused from his early days as a construction worker. His smile had charmed voters—especially women voters—since he'd first gotten into politics, as a city councilman in Pasadena. He had climbed the greasy pole up to the point where the news media claimed he had an excellent chance to become California's next senator. There were even whispers of him running for president later on. He was young enough for that.

But now he glowered at his campaign manager as he paced the spacious office, from its shuttered window to the big desk in the corner and back again.

His campaign manager, Howard McChesney, sat in a tense bundle of nerves in the armchair in front of the desk, his head swiveling back and forth, following his candidate's pacing.

McChesney was a wiry, edgy type, with a lantern-jawed face and cold blue eyes.

"They may be yahoos," he said, his voice scratchy as fingernails on a chalk board, "but they can throw the election into your lap. Or into Gionfriddo's."

"The Mafia candidate," Fry muttered bitterly.

"Mal, you've got to let them have their way with this," McChesney insisted. "If you don't, you lose the election. It's that simple."

Fry stopped his pacing and fixed McChesney with a look that had terrified labor gangs and corporate directors.

"Howie," he said in a quietly intense voice, "they want me to withdraw my support for science courses in the public schools. I can't do that! Hell, when I was on the school board I fought to keep science in the curriculum. They tried to slit my throat over that! Now you want me to buddy up to them?"

"If you want to be senator," McChesney replied.

"I can't do it."

"You mean you won't do it."

"That's right, I won't."

McChesney drew in a breath, then said, "Let me paint a picture for you, Malcolm."

Fry sat on the edge of his desk and folded his arms across his chest. When McChesney called him "Malcolm," he knew things were getting grim.

"So you stand up to the fundamentalists," McChesney said, his head tilted back as if he were talking to the ceiling. "You insist on pushing for more funding for science courses in public schools."

Fry nodded.

"The New Morality, the Catholic Church, and every Christian sect in this crazy state votes against you. You lose the election. Gionfriddo wins. What's the first thing he does when he gets to Washington?"

Sullenly, Fry answered, "He votes to cut federal funding for science classes."

McChesney spread his arms. "So there you are. What have you accomplished, except to lose the election?"

"I still don't like it."

"Neither do I. But there it is. It ain't going to go away. Those yahoos, as you call 'em, will work night and day for years and years to get what they want. They're patient, they're organized, and they're absolutely certain that they're right and anybody who's against them is wrong. They're certain that God's on their side."

Fry seemed to sag in on himself. "So I either give in to them or lose the election. Is that what you're saying?"

"That's what I'm saying."

"There's got to be some other way! Got to be!"

McChesney said nothing for several moments while Fry stared at him, silently pleading.

"Well, maybe . . ."

"What?"

The campaign manager pressed his lips into a thin line, gazed up at the ceiling again, then finally said, "Maybe we could try to outflank 'em."

"What do you mean?"

"The ultraconservatives are all worked up about this Mars business. They want to stop the program and bring all the scientists home."

"Stop the Mars program," Fry murmured. "Yeah, I've heard them bitching about how much it costs."

McChesney said, "It's more than the money. They don't like the scientists talking about finding intelligent life on Mars."

"It's extinct, isn't it?"

"Even so. They want to get everybody off Mars and forget the whole thing."

Fry shook his head. "Damn yahoos."

"Maybe so, but if you come out strong against Mars maybe you can finesse the science class issue."

"Against Mars?"

Breaking into a wide smile, McChesney explained, "The beauty of it is that it doesn't mean a thing. The government's already cut all the Mars funding to zero. So you can make a big splash about bringing those people back from Mars without making any difference at all to what's really happening."

Fry was silent for several moments, thinking. At last he asked, "I just make some noise against Mars and sidestep the school issue."

"Could work," McChesney said hopefully.

Another few moments of silence. Then, "Okay, let's do it."

McChesney slapped his hands together. "Good. I'll get Tilton and her people working on a statement for you to make. And I'll schedule a meeting with the head of the New Morality's California organization."

Fry gritted his teeth, but said, "Okay. Do that."

TITHONIAE FOSSE: THE CRATER

∎

Jamie's pocket phone was buzzing. He snapped awake and looked around, confused for a moment. Then he realized, I'm in the dome up on the plain. He sat up on his bunk and reached for the phone, buzzing away on the metal nightstand beside the bunk.

Vijay's smiling face filled the tiny screen, brilliant teeth against shining dark skin, big luminous eyes. "G'day, mate," she said brightly. "This is your six a.m. wake-up call."

"Good morning," Jamie said, yawning.

"How'd you sleep?" they asked simultaneously. Then laughed. As they chatted, Jamie heard coughing and snuffling from one of the other compartments, then water running.

"Time to get to work," he told Vijay.

"Me, too. One of the geologists came down with a bit of the jitters after you left. He started thinking about the meteor hitting the dome here. I had to sedate him."

"How's Billy Graycloud doing?" Jamie asked, and wondered why.

"Graycloud? Solid as a rock, that one. Like you, a stoic Navaho."

"No problems with the rest of the staff?"

"Nothing big enough to involve the resident psychologist," Vijay replied lightly.

"Okay," he said, pulling his legs out from under the twisted blanket and sheet. "Guess I ought to get to work."

"Go in beauty, Jamie."

He blinked with surprise, then smiled. "We'll make a Navaho out of you yet, Vijay."

IT TOOK THREE HOURS in the camper, trundling along full-out at thirty kilometers an hour, to reach the new crater. Jamie drove all the way, while DiNardo sat in the right-hand seat beside him and Hasdrubal hunched over them both.

"There it is!" DiNardo shouted, excited.

"Christ, it's *steaming*!" Hasdrubal blurted.

DiNardo shot an unhappy scowl at the American's blasphemy as Jamie braked the camper to a halt. All they could see of the impact crater was a raised rim of reddish gray stones. And a delicate wisp of steam rising from it and dissipating in the thin, clear air.

DiNardo felt his pulse thundering in his ears so loudly that he barely heard Jamie mutter, "I'll call back to base, let them know we're here."

"Yeah, yeah," Hasdrubal said impatiently. "Let's get out there and start setting up the instrumentation."

The biologist hurried back toward the camper's airlock, where their nanosuits were stored. Jamie made a swift, perfunctory call to the excursion controller, then pushed out of the driver's seat and also went to the rear of the camper.

DiNardo wondered if his legs would hold him erect. He had taken two of his heart pills once they'd bedded down in the dome, after the exertions of the climb up the cliff face and their hike through the bitter black night to the dome. Then he'd set his wristwatch alarm for two hours before sunrise so he could say his breviary before either of the other two woke up. Now he felt dull, dense and slow. I've got to be at my best, he said to himself. Lord, lend me strength.

Jamie felt excited, almost trembling with anticipation as he waited for Hasdrubal to close the seals on his nanosuit and inflate its hood into a helmet. Once the lanky biologist worked his long arms through the shoulder straps of his backpack, Jamie checked his suit and backpack connections, then started pulling on his own suit.

Monsignor DiNardo came slowly up the narrow aisle between the folded-up bunks and reached for the third suit. He looked pale to Jamie, his expression . . . what? Jamie asked himself: apprehensive, expectant, scared?

"Are you alright, Fulvio?" he asked.

DiNardo made a tight smile. "Yes. I am fine. Excited, of course."

Jamie made a mental note to ask Vijay about DiNardo's medical readouts. But Hasdrubal was already ducking through the airlock's inner hatch, eager as a child at Christmas to get outside and see the new crater.

Jamie ushered DiNardo into the airlock once Hasdrubal was outside. Then, finally, he went through himself.

The two men were standing on the circular rim, goggling down into the crater. Jamie stepped up to them, noting that some of the rim rocks were blocky, squarish. Then he looked down into the crater itself. It was a lot smaller than the Meteor Crater in Arizona, barely a couple of football fields across and only about twenty, twenty-five meters deep. Almost perfectly round. The rock must have come straight down at nearly ninety degrees, he thought. Steam was coming up from one slope, near the bottom, a weak little breath rising upward that disappeared almost immediately on the gentle breeze wafting by.

"Heat," Jamie murmured, although the Navaho in him thought the delicate cloud might be the spirits of dead Martians rising to join Father Sun at last.

"From the impact," said DiNardo.

Hasdrubal nodded inside his bubble of a helmet. "That rock dumped a helluva lot of kinetic energy into the ground."

"It penetrated to the permafrost layer," Jamie said.

"And it has remained hot enough to melt the permafrost even after the overnight cold," DiNardo agreed.

"Let's get the instruments planted," Jamie said. "And we'll need to bring back samples for the biologists."

"Damn straight," said Hasdrubal, fervently.

DiNardo turned sharply toward Jamie. "Do you think there might be organisms down there?"

"Or their remains," Jamie replied. "Either way, the bio people would crucify us if we didn't bring back samples for them to look at."

"Damn straight," Hasdrubal repeated.

"Yes," DiNardo agreed, his stubble-jawed head bobbing up and down. "Yes, of course."

"Wait a minute," Hasdrubal said. "Before we do anything we oughtta give this hole in the ground a name."

"A name, yes," said DiNardo.

"Or three names," Hasdrubal said, pointing to himself and the two others in turn.

"It should be your decision, Jamie," said DiNardo. "You are the senior among us."

Jamie knew instantly what he had to do. "Chang," he pronounced. "I name this crater for Dr. Chang Laodong."

DiNardo nodded. Hasdrubal muttered, "Rank has its privileges, don't it."

SO MUCH OF SCIENCE is physical labor, Jamie said to himself as he lifted a spadeful of dirt from the bottom of the crater and let it slide into one of the biology sample cases. Hasdrubal was a few meters away, worming sensor poles into the ground, unfolding their solar panels, actually singing to himself in a deep baritone as he worked. DiNardo appeared up at the crater's edge; the priest was trudging back and forth, carrying armfuls of sensor poles and sample cases from the camper to the crater rim.

He looks tired, Jamie thought as he looked up at DiNardo. For an older guy, he's doing his share of the dogwork. He hasn't said much, but he's actually smiling.

The sun was almost at the horizon when Jamie closed the last of the six sensor boxes.

"If you find any microbes in this dirt," he said to Hasdrubal, "you're going to have to figure out if they're native to Mars or were carried in on the meteor."

"That's a good problem," Hasdrubal said, grunting as he pushed one of the sensor poles into the churned-up slope of the crater. "That's the kind of problem a man could rest his career on."

"I'll give you a hand," said Jamie, reaching for one of the poles lying at the geologist's feet. He stepped carefully, as if trying to avoid treading on the spirits of the dead. "We don't have much time left before it gets dark."

Hasdrubal straightened up and said, "She's not steaming anymore."

Peering at the thermometer on his wrist pad, Jamie said, "Temperature's almost forty below. It hasn't been above freezing all day."

"Well, I'm sweatin'," Hasdrubal said.

"Me, too. I guess the suits give us enough thermal protection, after all."

"Guess so." Hasdrubal picked up one of the poles and began worming its pointed end into the ground, working it back and forth, back and forth. "We'll smell pretty gunky when we take these suits off tonight."

Jamie started pushing another pole into the ground. "Guess so. The badge of honor for working so hard."

"The priest must be takin' a break," Hasdrubal said, looking up. "Haven't seen him for damn near a half hour."

At that instant Vijay's voice came through Jamie's earphone, taut and anxious. "Jamie, Father DiNardo's heart readouts have spiked and then dropped into the red! I think he's flatlining!"

TITHONIAE FOSSE: DEATH STROKE

■

Despite reciting the rosary over and over again as he trudged wearily back and forth from the camper to the lip of the crater, Monsignor DiNardo found no peace, no solace, none of the tranquility that the repeated prayers usually brought him.

It was a foolish mistake to put on the nanosuit without putting the vial of pills into one of the suit's capacious thigh pouches, he realized. Now the pills rested in the hip pocket of his coveralls, mere centimeters from his grasp, but he could not reach them. Not without opening the suit, which was impossible out here in the open.

Excitement about the crater had smothered his usual good sense. Like a schoolboy, he admonished himself. You rushed out here to see the crater without thinking, without planning ahead. You allowed your enthusiasm to overpower your intelligence. A mistake. A serious mistake. The crater isn't going to disappear! You should have been more careful, more thoughtful, before pulling on the nanosuit and rushing out to see it.

He had volunteered to be the donkey, carrying instrument poles and sample cases from the camper to the crater's rim. Easy work, he thought. Waterman and Hasdrubal gave him the easiest task. I can recite the rosary as I walk back and forth. I can keep my loads light and walk slowly, deliberately, across the sands of Mars.

Still, his pulse thudded in his ears. He blinked beads of

perspiration from his eyes, felt sweat trickling down his ribs. Yet he felt cold, clammy and cold.

The rosary, he told himself as he pulled another armload of sensor rods from the camper's exterior cargo bay. Do it in Latin. *Pater noster . . .*

I could go back inside the camper, take off the suit, and get to the pills. I don't really need them, I'm fine at the moment. But it would be a relief to have them within my grasp.

And then what? he asked himself. Once you come outside again, how can you swallow a pill with this ridiculous plastic bubble over your head? Open it for a second and you'll die of decompression.

He lay the sensor poles on the ground at the crater's rim. It had stopped smoking, he saw. Peering down into the pit he saw Waterman and Hasdrubal laboring to set a network of sensor rods in the churned-up ground. A half-dozen insulated specimen cases lay off to one side.

"Father DiNardo?" The woman's voice in his earphone startled him.

"I am here," he replied, looking up into the cloudless butterscotch sky. Not entirely cloudless, he realized. Three little wisps floated high, high above. Like the Holy Trinity watching over him.

"Your readouts show a good deal of exertion." It was Mrs. Waterman's voice, he recognized. Of course. She is a physician. "Perhaps you should stop what you're doing and take a brief rest."

"Yes," he said gratefully. "Thank you."

I'll go back inside the camper and take a pill, DiNardo told himself. Then I'll be fine.

But halfway back to the camper he felt a sudden white-hot stab of pain at the base of his skull. He tried to call out, to scream, but his voice froze in his throat. I can't move! He willed his booted feet to take him to the camper but instead his knees buckled and he sank to the ground. The pain overwhelmed him.

He lay on the red sand on one side, his backpack preventing

him from rolling onto his back. He couldn't move. His arms, his hands, paralyzed. He tried to wiggle his toes inside the boots. Nothing. He lay there and stared at the distant horizon, reddish bare hills and endless barren wasteland.

Mother of God, he thought, I'm going to die on Mars.

JAMIE SCRAMBLED UP THE slope of the crater, knocking over a couple of sensor poles as loose stones rolled under his boots.

"Father DiNardo!" he shouted. "Fulvio! Are you all right?"

No response.

He reached the lip of the crater and saw the priest's body crumpled on the ground, halfway to the camper.

"He's collapsed!" Jamie called to Hasdrubal.

Vijay's voice came through his earphone, taut but calm. "It might be a stroke. Get him into the camper right away."

Jamie ran to the priest, Hasdrubal a few steps behind him. In the slanting light of the setting sun he peered at DiNardo's face. It looked ashen, sweaty.

He scooped up the body in his arms and trotted toward the camper.

"Lemme take his legs," Hasdrubal said, coming up beside him.

"It's okay. I've got him. Get the hatch open."

Hasdrubal sprinted to the camper, long legs covering the ground in loping strides as Jamie carried DiNardo's inert body. In the easy gravity of Mars the priest weighed only about thirty kilos. He pushed the body into the open airlock, then clambered up the little ladder and squeezed into the chamber with him.

Hasdrubal eyed him as Jamie slammed the control panel. It seemed to take hours for the hatch to close, the airlock to cycle, and the inner hatch finally to pop open.

"We're in the camper," he called to Vijay. "What should I do?"

She didn't answer.

As he opened DiNardo's helmet and unsealed the front of his nanosuit Jamie asked again. "Vijay! What should I do?"

"There's nothing you can do, Jamie," her voice replied. "According to these readouts, he's dead."

A PART OF FULVIO DiNardo's mind was angered at the silliness of it. I can see, I can hear, but I can't move, can't speak, can't even blink my eyes. This would be terrifying if it weren't so stupid.

He realized that he was about to die. The specialist he had seen privately in Rome had warned him more than a year ago that he was at risk for a cerebral hemorrhage. That's what the pills were for, weren't they?

But to die on Mars. What a cosmic irony. You spend half your life working to reach this place and you have a fatal stroke within a week of your arrival. What a test of faith this is!

Waterman is shouting at me. I can't make out the words. He's speaking in English, of course, but his voice seems slurred, distorted.

And I'll die without ever finding out why God wiped out the Martians. I'll have to ask Him personally. Assuming that I get to heaven. Of course I will. But that's the sin of presumption, isn't it. What did that American humorist say: It's not over until it's over. The devil waits, always. Satan bides his time and seizes the opportunity to drag souls down to damnation.

He had the feeling that they were carrying him, laying him down on one of the cots, straightening his legs and arranging his arms across his chest. I'm not dead, he tried to tell them. Not yet.

But they could not hear him.

Why did you kill them, Lord? They were intelligent. They must have worshipped You in some form or other. Why kill them? How could You—

And then DiNardo understood. Like a calming wave of love and peace, comprehension flowed through his soul at last. As Waterman and Hasdrubal fussed about him DiNardo finally understood what had happened on Mars and why. God had taken the Martians to Him! Of course. It was so simple, so pure. I should have seen it earlier. I should have known. My faith should have revealed the truth to me.

The good Lord took the Martians to Him. He ended their trial of tears in this world and brought them to eternal paradise. They must have fulfilled their mission. They must have shown their Creator the love and faith that He demands from us all. So He gave them their eternal reward.

DiNardo tried to blink his eyes. The light was getting so bright it was difficult to see Waterman and the other one. Glaring. Brilliant. I thought it would all go dim at the end, the priest thought, but it's getting brighter and brighter. Dazzling. Brilliant. Like staring into the sun. Like looking upon the face of . . .

JAMIE STRAIGHTENED UP, HIS arms and back aching after trying to pound DiNardo's heart back to life.

"It's no use, Vijay," he said.

"I can see that," she answered through the communicator still clipped to his ear. "You might as well give it up."

Jamie heard Hasdrubal, standing behind him, make a little grunt. "He looks peaceful enough. Almost like he's smiling."

BOSTON: TRUMBALL RESIDENCE

■

Commonwealth Avenue had gone through many cycles of urban evolution, from posh residential neighborhood for Boston Brahmins of the nineteenth century to seedy run-down apartments for students and welfare families, dangerous with drugs and street crime. Now, in the middle of the twenty-first century, the area was on the upswing again: the stately old houses had been gutted and remodeled; the wealthy and prominent had driven out the poor and needy.

Dex Trumball owned a whole block of residences on Commonwealth Avenue and used one of them himself as his town house. It saved him the helicopter commute from the family estate on the North Shore, near Marblehead, to the downtown financial district where he ran the Trumball Trust.

He sat in his darkly paneled entertainment center, surrounded by wall screens, nursing a tumbler of scotch as he watched the documentary segment that Monsignor DiNardo had recorded from the excavation site on Mars.

The priest was standing in the pit, amidst the low dark rows of building foundations that the digging had uncovered. Through the bubble helmet of DiNardo's nanosuit, Dex could see that his swarthy, stubble-jawed face was smiling happily. His hands were behind his back. To Dex he looked like a kindly uncle who was about to present a surprise gift to a favorite niece or nephew.

"I am on Mars," DiNardo said. "That is why I must wear

this protective suit. The air here is too thin to breathe. Besides, it contains very little oxygen."

Turning slightly, DiNardo gestured with one hand while keeping the other behind him. "This once was a village where Martian people lived. They built their homes here and grew crops nearby. A stream flowed past their village. They raised families and went about their daily lives here, in this place."

Dex nodded to himself. Good. He's being very positive, very firm about it. No maybes or probablies. Good.

The priest took his hand from behind his back and opened it. The camera view closed in on the object he held in his palm.

"This is a fossil. It once was part of a Martian's backbone. Once, some sixty-five million years ago, this was part of a living, breathing, intelligent Martian creature."

Terrific, thought Dex.

"What happened to these people?" DiNardo asked rhetorically. "They were wiped out in a cataclysm that destroyed nearly all the life on Mars, some sixty-five million years ago, long before human beings arose on Earth. At the same time, a similar cataclysm struck the Earth and destroyed many, many living creatures, including the mighty dinosaurs. Giant meteors struck both worlds, bringing death and devastation."

We'll need to splice in some computer animation, Dex said to himself. Show the village as it was before the meteors struck. Show what the Martians probably looked like.

The camera view had pulled back to show DiNardo's face again. "On Earth, more than half of all the creatures on land and sea perished, driven to extinction. On Mars, the people who built this village and every other form of life more complex than lowly lichen was wiped out."

Okay, Dex urged silently. Now get to the point.

"I am a priest of the Roman Catholic Church," DiNardo said, as if in answer. "I am here on Mars to learn more about God's creatures. To me, searching the universe to understand the works of God is a form of worship. The twenty-fourth psalm begins with, 'The Earth is the Lord's and the fullness thereof; the world and they that dwell therein.' To the men who wrote the Bible, the Earth was the only world they knew. To you and me, the universe is much larger, much grander, and God's immense creativity inspires us to seek out His handiwork wherever we may find it."

"Terrific!" Dex shouted as the screen went blank. "Just what we need." He thought about calling the priest, checked the computer's display of the local time at Tithonium Base. Five-fifteen in the afternoon there. Good enough.

But as he started to instruct the voice recognition phone system to put through a call to the base on Mars, it interrupted him.

"Incoming call, sir," the phone announced with the carefully modulated voice of a polished British butler. "From Dr. Waterman."

"Put him on," Dex said, leaning back in his stress-free recliner and reaching for the half-finished scotch with one hand.

Jamie's face looked awful. Dex immediately knew that something was terribly wrong.

"Dex, Monsignor DiNardo has died. He had a stroke. He was outside on an excursion with me and one of the biologists and he just sort of keeled over and died. There was nothing we could do for him."

Dex felt a sudden surge of hot anger. Dead? The priest's dead? How the hell are we going to use his footage if Mars killed him? Of all the stupid goddamned fucked-up asshole things to do, the dumb bastard dies on us!

"We found a bottle of pills on him," Jamie was going on, "and more pills in his personal effects. Heart medication of some sort, Vijay thinks. We're checking into it. Whatever his condition was, he kept it secret from us. He got through the physical exams without letting us know about it. We wouldn't have let him come to Mars if we'd known, of course."

Great! Dex smoldered. Just motherfucking great! Once the news media finds out that we let a sick priest go to Mars and he died there, we're toast. The whole fucking program will be just as dead as that idiot priest.

TITHONIUM BASE: FUNERAL RITES

■

I've made arrangements with the Vatican," Jamie was saying softly. "They'll beam a funeral mass to us. The Pope himself will say it."

Chang asked, "When?"

"Tomorrow morning. Nine a.m., Rome time."

"Eight in the morning here," said Nari Quintana.

Despite the fact that the Martian sol was slightly more than forty-one minutes longer than a day on Earth, Tithonium Base and all space operations kept to Zulu Time, the standard clock setting for Greenwich, England. The extra minutes were added each night, while most of the base personnel slept.

Immediately upon returning to the base Jamie had asked Chang to call Quintana and the team's contamination expert for a meeting to decide what to do with DiNardo's body. Now they sat glumly in Chang's office, in the sofa and chairs around the low serving table.

Jamie had been surprised to realize that Hasdrubal was the top contamination expert.

"I'm the man," the biologist had admitted, with a rueful smile. "Ustinov beat it back to Russia on the resupply flight last month."

"We have to decide," Jamie said, looking from Hasdrubal to Chang, "what to do with the body."

"Catholics prefer burial," said Quintana, unconsciously fingering the silver crucifix she wore around her neck.

"No way," Hasdrubal snapped. "We can't let his body decompose in the ground out there. I've got enough of a contamination problem with that garden Torok left."

Jamie felt surprised. "The garden's contaminated?"

"Other way 'round," said Hasdrubal. "I gotta make sure no terrestrial organisms get loose in the local environment."

Chang said, "I agree that we must not bury Dr. DiNardo outside."

"There are no scavenger microbes in the Martian soil," Quintana said.

"You know that for a fact?" Hasdrubal challenged.

Quintana's expression hardened. "None in the shallow layer in which we would bury the man. Besides, we could seal him into an empty cargo container."

Hasdrubal shook his head stubbornly. "Look, we gotta think about the long term here, centuries. That body already contains armies of microbes that'll decompose him. Those microorganisms will eventually worm their way out of whatever container you put him in."

Jamie almost grimaced at the word *worm*.

Quintana glared at the biologist. "Do you honestly believe that terrestrial microbes could survive in the superoxides that pervade the ground out there? Without water? Without oxygen?"

"We can't take the chance. Hell, bacteria have survived for years out on the Moon's surface without water or air!"

"I know that, but—"

Jamie broke into their growing argument. "The Vatican has asked that the body be shipped to Rome."

Chang looked relieved. "Of course. He must have a family."

"Or the Jesuits want him."

"There is a resupply flight due in two months," Chang said. "He can be sent home then."

The last resupply flight for a long time, Jamie knew. Most of the base personnel will have to go home on that one. All except fifteen of us. Unless I can come up with some alternative.

"We can't keep the body here for two months," Quintana said. "We have no means of embalming him."

"He'll rot away," Hasdrubal grumbled.

"That will be a health hazard inside the dome," Quintana pointed out, tapping a finger on the cushioned arm of the sofa. "We'll have to place him outside."

"Can't do that," Hasdrubal countered. "It's a contamination risk."

"Better to risk contamination than endanger the health of everyone here."

"No!" Hasdrubal insisted. "We have to protect the local environment. We can't spread terrestrial microbes out there!"

"And I will not permit his body to be kept here," Quintana declared, equally inflexible.

Chang scowled at them both. "The only alternative, then, is to burn the body."

"The Vatican'll *love* that," said Hasdrubal. "Besides, burning might not kill off all the microorganisms in his body. If even only a few survive we'll have problems."

"You're being foolish," Quintana said to the biologist.

"I'm doin' my job, lady."

Jamie suddenly grinned, understanding what they must do. "Wait," he said, raising his hands to calm them. "There's another alternative."

Chang turned toward him questioningly.

"Put the body in orbit until the resupply ship from Earth arrives," Jamie said.

"In orbit?" Quintana looked doubtful.

"Place him in a cargo container and fly him into orbit in an L/AV. Leave the container in space. The cold will preserve the body, won't it?"

A slow smile crept across Hasdrubal's face. "Like dunking him in a vat of liquid nitrogen. Better, even."

"Cryonic preservation," Quintana murmured.

Chang nodded. "Thank you, Dr. Waterman. We should have seen that possibility earlier."

Jamie grinned at the mission director. "Forests and trees, Dr. Chang. Forests and trees."

MARS ORBIT

∎

C huck Jones let his arms float weightlessly up from the lander/ascent vehicle's instrument panel.

"Orbital insertion," he said into the headphone clipped to his ear.

"Copy orbital insertion," came the voice of the mission controller, back at the base.

Turning to his copilot, Kristin Dvorak, Jones grinned and said, "Okay, let's unload the priest."

Dvorak was a Czech, so diminutive she barely made the minimums for an astronaut. Like Jones, she was wearing a nanofabric space suit, although neither of them had pulled the inflatable helmets over their heads. Her hair was the color of straw, thickly curled. Jones kept his thinning brown hair trimmed down to a buzz cut.

She slid out of the copilot's seat and floated toward the cockpit's hatch. Jones went after her.

"Never thought I'd preside at a funeral," he said as she slipped through the open hatch that led into the L/AV's cargo bay.

"This is not a funeral," Dvorak said, in heavily accented English. "We are merely placing his body in cold storage until the next flight from Earth arrives to take him home."

The cargo bay was empty except for a solitary cylinder, ordinarily used to hold supplies.

Jones was almost too big to meet the specifications for an astronaut. He always thought about one of the first Americans to go into space, Scott Carpenter: when informed that the height limit for astronauts was six feet, he wrote in his application form that he was five feet, thirteen inches tall. And he got away with it.

As they unhitched the cylinder from the straps holding it to the deck and floated it into the airlock, Jones mused, "You know, maybe when I die I'll have my body sent into space."

"Not buried?" Dvorak asked.

"Nah. Why stick yourself into the ground when you can go floating out to the stars?"

"Recycling," she said.

He shook his head. "I think I'd rather go into space."

Dvorak smiled slightly. "It makes no difference, really. Once you are dead, nothing matters."

As he swung the airlock hatch shut, Jones admitted, "Maybe so. But still . . ."

Once they sealed the inner hatch shut, Dvorak asked, "Will you return to Earth on the next resupply flight?"

Jones said, "No. I'll wait it out."

"We will all have to go back sooner or later."

"I guess so."

"I have applied for a job with Masterson Aerospace. At Selene."

"You want to live on the Moon?"

"Why not? It would be more interesting. Not so many jobs for astronauts on Earth."

"I'll go back to Florida," Jones said. "After a year on Mars, I want some sun and swimming."

"More jobs at Selene," Dvorak insisted.

"More women in Florida," said Jones, with a leer. "In biki-nis."

She smiled back at him. "Higher ratio of men to women at Selene. Intelligent men, scientists and engineers."

Laughing, they went back to the cockpit and launched the mortal remains of Dr. Fulvio A. DiNardo, S.J., into orbit around Mars.

BOOK IV
LIFEBRINGER

*The Old Ones knew that life is not rare, but precious;
not fragile, but vulnerable. Life is as deep as the seas
in which it was born, as strong as the mountains that
give it shelter, as universal as the stars themselves.
Yet life is always in danger, threatened by the very forces
that created it, imperiled by the whims of Coyote and
the implacable workings of time itself.*

*On the red world life was nearly extinguished by the howl-
ing Sky Demons. Yet life clung to existence. Life persisted.
But slowly, slowly, the spark was guttering out. One day,
inevitably, life would disappear from the red
world forever.*

Unless Lifebringer could return.

TITHONIUM BASE: THE GREENHOUSE

■

Jamie decided to hold the news conference in the greenhouse. He knew it was going to be grueling, but he wanted to show the viewers on Earth that the Martian explorers were safe and comfortable.

Edith Elgin had volunteered to moderate the news conference from Selene, for which Jamie was immensely grateful. She coordinated the reporters' questions and acted as hostess for the show. She relayed the questions to Jamie, who planned to respond to each one in turn, then wait for backup questions to reach him on Mars. It was tedious, but when the various segments were spliced together the conference would appear almost seamless, almost as though it had taken place in real time.

So Jamie stood in the greenhouse dome with the long hydroponics trays and their lush green plants behind him. Off to one side was Kalman Torok's little plot of a garden, tended now by Sal Hasdrubal and one of the new arrivals from Selene.

And up in orbit circling Mars, Monsignor DiNardo's body waited for the fusion torch ship that would come from Earth and return him to the land of his birth.

Edith's bright, youthful face filled the portable screen that one of the communications technicians had set up in the greenhouse. She couldn't look glum if she tried, Jamie thought, watching her as she introduced him and explained how the conference would be handled.

"To you viewers," she was saying, "it will look like this is a real-time interview. But remember that Dr. Waterman is really on Mars, about ninety-seven million kilometers from Earth as we record his statements."

Behind the screen stood a pair of comm techs running the cameras and Vijay, her dark face serious, her radiant eyes fixed on Jamie. He tried to smile for her, then decided it wouldn't look right for the cameras. "Serious, composed, distressed but determined," Edith had told him earlier, smiling encouragingly. "That's how you've got to come across. Show 'em some of that Navaho dignity and strength of character."

Strength of character, Jamie thought. How can I tell the world that DiNardo deliberately kept the knowledge of his cardiac problem from us? How do I tell them that the medics who examined him missed the fact that he was taking blood-pressure pills? It makes us all look stupid, or at least too anxious to have the priest here to do a really careful job of examining him. I've got to avoid that. I've got to keep that out of sight.

The first question was from the famous Orlando Ventura of World Wide News: "Dr. Waterman, we understand that Monsignor DiNardo had a preexisting cardiac problem, yet he was allowed to go to Mars. Do you feel some responsibility for his death?"

Are you still beating your wife? Jamie asked himself. The screen froze on an image of Ventura's lean, sculpted face. He looks like a coyote, Jamie thought: the same cold eyes.

Taking a breath, Jamie began, "The medical consensus is that being on Mars had nothing to do with Monsignor DiNardo's death. He might have suffered a fatal stroke in the Vatican."

Glad that there was no way for the interviewer to interrupt him, he went on, "Monsignor DiNardo wanted very much to come to Mars, to help in the exploration of this world. I guess you could say he gave his life for that purpose. He believed that he was doing god's work, exploring a world and a people that god had created just as he created Earth, created us. He died in my arms, and I can tell you that he was smiling when he died. He was at peace."

Ventura's second question, scripted days earlier, was predictable.

"Has Monsignor DiNardo's death forced you to reconsider the safety of all the other men and women on Mars? And if not, why not?"

So it went, for nearly four hours. Jamie stood there in the greenhouse, on Mars, answering their repetitive questions and trying to convince them—and ultimately their viewers—that the exploration of Mars was safe and important.

Over and again he stressed the same points as he answered the same questions.

"Our base here certainly isn't luxurious," he said, sounding weary in his own ears, "but it's comfortable and quite safe. As you can see, we grow a fair amount of our own food. We produce water from the permafrost underground. We get our oxygen from the Martian atmosphere. As much as possible, we live on local resources."

One reporter wanted to know how much it cost to run the operation on Mars.

Jamie forced a slow smile and replied, "Not nearly as much as Americans spend on pizza. And our funding comes entirely from private sources. No tax money is involved."

At last it was over. The screen went dark. The technicians started to fold their cameras into their carrying cases. Vijay rushed around them and into Jamie's arms.

"You look like a man who could use a drink," she said, after kissing him soundly.

"I wish we had some beer," he admitted.

They ate a brief, quiet dinner in the cafeteria by themselves, although Chang and several others came by their table to ask how the interview went. Jamie shrugged and said he thought it would be okay.

"It all depends on the editing," he said to each of the questioners, knowing that a clever editor can snip statements out of

context and make anyone look foolish, heartless, or even ma-
licious. Edith's doing the editing, he knew. She'll do a good
job. But once the vid is in the hands of the networks, what will
they do to it?

Dead tired, he went with Vijay to their quarters. By the time
they were crawling into bed a message from Selene came
through.

"Thought y'all'd like to see the rough cut," said Edith
Elgin, with a gleaming smile. "You did a good job, Jamie."

Almost two hours later, Jamie decided that Edith had done
a good job, too. The questions and his answers were now
arranged in a clear flow, with much of the repetition edited
out.

"She's awfully good, isn't she?" Vijay said, sitting in bed
beside Jamie.

"She sure is," he said, feeling dog tired, heavy lidded. But
he slid an arm around her bare shoulders. "You're a lot better,
though."

Vijay smiled at him. "And a lot closer, eh?"

SELENE: GOVERNING COUNCIL

■

It's funny, thought Douglas Stavenger as he took a seat toward the end of the long conference table. I haven't been chairman of the council in years; I'm not even a voting member anymore. But wherever I sit, everybody turns to me as if I were still in charge.

Power. Some people spend their lives scrabbling for power. Others run away from it, from the responsibilities and the never-ending pressure to make decisions. Stavenger shook his head in bemused wonderment. I never sought power. At least, I didn't consciously. It just sort of fell into my lap. And I can't get rid of it.

The conference room was in one of the two office towers that supported the massive concrete dome of the Grand Plaza. Through the long window that took up most of one wall, Stavenger could see the miniature trees and flowering shrubs that lined the plaza's winding walkways, the curving shell of the open-air bandstand, the Olympic-sized swimming pool with its thirty-meter diving platform.

As the other council members took their seats, Stavenger glanced up the table at the chairman, sitting at the head of the table. He was a retired engineer who had come to Selene originally on a one-year contract to work on the solar energy farms spread out across the floor of the crater Alphonsus. He had never left the Moon. Assigned to a term on the governing council by the computer-operated lottery that picked new members from the general population, he had stayed through three terms and risen to the chairmanship.

He was a round-faced, smiling Swiss who made friends easily and handled administrative chores mainly by delegating responsibility to his minuscule staff. He would have to step down from the council at the end of this term, unless the entire population of Selene voted by a three-to-one majority to extend his time in office.

"Are we all here?" he asked, looking up and down the table. Every seat was filled. "All those who are absent will please raise their hands."

A patter of weak laughs went around the table. It was the chairman's standard joke, part of his sense of humor that had apparently taken root in his mind when he was in high school.

Stavenger settled back in the comfortably cushioned chair as the meeting commenced. He noted with wry amusement that even the chairman focused on him when he spoke, as if he were still in charge.

The meeting ran smoothly enough. No major problems outside of the usual disputes over water allocations and proposals to enlarge the underground city so that still more refugees from Earth could become citizens of Selene.

"We have enough of these refugees," one of the council-women complained. "The more we let in, the more they influence our politics."

"Well, that's only fair, isn't it?" said another woman, sitting on the other side of the table. "If they're citizens they ought to influence our politics."

"It's time to shut the door," the first councilwoman said, looking squarely at Stavenger.

He straightened up in his chair. "It's hard to refuse people who've lost their homes on Earth."

"It's their own damned fault! They sat on their hands for years and years and let the greenhouse overwhelm them. Now they want to run away from it and come here."

The debate grew hot, with some council members insisting that no more refugees be accepted for citizenship.

As their voices rose, Stavenger held up his hand and asked the chairman to recognize him. The angry arguing stopped and all eyes turned to him.

"Do you think it would be possible," Stavenger asked mildly, "to have newcomers go through a waiting period before they're allowed to apply for citizenship?"

"They have to wait six months," said the chairman. "That's in our constitution."

"Could we stretch it to a few years? Give them enough time to learn how our community works? Let them integrate themselves into our society?"

The debate growled on for another half hour, but much more politely. Stavenger watched and listened, content that he had sucked the venom out of the argument. In the end, the council voted to extend the waiting period for citizenship to five years. And then immediately voted to enlarge the city's underground living area by twenty percent.

The chairman nodded happily, then said, "That leaves only one item on the agenda: Mars."

Again they all turned to Stavenger.

Clasping his hands together on the table, Stavenger said, "The explorers on Mars need our help. Funding from national governments Earthside has been cut to zero, and private donations to the Mars Foundation are running dry."

"What can we do about it? We can't spend billions on Mars, for god's sake."

"It won't take billions," Stavenger said, with a soft smile. "Basically, they need help with two things: transportation and supplies."

"How many people are we talking about?"

"At the moment there's just over two hundred people, all at one base in the Grand Canyon."

"We're supposed to feed two hundred people?"

"On Mars?"

"They grow some of their own food," Stavenger replied. "Two of our people are there right now, studying—"

"Who sent two people to Mars?"

"They volunteered. One's an agro-engineer and the other a logistics specialist—"

"A glorified accountant," somebody said in a stage whisper.

Stavenger waited for the snickering laughter to die out, then admitted, "He does have a CPA ticket, in addition to his engineering degrees."

"And he went to Mars?" asked the chairman, trying to move the discussion forward.

"Yes. He and the agro man want to see how the Mars base might be made self-sufficient, food-wise."

"And we paid for their transportation?"

"They went on a fusion torch ship that the Mars Foundation paid for."

"Hitchhikers, huh?"

A few council members laughed again.

"You might say that," Stavenger replied.

The chairman asked, "Just what does the Mars team need? And how much of it can we afford to give them?"

Stavenger hesitated a heartbeat. Then, "I don't think of it as giving them anything. I think we'd be investing in the exploration of a new world."

"Damned expensive investment."

"With no return."

"No return?" Stavenger snapped. "They've found the remains of intelligent life! They're uncovering villages and finding a whole ecology of living organisms! Isn't that return enough?"

"It doesn't buy any bread."

With a shake of his head, Stavenger replied, "It wasn't that long ago that we were the ones who needed help. This community of ours began as a collection of aluminum cans scattered across Alphonsus's floor. We needed help from Earth in those days. Now the people on Mars need help from us."

"That's all well and good," said one of the older men, "but the question remains: what's in it for us? We can't afford to run a charity operation."

"We're already doing that with the damned refugees," grumbled one of the other councilmen.

For several heartbeats Stavenger didn't reply. He looked up at the acoustic tiles of the ceiling, then broke into a grin as a teenaged girl flew past the window on colorful plastic wings. How to answer them? he was asking himself. How to make them see?

"Look," he said at last. "We're in a battle against the armies of ignorance."

The other council members stirred with curiosity. Even the chairman's perpetual grin faded into a puzzled, almost worried expression.

"Back on Earth most people are governed by those who are using religion to suppress freedom. They're the ones who ignored the warnings about the greenhouse, who denied that the Earth's climate was changing. They're the ones who allowed this catastrophe to overwhelm the Earth."

"What's that got to do with Mars?"

"Hear me out, please. Those people tried to rule us. They sent troops here to force us to bend to their authority. They killed our citizens. If and when they feel strong enough, they'll try it again."

"No!"

"I can't believe that!"

"Believe it," Stavenger said firmly. "All through history human civilization has been a struggle between individual liberty and the power of the state. Whenever a religious movement has gained the reins of governmental power, individual liberties are strangled. That's what's happening on Earth today. Now."

Several council members glanced uneasily at one another, but no one contradicted him.

"Why do you think so many refugees want to live here?" Stavenger continued. "If they're wealthy enough to come to Selene they're wealthy enough to take their pick of safe residences on Earth. They're coming here for freedom! Not because they want to live in cramped underground quarters. Not because they want to worry about water allocations and air pressure regulations. They want to be free: socially, intellectually, even religiously free."

The chairman said slowly, "Doug, I still don't understand what this has to do with Mars."

"It's part of the battle. Part of the long war for human freedom. Oppression thrives on ignorance. The explorers on Mars are finding new facts, new ideas, that challenge the ideas of the oppressors. That's why the fundamentalists are working so hard to end the exploration of Mars. That's why we've got to do everything we can to support that exploration."

For long moments the conference room was so silent that Stavenger could hear the faint whisper of the air circulation fans buried behind the ceiling's panels.

Then the youngest member of the council, a molecular biologist who had come to Selene University to study genetic engineering, asked, "How much can we do?"

"Not much," the chairman answered immediately. "But if I sense the feeling around this table, we'll do whatever we can. Right?"

One by one, the other council members nodded agreement.

"Very well, then," said the chairman. "In that case, we should listen to a proposal from one of our citizens who's just returned from Mars."

Stavenger felt his brows hike up. The chairman's got something up his sleeve, he realized. And he never mentioned it to me.

He caught the chairman's eye. The man was grinning slyly at him. Stavenger gave him a nod, admitting he was surprised.

"Would you ask Ms. McManus to come in?" the chairman said into his cell phone.

All eyes turned to the door as Doreen McManus, pencil thin and big eyed, looking almost frightened, entered the meeting room. Stavenger searched his memory and recalled that she was a nanotechnician.

"Ms. McManus has a proposal for enlarging the base on Mars, using nanomachines," the chairman said.

TITHONIUM CHASMA: THE DIG

■

Usually Zeke Larkin was the gentlest of souls, yet the normal expression on his sharp-featured face was somewhere between a glare and a scowl. People expected him to have a volcanic temper, and he did—but he had spent most of his adult life struggling to control it.

Still Zeke grumbled to himself as he worked at the excavation. He regretted volunteering for the dig. I'm a biologist, not a shit-shoveling day laborer, he told himself. I should be in my lab, studying the SLiMEs, not working out here like an extra in some "curse of the mummy" flick. Besides, we ought to be looking for the farming area instead of poking into these ruins. Seen one collapsed building, you've seen 'em all.

Larkin's expertise was in the forms of bacteria that lived deep underground, where they literally ate the iron-rich rock and excreted methane. When similar organisms had first been discovered on Earth, thriving in temperatures and pressures that biologists had assumed were far too extreme for living cells to survive, existing even without the need for sunlight, some waggish biologist had dubbed them *subsurface lithotropic microbial ecosystems*: SLiMEs. Deep drills had pulled up similar SLiMEs from kilometers below the surface of Mars.

Larkin's career goal was to study these colonies of underground bacteria, to determine how long they had been living deep below the surface of Mars, to study how they were different—and similar—to the SLiMEs of Earth.

He was a postdoctoral student from the University of Michigan, lean and wiry, with sapphire blue eyes that looked at the world warily, as if expecting trouble. He worked very hard at being friendly and sociable, especially with his fellow scientists. He had even developed a sense of humor that they variously described as wry, dry, or devilishly clever.

But on this sunny Martian afternoon he saw nothing humorous about being out at Carleton's dig, slaving away like an ordinary laborer with the rest of the volunteers. Instead of a pick and shovel, though, these laborers used digging lasers to break up the rock-hard ground, and then tiny chisels and whisks to slowly, carefully, patiently uncover the remains of the long-buried village.

There's nothing here, Larkin saw. Twenty meters behind him a pair of postdocs were delicately brushing eons of dust off the remains of a broken, uneven wall, a wavering line of blackened stone that once was the foundation of a building. A Martian home, Larkin mused. Or maybe a barn for their livestock. He grinned inside his nanosuit's bubble helmet. Maybe it was a bar, a saloon like in those western vids about the wild frontier.

But where he was standing there was nothing. No crumbled foundations, no remnants of ancient walls. No ancient pollen or seeds, even. Just bare, empty ground right out to the thirty-meter-high side of the excavation pit. Larkin leaned on the long-handled broom he had been using, wondering why he should bother to continue. We've run the dig out to the edge of the old village and beyond. There's nothing more here to uncover, and Carleton's too damned stubborn to move off to the area where the farms probably were. Time for me to get back to my lab and leave this bullshit behind me.

He saw Carleton standing off at the other end of the excavation, more than a hundred meters away, out where the village's neat gridwork of buildings gave way to a pair of meandering lanes. The anthropologist was unmistakable at any distance; he was the only person in the crew who still wore a hard suit. Larkin thought he looked like an alien robot who had enslaved all these nanosuited humans and forced them into stoop labor for him.

Well, this slave is revolting, Larkin told himself as he hefted the metal-whiskered broom and started off toward the ramp that led up to the edge of the pit. Then he chuckled as he remembered the old joke: Revolting? He's disgusting!

I suppose I could use a shower, he thought.

"You there!" Carleton's peremptory shout rang in Larkin's earphone so piercingly it made him wince. "Where are you going?"

"There's nothing more out here, Dr. Carleton. We've gone past the edge of the village."

"Let me see."

Annoyed, Larkin let the broom fall languidly to the ground and waited for Carleton, hands on his hips.

Once the anthropologist reached him, clunking through the rows of building foundations and the people hunching over them, Larkin pointed to the area where he'd been working.

"It's empty," he said. "We've gone beyond the limits of the village."

"What about the farm that you've been nagging me about?" Carleton said. He clumped past the biologist and looked out over the empty area.

"It's not here," said Larkin. "More likely on the other side of the village, upriver."

For several moments Carleton said nothing. Larkin couldn't see his face behind the tinted visor of his helmet, but he imagined the anthropologist was trying to find some reason to make him stay and work for him.

At last Carleton said, "You should go over with Macintyre and the others, then. There's more to uncover there."

"I'm finished for the day," Larkin said. "I need to get back to my own research."

"You agreed to work here," Carleton said.

"Not at the expense of my own research. I've got to get back to my lab."

"It's still a couple of hours before sundown. We've still got plenty of time to work."

"I've got to get back to my lab," Larkin repeated.

"There's still work to do here."

"Dr. Carleton, may I remind you, sir, that I am a volunteer. I don't owe you fealty and you don't have the power to command me."

Even though the gold-tinted helmet visor remained blank, Larkin could *feel* Carleton's fury radiating from it. "I have the power to write a negative evaluation for your dossier."

Once that would have worried Larkin, but now he was too tired to care. He let his anger seep through. "Go ahead and write whatever you want. Who's going to accept your word about anything?"

And he strode forcefully away from Carleton, toward the ramp that led up to the valley floor and the dome of the base, leaving the broom in the dust like the symbol of his independence.

"You can't leave while there's still work to be done!" Carleton shouted. "You can't just go!"

"The hell I can't," Larkin answered, without even looking back over his shoulder.

"I'll ruin you!" Carleton yelled.

"Go rape a student," Larkin retorted, without missing a step.

Carleton watched him go, white-hot rage boiling inside him. He tried to kick the broom but in the hulking hard suit all he managed was to scuff the ground and puff up a pathetic little cloud of dust. Glaring furiously, he saw that the other men and women working on the site all had their backs to him, all were bent over their tasks, none of them wanted any part of this conflict. They heard us yelling at each other, Carleton realized, but nobody's going to say a word about it. Not to me, at least. They'll talk about it among themselves, though, he knew. There won't be any other subject on their lips at dinner tonight.

Larkin hiked up the ramp to the lip of the excavation, telling himself that he'd never volunteer for Carleton again.

He doesn't own me! he said to himself. He thinks he's god almighty down there but he's nothing but a disgraced former scientist. What kind of a science is anthropology, anyway? Digging up bones and making guesses, that's all they do. Any real data they get comes from chemical analyses and radioactive dating.

The biologist walked alone along the edge of the excavation, heading for the dome. He glanced down into the pit, at the people working away down there. Slaves, he thought. You poor fools. You let him dominate you. He needs you a lot more than you need him. Maybe I should lead a slave revolt, Larkin said to himself. Let's see how far the high and mighty ex-professor could go without the rest of us toiling away for him.

The late afternoon sun slanted into the excavation, throwing sharp shadows of the low crumbled remains of the building foundations against the red, dusty ground. Larkin looked out at the blank area where he'd been digging. It didn't look exactly blank now, he saw. Some faint undulations here and there, just barely visible from up here with the sun at this angle. He shook his head. Too small to be building foundations; they're just tiny little squares. Oblongs, really.

I ought to tell Carleton about it, he thought. Then immediately answered himself, To hell with that and to hell with him. Let him find it out for himself. He's the big-shot anthropologist. Let's see how smart he really is.

TITHONIUM BASE: AIRLOCK HATCH

∎

Later that afternoon, Zeke Larkin was still irritated by his encounter with Carleton, but working hard to forget it. He saw the anthropologist in deep discussion with Sal Hasdrubal over by the suit lockers near the main airlock hatch and decided to go over and try to make amends with him.

I should've been more reasonable, he told himself. He's a jerk, but I did volunteer to help him, I guess.

As he approached them, he heard Hasdrubal say, "But your volunteers have found half-a-dozen different varieties of seeds in the dig. If you could ask them to try to locate the farmland beyond the edge of the village—"

"Not possible," said Carleton. "We've got our hands full as it is. We've only got about half the village uncovered."

"But the farm area'd be a tremendous find for the biological study—"

"I said no," Carleton snapped.

Larkin's temper got the better of him. "Don't waste your breath, Sal," he said. "The high-and-mighty professor isn't interested in biology or anything else except salvaging his own reputation."

Carleton whirled on him. "You're in a pile of trouble, mister! I'm your supervisor and—"

"Hey, I *volunteered* to help you," Larkin countered, his voice rising loud enough to echo off the dome's arched rafters. "I'm not your goddamn indentured slave!"

"You made a commitment, damn you!" Carleton hollered right back at him. "You can't go back on it now!"

The two men were standing nose to nose in front of the suit lockers, by the main airlock hatch, both of them red in the face and glaring at each other. Their shouting brought everything in the dome to a stop. Hasdrubal looked completely stunned; he didn't know what to say.

"You can't make me stay in that damned pit of yours one goddam minute longer than I want to!" Larkin yelled, his shoulders hunching, hands balling into fists.

"The hell I can't!" Carleton roared back.

Dr. Chang came scurrying across the dome and tried to get between them, but it was clear that he sided with Zeke. "All workers at the dig are volunteers," he told Carleton, shaking a finger in his face. "Not contract laborers."

Carleton threw up his hands. "I am a man surrounded by incompetence," he shouted. "This is the curse of my life, chained to fellows of little mark nor likelihood."

Chang started to get red in the face, too. "You are not director of this mission! I am!"

"You're nothing but—"

"Hold it!" Jamie jumped in, practically running from his quarters across the dome to get between Carleton and Chang. "Let's lower the voltage here before we start saying things we'll really regret."

Carleton glared at Chang, past Jamie's shoulder, and Chang glared back. Larkin stood off to one side, looking just as furious as the two of them.

Jamie said, "Dr. Chang, can we use your office to continue this discussion?"

Chang looked as if he was going to choke, but he nodded wordlessly. The four of them—Carleton, Chang, Larkin and Waterman—went into Chang's office and slid the door shut. Hasdrubal shrugged as he watched them go, then turned and walked away. Somebody's gonna explode, he said to himself.

Once he'd gotten the three of them seated in Chang's office,

Jamie said quietly, "I hope you've got the shouting out of your systems. This is no place for a schoolyard brawl."

Looking straight at Chang, Carleton said, "We had an agreement in place. The volunteers are committed to work the number of hours they agreed to. Nobody forced them to sign up to help me."

"*Volunteer* is the operative word," Zeke Larkin said, his voice much lower, though still quavering with anger. "A volunteer can put an end to his service whenever he wants to."

Sitting rigidly behind his desk, his face a frozen mask, Chang dipped his chin in the slightest gesture of agreement.

Jamie was still on his feet. "You both have reasonable points," he said. "But the important issue is this: there's work to be done. We have this village to uncover, and there will be more villages, in time. Carter can't get the job done without volunteers to help with the digging."

"Volunteers," Larkin repeated.

"But once you volunteer," Jamie said, trying to make it sound reasonable, "you've committed yourself to a certain amount of man-hours."

Chang puffed out a breath, then said, "I have spent many hours setting up work schedules for volunteers."

Larkin shifted uncomfortably on his chair. "I have my own work to think about. I should be—"

"You should be living up to your commitments," Carleton snapped.

Before the biologist could reply, Jamie said, "Look. We're a team here. A family. Families have arguments all the time, but we shouldn't let an argument get in the way of doing what we came here to do."

"What we're doing here," Larkin said heatedly, "is rearranging the deck chairs on the *Titanic*."

Jamie stared at him.

"This world is dying," the biologist went on. "The endolithic lichen are dying off. There's not enough water available to support—"

"Permafrost contains oceans of water!" Chang interrupted.

"Frozen. The SLiMEs can tap the permafrost, but nothing on the surface of Mars can. Eventually the last of the lichen will die off and the surface will be totally sterile. Then the SLiMEs'll be next."

He's right, Jamie thought. Mars is dying. But he heard himself ask, "How long is 'eventually'?"

Larkin shrugged his thin shoulders. "A hundred thousand years. A million. What difference does it make? The planet's dying and there's nothing we can do about it."

Carleton said, "All the more important, then, to excavate what remains of the village. And anything else we can find."

"Digging up the dead," Larkin muttered. "While I ought to be seeing how long the SLiMEs can last."

"It's important!" Carleton insisted. "Vital!"

"So's my own work," Larkin retorted.

Surprisingly, Chang said, "I can rearrange schedule. It can be altered."

"What?" Larkin looked astounded.

Chang almost smiled. "You will work same number of hours at the dig. I will stretch out your commitment, give you more time in your lab."

Jamie asked, "Carter, is that agreeable to you?"

Carleton hesitated, then mumbled, "As long as I have the manpower I need to keep the excavation work going."

"Zeke?"

Reluctantly, Larkin nodded. "Yeah, I suppose so. If I can spend more time in my lab."

"Good," said Chang.

"Thank you, Dr. Chang," said Jamie gratefully. "You've solved the problem." Silently he added, For the time being. Until the next flare-up.

Then Larkin muttered, "It doesn't make any difference, anyway. We'll all be packing up and leaving here before another year is up."

Jamie didn't have the heart to contradict him.

* * *

FROM HER DESK JUST inside the infirmary's entrance Vijay could see just about the whole interior of the dome. She watched Larkin and Carleton leave Chang's office and walk toward the cafeteria without so much as glancing at each other. As if each one of them is totally alone, she thought. Neither one of them wants to acknowledge the presence of the other. Well, at least they're not screaming at each other.

Jamie was still in the mission director's office with Chang. He'll prob'ly be in there for a while yet, Vijay realized. They must have a lot to hash over.

Turning slightly, she saw Larkin get in line at the cafeteria's counter. Carleton went past him to the coffee urn, poured himself a mug, then looked around for a place to sit. He found an empty table by the curving wall of the dome and sat there, alone, while Larkin filled his tray and joined three other men and women at a table on the other side of the cafeteria. As far away from Carleton as they could get, Vijay saw.

The cafeteria seemed unusually quiet, she thought, conversations muted, little knots of men and women talking in subdued tones, as if they were afraid of being overheard.

It took Vijay a few moments to decide, but then she shut down her desktop computer and went to the cafeteria's trio of urns to make herself a cup of tea. The water wasn't much more than tepid and the urns themselves looked dull, almost grimy. Maintenance is slipping, she thought, as she made her way through the tables toward Carleton.

"Mind if I join you?" she asked as she took the chair across the small table from him.

Carleton smirked at her. "You're not afraid of catching it?"

"Catching? What?"

"Carleton's disease. It's something like leprosy. Nobody wants to be near you." He gestured with one hand; all the tables next to theirs were empty, unoccupied.

"That's a bit melodramatic, i'n't it?"

"A bit, perhaps," he admitted with a slightly sheepish grin. "But they all think of me as some kind of ogre now. The big, bad taskmaster who's abusing his volunteer helpers."

Vijay took a sip of the lukewarm tea, then asked, "How do you feel about it?"

He stared at her for a long moment. "This is a psych quiz, isn't it?"

She lowered her eyes, then replied, "The emotional stability of this group is as important as its physical health. You know that."

"And I'm a threat to the group's emotional stability," he muttered.

Vijay smiled at him. "It's not about you, Carter."

"Isn't it?"

"Not entirely. There are two hundred and some other people here, y'know."

"Most of whom would gladly push me out the airlock in my Jockey shorts."

"You *are* a narcissist," she said, laughing.

He cocked his head to one side. "It is the stars, the stars above us, govern our conditions."

"What's that from? Shakespeare?"

"*King Lear*, if I remember correctly."

"Di'n't Shakespeare also say that the fault is not in our stars, but in ourselves?"

Nodding, Carleton said, "That's from *Julius Caesar*."

"So which is it? The stars or ourselves?"

"Both," he said, with a tired sigh. "Neither."

More seriously, Vijay asked, "Are you going to be all right?"

"Me? I'm fine. Go do a psych profile on that hotheaded biologist if you're looking for a troublemaker."

"Maybe I should," she said.

"There you are!" Turning, Vijay saw Jamie approaching their table. She broke into a big smile.

"I thought you were going to stay in Chang's office all night," she said.

Jamie pulled a chair from one of the unoccupied tables and sat between Carleton and Vijay. "He needed to have his feathers smoothed a little. He doesn't show it much, but he gets just as worked up as any of us."

"You don't," Carleton said. "You're always as cool as a sea breeze."

"Not inside," Jamie said. Turning to Vijay, "Had dinner yet?"

"Not yet."

Looking back at Carleton, Jamie asked, "Would you like to join us?"

Carleton's eyes flickered from Jamie to Vijay and back again. Then he said, "No thanks. I'm not very hungry this evening."

He got to his feet and walked away without another word.

Vijay watched him go. "He's a ticking bomb," she murmured.

"Just what we need," said Jamie.

Heading toward his quarters, Carleton had to pass the table where Larkin was sitting with another man and two women. He nodded graciously to them; the lean-faced biologist gave him a wary nod back.

Halfway across the dome, Carleton looked back over his shoulder at Waterman and his wife, standing at the service counter loading their trays, smiling at each other.

She's beautiful, and therefore to be woo'd, he quoted to himself. She is a woman, therefore to be won.

TITHONIUM BASE: MIDNIGHT

■

Billy Graycloud sipped at a lukewarm mug of coffee as he watched the computer's latest run scroll down the desktop monitor screen. Outside the partitions of the comm center the dome was dark, shadowy. Everybody else was asleep, Graycloud thought. He had volunteered for the night shift at the comm center so that he could work on his attempt to translate the Martian pictographs. No disturbances. The dome's life-support systems were running smoothly enough and the occasional message from Earth was never so important that it couldn't wait until morning to be read and acted on.

Volunteered. Graycloud mulled the word around in his mind. The idea of volunteering had caused a big blowup a few hours earlier. Zeke Larkin and Dr. Carleton were sore enough to start socking each other, Graycloud thought. Right there at the lockers alongside the main airlock. In front of everybody. For a while Graycloud thought that maybe one of them was high on drugs. Maybe both of them.

Even Chang got into it. But then Dr. Waterman came on the scene and calmed them all down. Sitting bleary eyed at the central console in the communications center, Graycloud wondered what Dr. Waterman had done, what he had said, to put an end to the fight. He had no doubt that Dr. W had been the peacemaker. No doubt at all.

Graycloud had been one of the volunteers out at the dig when Larkin had exploded. Dr. Carleton had been pretty bossy, Graycloud thought, but the anthropologist was always a hard-ass out there. He called it *his* dig and that's the way he thought of it. Volunteers like me are just supposed to do what we're told and not talk back.

So what? he asked himself. Why did Larkin get so uptight? Graycloud yawned and stretched his arms over his head. Forget about it. Dr. W smoothed things over. Get back to your own work and stop rehashing what happened this afternoon.

Yesterday afternoon, he corrected himself. It's past midnight.

He returned his attention to the words scrolling down the desktop screen. Gibberish. No sense to them. "Sun, cook river, make house unknown word, unknown word." With a shake of his head Graycloud decided that his latest stab at assigning words to the Martian symbols was a complete flop. With a touch of a key he blanked the screen, then called up the images of the Martian pictographs.

They mean something, Graycloud told himself. But what? He yawned again and noticed that it was actually well past one A.M.

Get some sleep, he told himself. The comm center doesn't need you sitting here all night. Messages from Earth are routed automatically, and we don't have anybody out on an excursion so there won't be any calls from outside the dome. If anything goes wrong with the life-support systems the alarms will whoop everybody wide awake in two seconds.

He reached for the keyboard to shut down the computer, but the Martian images entranced him. They've been sitting on that wall for millions of years, he told himself. They can wait another couple of hours. Yet he kept staring at them as if he could make the symbols speak to him. He fell asleep in his chair in front of the computer screen.

BRIGHT MORNING SUNLIGHT SLANTED through the dome's transparent walls as Jamie stared at his desktop screen. His cubbyhole of an office was bare except for the laptop computer resting on the shaky folding table and the other, empty chair. The thin, flexible smart screens that he had taped to the cubicle's partitions were blank, gray. Only his laptop showed Dex Trumball's earnest face.

Dex had warned him to plug in the earphone for this message; he didn't want anyone to overhear it. Now, as Jamie sat listening to his proposal, he understood why.

"I know it goes against the grain, Jamie," Dex was saying, "but we've got to face the facts. If you want to keep the program going, this is the only way to get the funding you need."

Dex was at his home on Boston's North Shore, Jamie could see: in his darkly paneled den. Through the narrow window behind Dex, Jamie could see thickly leaved maple trees glowing red and gold in the afternoon sun. It must be autumn in New England, he thought in a separate part of his mind as he tried to digest what Dex was saying.

"It won't be like a swarm of tourists, Jamie. This'll be strictly a high-end operation. Rollie Kinnear figures he can get fifty million a pop. Fifty million each! If we ferry ten people to Mars for a week's visit, that's half a billion dollars, gross. Do that three, four times a year and we can support your people indefinitely."

Ten wealthy tourists, Jamie thought. Then ten more. Then twenty, twenty-five. A hundred. A thousand. They'll trample around here and ruin everything. We won't be able to get any work done. They'll want souvenirs: *Be the first in your crowd to bring back a rock from Mars! Look, I brought a piece of pottery from the Martian village!* Jamie shuddered.

"I've talked it over with the Navaho president and her council," Dex was going on. "They're not crazy about the idea but they'll go along with it because it can bring in money for them."

Let the palefaces have their little settlement by the water's edge, Jamie thought with the bitterness of tribal memory. There's only a few of them and the land is wide and free.

Dex was saying, "Um, the council voted to approve the plan, but only providing that you handle the operation from your end. You personally. They don't trust anybody else to take care of the tourists properly, see that they don't mess things up over there."

You want me to be the Judas, Jamie answered silently. Open up Mars to tourism and let Jamie take the responsibility.

He listened to Dex's words and watched his erstwhile friend's face closely as the man spoke. Dex's expression alternated from earnest enthusiasm to worried apprehension to an almost truculent insistence.

"I know you won't like this idea, Jamie, but it's the only way we can raise enough money to keep you guys going. Otherwise we're going to have to shut down the whole operation and bring you all back home."

And once we leave, your friends can come in and set up a wide-open tourism operation. *See the Martian cliff dwellings! Plant your footprints where no human being has stood before! Walk through an ancient Martian village!*

Strangely, Jamie felt no anger. Only a deep, aching, sullen remorse, the kind of pain that grips the heart when a dream is shattered.

Dex had finished talking. His image waited frozen on the laptop's small screen.

Jamie looked out through the open doorway of his cubicle toward the rusty red, rock-strewn ground. Mars is dying, he heard Zeke Larkin say. And he knew that Zeke was right. This is a dying world. And we're dying with it.

Fingering the communicator clipped to his ear, Jamie said, "Dex, the answer is no. Thanks for your effort. I know you think you're doing what needs to be done. But no. Not now. Not while I live."

He turned off the laptop, knowing it would take more than ten minutes for his reply to reach Earth. God knows how long it'll take Dex to react. Jamie shook his head. It doesn't matter what his reaction is. It doesn't matter if he quits the program altogether and cuts off his foundation's funding completely. None of that matters.

Yet Jamie feared he was wrong. He was cutting off the exploration team's lifeblood. While it might take a million

years for the last Martian lichen to shrivel and die from lack
of water, the human explorers on Mars would disappear in a
matter of months, for lack of funds.

BILLY GRAYCLOUD HAD RAISED his fist to rap on the partition of Dr. Waterman's office, but saw that Jamie was staring intently at his laptop screen, comm unit clipped to his ear.

He won't want to be disturbed, Graycloud thought. He
turned and went to the cafeteria, sipped briefly at a mug of
weak coffee, then walked back to the cubicle. The laptop was
closed now; Dr. Waterman was sitting stiffly in his little chair,
staring at infinity.

"Uh . . . Dr. W?"

Jamie stirred and focused on Graycloud. "Billy. What is it?"

"Got a minute?"

With a nod, "Sure. Come in."

Graycloud settled onto the only other chair in the cubbyhole, his long legs bumping the wobbly little table on which
the laptop sat, his knees poking up awkwardly.

"It's the translation, sir."

"What about it, Billy?"

"It's not goin' anyplace. I've tried about a hundred sets of
words, you know, definitions for each of the symbols—but
they don't make any sense."

Jamie smiled tiredly. "Maybe the hundred and first."

"Maybe."

"Or the thousandth."

Graycloud started to reply, hesitated, then asked, "Are we
gonna be here that long?"

SELENE: NANOLAB

∎

I haven't been in here since Kris Cardenas left for the Saturn habitat," said Doug Stavenger.

"She was a great scientist," Doreen McManus said.

"Still is, I suppose," Stavenger replied. "Way out there in orbit around Saturn."

Selene's nanotechnology laboratory was quiet and almost empty at this time of the evening. All the regular staff had left for the day. The reactors where virus-sized nanomachines were working ran silently, turning raw materials such as carbon powder into sheets of pure diamond structural material for spacecraft. New nanomachines were incubating in other reactors, behind sealed hatches.

Faint bluish light strips ran along the ceiling: ultraviolet lamps whose light could deactivate any nanodevices that somehow escaped the confinement of the reactors and incubators. Safety was a paramount concern in the nanolab, even after many years of secure operation. No one wanted an accident that unleashed all-consuming nanomachines into the underground community of Selene. No one dreaded the "gray goo problem" more than the scientists and technicians of the nanolab staff.

"This is my cubbyhole, here," Doreen said as she led Stavenger to a small desk at the end of a workbench.

He nodded, looked around, and pulled up a small wheeled chair as she sat in the padded desk chair.

She looks nervous, Stavenger thought: big gray-green eyes staring out like a frightened kid's.

"There's nothing to be frightened of," he said, trying to reassure her. "Dex Trumball isn't an ogre."

She tried to smile. "I know. It's just that . . . well, I know enough about Dr. Waterman. He's not going to like my proposal. Not at all."

Stavenger made a nonchalant shrug. "That's his decision. Right now I think you owe it to the people working on Mars to let Trumball know what you can do."

"Dr. Waterman's going to hate it," Doreen said in a small, almost whispering, voice.

"Be that as it may, your idea may save the entire Mars operation."

The desk phone chimed. Doreen flinched visibly at the sound. Stavenger glanced at his wristwatch. "He's right on time."

Dex Trumball's face took form on the phone screen. Stavenger introduced himself, then gestured toward Doreen. After the usual pleasantries, Stavenger got down to the point.

"Ms. McManus made a very interesting presentation to our governing board about the possibilities of using nanotechnology to enlarge the area on Mars where people can live and work. I thought that you and your Mars Foundation people ought to hear about it."

Trumball's sharp, hard eyes flicked from Stavenger to Doreen and back again. "Okay, I'm listening."

Doreen began to speak, hesitantly at first but then with growing confidence and enthusiasm.

After half an hour, Dex interrupted, "Wait a minute. You're saying that you can create a completely earthlike environment that's *kilometers* wide?"

"As large as you want it," Doreen said, nodding vigorously. "You can make it an ongoing operation, constantly enlarging the earthlike area."

"Under a dome," said Dex.

"Yes. It would have to be enclosed, of course."

Stavenger interjected, "It wouldn't be totally earthlike. The gravity would still be at the Martian level."

"That's not a problem," Dex said. "As long as people could live under the dome in a shirtsleeve environment."

"They could wear bikinis!" Doreen said.

Dex smiled. "Most of the tourists we'd bring to Mars would look awful in bikinis. But on the other hand . . ."

BOSTON: TRUMBALL TRUST HEADQUARTERS

■

More in sorrow than in anger, Dex said to himself. Remember that: more in sorrow than in anger. Jamie's a stubborn sonofabitch but that's who he is and there's no sense getting sore about it. You just have to do what you have to do.

Despite the brilliant sunshine and crystal blue sky, it was chilly up on the windswept roof of the Trumball Tower. Roland Kinnear was trying to smile bravely, but it was clear that the gusts whipping in from the harbor cut through his light summer-weight suit jacket and turned his perpetual smile into something of a grimace.

"Not like Hawaii," he said to Dex, raising his voice over the rush of the wind.

"You want to go back downstairs?" Dex asked.

Kinnear shrugged. "In a minute or two. I figure you brought me up here for a reason."

Dex studied his old schoolmate's round, normally cheerful face. "I wanted this conversation to be strictly private, Rollie. Just between you and me."

Kinnear's light blond brows furrowed. "You don't trust your staff?"

"Sure I do," Dex said. "But I don't want to run the risk of somebody accidentally overhearing us."

Kinnear thought that over for a moment, then asked, "Can we get out of this wind, at least?"

Dex laughed, then took Kinnear by the elbow and led him to the other side of the roof where they were sheltered by the bulk of the structure that housed the building's cooling tower. From this angle he could see the city's busy streets, and across the Charles River the gray, utilitarian buildings of the Massachusetts Institute of Technology. Harvard's redbrick Colonial-style campus was off to their left, half hidden among the flaming trees in their autumnal colors. Farther on toward the horizon, past more colorful trees and stately slim white church steeples, was Lexington and the common where a handful of Minutemen had tried to make a stand against the British army.

"It's pretty," Kinnear said, "with all the trees in color."

"They say we might even get some snow this winter," Dex said, wistfully. "It looks beautiful all in white."

Out of the wind, Kinnear relaxed enough to put his pleasant smile back on. "So what do you want to talk about, Dex?"

"Mars. What else?"

"You're in bad shape, from what I hear."

"We're bleeding to death," Dex admitted. "That damned priest's just about killed us."

"He didn't do himself any good, either." Kinnear grinned.

"Yeah, yeah, but now we've got people blaming *us* for his death. We're getting really nasty mail, calling us priest killers, making threats."

"Anything serious?"

"I've doubled our security. There's a lot of nuts out there." Dex shook his head. "Priest killers," he muttered.

"So your money flow . . . ?"

"Down to a trickle. Less."

"I still think the tourism idea could fly," Kinnear said, obviously trying to brighten Dex's mood.

"That's what I want to talk to you about."

"My people tell me Waterman turned you down flat."

"You've got a line into my private office," Dex said. "I figured as much."

Widening his smile, Kinnear said, "We're talking a ton of money here, Dex. I have to protect my investment."

"You haven't spent a dime, Rollie."

"Well, I might have. But the Navaho chief nixed it, did he?"

Nodding, "I expected he would."

"So, do you go over his head?"

"Can't. The Navaho council has the final word on what we can or can't do on Mars."

"But they voted in favor of the tourist plan, didn't they?"

"Yes, but they won't go against Jamie. If he says no they'll go along with him."

"Shit. They'd turn down all that money?"

"They would and they will."

Kinnear pursed his lips. "Well, that's that, I guess."

A jet airliner from Logan Aerospaceport, across the Inner Harbor, roared over them, making conversation impossible for a few moments. Dex used the time to frame the words he had to speak.

"Rollie, there's a way we can get this done," he said, as the airliner's thunder diminished in the distance.

Kinnear looked askance at him.

"It works like this," Dex said, wondering if he could really go through with it. "Without your tourist money, the Mars Foundation goes bust."

"But you've got other sources of funding, don't you?"

"It's not enough. We've got enough in the bank to finance one more resupply flight to Mars. After that, if we don't get an injection of new funding we're going to have to shut down the operation on Mars and bring everybody home."

"And that's that."

Dex shook his head. "No, that's just the beginning. I'll see to it that when the people leave Mars they mothball their base, you know, wrap up all the equipment, seal the domes they've been using, keep it all ready for somebody else to use."

Kinnear's smile widened. "You're starting to interest me, Dex."

"Once the last of them has left Mars, the Navaho no longer have their claim to the place. It's open for grabs."

"And we grab it!"

"We send a skeleton team to the base and reopen it, then claim exclusive use of the area for Kinnear Travel, Inc."

"Holy shit! Would that be legal?"

"Perfectly legal. The Mars Foundation will be your partner, Rollie. You and me together. What's more, I've got some experts from Selene who can build a completely shirtsleeve environment for the tourists. Let 'em wander through the village and the cliff dwellings without using a spacesuit."

"Tourists on Mars. Hot damn!"

"Scientists, too," Dex said quickly. "We'll bring scientists back, but they'll be working under our direction."

"Sure, sure, we'd need a few scientists to work as guides for the tourists."

"And to continue their own studies, Rollie. I want to carry on with the work they're trying to do now."

"Yeah, okay. We could even bring your pal Waterman back—but under our terms."

"Jamie?" Dex was truly surprised at the thought. "No, he won't go back. Not if we're running the show. He hates the whole idea of bringing tourists to Mars."

"So? What's he going to do?"

Feeling truly sad, Dex said, "He'll probably commit suicide. Or murder."

■

Sitting tensely in the little bungee-cord chair in his office cubicle, Jamie asked, "So what do you think?"

Maurice Zeroual looked equally tense. He was a logistics specialist from Selene who had come to Tithonium Base on the resupply flight a few weeks earlier. Born in Algeria, Zeroual had fled to the Moon when his nation dissolved into murderous sectarian violence. He had volunteered to study the possibilities of making the Mars base self-sufficient.

He did not look happy. Zeroual was a smallish man, wearing a loose-fitting white shirt and gray slacks. His skin was as dark as scorched tobacco leaf. A thin fringe of a beard outlined his jaw. Jamie thought he smelled a strange cologne: like mint, or some oriental spice.

"I haven't completely finished my analysis," Zeroual began, in a soft tenor voice with a definite British accent.

"But you've learned enough to ask to meet with me," Jamie said, also softly, trying to encourage the younger man to speak freely.

"I can see the general picture clearly enough, yes."

"And?"

Zeroual's dark brown eyes shifted away from Jamie's. "There's no way you can continue to support two hundred people here. Not with the resources available to you."

Jamie took in a breath. I expected that, he said to himself. Aloud, he asked, "How many?"

"At best, maybe thirty."

"Thirty?"

"The optimal number would be somewhere around half that. Say, fifteen people. You could support fifteen people here indefinitely with the food you raise in the greenhouse and the amount of additional supplies that Selene can afford to send you."

"Fifteen people."

Zeroual leaned forward, rested his palms on his knees. "Of course, if you can obtain some continued funding from your Mars Foundation you could enlarge that number slightly."

Nodding, Jamie said, "The Foundation can provide a trickle of money, I suppose. I don't know for how long, though."

"I'd advise that any funding you get from the Foundation should be devoted to enlarging your greenhouse," Zeroual said earnestly. "If you can enlarge your resource base, even just a little at a time, you can support more people."

"Like the Old Ones," Jamie muttered.

"Excuse me?"

"The original people who settled in the southwestern United States, a thousand years ago or more," Jamie explained. "They had to survive in a very harsh, very arid environment. They learned how to grow crops with precious little water. They learned to survive."

Zeroual nodded. "Ah. Yes. Something like that. You'll have to learn to survive in a harsh environment. With very little help from outside."

WASHINGTON, D.C.: SENATE INVESTIGATION COMMITTEE

∎

S tate your name and affiliation, please."
"Franklin Haverford Overmire. I have the honor to be archbishop of the New Morality Church."

Archbishop Overmire looked tanned, vigorously healthy and completely at ease at the witness table, smiling at the senators arrayed across the front of the room. He wore his customary custom-tailored black suit. His light brown hair was cut just short of his clerical collar.

The clerk offered a Bible to Overmire; the archbishop placed his beringed right hand lightly upon it.

"Do you swear that the testimony you are about to give this committee will be the entire truth?"

"Of course."

Morning sunlight beamed through the long windows of the committee chamber. At the head of the room sat the senators; every member of the committee was there. Every row of spectators' benches was filled. The side aisles were crammed with news media camera teams.

The committee chairman, a crusty white-haired veteran of decades of Washington infighting, hunched over his pencil-slim microphone and announced in a grating voice, "The purpose of this investigation is to determine if the death of a member of the exploration crew on Mars was caused by negligence."

He paused dramatically, then added, "Or if the conditions

on Mars are too dangerous to allow human exploration there to continue."

Sitting in the front row of benches directly behind the witness table, Dex Trumball fingered the subpoena he had folded into his jacket pocket. The committee lawyer who had personally presented the subpoena to him in Boston had promised that Dex would be called on the first day of the hearings. But he wondered why Archbishop Overmire had been asked to appear. What's he got to testify about? Dex asked himself. All he knows about Mars is that he's against our exploring it.

Besides, this committee can't shut down our program. The government isn't funding us and they can't stop us. This hearing is strictly public-relations crap, a chance for these politicians to get their faces on the news.

Sure enough, after the first few powder-puff questions, the senator from Overmire's state of Georgia was granted the floor. She was a youngish-looking woman with ash blond hair, slightly plump, with a high voice that reminded Dex of the whining of a handheld power drill.

"Archbishop Overmire," she began, smiling broadly enough to make dimples, "the official report of Monsignor DiNardo's death on Mars states that he suffered a paralytic stroke."

"So I understand," said the archbishop.

"Our investigation has determined that he had a preexisting cardiac problem, yet he was allowed to make the journey to Mars."

"Scientific hubris," the archbishop replied.

"You mean that the scientists directing the exploration of Mars didn't investigate his health deeply enough to determine that he was suffering from cardiac disease?"

"Not exactly."

"Or they ignored the fact that Monsignor DiNardo was ill? They allowed him to risk his life knowingly?"

Overmire shook his head slightly. "I'm afraid that the late Monsignor DiNardo thought of himself as a scientist ahead of his being a priest of the Roman Catholic Church. He wanted to work on Mars so badly that he was willing to tempt God."

Dex felt his face flame.

"Tempt God, Archbishop?" prompted the senator.

"Matthew, chapter 4, verse 7: Thou shalt not tempt the Lord your God."

The senator's smile changed subtly. "You believe that Monsignor DiNardo tempted God by going to Mars, despite his illness?"

"What else? He chose secular humanism over his Lord and Savior and suffered the consequences."

"Then his death wasn't an accident?"

"It was divine justice."

Dex fought down a sudden urge to puke. This isn't an investigation, he realized. It's a fucking inquisition.

TITHONIUM CHASMA: THE DIG

■

Zeke Larkin laid his digging spade on his shoulder as he and Alonzo Jenkins trudged through the morning sunshine from the dome's main airlock toward the dig.

Lonzo, a stubby, dark-skinned postdoc geochemist from Toronto, was singing his usual lament, ". . . picked up my shovel and walked to th' mine. Loaded sixteen tons of number nine coal and th' straw boss said—"

"Don't you know any other songs?" Larkin asked, half annoyed, half amused.

"None that's so appropriate."

The rest of the digging crew were already standing around the edge of the pit in their nanofabric suits. Carleton was nowhere in sight.

"Where's our taskmaster?" Larkin asked, turning back toward the airlock.

Sure enough, Carleton came through the hatch in his bulky hard-shell suit. He's too goddamned stubborn to switch to a nanosuit, Larkin thought. Like it's going to damage his reputation if he gives in and admits the nanos are better.

Carleton strode to the edge of the dig, his face hidden behind the reflective visor of his helmet. "All right," he said, "let's get to work."

Larkin realized that Carleton didn't give him any specific instructions. After his blowup with the anthropologist two days earlier, he'd stayed away from the dig. But Jamie Waterman had stepped into his lab the previous evening to tell him that Dr. Chang had rearranged his schedule and he was expected at the excavation site the next morning.

So he stood with his spade on his shoulder, like an infantryman with his rifle, as all the others started down the ramp and into the pit.

"Larkin, you go with Jenkins and help him with the digging out by the old riverbed," Carleton said, his voicing sounding tight, edgy in Larkin's earphone.

Suppressing an instinct to give the anthropologist a military salute, Larkin said merely, "Right. Okay."

But he hesitated. "Dr. Carleton . . ."

"What?"

"Over on the other side of the village, where I was digging a couple of days ago—"

"When you decided to quit?" Carleton snapped.

Larkin sucked in a breath.

"Well?" Carleton demanded.

"Nothing," said Larkin. And he started down the ramp to catch up with Jenkins. Why bother? he thought. So there's some bumps in the ground out there. So what? It's probably not important. And even if it is, he's too pigheaded to listen to me. I'm on his shitlist, big time.

AS THE DAY WORE on, though, Larkin kept thinking about the seemingly empty ground on the other side of the village. He and Jenkins were just going through the motions, he realized. They were digging through the layers of accumulated stone that had once been the bed of the river that flowed through the valley.

Look for possible fossils, Carleton had told them. Yeah, sure, thought Larkin. Like we'd be able to tell what's a fossil from what's an ordinary rock. On Earth you might turn up a fragment of a seashell, or the bones of some animal. But on Earth you'd recognize them for what they are. What do Martian seashells look like? How can I tell if this flat rock is just a rock or maybe it was once a turtle's shell? No way to know.

Like trying to decipher those hieroglyphics from the buildings up on the cliff. We've got nothing to compare them to.

Still his mind kept returning to the memory of those slight, barely perceptible ridges in the ground out in the empty area on the other side of the village. You can hardly make them out, Larkin said to himself. Only when the sunlight slants in at the end of the day, that's when you can see them.

Do they mean anything? Probably not. And yet—they're *regular*, like a pattern. Not random.

His spade struck a hard, stubborn layer of rock with an impact that sent a shudder up his arms. Damn! Like the pirates in *Treasure Island* when they hit the buried treasure chest.

"Hey, Lonzo," he called. "Gimme a hand here."

"Whatcha got?" Jenkins asked, straightening up tiredly from his own digging.

"Maybe a whale," Larkin wisecracked.

Jenkins came over and the two of them began digging carefully around the hard object. It took more than an hour, but they finally cleared all the compacted dust from it.

"Some whale," Jenkins grumbled, panting from the exertion. "It's just a goddamned big flat rock."

Larkin stared at it. Maybe a geologist could make something out of it, but he had to agree with Lonzo: it was nothing more than a big flat rock.

"A lot of work for nothing," Larkin said.

"Yeah, but you never know. Might've been a whale. Or a dinosaur. You don't know till you've done the work to uncover it."

Larkin shook his head inside the inflated bubble of his helmet. "What's that song of yours say? 'Another day older and deeper in debt'?"

"Exactly." Jenkins looked up at the sky. "Well, this day's just about over. We've loaded our sixteen tons, right?"

"Right. Let's head for the showers."

But when they got to the ramp that led up to the lip of the excavation, Larkin told his partner, "You go on, Lonzo. I want to look at something."

Jenkins shrugged inside his nanosuit and started up the ramp. Larkin walked through the remains of the village, past the dark square shapes of building foundations laid out in neat geometric order, and out to the edge of the empty space.

The sun was low enough to throw those slight banks of ground into high relief. Another few minutes and the sun'll sink down past the edge of the pit, Larkin thought. Then it'll all go into shadow.

He hunkered down to his knees, then leaned forward and put his head on the ground, squinting at the faint, faint rows of raised mounds.

"What are you doing?" Carleton's voice sounded more annoyed than curious.

Getting up to a kneeling position, Larkin called back, "There's a pattern here."

"A pattern? What are you talking about?"

"Come over here and take a look. Quick, before the sun goes down too far."

Turning to look over his shoulder, Larkin saw Carleton's cumbersome hard suit clumping slowly toward him, like some robot monster from a horror vid.

"Come on," Larkin urged. "Faster."

Carleton lumbered up to him. "What pattern? I don't see any—"

"Get down. You can barely make it out, but if you get down you can see the shadows."

Muttering to himself, Carleton slowly, awkwardly lowered himself to his hands and knees. "If this is some kind of a practical joke . . ."

"Lower. Quick, the sun's almost down."

Carleton slowly, carefully got down flat on his belly. Larkin fought back a laugh. The anthropologist looked like a beached mechanical whale.

"What pat—" Carleton's breath caught in his throat.

"You see it?" Larkin urged.

"Rectangles! Laid out in orderly rows!"

"Yeah!"

"Do you know what this is?" Carleton's voice was brimming with excitement.

"Their farm?"

"Farm, hell! This is their cemetery! I'll bet my life on it! We've found their cemetery!"

Larkin started to frown at the word "we," but then he thought, What the hell. He wants to horn in on the credit, so what? If he's right . . .

He sat there, squatting on his knees with Carleton stretched out prone beside him in the bulky hard suit, until the sun dipped below the edge of the excavation and the area darkened into shadow.

"All right," Carleton said, sounding excited. "All right. Now what we've got to do is—ugh!"

"What? What do we have to do?"

"Get me back on my feet! I can't get up in this damned hard-shell."

Larkin laughed and tried to pull Carleton up. He had to call two other men to help him.

TITHONIUM BASE: DISCUSSION

■

J amie asked to use Chang's office for this meeting of the team's three key people to decide on the future of the exploration effort. He began by explaining the conclusions of the logistics study that Maurice Zeroual had headed.

"We can afford to maintain fifteen people on Mars," he told them. "That's all that the Mars Foundation can support, even with help from Selene."

"Fifteen people?" The shock broke through Chang Laodong's normal impassivity. "Not enough. Impossible."

"That would really be a skeleton crew," quipped Carter Carleton.

Jamie nodded grimly. "Skeleton, as in dead."

Carleton nodded.

The other person in Chang's office was Nari Quintana. She sat in one of the chairs that flanked the low coffee table, her legs tucked under her, her brown eyes flicking from one man to the next.

Jamie, on the sofa beside Chang, asked her, "Dr. Quintana, would reducing the number of people here to fifteen or so present any special medical problems?"

She hesitated a moment, then replied, "I can't see where it would. Except that I would probably have to help in some of the other work, like Carter's excavation."

"You would stay?" Jamie asked. "Under those circumstances?"

Quintana nodded slowly.

"Indefinitely?" Jamie prodded. "I don't know how frequently we'd be able to bring resupply flights in."

"There's a flight due in next month, isn't there?"

Chang said, "That is the last scheduled flight."

"There'll be one more," Jamie said, his voice almost choking. "To take most of the staff home."

"Evacuation flight," said Chang. "Yes. But no further resupply flight for at least one year."

"One year," Quintana echoed. She took a deep breath, obviously juggling several possibilities in her mind. "I will stay. But not forever, of course."

"Of course."

Chang said, "I will have to return to Earth."

Jamie turned toward him. "No, that's not necessary."

Chang closed his eyes briefly. "Very necessary. I am an administrator, not a working scientist. I cannot dig in Dr. Carleton's pit. I should not fill a position on a geology team that a younger, more vigorous man could occupy. When the evacuation flight comes, I will leave on it."

Jamie wanted to say something, but he could not think of any words.

"All right," Carleton said impatiently. "Are we finished? I've got to get out to the dig. We're starting to probe their cemetery."

Jamie held up one hand. "Be patient a bit, will you?"

"But—"

"Your wife should be part of this discussion," Quintana said. "She's our psychologist. Emotional questions will be just as important as medical, if you plan to reduce the staff here to fifteen."

"You're right," Jamie said. As he fished for his phone in his shirt pocket he couldn't help thinking, We're shriveling away, just like the lichen. But it won't take a million years for us to disappear from Mars.

Carleton, sitting across the low table from Quintana, shook his head impatiently. "Just when we're about to hit pay dirt. We've located their cemetery. I've got an engineering team rigging up a deep-radar set so we can use it to see what's buried there before we start digging."

"Do you really believe it's the cemetery?" Quintana asked.

"I'm certain of it." Jabbing a finger at her, Carleton went on, "In another week we'll be uncovering the remains of the Martians who lived in that village. We'll be making epochal discoveries, learning what they looked like, how they treated their dead. And now this. Reduce our work force to fifteen. It's as if they don't want us to find anything."

"They?" Quintana asked.

"The fundamentalists. The idiots who're running the governments back Earthside. And everything else."

Chang almost smiled. "Perhaps they are right. Perhaps God does not want you to make discoveries."

Carleton glared at him.

"I was joking," Chang said.

Jamie clicked his phone shut. "Vijay will join us in a few moments."

Chang sighed, then said to Carleton, "Many discoveries will remain undone. The new crater that the meteor impact made. The search for other villages. Stratigraphy mapping. South polar cap's melting. None of that. With fifteen people they can only stay here at base. No excursions."

"My excavation will slow down to a crawl," Carleton muttered.

Someone tapped at the office door, then slid it open. Vijay stepped in, wearing coral coveralls with a bright orange and yellow scarf tied around her waist. Jamie moved over on the sofa to make room for her to sit between him and Chang.

"We're discussing the problems that might arise when the staff here is reduced to fifteen people," Jamie explained.

"The question of psychological problems came up," said Quintana.

Vijay glanced at Jamie, then turned to face the others and began, "Yes, the emotional pressures of having only a dozen or so people will certainly increase. 'Specially at the outset. It'll be painfully clear that we're here on a shoestring."

"What do you see as major problems?" Chang asked.

"Fear," she replied immediately. "We've all got a certain amount of fear to deal with, but most of the time we keep it bottled up inside. Remember when that meteor hit, a couple weeks ago? The fear came out then, di'n't it?"

Quintana mused, "With only fifteen people . . ."

"The fear quotient will grow, of course. It'll show up in different ways. Moodiness. Irritability. Aggression, in some." She looked directly at Carleton.

"Physical aggression?" Jamie asked.

"Maybe sexual," Carleton said. "Fifteen people is a damned small gene pool."

THAT NIGHT, AS JAMIE climbed wearily into bed, Vijay asked, "Well, d'you think your meeting accomplished anything?"

"A little," he said, pulling the thin cover over himself. "Chang said he'd leave. Carleton figures that digging up his village is about all we can do with just fifteen people."

"Nari's planning to stay?"

He turned toward her. "Yes. She said she'd stay indefinitely."

"Good."

Jamie turned off the lamp on the night table. Their bedroom went dark, except for the faint greenish glow of the digital clock's display.

"You di'n't tell them about the other option, did you," Vijay said. It was a statement, not a question.

Jamie didn't reply.

"Dex's plan," Vijay added. "You could keep more'n a hundred scientists here if you let Dex have his way."

"I'm not turning Mars into a tourist resort."

For a heartbeat or two Vijay didn't reply. At last she murmured, "You could at least consider it, love. You could be a bit more flexible."

"No."

She slid her body against his and ran a hand down his abdomen, to his crotch. "Y'know, love, a hard man is good to find, true enough. But sometimes you've got to bend a little."

Jamie closed his eyes as he felt his body tingle beneath her hand. "You're using your feminine wiles on me."

"Just asking you to think clearly, love. Look at all your options. Don't make up your mind until you've explored the different paths that're open to you."

He grunted. "You sound like my grandfather."

He could hear the smile in her voice. "I make you think of your grandfather?"

Jamie reached for her. "You're a damned good psychologist, you know."

"That's right, love. And now it's time for some physical therapy."

IN BOSTON IT WAS well past seven P.M.

"Are you going to hide in here all night? We're almost ready to serve dinner and you haven't even said hello to our guests yet." Dex's wife was frowning at him from the doorway of the big old house's library. Wearing a skintight, low-cut gown of gold lamé, she held a stemmed martini glass in one hand.

Dex looked up from the phone screen and forced a smile. "Just another minute or two. Tell the cook that he works for me, not the other way round."

His wife's frown deepened, but she said nothing further, just turned and swept grandly out of his sight.

"Sorry for the interruption," Dex said to the image in the phone screen.

Rollie Kinnear grinned at him. "Hey, I've got a wife, too."

Dex could see it was midafternoon in Hawaii. Rollie was stretched out on the lanai of his beachfront home, dark glasses over his eyes, garishly bright shirt flapping in the sea breeze.

"She's throwing a dinner party," Dex muttered.

"Trying to raise money for you?"

"I wish. She couldn't care less about Mars."

"So when do you tell your Indian pal that you're shutting down the whole operation?"

Dex sucked in a breath. "It's going to just about kill Jamie, you know."

"Hey, you know what general Sheridan said about good Indians." Kinnear laughed.

"I can't do it in a goddamned message," said Dex, surprised at his own words. "This is something that's got to be done face-to-face."

"So bring him back home and tell him," Kinnear said, his smile shrinking. "I've got investors who're hot to trot. But they won't stay hot forever, you know."

"I know," Dex said, as he realized what must be done. "There's a flight going to Mars in three weeks. I'll go out on it and tell Jamie what's going down."

"To Mars? How long's it going to take you to get all the way out there?"

"Less than a week. The fusion torch ships are fast."

"Can't be fast enough," Kinnear said, totally serious now. "I want to get this deal finalized, Dex. We're talking major bucks here, pal."

"I know," Dex replied. Silently he added, And we're dealing with a man's life.

THE VILLAGE

∎

It was the same dream.

Jamie walked through the village, an unseen ghost among the Martians. They were going about their various businesses as the warm sun baked their adobe structures. Try as he might, Jamie could not get a clear vision of them. He knew they were all around him, moving through the narrow packed-dirt streets, but he couldn't quite make out what they looked like.

Up on the cliff face far above him the temple buildings stood white and clear in the sunshine. Jamie stood for a long time in the village's central square and stared up at the temple complex.

Maybe I can go up there and ask them what their writing means, he said to himself. He saw that there were steps carved into the nearly vertical cliff wall. A rugged climb, he thought. They must be terrific climbers.

"Ya'aa'tey!"

Whirling around, Jamie saw his grandfather Al, once again in his best black leather vest and the hat with the big drooping brim and silver band circling its crown.

"Ya'aa'tey," Jamie replied happily, reaching both hands toward his grandfather.

"How's it goin', Jamie?" Al asked. "Makin' any progress?"

"The whites want to bring tourists here," Jamie said. In his own ears his voice sounded as if he were nine years old.

"Naw, they can't get here. Not here."

"That's right," Jamie said, feeling relieved. "This village doesn't exist anymore, does it?"

Al grinned at him, dentures white and even in his weathered, seamed face.

"You don't get it, do you, grandson? They can't come here because this village don't exist yet."

TITHONIUM CHASMA: THE GRAVEYARD

∎

Fifteen people, Jamie thought as he stared at his computer display. Fifteen men and women. Who's going to stay? Who'd want to stay, under these conditions?

I can't ask Vijay to risk it, he told himself. She'd want to stay with me, but it's not fair for me to keep her here. But I can't send her away, either. I promised her we'd be together, whatever happened. If I stay, she stays. She won't want to leave, not without me. And I've got to stay here. I've got to.

His pocket phone buzzed. Flicking it open, he saw Billy Graycloud's face in the tiny screen. The kid was outside at the dig, clear nanofabric bubble over his head.

"Dr. W, we've cleared one grave. You oughtta see it before they start takin' the bones out."

"Right," said Jamie. "I'll be there in a minute."

He jumped up from his chair so fast he banged a knee against the wobbly folding table and nearly knocked his laptop to the floor. Stuffing the phone back into his shirt pocket, Jamie rushed to the suit lockers by the main airlock hatch and hurriedly pulled on a nanosuit.

"Not so fast, please."

Jamie looked up and saw the diminutive Kristin Dvorak, one of the astronauts.

"I am the safety officer today," she said, in her Middle European accent. "You rush too much, you kill yourself."

Jamie smiled sheepishly. "I know. It's just—"

Kristin held up a finger. "I'll check you out. Make sure you're sealed up good."

He stood there like a suspect in a police shakedown while she walked all around him, checking his suit seals, his life-support backpack and their connections to the suit's metal collar.

"Hokay," she said, her ballerina-slim face utterly serious. "Now pull up the hood and inflate it."

Jamie did as he was told. Then she checked the transmission from the radio clipped to his ear. At last Kristin smiled and said, "You are clear for excursion. Have a pleasant day."

Jamie grinned at her and ducked through the airlock hatch.

Once outside he loped across the stony ground to the edge of the excavation and down the ramp to its bottom. A small crowd was standing off at the far side of the pit, where the cemetery lay. Jamie couldn't see Carleton among them.

"Dr. W!" Graycloud's voice. "Come and see this!"

Jamie made his way along the central street of the long-buried village, ancient building foundations dark and low against the reddish ground on either side of him. Nobody was working among them, he saw. They're all at the graveyard.

"We waited for you, Jamie," said Carter Carleton. Jamie was surprised to see him in a nanosuit instead of his usual hard-shell.

"I'm sorry if I held you up," he said, panting a little from his trotting.

Carleton seemed strangely subdued. "He's waited sixty-five million years. A few more minutes won't bother him."

There were eight men and women standing at the edge of the grave, Billy Graycloud among them. Jamie was surprised to see Mo Zeroual, too. What's a number cruncher from Selene doing out here? he asked himself. He must have volunteered.

Jamie looked down into the uncovered grave. It was filled with odd-looking bones, crushed by the weight of eons, flattened, distorted. But he thought he could make out what looked like a spine, and maybe those were limbs. Six of them?

"That's a Martian?" he whispered.

"That's a Martian," Carleton replied, his voice also hushed, choked. "And more."

Jamie glanced at the anthropologist, then looked back into the grave.

Pointing, Carleton said, "Those look like beads, don't you think? And that little object there might have been a small vase or a cup of some sort."

"It's hard to tell," said Jamie.

"It's all been flattened by the overburden," Carleton said, still half-whispering. "It's going to take some time to put it all together and find out how they were actually built."

"Six legs?" Jamie asked.

Carleton nodded inside his bubble helmet. "At least. Two of them end in grasping appendages. Hands. See?"

"Hard to tell," Jamie repeated.

Graycloud spoke up. "They must've been built close to the ground. Like turtles."

"Not necessarily," said Carleton. "The skeleton's been flattened by the weight of thirty meters of soil pressing down on it."

Someone else made a comment, and Carleton answered. But Jamie stared into the grave and saw at last the Martians that he had dreamed about. They didn't look human at all, but they had legs and arms and hands, eyes and ears, they spoke a language and wrote pictographs and built this village and the shrine high up on the canyon wall. They had minds. We could have communicated with them, if only . . .

Carleton sank to his knees and bent to reach into the grave.

"Careful!" one of the group gasped.

"I know," said Carleton, leaning over. His gloved fingers reached for the flattened, odd-shaped bone at one end of the skeleton. It was only slightly larger than his hand, mottled rusty gray, hard looking.

Holding it up in his hands like a kneeling worshiper raising a holy grail, Carleton said, "This is a cranium. Got to be."

"The brain case isn't all that big."

"Are those eye sockets?"

"They look straight ahead. Binocular vision."

"They saw things in depth: three-dimensional vision, just like us."

Resting back on his haunches, Carleton turned the fossil around in his hands. "Ha. See this?" He pointed with his free hand.

Jamie saw a hole in the back of the skull.

"Foramen magnum, I'll bet my last breath on it," Carleton said in a strangely hushed, almost worshipful voice. "This is where the spinal cord went through the cranium to connect with the brain."

"If its brain was in its cranium," one of the biologists said.

Ignoring the remark, Carleton went on, "It must have been four-legged."

"Or six?"

"It held its body horizontal to the ground. It didn't stand upright, the way we do."

Jamie thought that was a lot to assume in the first five minutes of examination, but he said nothing. This was Carleton's moment and he was entitled to his surmises. Who knows? Jamie asked himself. He might even be right.

Carleton slapped his gloved hands together, startling Jamie out of his musings. "All right," he said, his voice loud and commanding now. "We start removing the bones, one piece at a time. I want a complete photographic record. Every clod, every molecule we remove has got to be recorded down to the nanometer. This is history, people! Let's get to work!"

And Jamie heard his grandfather's enigmatic words: *This village don't exist yet.*

TITHONIUM BASE: THE TRANSLATION

■

Jamie helped Carleton and his team to tenderly lift the fossilized bones out of the grave, together with the beads and shards of pottery that lay with the body, and carry them inside the dome. Under Carleton's exacting direction, they laid everything on the big stereo table in exactly the same positions as they had been in the grave.

Two technicians spent the next hour taking stereo photographs of the remains, while Carleton's people gathered in the cafeteria to relax after a long, exciting, tension-filled day. Jamie went with them.

"Well, they buried their dead, all right," said Alonzo Jenkins as he lounged back in a cafeteria chair, legs stretched out and a plastic glass of fruit juice in his hand.

"With trinkets," added Shirley Macintyre, one of the medical technicians who had volunteered to help at the dig. She was in her midtwenties, and had dropped out of astronaut training in Britain to join the medical team on Mars. Tall, lean and muscular, she had been pursued by several of the men but stayed aloof from them all.

"They must have believed in an afterlife," Billy Graycloud said softly. Eyebrows went up; people looked surprised that Graycloud would speak up.

Jamie smiled at the young man and said, "So they must have had some form of religion."

Everyone nodded.

"I wonder how much they were like us," murmured one of the men.

"Or we're like them."

"Not physically," said Jamie. "We don't look anything alike."

"But mentally?"

"Spiritually?"

"They lived in villages," Jamie said, ticking off points on his fingers. "They had a rudimentary form of writing. They buried their dead—"

"With beads and pottery," Macintyre interjected.

"Like Billy said, they believed in an afterlife," said Jenkins. "So they must have had some kind of religion."

"That's the basis for religion, sure enough."

They looked up to see Carter Carleton walking toward them from the juice dispensers, a glass in his hand, a happy smile on his handsome face.

"The promise of life beyond death," Jenkins said. "That's what religion's all about."

"It's a powerful lure," Carleton said, joining the conversation as he sat himself next to Macintyre. "It's pure nonsense, of course, but it's certainly suckered people into accepting religion everywhere, even on Mars."

"What do you mean, it's nonsense?" Macintyre asked. "How can you be sure?"

"Catholic, aren't you?" said Carleton, frowning slightly. "You've had it pounded into your skull since before you could walk."

Jenkins objected, "That's not fair, Dr. Carleton. Everyone's entitled to their beliefs."

"Besides," Macintyre said, "there's a lot more to religion than the promise of an afterlife. There's the whole ethical basis. Society would be impossible without religion's ethical teachings."

Carleton smirked. "Like 'Thou shalt not kill'? Except when your church says it's okay. Like the Crusades: kill the Saracens! Or the suicide bombers: kill the unbelievers!"

"They were extremists."

"Were they? How about the good Christians back in the USA who've made homosexuality a crime in their states? Outlawed abortion. Hell, they're even trying to make all forms of family planning illegal."

"They're acting on their beliefs," Macintyre insisted.

Jamie got to his feet and left them arguing. To himself he thought, How about the religious believers who don't want us here on Mars? How about the terrorists who set off those bombs back at the university? How about—

"Dr. W?"

Jamie broke out of his thoughts and saw Billy Graycloud walking beside him.

"Had enough of the debate?" he asked.

Graycloud smiled shyly. "I figure they'll start asking me about my religious beliefs pretty soon. I don't want to get involved in it."

"Smart lad," Jamie said. "We've got enough to do without getting into arguments over religion. They'll start yelling at each other pretty soon."

"I guess. Nothing like religion to start people fightin'."

Jamie smiled bitterly. "When you're sure you're right, when you've been told all your life that these beliefs are the absolute truth . . ." He shook his head. "People have done horrible things in the name of religion."

They walked side by side toward Jamie's quarters.

"I guess that's why they're scared of science," Graycloud muttered, as much to himself as to Jamie. "Scientists don't talk about truth. They look for facts."

"And we change our minds, too, when new facts contradict what we believed."

Graycloud nodded. He looked to Jamie as if he was about to say something, but he stopped himself and remained silent.

"Is there something else?"

Graycloud pursed his lips, as if searching his memory. "Well, yeah, there is."

Jamie waited for the youngster to go on. After several silent steps he prodded, "What is it, Billy?"

Frowning slightly, Graycloud said, "The translation."

"Getting anywhere?"

"Kinda. Maybe. I'm not sure."

"What's the problem?"

"Could you come over to the comm center? I can show you what I've done so far."

Nodding, Jamie changed course and walked with Graycloud to the communications center. The place was silent except for the hum of the consoles. Two women were on duty, chatting quietly together, headphones clipped to their ears while their display screens flickered with routine messages. Graycloud sat at an unused console and booted up the computer. Jamie pulled one of the little wheeled chairs over beside him and sat on it.

The screen showed the inscriptions carved into the wall of the cliff structure. Graycloud scrolled the screen's cursor to the image of a circle with short lines emanating from it, north, south, east and west.

"Okay," Graycloud said, licking his lips. "That one I call the sun."

"Father Sun," Jamie murmured. "Like the Navaho sun symbol."

"Right. Okay. That one's easy. Now this one . . ." The cursor drifted to a wriggly pair of lines and stopped. "This one might mean 'water.' Or 'river.'"

"That's reasonable," said Jamie.

"And this one . . ." The cursor swung to a bulbous symbol that reminded Jamie of a head of broccoli. "Might be 'tree' or 'plant.'"

"Or 'crops,'" Jamie suggested.

Graycloud's brows hiked up. "Yeah. Crops. Could be."

Jamie patted the younger man's shoulder. "You're making progress, Billy."

"Am I?" Graycloud turned toward him and Jamie could see the doubt and worry in his eyes. "Or am I just screwin' around?"

"Progress," Jamie said firmly.

Graycloud shook his head warily. "I don't know, Dr. W. All I'm really doing is assigning our words to their symbols. Arbitrarily. How do we know the circle means the sun? It might mean 'crater' or 'beach ball,' for all we know."

Jamie almost laughed. "Probably not 'beach ball.'"

"But you see the problem?" Graycloud said, almost pleading. "I'm just assigning *our* meanings to *their* symbols. It's GIGO: garbage in, garbage out."

For a moment Jamie said nothing, thinking hard as he looked at this earnest young man and considered his problem. At last he said, "The proof will be in the message you get out of the symbols, Billy. When you run these meanings through the computer, will a meaningful message come out of them or will it be meaningless nonsense?"

"But we could be fooling ourselves."

"How?"

"I mean, even if we get a message that seems to have some meaning to it, it could be just the meaning we put into it. It could have nothing to do with what the Martians wanted to say."

"I see."

"I could be wasting my time here."

Jamie smiled. "Billy, you've got thesis blues."

"Huh?"

"Every graduate student goes through this when they have to write their thesis. At some point in the project it all starts to look like nonsense, garbage, junk. You feel certain that you're wasting your time, that what you're doing is all gibberish and it's never going to go anywhere. You start to wonder if you shouldn't just toss it all down the chute and go out and sell used cars or paint houses or do something, *anything*, that's more useful than the crap you're working on."

Graycloud stared at him for a long silent moment. Then, "Did you ever feel that way?"

Jamie nodded, remembering. "With my master's thesis. And especially with the doctorate. *Stratigraphy of the Potential*

Oil-Bearing Deposits of Northern New Mexico. I almost quit school altogether when I was working on that one."

Blinking, Graycloud said, "But there aren't any oil-bearing deposits in northern New Mexico. Are there?"

"Not much. Plenty of dinosaur fossils, though. I damned near changed my major to paleontology."

"Really?"

"I thought about it. But I stayed with geology and that thesis earned me my Ph.D."

Graycloud looked uncertain, troubled.

"Keep plugging at it, Billy. I know it looks like a mess now, but you'll get there. It'll be worth it in the end."

"I sure hope so."

Silently, Jamie replied, So do I, kid. So do I.

TITHONIUM BASE: THE PATH

■

"Must've been some dreams you had, love," Vijay said as she dressed for the day.

Freshly showered, Jamie looked up at her as he pulled on his softboots. "What do you mean?"

"You were tossing all night. Nearly pushed me out of the bed, you did."

"No!"

She sat on the edge of the bed beside him and put a hand on his shoulder. "What was it, Jamie? What were you dreaming about?"

Jamie tried to remember. "It was all pretty confusing."

"You called out to your grandfather. More'n once."

Nodding, he replied, "Yes, Al was there. And Billy Graycloud. And you, too."

"That's what you were moaning about?"

"It's a jumble. It doesn't make any sense. The more I try to remember it the blurrier it gets."

Vijay got to her feet, smiling. "Well, whatever it is, I hope you resolve it. Kept me up most of the night."

She waited while he finished dressing. As he took the bear fetish from atop the bed table and slipped it into his coverall pocket, Jamie thought about his dreams.

There was more than one, he remembered. I was with Al and Billy in the village, then I was at an airport somewhere with Dex. And then with Vijay, here on Mars again. And they were all dying. Everything was dying. The people in the village, Al, Billy, Vijay—everybody was dying and there wasn't anything I could do about it.

"Where are you, love?"

He twitched with surprise and realized that he'd been standing by the bed table for several minutes, lost in thought.

"I'm sorry," he mumbled.

Vijay smiled again. "Come on, mate. Breakfast time. Then I've got to write up a half dozen psych profiles."

"And I've got to sort out the personnel files, see who wants to stay and who has to go."

They left their quarters and started across the dome toward the cafeteria, Jamie plodding along like a schoolboy trudging unwillingly to class. Morning sunlight filled the dome with brightness.

"How are you and Dr. Quintana getting along?" he asked as they got into line at the serving counter. Somebody was cooking up pancakes; Jamie savored the aroma of baking and maple syrup.

"No worries with Nari," said Vijay. "We're writing this paper together and I help her on her regular rounds in the infirmary. She likes to pretend she's a tigress, but under it all she's more like a little koala bear, actually."

"No more lice patrol?"

Vijay laughed. "Not until the next resupply mission lands."

In two weeks, Jamie knew. They'll take back a few dozen people. Then Dex'll send the evacuation flight to take the rest of the staff. We'll only have fifteen people left here. Fifteen people. Unless . . . Unless . . .

AFTER BREAKFAST JAMIE WENT to his cubicle of an office and pulled up the logistics and financial data that Mo Zeroual had amassed. Fifteen people, he thought. Fifteen men and women. Working here at the dome indefinitely, maybe for a year or more before we can afford another resupply flight.

Then he called up the detailed proposal that Dex had sent from Boston. Tourists. Jamie's blood ran cold at the thought.

Only ten at a time. Three times a year. Or four. If we go with four it could bring in two billion dollars a year. Enough to keep us going. We'd have to shave the operation a little, cut the number of people here by ten percent or so. But we could keep nearly two hundred people working here. We could keep going—as long as the tourists keep coming.

But now Dex wants to terraform the whole area here. Put a big glass dome over the village and the cliff structures so the tourists can tramp around in their shirtsleeves.

Damn! Jamie wanted to slam a fist on his desktop, but he knew that the flimsy folding table would collapse if he did. Instead, he got to his feet and paced out of his cubicle, walking blindly across the dome, wondering what to do, what to do.

We're digging up the fossils of Martians! he screamed silently to himself. We're learning how they lived, what they felt, the meaning of the pictographs they carved into the wall of their temple.

And nobody on Earth cares! Nobody gives a damn! Nobody who matters, at least.

How can I get us through this? Jamie asked himself. Fingering the fetish in his pocket, he wondered, What path should I choose, Grandfather?

"Jamie? Dr. Waterman?"

Jamie blinked to see tall, gangling Sal Hasdrubal looming before him, his dark face set in a hard, troubled frown.

Pulling himself out of his thoughts, Jamie said, "Sal. Good morning."

"Can I talk with you? In private?"

"Sure." Jamie gestured back toward his cubicle. "In my office."

Hasdrubal's lanky form nearly filled the cube; his long legs stretched almost the width of the small compartment.

"What's on your mind, Sal?" Jamie asked. He had slid his own chair as far into a corner as he could.

"It's the crater," said Hasdrubal. "The one that the meteor impact made."

"Crater Chang," Jamie said.

Hasdrubal almost smiled. "Yeah, Chang."

"What about it?"

Hasdrubal pointed toward Jamie's laptop, resting on the folding table against one of the partitions.

"Can I use your computer?"

"Go right ahead."

Within a few seconds the laptop's screen displayed a series of graphs. Before Jamie could ask what they represented, Hasdrubal explained: "The crater's still outgassing." He traced one of the curves with a long, slim finger. "See, here's the data from the sensors we left there. Water vapor, some trace elements. But no superoxides."

Jamie understood. "The bottom of the crater is deep enough so that it's below the superoxide layer near the ground's surface."

"Right. And there's still enough heat to be boilin' out some of the permafrost down there."

"How deep is the crater?" Jamie asked.

"Twenty-eight meters at its deepest point."

"And the permafrost is still boiling off? That can't be from the heat of the impact, not after this many weeks."

"Don't know," Hasdrubal said, with a shrug. "But I have a hunch."

Jamie waited.

"It could be that the bacteria living that deep are melting the permafrost."

"Bacteria?"

"Yeah. You know, SLiMEs. They get their water from the permafrost. They must be able to liquefy the ice."

"How could they do that?"

"That's one of the reasons I want to go back."

"Chang won't permit it?"

"I've tried to get him to okay a trip back to the crater, but he says you decided we hafta put all our efforts into Carleton's dig."

Jamie hesitated, then nodded. "That's right. I did."

"But that crater's *important*," Hasdrubal insisted. "Look. Look at this."

The biologist flicked his long fingers across the keyboard of Jamie's laptop. Photomicrographs appeared on the screen.

Squinting slightly, Jamie said, "Those look like bacteria."

"That's right! That's just what they are. SLiMEs. From the soil at the bottom of the crater."

"Living?"

Hasdrubal's dark face was intense, demanding. "Not for long. They're desiccating, drying out. Their natural environment is underground, where it's safe from the radiation hitting the surface. And warmer. Now they've been exposed and it's killing them."

"So what can you do about it?"

Gesturing with his long arms, Hasdrubal replied, "Go to the crater, pack up some samples and bring 'em back here where I can keep them in an environmental chamber."

"And study them," Jamie finished for him.

"And study them, right," Hasdrubal agreed. "They'll be in a simulated environment instead of the real thing, but we can watch how they react, how they grow and reproduce, how they melt the permafrost."

Jamie thought about it for a moment. "They eat rock?"

"Iron. These SLiMEs are siderophiles. But they need to be in a high-pressure environment, and protected from solar radiation."

"And the harder stuff, too," Jamie added. "X-rays and gammas."

"Yeah," said Hasdrubal. "Exposed on the surface they get a full dose of whatever hits the ground, even at the bottom of the crater."

Looking up from the screen, Jamie asked, "So you want to go back to the crater and scoop up some samples of the bacteria."

"I need to!" Hasdrubal said fervently. "It's important for

our work here. I mean, why the hell are we here if we can't study the indigenous life forms?"

Jamie smiled, remembering when his two-year-old Jimmy discovered the difference between "I want some candy, Daddy" and "I *need* some candy, Daddy."

"How long would you have to stay at the crater?"

"Half a day, at most. Well, maybe a whole day."

Nodding wearily, Jamie said, "Let me talk to Chang about it. Maybe we can squeeze in a quick excursion for you before the resupply ship arrives."

Hasdrubal nodded knowingly. "And we start packing up to leave."

BOSTON: TRUMBALL RESIDENCE

■

Y̲ou really don't have to do this," she said.

Dex looked up from the small pile of data discs he was stuffing into his travel bag. "Yes I do," he said tightly.

His wife sighed, a maneuver that never failed to stir Dex, even though she was wearing a loose-fitting casual blouse over a comfortable pair of dark slacks.

"Two weeks?" she bleated.

"Five days out, three days on Mars, five days back," Dex replied. "Thirteen days, total. I'll be back in time for election day."

"And what am I supposed to do while you're gone? Have you thought about that?"

Dex recognized the slightly veiled threat. He made himself grin at her. "Read our prenup," he suggested.

"You're rotten!"

"I know. I'm sorry. I told you you could come with me."

"To Mars?" Her china blue eyes went wide.

"Sure. I've been there. It's fascinating. It'd be fun to have you there with me."

She shook her blond head. "Not me! I'll stay home and wait for you, like those wives of whaling sailors in the old days."

"Maybe I should build a widow's walk up on the roof," Dex muttered as he zipped up the travel bag.

"You're really leaving?" she said, her voice going small, almost frightened.

"I'll be back."

"You're risking your neck because of your Apache friend."

"Navaho."

"Whatever. I hate him."

Dex looked squarely at her. She was really upset. "Look, honey, it's no more dangerous than flying to London. Really."

"But why do you have to go to frigging Mars just to tell him you're sending everybody home?"

With a sadness that he'd kept under control until this moment, Dex said, "I can't tell him any other way. It's got to be face-to-face, man-to-man."

"Stupid macho bullshit," she muttered.

Dex shrugged. "When you have to kill a man," he quoted Churchill, "it costs nothing to be polite about it."

His wife dabbed at her eyes as he brushed past her and headed for the limousine waiting to take him to the aerospaceport.

IT WAS THE FIRST time in more than two months that the president had invited Francisco Delgado to the Oval Office, and she wished she hadn't.

The president of the United States sat behind her broad dark mahogany desk, smiling at Archbishop Overmire, who seemed perfectly at ease in the cushioned leather chair next to Delgado's. Behind the president, through the long windows that looked out on the Rose Garden, the science advisor could see that last night's rainstorm had stripped the last leaves from the trees. The Weather Service predicts a colder-than-normal winter, Delgado thought idly; maybe even a little snow up in New England.

"I'm very pleased that you could find the time to attend this meeting," the president was saying to Archbishop Overmire. Her smile seemed genuine enough; much warmer than she had ever vouchsafed to her science advisor.

Overmire smiled back graciously. "Madam President, your slightest wish is my command."

Three of Overmire's aides sat back on the sofa by the unused fireplace, dressed, like the archbishop, in black clerical suits. Delgado thought they looked like clones: each of them ascetically thin and pale. Overmire himself glowed with pink-cheeked health and happy good cheer. On the facing sofa sat the president's chief of staff and her chief counsel.

Delgado had wanted to bring a couple of his assistants to this meeting, especially the young geologist who monitored the work on Mars and the head of the Georgetown University anthropology department, a Jesuit who was closely following Carleton's excavation of the Martian fossils. But the president's assistants had said no: this was a small, informal meeting. No staff people.

Except for the archbishop's three clones and the president's two staff members. What they meant was that Delgado was not allowed to bring his own people with him.

After a few minutes of meaningless pleasantries, the president said to Overmire, "I take it you've seen the images from the Martian graves."

"I have indeed," said the archbishop. "They look more like the skeletons of dogs or pigs than people."

"They're Martians," Delgado said. "We shouldn't expect them to look like human beings."

Overmire smiled tolerantly. "I'm not a scientist, of course, but it looks to me as if your people on Mars have uncovered a pet cemetery, not a graveyard where people are buried."

Delgado felt his cheeks flame, but he immediately clamped down on his anger. The man's trying to bait me, he told himself. Turning to the president, he said, "Whether the skeletons uncovered so far are the remains of the people who built the village or their pets, the fact remains that intelligent creatures lived on Mars, built their homes on Mars, and even believed in some form of afterlife."

"They worshipped God," the president breathed.

Overmire corrected, "They worshipped false gods, of course. They had no knowledge of our Lord and Savior Jesus Christ."

"How can you know that?" Delgado demanded. "What evidence do you have—"

"Gentlemen," said the president, "we're not here to discuss religion. Or archeology, for that matter."

"Of course," said Overmire, smiling again.

Just what are we here to discuss? Delgado wondered silently.

As if to answer his unvoiced question, the president explained, "My secretary of education is making a fuss about these Martian fossils. She wants to encourage schools around the country to study what the scientists are discovering."

Ahh, thought Delgado. Education's doing her job and that's got the president worried.

Overmire's smile disappeared. "Use federal tax dollars to popularize godless humanism?" he said, his voice low and tight. "It's bad enough that secular university scientists are giving seminars and holding conferences about these alleged Martians—"

"Alleged?" Delgado snapped.

"There's no proof that the Martians were intelligent."

"No proof?" Delgado's temper snapped. "They built that village! They buried their dead! With funeral adornments! They built those structures up in the cliff! They carved writing into the walls!"

"One wall," said Overmire. "And, quite frankly, it's just as easy to believe that this Navaho scientist put up all these so-called structures just to wheedle more money out of us."

Delgado sputtered, "That's . . . that's . . . it's a goddamned lie and you know it!"

Unruffled, Overmire lifted one hand and replied, "You scientists have a saying about Ockham's razor, don't you? If you have more than one possible explanation for something, then the simplest one is the right one? Well, which is simpler, assuming that there was a race of intelligent people on Mars sixty million years ago, or assuming that some fanatical scientists have faked the evidence for them?"

It took all of Delgado's willpower to keep from leaping at the archbishop's throat and throttling him.

The president, behind her massive desk, made a curt gesture. "Now, listen," she said. "My education secretary is priming herself for a run for the presidency in two years. I can't let her use Mars as ammunition against me."

Overmire's smile turned crafty. He eased back in his chair and said, "Madam President, your administration has not been as fully cooperative with the Lord's work as it might be."

"I admit that," said the president. "And I'm taking steps to change it."

The archbishop beamed. "In that case, be assured that you will have the full backing of the New Morality—and every right-thinking, God-fearing voter in the land."

The president smiled back at him.

"That is, *if*," Overmire continued, "you ask for the resignation of your secretary of education and replace her with someone we can both work with."

The president's smile started to look forced, but she nodded.

"By their fruits you shall know them," Overmire murmured.

Trying to contain his temper, Delgado said, "Madam President, you've got to see the whole picture here. We're dealing with the difference between science and misplaced religious faith."

"Misplaced?" Overmire looked shocked.

"We're dealing," Delgado went on, his voice rising, "with the struggle between free scientific inquiry and dogmatic dictates from people who cherish ignorance over understanding. It's bad enough that we've stopped supporting the exploration of Mars, and we've got congressional committees investigating that priest's death. Now you're talking about preventing the Department of Education from helping school children learn about the cutting edge of scientific exploration!"

"I resent your attitude," said the archbishop.

The president agreed. "You could notch it down a bit, Dr. Delgado. An apology wouldn't be out of order."

"Apologize? For the truth? I'd sooner resign!"

With a shrug, the president said, "If that's the way you feel, I'll expect your resignation on my desk before the end of the day."

Overmire's smile turned smug. And Delgado finally understood why he'd been invited to the Oval Office.

TITHONIUM BASE: RESUPPLY FLIGHT 082

∎

For the five days of the fusion torch ship's flight to Mars Dex felt a growing apprehension about seeing Jamie again. He'll try to talk me into keeping the operation going, Dex told himself. He's got this cockamamie scheme for keeping fifteen people at the base and depending on Selene for supplies. He'll never agree to shutting down the operation completely. He won't want to leave Mars. Christ, when it comes down to it I'll probably have to get a couple of guys to literally pick him up and carry him off.

Not this flight, thank god. All I've got to do on this flight is tell him we're giving up. Tell him it's finished, over. All I've got to do is rip his guts out.

By the time the torch ship took up an orbit around Mars Dex was in a thoroughly depressed mood. Not even the sight of the red planet gliding past the observation port of the ship's lounge gladdened him.

JAMIE WAS ALSO APPREHENSIVE about Dex's arrival. He paced tensely from his tiny workspace to the cafeteria, poured himself a mug of coffee, checked with the flight monitors in the communications center.

"Oh-eight-two is right on the mark, Dr. Waterman," the flight controller told him, smiling up at him from her display screen. "I hope they remembered to bring the cosmetics we ordered."

Jamie tried to smile for her. His thanks came out more as a grunt than anything else. Cosmetics, he said to himself as he headed back toward his cubicle. She must just be kidding, trying to cheer me up.

Hasdrubal's excursion to Crater Chang had been okayed. Jamie himself would go with the biologist. He was looking forward to it, looking forward to doing something useful, something more than scowling at logistics numbers that wouldn't change and hoping for a miracle.

Unbidden, Zeke Larkin's bitter words rang in his mind. *What we're doing here is rearranging the deck chairs on the* Titanic.

The PA speakers blared, "L/AV HAS MADE RENDEZVOUS WITH RESUPPLY FLIGHT 082."

When they come down, Jamie knew, Dex will be with them. And he'll be carrying our death warrant.

THE TIME SEEMED TO stretch endlessly. In the weightlessness of orbit, Dex stayed in his compartment and tried not to make any sudden motions. His head felt stuffy, as if he were coming down with a bad cold. His guts felt woozy.

That's all normal, he told himself. You've been through this before. Twenty-three years ago, he remembered. It's been twenty-three years since I left Mars. I swore I'd never return. Once was enough. But here I am. Why? For Jamie. Because of that goddamned stubborn redskin.

Because he's my friend, Dex realized. Over all these years he's been the one real friend I've got. Dex sat on the edge of his bunk, gripping its sides with both hands, suddenly aware of the truth of it. Rollie Kinnear, all the people he knew from business, from the Foundation, his social acquaintances, even his various wives—Jamie's the only one among them who's a real friend. A pain in the ass, that's true, but all he's ever wanted from me is to help him explore Mars. Nothing for himself, just Mars.

And I'm here to take that away from him.

* * *

"L/AV LANDING IN TEN minutes," THE PA SPEAKERS AN-
NOUNCED.

Jamie looked up from his laptop's display. He'll be here in
ten minutes. Slowly he got to his feet and started for the
main airlock hatch. Then he hesitated, and made a detour toward the infirmary.

Vijay was at the desk that they had shoehorned in next to
the accordion-fold door.

"Would you like to come and greet Dex?" he asked her,
trying to make it sound light.

"Need some moral support, love?" she countered.

He grinned despite himself. "Only a couple tons
worth."

Vijay closed her laptop gently and got to her feet. He saw
that she was wearing a light peach-colored sweater and a
knee-length skirt instead of her usual coveralls.

"You expected this, didn't you?" Jamie said.

She smiled at him, dazzling white teeth against her dark
skin, and he realized all over again how much smarter she was
than he.

They stood off to one side of the airlock hatch, where they
could look through the dome's transparent wall out onto the
bare, rust-red ground and the towering cliffs off in the distance.
A broad area had been cleared of rocks and scoured smooth by
uncounted landings of L/AVs. A pair of the spindly vehicles
stood off by the edge of the landing area, looking like big
metallic spiders. Sunlight glinted off their bulbous glassteel
canopies.

"L/AV LANDING IN ONE MINUTE," the overhead speakers
announced. Then it switched to the computer synthesized
voice of the automated countdown. "FIFTY-FIVE SECONDS . . .
FIFTY-FOUR . . . "

Jamie felt his palms sweating. What if there's a malfunc-
tion? What if they have to abort the landing? What if the
landing struts fail? What if—

Vijay squeezed his arm and pointed with her other hand. "Look! There it is!"

The L/AV grew from a black dot against the yellowish sky and took on solid form. Jamie could even see the skinny landing struts sticking out from the corners of the boxy main body. The craft seemed to stagger momentarily as a burst of rocket exhaust flared from its main nozzle. Then it straightened, turned slightly in midair, and descended straight down. Even through the insulated wall of the dome Jamie could hear the thin screeching of its altitude jets. Dust and pebbles flew from the landing field as the L/AV settled down softly, its thin legs flexing.

"They're down!" Vijay exclaimed.

Jamie let out the breath that he'd been holding for the past dozen seconds.

It took a seemingly endless time for the access tube to crawl out and connect with the L/AV's airlock. The few dozen people clustered around the dome's airlock hatch faded back as Jamie and Vijay went to the hatch. Jamie saw that Chang was already there, in a crisply fresh set of sky blue coveralls.

"Dr. Waterman," said the mission director, with a slight bow.

"Dr. Chang," Jamie replied, dipping his chin in return.

Jamie found himself licking his lips as a pair of technicians swung the airlock hatch open. What should I say to Dex? Should I let Chang greet him first? How's he going to be after coming all this way?

Dex Trumball was the first person to come through the access tunnel. He was wearing a short-sleeved sports shirt of pale lemon hanging loosely over dark slacks, and carrying a black soft-sided travel bag in one hand.

He stepped over the sill of the hatch, glanced around. Jamie suddenly realized that Dex had worked just as hard as he himself to keep the exploration of Mars alive. He's come all this way when he could have stayed home. He—

Dex walked past Chang and straight to Jamie. Jamie took a step toward him. Dex dropped his bag and the two men suddenly clasped each other in a profound embrace of warm friendship.

"Welcome back to Mars," Jamie said, his voice strangely throaty.

Dex grinned the way he had twenty-three years earlier, when they had first explored the cliff structures together.

"I didn't think it'd hit me this way, Jamie, but it's good to be back. Damned good."

TITHONIUM BASE: EXCURSION

■

Jamie clutched Dex's shoulders for several wordless moments. At last the two men stepped back from each other, both of them grinning broadly.

Dex recognized Vijay. "Well, how are you, gorgeous?"

"I'm fine, Dex. Glad to see you here." She put her hands on his shoulders and bussed him on the cheek.

"And you know Dr. Chang, of course," Jamie said, gesturing toward the mission director.

Chang stepped forward stiffly and offered his hand.

"A pleasure to see you again, Dr. Chang," Dex said.

"Welcome to Trumball Exploration Center," said Chang, using the base's official name.

Dex nodded, then glanced around. "My father'd be very impressed with all this."

"Please allow me to show you our humble base."

Dex glanced at Jamie.

"Go ahead," Jamie said. "I'll take care of your baggage."

"Hey, this is it," Dex said, bending to pick up his travel bag. "I leave when the torch ship goes."

A sudden idea struck Jamie. "In that case, why don't you come with us this afternoon?"

Chang's eyes narrowed, but he said nothing.

"Come? Where?" Dex asked.

"We're going out on an overnight excursion. To Crater Chang."

"Safety regulations," Chang murmured. "It is necessary—"

Dex interrupted, "Dr. Chang, I'm an experienced geologist. I've driven a camper more than a thousand kilometers overland."

"More than twenty years ago," Chang pointed out.

"The campers haven't changed that much. And I've passed all my physicals."

"So did Monsignor DiNardo."

Dex's expression tightened slightly. "I'm not going to die on you, Dr. Chang. And I'd like to get outside—after you show me around the base."

Chang looked from Dex's blue-green eyes to Jamie, then back again. "I know of your experience in overland excursion. No one has driven a camper farther."

"Then it's okay?"

"If the scientific director agrees."

Jamie said, "I think it will be good for Dr. Trumball to accompany Hasdrubal and me on the excursion. It's only overnight. We'll be back tomorrow."

"In time for the torch ship's departure," Dex added.

With a laugh, Jamie said, "We won't leave you stranded here, Dex."

"Good." He hefted his travel bag. "I only brought a couple days worth of underwear."

WHILE CHANG ESCORTED DEX on a tour of the base dome, Jamie took Dex's bag and, with Vijay beside him, carried it to the compartment that would serve as Dex's quarters.

"D'you think it's all that good an idea, taking him out on your excursion?" she asked.

Jamie tossed the bag on the compartment's bunk, noting almost unconsciously how lightly it floated in the gentle Martian gravity.

"A very good idea," he replied as they started back toward the infirmary. "I want Dex to see what we're doing here."

"But what about the village?"

"We'll take a look at it on our way out to the cable lifts."

Vijay shook her head ever so slightly. "Carleton's going to be disappointed."

"We'll look at the village," Jamie repeated. "But I want Dex to see this new crater and the work that Hasdrubal's doing."

"I hope you know what you're doing."

"Me, too," Jamie said.

AFTER A BRIEF LUNCH with Chang in his office, Jamie bustled Dex to the main airlock, where they pulled on nanofabric suits.

"These things really work?" Dex asked, looking dubious.

Jamie nodded. "Everybody uses them now."

"Pretty flimsy."

The astronaut serving as safety officer almost scowled at him. "They're the best damned protection you can have," he said firmly. "A helluva lot better than those old clunkers. Even Dr. Carleton is using 'em now."

As if on cue, Carter Carleton came striding up toward them. Jamie introduced the anthropologist to Dex.

"Coming out to see the excavation," Carleton said as he reached for one of the suits hanging limply in their locker. It wasn't a question.

"We'll stop by and take a look," Jamie replied. "We're on our way out to see Crater Chang."

"Chang." Carleton's voice went flat.

"I've been following your work on the village," Dex said, suddenly diplomatic. "Fantastic stuff, especially the graveyard."

"Yes," said Carleton.

"Complete skeletons," Dex went on, shrugging his arms into the suit's backpack. "We're trying to get the news nets to carry a special on your work."

Carleton said nothing. He stepped into the leggings of the suit he'd chosen, pulled them up over his hips and then worked his arms into the sleeves.

Once all three of them were in their suits with the bubble helmets inflated and the astronaut satisfied that they were properly sealed up, Carleton asked:

"Just how much time can you spare to examine the village?"

Jamie recognized the sarcasm in his voice. The anger.

"An hour," he said, stepping to the airlock hatch. "Then we've got to go up the cable with Hasdrubal and spend the night in the dome up on the plain."

"One hour," Carleton muttered.

Jamie glanced at Dex. From the expression on his face Jamie could see that even Dex recognized the bitterness in Carleton's tone.

"THAT'S ONE PISSED-OFF ANTHROPOLOGIST," Dex said as he walked between Jamie and Hasdrubal toward the cable lifts running along the cliff face.

"Did you want to stay longer?" Jamie asked.

With a small shrug, Dex said, "Might've been interesting, poking around those building foundations, looking into the graves."

Hasdrubal said, "Carleton wouldn't let you touch anything."

"Yeah. I can understand why."

And maybe, Jamie thought silently, you'll be able to understand why we can't have tourists poking around the village.

They reached the base of the cable and started to clip the harnesses over their suits. Jamie watched Dex closely. He had no problems with the harness and he seemed to be more at ease wearing the molecule-thin nanosuit.

"We gonna stop and look at the cliff structures on the way up?" Dex asked.

"Tomorrow," said Jamie. "On the way down."

Hasdrubal made a low, chuckling sound. "If we stopped now to look at the structures Carleton would shoot us in the back with one of the digging lasers."

Jamie laughed, but when they started up on the cables he could see the team of people digging away industriously at the excavation. One person, though, was standing at the edge of the pit watching them, fists on his hips. Even at this distance Jamie could sense the anger radiating from the anthropologist.

TITHONIUM BASE: EVENING

■

Jamie's gone daft, Vijay said to herself as she watched her husband, Dex and Hasdrubal striding from Carleton's excavation out toward the buckyball cables that ran up the seamed sheer face of the cliff to the plain up at the top. It was almost sunset, and the shadows of the three men stretched out across the uneven, rock-covered ground like fingers straining for a prize they could not reach.

The three of them had stopped briefly at the excavation; at the edge of the pit Jamie pointed here and there while the other two stood beside him. Then they moved on. Jamie wants to get to the cable lifts before it gets dark, Vijay told herself.

But Dex is only here for two more days and Jamie's spending more'n half that time trotting him out to that crater, Vijay thought. Why's he doing that? With a shake of her head, she kept staring through the transparent wall of the dome, watching the three nanosuited figures walking away. Like three little boys going out on an adventure, she realized. Jamie's turning his back on his responsibilities. Dex is, too. They ought to know better.

With a helpless sigh, Vijay commanded herself, Go back to your room. Wash your face. Get ready for dinner. Alone.

Yet she stood there and watched the three men moving away from her.

"He's really a fanatic, isn't he?"

Turning, she saw Carter Carleton standing beside her, his usual self-assured smile totally gone. He looked angry.

"No, Jamie's not a fanatic," she said. "He's dedicated."

"He's supposed to be showing Trumball the work we're doing here. Look at them. They hardly glanced at my excavation."

"I know," Vijay said. "I really don't understand what Jamie's up to."

"Whatever it is, he doesn't think my work is very important, does he?"

"It's not that. There's something going on inside his head but I don't know what it is." Vijay kept staring at the dwindling figures as she spoke. "I wonder if Jamie himself knows what it is."

"A fanatic," Carleton muttered. She could hear the resentment in his voice.

"Dedicated," she repeated.

Carleton fairly glared at her. But then he made a tentative smile and said, "I see. *I* am dedicated. *You* are a fanatic."

Vijay shook her head. "A fanatic is someone who doubles his efforts after he's forgotten his aim. Jamie hasn't forgotten his aim."

"'For if I should despair, I should grow mad,'" Carleton quoted.

"Jamie hasn't despaired."

"Not yet."

"Not ever."

He touched her back lightly, with just the tips of his fingers, and gestured toward the cafeteria with his free hand. "May I invite you to dinner?"

Vijay thought about it a moment, glanced again at the dwindling figures of the three men, then back at Carleton's handsome face. The anger was still in his eyes, but he was making himself smile at her.

"I don't like to eat alone," he said, almost gently.

"Neither do I," said Vijay. "Let me wash up first."

"Certainly." His smile broadened. "Meet you in the cafeteria in half an hour?"

"Fine."

All through dinner Vijay tried to get a reading on Carleton. She knew his dossier by heart, knew how he'd been ruined by a charge of rape that he strenuously denied. He had been stripped of his professorship and tenure, his wife had left him, his fellow anthropologists treated him as a pariah. His career, his life, were ruined. So he came to Mars and made the biggest discovery since somebody stumbled over the bones of Neanderthal Man. The irony was cosmic.

"Something's amusing you?" Carleton asked from across the table. Their dinners were long finished. Even the fruit pies they had taken for dessert were nothing more than crumbs now.

"Just thinking about the weird turns that fate takes," she said. "You had to come all the way out here to Mars to find vindication."

He steepled his fingers in front of his face. "Vindication? That's a strange word to use."

Vijay said, "I mean, if the fundamentalists believe in divine guidance, then they've got to admit that your discovery of the village here must be God's way of showing that the accusations against you were false."

Still half-hiding his face, Carleton replied in a low, strained voice, "No, they'd never admit that they were wrong. That they got that woman to perjure herself. Never."

"But—"

"They're the fanatics, Vijay. Real fanatics. They'd do anything to further their cause. Give them enough power and they'll start burning people at the stake again."

There was real fury in his tone now. Hatred. Good, she thought. Don't repress it. Let it out.

"You'll be cock of the walk when you return to Earth. You can wave your discovery under their noses."

"If I return to Earth."

"If?" Vijay felt startled.

"I decided when I came here to Mars that I wasn't going to look backward, I wasn't going to let them turn me into a bitter old man. Now—well, why should I go back? What's back there for me except pain and sorrow?"

He feels sorry for himself! Vijay realized. Can't say I blame him.

She said, "But you can go back in triumph. You can have your pick of university posts."

He thought a moment. "I wonder. The New Morality controls most of the academic establishment these days."

"But you—"

"Don't you know that the Mars Foundation can't even get the news nets to carry a documentary about my village? They're blocking us out."

"Jamie mentioned something about that," she murmured.

"No, I think I'll stay right here," Carleton said. "I can do some really important work here, no matter how they ignore me back home. I can have some respect here, despite clowns like Larkin."

Better to reign in hell, Vijay thought, than to serve in heaven.

But she asked, "What if Jamie has to close down the whole operation?"

With a shrug, "We'll cross that bridge when we come to it."

Vijay couldn't think of anything to say, except, "I don't think that's a very healthy attitude. You've got to prepare for problems before they hit you."

He turned on his smile, but there was sadness in it. "Don't worry about my attitude. I'm a healthy enough man, Vijay."

She thought she detected just the slightest emphasis on the word *man*.

They picked up their dirty dishes and deposited them in the slowly revolving drum that fed the microwave cleaning unit.

As they started out of the cafeteria, toward the living units on the other side of the dome, Carleton asked, "My place or yours?"

Vijay looked sharply at him. He was smiling again, but it looked just a bit forced to her. You'd better stop this right here and now, she told herself. Don't let him get any ideas about you. A different voice in her mind countered, Not that he doesn't have ideas already.

"You go to your place and I'll go to mine," she said firmly.

Keeping pace beside her, Carleton said, "I thought we might have a nightcap. I still have some of that single malt I told you about."

"No thanks, Carter."

"Scared?"

She hesitated a heartbeat, then admitted, "Yes. A little."

Strangely, he chuckled. I've stroked his machismo, Vijay thought. But that's as far as this goes.

As they approached the living quarters, he gripped her arm and asked again, "Just a little scotch?"

"You are a persistent one, aren't you?"

"But not a fanatic."

Still walking toward her quarters, Vijay said, "Carter, there are lots of women here who'd be happy to share your bed."

"Maybe. But none as beautiful as you."

"Lots of unmarried women."

Carleton grunted softly. "He's run off with his buddy and left you here to fend for yourself."

"'Kay. So now I'm fending." Vijay tried to pry his fingers off her arm. He tightened his grip.

"I want you, Vijay."

"No, Carter. Please let go of me."

Vijay placed her back against the flimsy accordion-fold door of her quarters. Carleton took her other arm and pinned her against the door. She felt it shuddering behind her.

She could see the need in his eyes. Stand up to him, she told herself. Stay in control. If that doesn't work, knee him in the groin.

"Come on, Vijay. Nobody's going to get hurt." He was pressing her against the sagging door, speaking faster now, his voice low and urgent. "Jamie won't know. You've seen my medical dossier; you know I had a vasectomy more than twenty years ago."

Vijay could see a few other people scattered across the

dome. No one was looking their way, but a single shout would focus everybody's attention on her.

Very firmly she said, "Carter, the answer is no. Now please let go of me."

For a long moment he stood there frozen, leaning against her, staring down at her. Then he seemed to change. She saw the fire in his eyes tamp down. He released her arms and took a small step back from her.

"Thank you," she whispered, rubbing her arms where his hands had clamped her.

"Sorry," he muttered. "I got carried away."

"Good night, Carter," she said.

He nodded. "I'm not a rapist, Vijay."

"I never thought you were," she half-lied.

He turned and walked away, toward his own quarters, moving with the exaggerated precision of a man who's trying to show the world he isn't drunk.

Vijay slid her door open and quickly stepped into the quarters she shared with Jamie. She pushed the door shut again and clicked its flimsy lock, knowing that it would never stop a determined man.

Before undressing for the night she searched both bed tables until she found the emergency flashlight. Hefting it in one hand, she told herself it would make a decent weapon, if push came to shove.

Then she picked up the phone and asked the communications tech to contact Jamie. He ought to be in the dome up on the plain by now, she thought. Vijay had no intention of telling her husband about Carleton. Nothing happened, really, she told herself.

But she picked up the flashlight again with her free hand as she waited for her call to go through.

TITHONIAE FOSSE: EXCURSION

■

Jamie woke early, blinked a few times, then sat up in the bunk and remembered last night. He and Dex and Hasdrubal had reached the dome just a few minutes after sundown. Jamie had kept Dex outside long enough to see the aurora; he made some oohs and aahs but Jamie got the firm impression that the Sky Dancers didn't impress Dex all that much. Then the three of them had a bland meal microwaved from the dome's supplies and had gone to bed. Vijay had called, as he'd expected. She sounded a little tense, but Jamie ascribed that to her being worried about him being away on this excursion.

The last excursion we'll be able to make, Jamie realized as he got out of the bunk and padded toward the communal lavatory. Unless Dex can find some more money for us.

No. He shook his head at his reflection in the lavatory's metal mirror. Don't put it on Dex. You've got to make the decision. This is your responsibility.

Through their brief breakfast in the dome Dex eyed Jamie warily, like a man trapped in an office with an insurance salesman, Jamie thought. He's waiting for me to put the pressure on him. I guess I look the same way, come to think of it, waiting for him to try to sell me on his tourist scheme. We've got to decide on the future of our work here. Life or death.

After checking out the camper they were going to use in strained silence, Jamie, Dex and Hasdrubal started out for Crater Chang. The sun was barely above the ragged horizon as they slowly drove out of the dome. Hasdrubal did the driving; Jamie sat in the right-hand seat beside him, and Dex stood behind them, hunched between the two seats so he could watch the landscape rolling by.

For more than an hour Jamie tried to open the conversation he wanted to have with Dex. But the words just wouldn't come out. He sat in the cockpit and inwardly struggled to find the right words while Dex hung over his shoulder, equally quiet. Hasdrubal drove the camper in silence, wrapped in his own thoughts.

"Hasn't changed much," Dex said at last. "Rocks, rocks and more rocks."

"Like watching a golf tournament on video," said Hasdrubal. "They all look the same."

"Miles and miles of nothing but miles and miles."

Hasdrubal glanced over his shoulder at Dex. "You did that long-range trek, didn't you, back on the Second Expedition. You and what's-his-name."

"Craig. Possum Craig. That was more than twenty years ago," Dex said. "But it still looks the same. Mars doesn't change very quickly."

"Well, you're gonna see somethin' new in half an hour or so," said Hasdrubal.

"The new crater. Bet it looks like all the other craters around here."

"You're a geologist, right?" Hasdrubal asked.

"Was, back in the day. Haven't picked up a rock in a long time."

Jamie listened to them chatting back and forth. Dex is pretending to be bored, he said to himself. Maybe it's not a pretense. He's spent half his life working to support the exploration of Mars but it just doesn't excite him the way it gets to me. It's not in his guts, not in his soul. Or if it is, he hides it a lot better than I do.

Dex tapped his shoulder. "Don't you have anything to say, Chief?"

Jamie grimaced. He hadn't heard Dex use that half-derogatory term in more than twenty years. Okay, he told himself, time to face the music.

Pushing himself up from the seat, Jamie said to Dex, "I have a lot to say, Dex. And I guess you do, too."

He gestured to the cots that faced each other like benches. The upper cots were folded back against the camper's curving walls. Dex went back and sat on one of them, Jamie took the one opposite.

With a knowing grin, Dex said, "I figure you brought me out here so we could talk."

With a glance at Hasdrubal, up in the cockpit concentrating on the driving, Jamie said, "We have a lot to talk about."

"Jamie, I know you hate the idea of tourists coming here, but—"

"We can't do our work with tourists tramping through the base," Jamie said.

Raising a hand, Dex said, "Hear me out, Jamie. Let me give you the full picture."

Jamie pressed his lips into a tight line. He saw the quiet intensity on his old friend's face. *He's dropped his mask. I was wrong: this is hitting him just as hard as it's hitting me, almost.*

"So give me the full picture," Jamie said, almost in a whisper.

"There just isn't any money!" Dex said. "The government, the private donors, even the big foundations—none of them are willing to put up funding for Mars."

"The greenhouse warming . . ." Jamie muttered.

"That's just a bullshit excuse. What we need for Mars is small change compared to the trillions they're spending on the greenhouse effects."

"But then why are we being shut out?"

"They're out to get us."

"They?"

"The fundamentalists. The New Morality. They're taking control of the government. They're putting pressure on our donors, on the universities and the foundations. They're even shutting us out of the news nets!"

Jamie said, "Selene's willing to help. It's not much, but we could keep a dozen or so people working here. Fifteen, tops."

"Big fucking deal."

"It's better than nothing."

Dex shook his head. "Jamie, that's why this tourism deal is so important. It could save the whole operation! You could keep a couple hundred people on Mars."

"If we let tourists come here." Jamie felt a lead weight in his guts.

"Only a handful," Dex said, almost pleading. "Five at a time. Ten, tops."

"And then twenty. And then—"

"No! Ten at a time, maximum. I swear it! No more than that, ever."

"Dex, I know you mean that, but once people start paying that kind of money to come here, how are you going to control them? They'll turn the place into another Disney World."

"Not if—"

"You want to terraform the area," Jamie said, almost hissing the words. "You want to change it so the tourists can walk around in their shirtsleeves."

"Would that be so bad?"

"And what happens to the Martian organisms? The endolithic lichen. It'll kill them."

"Move the damned rocks outside the terraformed area," Dex said.

"And the village? The cemetery? The cliff structures?"

"Let the tourists see them! They'll pay enough so you can send out teams to find other villages. There must be more of them."

"I'd rather cut my arm off."

Dex took a deep breath. "Christ, you've got to be the stubbornest goddamned redskin in the world. Jamie, you've got to listen to reason!"

Jamie closed his eyes and pictured the base with only

fifteen people working in it. What could they do, what could they accomplish? he wondered. We wouldn't be able to do much useful work. Just help Carleton clear away more of the village. No excursions beyond the immediate area around the dome. No new discoveries.

As if he could read Jamie's mind, Dex said, "You know you can't accomplish diddly-squat with just fifteen people. They'll be caretakers, nothing more."

"At least they'll be taking care of the place, not trampling it into the dust."

"Aw, shit, Jamie," Dex groused.

Leaning toward him, Jamie asked, "How many of your billionaire friends will come to Mars, Dex? At fifty million a pop, how many will come?"

Taken aback somewhat, Dex muttered, "A couple dozen or so, at least. Forty, fifty, maybe."

"Okay, that's two and a half billion dollars."

"That'll keep you going for years."

"How many years?"

Dex did some swift mental arithmetic. "Three, four. Maybe five."

"And then what?"

"Then what?"

"After the high rollers have come and gone. How do we fund the operation then?"

Dex hesitated.

Jamie said, "I'll tell you how. You'll lower the price, right? Get more customers to come. More tourists visiting Mars. Lower prices means more people. That's what you'll have to do to keep the money flowing in."

"Okay, but by then you'll probably be finished excavating the village. You can leave it for the tourists and move on."

"No! Never! That village isn't a tourist attraction. It was the home of living, breathing, intelligent people! We have to protect it, honor it."

"For chrissake, Jamie, this isn't some goddamned religious crusade!"

"The hell it isn't!"

Dex's voice turned cold and hard. "Okay. You turn down the tourist idea and you run out of funding. What then?"

"Selene will keep us alive."

"Barely."

Jamie nodded, admitting it. "We'll manage. Somehow."

"For how long? A year? Two? Selene's not going to support you indefinitely, especially if you're not producing new results. They'll shut you down sooner or later."

"Maybe," Jamie conceded.

"And you know what'll happen once you shut down the base and bring everybody home?"

This is home, Jamie replied silently.

"Once the Navaho presence on Mars ends," Dex went on remorselessly, "the Navaho Nation loses its right to control the territory. Somebody else will come in."

"Your friends with their tourist operation," Jamie replied woodenly.

"Damned right. And they won't be interested in scientific exploration at all. They'll be your worst nightmare come true, Jamie."

Sullen resentment burning inside him, Jamie muttered, "And you'll help them."

"Damned right I will," said Dex, with some heat. "You know why? Because I don't want to see this work abandoned. I want to keep the exploration of Mars going."

"By selling out to tourists."

"Right! You think you're the only one who cares about what we're doing here? You think you've got a monopoly on righteousness? I'll make a deal with tourists, I'll make a deal with anybody, the devil incarnate, if I have to. The important thing is to keep this operation going—even if your people have to put up with tourists."

Jamie stared into his friend's face. He *does* care, Jamie realized. He's so damned dead wrong, but he cares.

Then he heard his grandfather's voice in his mind. *There's always more'n one path to get where you want to go, Jamie.*

Finding the right path is important, but sometimes you've got to travel a path that's tougher, more roundabout. The important thing is to get where you want to go.

Before he could make up his mind to say anything, Hasdrubal called from the cockpit, "We're almost there. Another ten minutes."

"Think about it," Dex whispered to Jamie. "Don't be so goddamned stubborn."

Jamie nodded wordlessly, but in his heart he knew he could never allow Dex or anyone else to ruin his life's work.

TITHONIAE FOSSE: CRATER CHANG

■

"They're dead. They're all dead."

Sal Hasdrubal was on his knees in the bottom of the crater, half a dozen sample cases scattered across the broken rocks. The steep sides of the crater were studded with sensor poles. Hasdrubal had scraped a meter-long trench in the looser ground between the rocks and was pouring some of the dirt into one of the insulated plastic boxes.

But as he worked he grumbled, "It's useless. We're too friggin' late. They're all dead."

From up at the lip of the crater Jamie asked, "How can you be sure?"

Hasdrubal looked up at him, then shook his head. "They couldn't take the radiation. The cold. The low pressure."

"But maybe some of them—"

"Naw. We're too damned late. They're all dead."

Dex came up beside Jamie in his nanosuit and peered into the crater. They could see Hasdrubal's bootprints weaving through the sensor poles. The biologist had insisted on going down to the bottom alone, afraid that too many boots might damage the microbes living in the ground down there.

"They formed a crust of dead cells," he said mournfully. "Like they were trying to shield themselves."

"Then maybe some of them have survived," Jamie said hopefully. "Beneath the protective crust."

Dex added, "Bacteria have survived on the surface of the

Moon for years, with no air, no water, and hard radiation pouring in on them."

"Yeah, I know," said Hasdrubal. He clicked the last of his sample cases shut. "Maybe you're right. Maybe some of 'em have gone into a spore state."

"You'll have to get them under a microscope," Jamie said, trying to sound encouraging.

"Yeah," Hasdrubal replied glumly.

"Can we give you a hand carrying the cases back to the camper?" Dex asked.

Slowly rising to his feet, Hasdrubal said, "Sure. 'Preciate it. Come on down."

Jamie and Dex scrambled down the loose rocks and soil of the crater's steep walls. With each of them carrying a pair of sample cases, they made their way back up to the surface and trudged to the camper.

"Stow 'em in the outside bay," Hasdrubal said. "Keep 'em at ambient temperature."

Jamie glanced at the sun, still climbing in the yellowish sky. A few thin wispy clouds rode near the horizon. Nothing to worry about, he thought. No sign of a dust storm. Wrong season.

With a glance at the digital watch on the wrist of his nanosuit, Jamie said, "It's not even noon yet. We could get back to the dome before sunset if we start out now."

"Might's well," Hasdrubal agreed. "Nothin' more here for me to do."

Once they had vacuumed the dust off their suits, Jamie took the driver's seat, with Hasdrubal at his right.

"I thought we had jump seats in the old campers," Dex said, leaning in between them again.

"Nope," said Jamie, engaging the superconducting electric motors that drove each individual wheel. "We always had to scrunch down like that."

"Well I'm going to make a note about it. A jump seat would be a helluva lot more comfortable."

"Do that," Jamie said, thinking, That's the least of our worries.

Hasdrubal looked morose, Jamie thought.

"Too bad we didn't get here soon enough to study the microbes alive," Jamie said.

"Yeah. I had hoped to bring 'em back to the dome, put them in a simulated environment, see how they made out, watch them adapt. But we were too late. Now we'll never know."

Dex said, "Don't give up. Maybe some of them survived."

The biologist made a halfhearted shrug. "Like you said, I'll put 'em under the microscope, see what there is to see."

"Then what?" Dex asked.

"Then I pack 'em up and ship 'em back to Chicago."

"The University of Chicago?"

"Yeah. Biology department."

"Who'll be studying them there?" Jamie asked.

"Me. If I still have a job there."

Jamie felt his brows hike up. "You? You're leaving?"

"Not on the ship in orbit now," Hasdrubal said, his voice heavy and slow. "The next flight."

"The evacuation flight," Jamie said.

"Yeah. Right."

Dex asked, "What did you mean, if you still have a job there?"

"I been gettin' messages from the university, and from a few friends in the bio department. I'm supposed to be up for tenure, but the university brass is puttin' tenure appointments on hold."

"Why the hell would they do that?" Dex asked.

Jamie said, "I'd think your work on Mars would guarantee you an appointment."

Shaking his head, Hasdrubal said, "Just the opposite. There's a move on to deny tenure to anybody who's been away from the campus for more'n a year."

"That's ridiculous!" Jamie snapped. "You got a sabbatical for your time on Mars, didn't you?"

"The sabbatical was up last year. My department head said

he'd handle the paperwork so's I could stay on Mars long as I needed to. But now the university administration is cutting the legs out from under him. Me, too, looks like."

Jamie glanced back at Dex. He looked grim.

Hasdrubal went on, "If I can get back before the academic year ends next spring I oughtta be okay. But I can't stay on Mars and keep my job. They've made that clear enough."

"Son of a bitch," Dex said softly, carefully pronouncing each word.

"I could talk to them. . . ." Jamie started to say.

"Wouldn't do any good," Dex said. "The university's caving in to the fundamentalists. Just like Penn did to get rid of Carleton."

"I can't believe that," Jamie said.

"Believe it. This is just another one of their cute little tricks to kill the Mars program." Dex's voice dripped acid. "I'll have to start checking some of the other schools. Cute: stay on Mars and lose your job. Real cute."

"That's what I'm up against," Hasdrubal said.

"That's what we're all up against," said Jamie, feeling hollow inside.

"Naw, you got tenure," Hasdrubal said. "You're okay."

Dex grunted. "How long do you think it'll be before those psalm-singing sons of bitches get the universities to start reviewing their tenure appointments?"

TITHONIUM BASE: RETURN

■

They were a glum trio as they rode the buckyball cables down to the valley floor and trudged to the dome, toting Hasdrubal's sample cases. Jamie glanced at the people working on Carleton's excavation as they passed by the pit in the dying light of the day. They all were working busily away at the dig. Like ants, Jamie thought.

The three men hardly spoke a word to each other as they went through the airlock, vacuumed the dust off their nanosuits, and then pulled the suits off and hung them on their racks.

Dex muttered something about meeting with Chang and headed off for the mission director's office. Hasdrubal put all six sample cases on a cart and pushed it toward the biology laboratory. Jamie stood alone by the airlock hatch and gazed out across the dome. The place looked quiet, subdued. No excitement, no *purpose* to any of it. They all know they're going to leave soon, he thought. They all realize that the best we can hope for is a caretaker operation. Their work here is finished. Their careers aren't on Mars anymore. Their lives aren't on Mars. He felt tired, utterly weary, defeated.

Where's Vijay? he wondered. She's usually at the airlock when I come back from outside. She knows we're coming in. We sent the word to the excursion controller. Why isn't she here?

Because she has her own work to do, the other side of his

mind answered. She's got more to do than run into your arms every time you come back from an excursion.

Still, he felt disappointed. She's always there to greet me. Even when I'd fly home to Albuquerque she'd be at the airport. Even when I came back after Jimmy died.

He started out across the dome toward the infirmary, telling himself, She must be working. Maybe some emergency came up, somebody got hurt or something.

Several people nodded hellos at Jamie as he strode across the plastic flooring. He nodded back and gave perfunctory greetings.

"Hey, good to see you back, Dr. W," said Billy Graycloud. "I've got something to show you—"

"Not now, Billy," Jamie said, brushing past the young Navaho, not looking back to see the hurt expression on the kid's face.

As he neared the entrance to the infirmary a new thought struck him. What if something's happened to her? What if she got sick, or had an accident? He hurried to the infirmary.

Vijay was in Nari Quintana's office, deep in earnest conversation with the chief medical officer, their two heads bending toward each other over Quintana's little desk like two schoolgirls sharing a secret.

Jamie stopped at the office's open doorway, feeling immensely relieved and more than a little exasperated. She's all right. Nothing's happened to her. Then why—

Before he could speak a word, Quintana noticed him and flinched like a woman caught by surprise. Vijay turned. Her eyes went wide and she leaped out of her chair.

"Jamie!" She flung herself into his arms. "Oh my god, I completely lost track of the time. I'm so sorry. I really wanted to be at the airlock when—"

He wrapped his arms around her and kissed her soundly.

"I'm sorry, Jamie," Vijay repeated. "You must think . . ." She glanced at Quintana, who was leaning back in her desk chair with a knowing grin on her lean face.

"It's okay," he said. "I just wondered where you were."

"Nari and I got to talking," Vijay said, speaking faster than usual, embarrassed or upset or—what? Jamie wondered.

Quintana made a show of looking at her wristwatch. "It's almost the dinner hour. You two go off and get something to eat. I have a lot of paperwork to do here." She made a show of pecking at her keyboard and peering at her computer screen.

Arm in arm, Jamie and Vijay headed for the cafeteria. Jamie noticed that Carleton's people were coming through the airlock. It'll be sundown in a few minutes, he realized. The cafeteria was almost empty; dinner hour was just starting. He realized he was famished.

"How'd it go?" Vijay asked as they loaded their trays.

"Not good," said Jamie. "Hasdrubal's bugs have either died off or gone into a spore state."

"I mean with Dex."

"Even worse," Jamie said. They walked through the mostly unoccupied tables, found a small one near the dome's curving wall. As they pulled out their chairs the wall turned opaque for the night; suddenly there was nothing to see outside.

"The only way Dex can get any reasonable funding is to bring his big-spending friends here and turn this base into a tourist center." He plopped down in his chair, his appetite suddenly gone.

Vijay started to reply, hesitated, then went ahead. "You'll have to let him do it, then, won't you?"

"No," Jamie snapped.

She leaned toward him, placed her dark hand on his coppery one. "Jamie, if you want to stay here, if you want to keep on with the work you're doing here, you're going to have to make a compromise."

He said nothing.

Vijay went on, "There must be some way to allow a few tourists here without ruining everything."

"They'll want to put up a huge dome to cover the whole area and fill it with air at Earth-normal pressure," he said grimly. "That'll kill the lichen. God knows what the oxygen will do to the ruins of the village, the bodies in the graves."

It was Vijay's turn to go silent.

Bitterly, Jamie said, "Those buildings in the cliff have stood there for sixty million years and more. How long do you think they'd last in a terrestrial atmosphere? With tourists chipping pieces off them? Writing graffiti on the walls?"

"Oh, come on, now, Jamie. It won't be like that and you know it."

He tried to frown at her, found he couldn't. "Well," he said softly, "maybe I'm exaggerating. A little."

He saw Vijay look up and, turning, there was Billy Gray-cloud standing at his elbow.

"Uh, I'm sorry to interrupt, Dr. W, but if you have a couple minutes after you're finished eating could you come over to the comm center? I've got something I want to show you."

A little irritated at the interruption, Jamie nodded. "Sure, Billy. After dinner."

"Thanks!" The young man beamed a grateful smile and then quickly walked away.

Jamie noticed Carter Carleton and several others pushing two tables together. Carleton sat at the head, with several young women sitting at the places closest to him.

Vijay smiled. "Carter's taking my advice."

"Advice?"

"We had dinner last night." Before Jamie could say anything she went on, "I told him there were plenty of young women here who'd be glad to be with him."

"In bed," said Jamie.

Vijay nodded.

"You had dinner with him. Did he come on to you?"

"Nothing serious. Nothing that I couldn't handle," she said. But she looked down at her plate of soymeat.

Jamie half-joked, "Should I go over there and punch him out?"

Vijay looked up. Totally serious, she replied, "No need for that, Jamie. His reputation is much worse than he really is. I can handle him, no worries."

"Really?"

"Really."

Jamie looked into her midnight eyes and decided to let the subject drop. *I can trust Vijay. She's the one person in the world I can rely on. The one person in two worlds. No, make it three, if we count Selene.*

"The wheels in your head are turning," Vijay said, with a smile that was almost impish.

He shook his head. "They're spinning, but I'm not getting anywhere."

"You will, love," said Vijay. "You will."

But when they were leaving the cafeteria, Jamie saw Sal Hasdrubal morosely pushing a half-filled dinner tray along the counter.

"What did the microscope show, Sal?" he asked.

The lanky biologist gave Jamie a somber stare. "They're all gone. Just a few weeks out in the open killed them all."

"They're all dead?"

"Every last one of the cells. Dead."

And so are we, Jamie said to himself. *So are we.*

TITHONIUM BASE: MIDNIGHT

■

Midnight. Jamie stared at the numerals on the digital clock beside the bed. He couldn't sleep. He couldn't remember being so tied up, so tense. Never in his life. Not even when he was pouring every milligram of sweat and determination in him to get picked for the First Expedition. It had never been like this. Not all this pain. All this anguish.

He turned and looked at his wife, breathing softly beside him. In the shadows of the darkened room he could just make out the curve of her shoulder against the sheets. He'd been too wired even to try to make love with Vijay. Everything is falling apart, Jamie told himself. Everything I've ever wanted, ever worked for. It's all falling apart.

It's such a mess, Jamie thought. I can't ask her to stay here when there'll only be fifteen of us on Mars. That's not enough people; it'll be too risky for her. But she won't want to leave if I stay.

He realized he'd said *if* I stay. For the first time he'd used that deadly little word. If. And he remembered his conversation after dinner with Dex. Maybe his last conversation with Dex, ever.

After dinner, as he and Vijay were walking back to their quarters, he had seen Dex leaving Chang's office.

"I've got to talk to him," he'd said. Vijay had nodded her understanding and continued walking to their quarters.

"Dex," Jamie called, hurrying toward him. "Wait up a minute, will you?"

Trumball stopped and eyed Jamie, a quizzical expression on his face. "The final arm-twisting session?" he asked.

Jamie tried to smile, failed. "You're leaving tomorrow."

"Right. And so will you, buddy, sooner or later."

He gripped Dex's arm and led him aimlessly across the big dome, steering him unconsciously away from the busy cafeteria, toward the empty labs on the other side.

"Chang's making preparations for the evacuation flight," Dex said, his voice low, tight. "Looks like just about everybody's going to leave in a couple of months."

"Dex, isn't there any way—"

"There is, Chief, but you won't allow it. You'd rather sit here with a couple of dozen people and twiddle your thumbs until even Selene's funding runs out and you have to abandon this place altogether."

Jamie felt a hot iron smoldering in his guts. "And then you move in. With your tourists."

"Damned right. Better than leaving Mars abandoned altogether."

"Turn this place into a Disney World."

Dex pulled his arm free of Jamie's grip. "You just don't get it, do you, Jamie? You're just as fanatical as those suicide bombers who hit your campus. You'd rather die than bend a little."

"Maybe," Jamie said tensely.

"And you're willing to risk Vijay's life, too."

"That's not fair!"

"Fair my ass! You want everything your own way. Well, there's more than one way to run this operation and once you're gone from Mars I'll come back and do what needs to be done to keep exploring this planet."

"With tourists."

"With the frigging Seventh Cavalry, if that's the only way to do it."

"Yeah, I imagine you would."

"This isn't some holy crusade, Jamie," Dex insisted. "You see Mars as some kind of sacred shrine. Only the truly devout may set foot upon it. Well, that's not the way the world works, friend. Never was and never will be."

"I believe it's our duty to preserve this place from people who'd wreck it."

"Christ, you're like a father who'd rather send his daughter to a convent instead of letting her live in the real world."

"This is the real world!" Jamie fairly shouted, spreading his arms out wide. "I don't want to see it ruined!"

"Then stay here and help protect it. Stay here and take charge of the tourists who'll bring in the money you need to keep going."

"I can't. Dex. I just can't do it!" Jamie pleaded, his insides knotting.

"Then we'll do it without you, after you leave."

"I'm not leaving."

Dex drew in an exaggerated, exasperated sigh. "So you're going to stay here. You and fourteen other fools."

"As long as I can."

With a shake of his head, Dex said softly, "I just hope you don't kill yourself, pal. Or your wife."

He turned abruptly and strode away, leaving Jamie standing there, furious, his insides clenched. He realized the dome was utterly silent. The people in the cafeteria were as immobile as rocks, staring at him. Feeling alone and friendless, Jamie walked off toward his quarters.

Now he lay in bed, realizing that he might never speak to Dex again. He also realized that Dex was right. There was no other way: no other path that led out of this quagmire. But it was a path he could not take.

As quietly as he could, Jamie slipped out of bed. He padded to the lavatory and pulled on a fresh set of coveralls, then tiptoed to the door.

"Jamie?" Vijay called drowsily.

"I've got to go out for a little while," he whispered to her. "I'll be back. Go to sleep."

Without waiting for her reply he slid the door back and stepped out into the dome's open common area. Barefoot.

Like a skulking redskin, he said to himself. Sneaking around in the night.

The dome was dimly lit. Just about everybody was asleep, except for the people monitoring the communications equipment. No one was outside in the bitter Martian night. No one was out on an excursion. They were all asleep, Jamie thought, waiting for the inevitable day when they would leave Mars. For good.

As he padded softly toward his office Jamie heard the soft sighing of the breeze wafting by. On any other night it would have comforted him. Not tonight. Mars is saying good-bye to us. Good-bye to me.

He reached his office, sat on the yielding little chair, and sank his head in his hands.

It's finished, he thought. Dex is right. What can fifteen people do here? I'd be putting Vijay's life in danger. I can't do it. I can't do it.

They win, Jamie told himself. I have to leave Mars. Forever.

He wanted to cry. He wanted to sob and tear his hair and mourn the death of all that he had hoped for, all that he had worked for. But tears would not come. Not even that solace was allowed him.

"Uh . . . Dr. W?"

Jamie looked up, feeling his cheeks flare hot with embarrassment.

It was Billy Graycloud standing at the entrance of his cubbyhole, looking more than a little embarrassed himself.

TITHONIUM BASE: THE PRAYER

■

Billy," Jamie said softly, suppressing an urge to wipe his face, straighten his hair.

"I . . . uh, saw the light on in your office. . . ."

Some office, Jamie thought. A cubicle with flimsy partitions that'll collapse if you lean on them.

"Do you have a minute?" Graycloud asked. His voice was soft, but Jamie heard some urgency in it.

Remembering, Jamie apologized, "I said I'd see you after dinner, didn't I? I'm sorry. I got . . . tied up, sort of."

Graycloud nodded minimally. "You and Mr. Trumball."

Jamie nodded back, realizing that everybody in the dome must have heard their shouting.

"So what do you want to tell me, Billy?" he asked wearily.

Shifting uneasily on his feet, Graycloud replied, "Can you come over to the comm center? It'd be easier if I show you what I've got so far."

"The translation?" Jamie got up out of his chair.

"I'd like to get your reaction to it, if you've got a couple minutes."

"Okay." Jamie got to his feet slowly.

As they started across the shadowy dome, Graycloud said, "I think maybe I'm getting some sense out of the writings."

"You are?" Despite himself, Jamie felt a tendril of excitement pulse through him.

"I think so. I might be foolin' myself, you know, putting words in their mouths, kinda. . . ."

"Let's see."

Leading the way toward the comm center, Graycloud explained, "I assigned specific words to each of the symbols, and then sort of filled in to make sense of each line. Like the Egyptologists did to translate the ancient Egyptian hieroglyphics, back in the nineteenth century."

Jamie felt an increased respect for the young Navaho. "You've been doing some research, haven't you?"

Graycloud lowered his eyes bashfully. "Yessir. Some."

Two women were monitoring the consoles in the communications center. Graycloud booted up an unused computer while Jamie pulled over a wheeled chair and sat beside him.

"It's pretty rough," Graycloud said, his fingers working the keyboard. "And like I said, I'm prob'ly putting words into their mouths, kinda. But I haven't changed the sequence of their pictographs; each word stands in the same place as its symbol carved on the wall."

"Let's see what you've got, Billy."

The display screen showed an image of the Martian pictographs. Then words in English began to print over it.

"The words in brackets are what I put in. The rest is straight from the symbols themselves, in the same order as they appear on the wall," Graycloud explained.

Jamie barely heard him. He was focused on the translation as it came up on the screen.

```
[We are] the People. The People [live] under Fa-
ther Sun. Father Sun [is] life. Father Sun
[makes] the crops [grow]. Father Sun [is] Life.
Father Sun [makes] the river [flow]. Father Sun
[makes] the river [bring] water [to or for] the
People. Father Sun [is] life. Father Sun [makes]
the wind [blow]. Father Sun [makes] the clouds
[bring] rain. Father Sun [gives] life [to] The
People. Father Sun [is] life. The People [wor-
```

```
ship? adore?] Father Sun. Father Sun [gives]
life [to] the People. Father Sun [is] life.
```

"The rest is pretty much the same," Graycloud said, almost whispering. "Lots of repetition. It's kinda like a poem, sort of."

"It's a prayer," Jamie said, also in a near-whisper, his eyes still staring at the words.

"A prayer," Graycloud echoed. Then he raised his voice slightly, breaking the spell. "Or maybe it's just all garbage. You know, maybe I just put in words that have nothin' to do with what the Martians really meant to say."

"No, Billy, I don't think so. You've made contact with them. You've touched their spirit."

"You think so?"

More excited now, Jamie said, "You've got to write this up and get it published. And let Dex Trumball see it, too, before he takes off tomorrow."

Graycloud looked embarrassed. "Dr. W, the professional journals won't publish this. The real philologists will say it's crap—by an amateur."

"Then we'll have the Foundation publish it. We'll get it in front of the public. Get it on the Net, in the news."

"You really think . . . ?"

Jamie patted the youngster's shoulder. "Billy, you're going to become famous. Your translation's going to cause a stir, one way or the other. The more controversy, the better."

"But they'll say I don't know what I'm doing! They'll laugh at me."

"Pioneers always get laughed at. Look at Wegener and the theory of plate tectonics. The geologists laughed him to scorn, but he turned out to be right."

Graycloud looked down at his shoes and muttered, "I don't know if I could deal with that, Dr. W."

"You will, Billy." Silently, Jamie added, You'll have to.

His face showing clearly the conflict inside him, Graycloud

asked, "If I write this up, you know, make a formal paper for publication, would you put your name on it, too?"

Jamie felt surprised. "I didn't do any of this work, Billy."

"I did it under your supervision. And if your name's on the paper people'll take it more seriously."

"And I'll take some of the heat," Jamie said with a smile.

"Yeah. I guess."

Nodding, Jamie said, "Okay, Billy. I'll write a preface for your paper. Explain the background. We'll include images of the pictographs and the cliff structures."

"And you'll put your name in as coauthor?"

"If that's what you want."

"Thanks, Dr. W!"

We've got to get this to Dex before he leaves, Jamie thought. Maybe it'll turn him around, convince him we've got to push ahead with our work here.

But then the reaction set in. Billy's right. The academics will rip this translation to shreds. Nobody will pay any real attention to it. The news nets will claim it's a desperate attempt to draw support for exploring Mars. A dying gasp. Which it is.

Graycloud broke into his dismal thoughts. "Dr. W? How long do you intend to stay here? On Mars?"

Jamie looked into the youngster's earnest face. "As long as I can, Billy."

Graycloud's eyes shifted away momentarily. Then he said, "I'll go back on the evacuation flight, then. You'll be the resident Navaho, okay?"

Wearily, Jamie said, "Going back to Arizona?"

"New Mexico first. I'll take a little vacation in Taos. That's where my family lives."

"Not on the Navaho lands?"

"Naw. My father owns an art gallery in Taos."

Jamie almost smiled. "My grandfather had a shop on the Plaza in Santa Fe."

"You wouldn't recognize Taos," Graycloud said. "Last time I was there the whole state was green as Ireland, just about.

You couldn't walk along the sidewalks in town because the bushes had grown so thick."

"From the greenhouse climate shift," said Jamie. "Some regions get drought, some get floods, but the southwestern desert is getting good rain." He thought about the president of the Navaho Nation and her problems with squatters encroaching on their land.

"Yep. Just give that old desert scrub some rain and it blooms like the Garden of Eden."

A memory popped into Jamie's consciousness. "When Arizona was admitted to the Union, back around nineteentwelve, one of the men appointed to the U.S. Senate gave a speech about the new state. He ended it by saying, 'All that Arizona needs to make it heaven is water and society.' "

Graycloud grinned. "And somebody in the audience said, 'That's all that hell needs to make it heaven.' "

They both chuckled at the story.

"Wish we could say the same for Mars."

"Water and society," Graycloud echoed. "Yeah."

For several moments neither of them said anything. Jamie looked past Graycloud, at the two communications technicians sitting at their consoles, at the humming, blinking screens, at the curved beams of the dome high above, lost in shadows. How long will we stay here? he asked himself. How long can we hold on?

He had no answers. At last he got to his feet.

"You've done a good job, Billy," he said to the younger man. "I'm proud of you, son."

Graycloud actually blushed.

Jamie left the younger man sitting there, with his translation on the display screen, and padded barefoot and alone back to his quarters.

TITHONIUM BASE: THE PATH

■

Jamie tried to enter the room as quietly as possible, but still Vijay stirred awake.

"You okay?" she asked drowsily.

"More or less," he replied.

She lifted her head slightly and squinted at the digital clock. "Try to get some sleep before the sun comes up, love."

"Billy Graycloud's translated the pictographs," he said, sitting on the edge of the bed. "He might be on to something."

"That's good."

"He's going back on the evacuation flight. Back to New Mexico."

"Almost everybody is."

"Yeah." Jamie stretched out on the bed beside her, too tired and worn down even to take off his coveralls. But something was playing in his mind. A thought, an idea, fragile, elusive. He almost had it, but it kept slipping away from his conscious grasp. Something Billy said, he remembered. Something about rain and the desert . . .

Just give that old desert scrub some rain and it blooms like the Garden of Eden.

Turn the desert into a Garden of Eden, Jamie said to himself. Easier said than—

He sat bolt upright in the bed. "Why not?" he said aloud.

Vijay turned toward him. "Why not what?"

"We could do it!"

"Do what?" She sat up beside him.

"We could do it!" he repeated, almost shouting. "I've got to tell Dex! And Hasdrubal."

Jamie jumped off the bed and ran to the door, leaving Vijay in the bed, startled and confused.

"CHRISSAKE, JAMIE, IT'S NOT even six o'clock!" Dex complained.

Jamie had waited as long as he could. He'd never felt so excited, not since the moment when he'd first set foot on Mars, back in the First Expedition.

Still barefoot, Jamie had gone from his bedroom to the cafeteria and started up the coffeemaker. He fidgeted around impatiently, mentally reviewing what he had to do. Billy Graycloud came out of the comm center, yawning, together with the two technicians who had been on duty there. Their replacements shuffled in, looking surprised that the aroma of brewing coffee was already wafting through the dimly lit dome.

Jamie had laughed and waved at Graycloud, then taken a mug of coffee and sat impatiently in the cafeteria, thinking, planning, hoping, waiting for the sun to come up. At last the dome's wall depolarized and became transparent again. Jamie saw the rusty surface of Mars out there, rocks scattered everywhere, the massive cliffs rising almost perpendicularly, so high their top was cut off by the edge of the dome's transparent section.

He couldn't wait any longer. Sitting at the cafeteria table, his insides fluttering, he yanked out his pocket phone and buzzed Dex.

A sleepy, "Whassamatter?"

"Come on out to the cafeteria, Dex. I've got something to tell you. Something important."

"Jamie?"

"Yes! Get up! Now!"

"Chrissake, Jamie, it's not even six o'clock!"

"Coffee's waiting for you."

Dex mumbled something and cut the connection. Jamie laughed inwardly. If he doesn't come out in a few minutes I'll go over and drag him out of bed.

He thought about calling Hasdrubal. And Chang. No, Jamie said to himself. Dex first. Just Dex. One-on-one. I'll tell the others afterward.

Dex came out of his quarters, squinting unhappily at the sunlight lancing through the dome as he trudged slowly toward Jamie in the cafeteria. Jamie bolted out of his chair and sprinted toward him.

"What's going on? What's happened? Christ, you don't even have shoes on!"

Steering Dex toward the coffee machine, Jamie said eagerly, "We've been looking through the wrong end of the telescope! All this time you've been thinking about terraforming the area for your tourists."

"And you've been dead against it," Dex muttered.

"I was wrong. We both were wrong. We don't terraform Mars for human visitors. We terraform for the Martians!"

Dex squeezed his eyes shut for a moment. "It's too damned early for jokes, Jamie."

"It's no joke! Take a piece of Mars and terraform it so that Martian organisms can live in it!"

"Terraform for Martians?"

"Terraform's the wrong word. Areform it. Ares is the astronomical term for Mars, isn't it?"

Dex reached for the coffeepot with one hand, a mug with his other.

"Jamie, what the hell are you talking about?"

"You went out with us to Hasdrubal's crater yesterday."

"Yeah. His bugs are all dead."

Guiding Dex to a table, Jamie said, "Well, suppose we had another crater, deep enough to expose the microbes living below the permafrost."

"They'd die off from the cold and radiation, just like the ones—"

"Not if we domed over the crater!" Jamie said as they sat

down. "Let the air pressure build up inside it naturally. Protect it from the cold and radiation."

Dex opened his mouth, closed it. At last he said, "You think the bugs could live?"

"In a Martian environment! Yes!"

With a slow shake of his head, Dex asked, "How do you know what kind of environment they'd need? They live deep underground, don't they?"

"We'll make several craters. Five, ten, whatever. Make slightly different environments in each of them. Vary the air pressure, the temperature—and watch the microbes adapt to the new conditions."

"They'll all die."

"Hasdrubal's microbes survived for a couple of weeks," Jamie countered. "If we protect them, give them better conditions, some of them might survive. It's worth trying!"

"And study them as they adapt," Dex muttered.

"It's a chance to begin repopulating Mars!"

"They're only bacteria, Jamie."

"But they'll evolve, over time."

"Millions of years."

"So we do a long-term experiment!"

Dex leaned back in his chair and took a long swig of coffee. "You're crazy, you know."

"So was Archimedes," Jamie said, laughing.

"Eureka and all that."

"We can do it, Dex! The greatest experiment of all time! We can bring life back to Mars! Instead of watching the planet die, we can repopulate it!"

"And who's going to pay for it?"

Jamie hesitated, then answered, "Your tourists, I guess."

Sitting up straighter, Dex said, "You'll let tourists here?"

"This area only," Jamie said, his old reluctance giving way only slightly. "The village, the cliff structures. Five at a time. They stay for one week."

Before Dex could respond, Jamie added, "And no terraforming. They go out in nanosuits, just like the rest of us."

Dex pursed his lips, then said, "Might make them enjoy the trip better, using the suits, make them realize they're really on Mars."

"I'll take charge of the visitors," Jamie said. "Personally." That's the price I'll have to pay, he told himself.

Dex grinned at him. "Yes, warden."

"And, Dex, can you add into their price a fellowship for students who want to spend a year on Mars?"

"Maybe." Dex thought about it for a moment. "Yeah, I don't see why not."

Jamie sucked in a deep breath. "Okay. Now let's tell Hasdrubal. And Chang."

"You tell them," said Dex. "Soon's I finish this coffee I'm going back to my room and pack."

With a laugh, Jamie said, "I've got something for you to take back with you. Billy Graycloud's translated the Martian writing."

"Translated—?"

"It's a prayer, Dex. A beautiful Martian prayer to the sun."

"Jesus Christ."

"You can stir up some interest with it. Get some media attention."

Dex nodded slowly. "Sure."

"Good."

Getting slowly to his feet alongside Jamie, coffee mug in one hand, Dex asked, "Can I go pack my bag now?"

"You don't want to stay?"

"Hell no. I've got a lot to do back on Earth. You stay here, Jamie. This is home for you."

TITHONIUM BASE: THE MILLION-YEAR
EXPERIMENT

∎

Jamie fingered the bear fetish in his coveralls pocket as he stood between Chang Laodong and Carter Carleton watching the access tube disconnect from the squat, squarish body of the L/AV and roll back toward the dome.

So long, Dex, Jamie said silently. Pick your tourists carefully. I'll be here waiting for them.

"LIFTOFF IN FIFTEEN SECONDS," the overhead speakers announced. "FOURTEEN . . . THIRTEEN . . . "

Saleem Hasdrubal came up beside them. Looking out at the L/AV, he said, "I hear you've been talkin' about my work."

" . . . TEN . . . NINE . . . EIGHT . . . "

Jamie said, "That's right."

"Mind tellin' *me* about it?"

" . . . FIVE . . . FOUR . . . "

Jamie held up a finger, his eyes on the landing/ascent vehicle, his other hand squeezing the fetish. Rocket launches always had an element of danger, he knew.

" . . . TWO . . . ONE . . . LIFTOFF."

The L/AV hurtled out of sight, the hot exhaust from its ascent engine spraying grit and pebbles across the landing area.

"Liftoff nominal," they heard the astronaut pilot's voice, almost as emotionless as the computer. "On track for orbital rendezvous."

Jamie relaxed his grip on the stone bear. Turning to Hasdrubal, he began explaining his idea for repopulating the dying Mars. Together with Carleton and Chang they started walking slowly away from the airlock area.

The biologist's eyes widened as he grasped what Jamie was saying. "It'd take a million years before you saw any development," he said, his voice slightly hollow with awe.

Jamie replied, "It'll be a long-term experiment, that's for sure."

Chang asked, "Can it be done?"

"Blasting out some new craters and doming 'em over?" Hasdrubal asked. "Yeah, sure. Make 'em deep enough to expose the SLiMEs. Why not?"

The mission director almost smiled. "Then watch bacteria adapt to new conditions."

"Watch them evolve," said Carleton. "The fundamentalists are going to go wild over that."

"Let them," Jamie said tightly. "Tourism will keep us funded." And he realized, "Every tourist who comes here will be a walking advertisement for our work when he gets back home."

Carleton grinned mischievously. "I'll put them to work at the dig. That should give them something to talk about when they return to Earth."

"Let them take souvenirs home?" Jamie asked.

The anthropologist shrugged. "Martian rocks. Or pebbles, more likely."

Chang spoke up. "When a tourist digs up something of significance, artifact or fossil, attach his or her name to it. Give them pride."

"Good idea," said Carleton. "We'll keep a running catalogue of all the bits and pieces, with the names of the people who found them."

Hasdrubal still seemed somewhat dazed by Jamie's idea. "A million-year experiment. There's never been anything like it."

"Yes there has," Jamie replied. "You and me, all of us, all the life on Earth."

"And Mars, too, I guess," the biologist admitted.

"But now we can do a controlled experiment."

"And take notes." Hasdrubal laughed, a little shakily.

They had reached the cafeteria.

Chang gestured to the nearest table. "A proper ceremony is in order," he said. "Please wait here."

The mission director hurried back toward his office.

"What's he up to?" Jamie wondered.

Carleton said, "I bet I know."

Chang reemerged a moment later, carrying a slim green bottle in one chubby hand.

"Rice wine," he explained once he reached their table. "From my home province."

They drank a toast to the new project: Chang, Carleton, Hasdrubal and Jamie. To the future. To the million-year experiment.

Then Carleton got to his feet.

"Going to excavation?" Chang asked, an almost amiable smile on his chunky face.

"In a while," the anthropologist said. "First I'm going to put in a call to Selene. We're going to need a nanotechnology expert to oversee building the domes over the craters. I know just the right person."

As he hurried off toward his quarters, they heard Carleton almost singing, "Let me not to the marriage of true minds admit impediments. . . ."

IT WAS A LONG and exhilarating day. Chang actually laughed as he cancelled the evacuation flight. Carleton and his crew went out to the dig with renewed spirit. Hasdrubal gathered most of the biologists and began planning the first steps of what they all called the million-year experiment.

As darkness fell and the dome's transparent windows went opaque, Jamie stood by the entrance of his office cubicle and listened to the hum of activity. The cafeteria was filling up. People were laughing and joking. The overhead speakers blared up-tempo pop tunes.

He and Vijay had dinner with Hasdrubal and Zeke Larkin.

"I asked Carleton about blowing out new craters," Larkin said over his plate of soymeat. "He's the local expert on explosives."

"And?" Jamie prodded.

"He said he'd help us all he could."

Hasdrubal chuckled. "Maybe he's hopin' you'll blow your head off."

Larkin grinned back at him. "Yeah. Maybe so."

"The important thing," Jamie pointed out, "is that you can work together on this."

"That we will do," Hasdrubal said firmly.

All through dinner Vijay said very little, and as she and Jamie walked back to their quarters he asked, "Anything wrong? You've been a quiet little mouse all evening."

"You had a lot to say," she countered.

"Guess I did," he admitted.

Vijay slid her arm into his. "You've done it, Jamie. You've found the right path."

The memory of his grandfather flickered through Jamie's awareness. *This village don't exist yet*, Al had told him in his dream. But it will, Jamie said to himself. We'll bring it to life.

"I don't know if it's the right path," Jamie replied to Vijay, "but I think it's a path that we can all follow. A path that will lead to where we want to go."

"Even if it takes a million years?" she teased.

"Even if takes longer," he said, totally serious.

"The important thing is, you're going to keep the operation going," she said. "You're going to make it better than ever."

Jamie nodded. "At least we'll be able to stay on Mars."

"People will be on Mars all the time."

"Even tourists," he said.

"You'll handle them. You'll put them to work, won't you?"

"That's the plan."

Later, as they were undressing for bed, Jamie came to a realization. "You know, all through dinner you were looking at me in a kind of funny way."

Vijay's brows rose questioningly.

"It wasn't just that you were quiet most of the time. You had this funny expression on your face."

As she slipped her naked body under the sheet Vijay asked, "A funny expression?"

"Funny as in strange." Jamie sat on the edge of the bed, then stretched out beside her and pulled up the sheet. He switched off the light. Vijay cuddled her body against his.

"What kind of expression?" she whispered into his ear.

He turned toward her, and in the darkness he answered, "I don't know. Kind of like you knew something I didn't. Kind of like you had a secret."

"I don't have any secrets from you, love."

"I know. It's weird, isn't it?"

For a moment Vijay said nothing. They lay together, bodies pressed tight.

Then, "We'll be staying on Mars permanently, won't we, Jamie?"

"Looks that way."

"I've been talking it over with Nari. There's no reason why we shouldn't have another baby."

"Another . . . ? What? Here on Mars?"

Vijay laughed softly in the darkness. "Think of it as a biology experiment; a nine-month experiment."

"That's some experiment," Jamie muttered. "It's a big decision, Vijay. Are you sure—"

"I was sure when we left New Mexico, love. I just had to wait until you got everything sorted out in your head. And now you have, so . . . why not?"

"At our age?"

"That's no problem."

"But . . . on Mars?"

"Children have been born on the Moon. It's perfectly natural."

"But—"

"Nari will take good care of me. I'll be fine and we'll have a healthy child. It'll be good publicity for Dex to use."

Despite himself, Jamie laughed. "A publicity stunt."

"A baby. Our baby. It's time we did it."

"A nine-month experiment."

She nuzzled her cheek against his. "Mars forever," Vijay whispered.

"Forever," he whispered back.

EPILOGUE: DEPEW, FLORIDA

■

Bucky Winters sat at the old wooden desk in the bedroom he shared with his two older brothers. They were both out somewhere, so he had the room to himself for a change.

On the screen of his notebook computer was an image of the writing that the Martians had chiseled into a wall of the buildings they had left behind. And superimposed over the strange symbols were words:

```
[We are] the People. The People [live] under Fa-
ther Sun. Father Sun [is] life. Father Sun
[makes] the crops [grow]. Father Sun [is]
Life. . . .
```

He stared at the screen as the words scrolled past his goggling eyes.

They wrote those words! Bucky marveled. There really were Martians and they built villages and wrote prayers. There are scientists on Mars exploring the planet, digging up the old villages, translating the Martian writing.

Trembling with excitement, Bucky got up from the wobbly desk chair and went to the window. He slid it open and crawled out onto the porch roof. Moonlit clouds were drifting across the stars, silvery against the black of night. The stars twinkled and blinked as the clouds drifted past them.

His tongue between his teeth, Bucky looked toward the

southwest, hoping that the clouds weren't so thick that they covered . . .

There it is! Mars, shining red and steady against the infinity of space. Bucky stared at it, thinking:

I'm going to get all As in high school. I'll take whatever classes they want me to take and study Mars here at home; I won't let anybody at school know about it. I won't say a word to anybody, not even Mom and Dad. I'll get the best marks anybody can get all through high school and win a scholarship to college. I'll study astronomy in college and when I graduate I'll go to Mars. I'll help them explore. I'll get there no matter what.

In the dark night Bucky smiled at the steady red beacon of Mars. Wait for me, he asked. I'm coming to you.

Turn the page for a preview of

THE RETURN

BOOK IV OF VOYAGERS

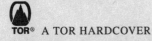

Available August 2009
from Tom Doherty Associates

TOR® A TOR HARDCOVER   ISBN 978-0-7653-0925-9

CHAPTER 1

∎

"You've changed."

"*I've* changed?" Raoul Tavalera cast a surprised look at Evelyn Delmore, sitting on the sofa next to him.

The party had pretty much drifted away from the living room. The old-fashioned, overfurnished room was almost empty, except for a few of his mother's white-haired friends and Evelyn, who'd been at Tavalera's side since the instant the party started, just about.

His former neighbors and old schoolmates had gathered in his mother's house to celebrate his returning home after nearly six years in space. But it was a strangely quiet, subdued sort of party. Hardly any alcohol, for one thing. When Tavalera had asked for a drink his mother had handed him fruit punch. He had to get one of his old college buddies to spike his glass with a dollop of tequila. The guy poured the booze surreptitiously out of a pocket flask, eyeing the tiny red light of the security camera up in the corner of the ceiling.

And not all of his classmates and former buddies had shown up. When he asked where Vince Tiorlini was, Tavalera got shifty looks and embarrassed mumbles about work camps in the flooded Pacific Northwest. Zeke Berkowitz, too: re-education center for him. They said he'd be out in another few months, maybe. Even Ellen O'Reilly. Her flaming temper had gotten her sent away somewhere, nobody seemed to know where.

Six years, Tavalera thought. A lot had changed in six years.

Or maybe, he thought, it's just that I'm looking at everything through different eyes, after being away for so long.

There had been dancing, of sorts. Very subdued shuffling around the floor of the dining room, which had been emptied of furniture for the evening. Dull, old-fashioned music from individual phones that each dancer clipped to his or her ear. So that the noise won't disturb any of the older people, Tavalera's mother had explained. He had tried to tune the phone to something livelier but got only a god-awful shriek in his ear; the phones were restricted to one single channel, bland and boring. Finally Tavalera had given up in numbed disgust and returned to the living room. That wasn't dancing, he told himself. He'd had more fun in kindergarten when the teachers made them all march in time to patriotic songs.

Looking around the hushed living room, Tavalera found that most of the partygoers his own age had crowded into the kitchen, but even there they were a pretty quiet crowd, he thought. He remembered impromptu parties aboard the *Goddard* habitat, all the way out by the planet Saturn, where'd he'd spent a couple of involuntary years and fallen in love. They were noisy, cheerful bashes, fueled by home-brewed booze everybody called rocket juice. People danced to music that made the walls vibrate, for crying out loud. This homecoming gig was more like a wake than a party.

I've known these people since I was a little kid, he mused. We all went to school together, right through college. But they're different now. Strangers. Maybe it *is* me, he repeated to himself. They haven't changed. I guess I have.

Tavalera was a compactly built middleweight, exactly one hundred and eighty-two centimeters tall. He had a long-jawed, melancholy face with a set of teeth that made him look, he knew, like a caricature of a horse. Not handsome, but not entirely unattractive, either. Somber brown eyes, dark hair that he kept cropped short after years of living and working aboard spacecraft.

"Yes, you've changed," said Evelyn Delmore, peering nearsightedly at him as she sat beside him on the sofa. The crumbs of his homecoming cake were scattered over the big tray on the coffee table, the table itself, much of the floor, and Tavalera's travel-weary slacks. He realized how old-fashioned the living room was, with its fake fireplace, overstuffed furniture, and the wall-sized TV screen that was never off. There were only a few of the older neighbors in the living room now, all of them placidly watching the TV news.

The big wall screen over the mantlepiece was showing bulky, ungainly robotic soldiers clanking through some village in a jungle. Might's well be the same newscasts they were running before I left, Tavalera thought. The info bar running along the top of the screen read: **Medellín, Colombia**.

That red unblinking eye of the security camera bothered him, up there in the corner of the ceiling, by the old-fashioned crown molding that his mother loved so well. It seemed to be staring at him. Why does Ma need a security camera? Tavalera wondered as he sat on the sofa. She's got one in every room, for chrissake, even the kitchen.

He heard somebody yowl with laughter, back in the kitchen, where almost everyone had moved to. Except for Evelyn, all the people of his own age had squeezed in there. That's where the food is, he thought. The laughter quickly cut off, as if some teacher or librarian had hissed out a warning shush.

He got up and headed toward the back of the house, Evelyn half a step behind him. Tavalera felt almost annoyed. I don't need her hanging on me! He thought of Holly, back at the *Goddard* habitat. I wonder what Holly's doing right now.

The kitchen was jammed: people were sitting on the counters, crowding into the mudroom, couples sitting on the back steps that led up to the bedrooms. But their talk was subdued, low-key. They were almost whispering, as if they were in church, or afraid to let anyone hear what they were saying. It unnerved Tavalera.

His brother, Andy, was entertaining them all with an impromptu display of juggling. Impromptu and inept, Tavalera thought. Andy had a big grin on his face as he tossed pieces of fruit in the air. The floor around his feet was littered with oranges, apples, and something that had splattered and made a pulpy mess.

It didn't bother his mother at all, Raoul saw. She seemed dazedly pleased at all the friendly faces crammed in around her. She was standing by the stove, looking kind of dumpy and round and as white as bread dough, smiling vacantly, hardly changed at all in the years Tavalera had been away. Except that now her white hair was dyed ash-blond.

Why in hell did she dye her hair? he wondered.

He realized that Evelyn was staring intently at him, as if trying to read his thoughts.

Embarrassed at her attention, he asked, "I've changed, huh?"

"Yes. Definitely." She kept her voice low, just like all the others.

"How? For the better?"

"I don't know yet." She was about Tavalera's age, pretty in a pale blond way, even though she was decidedly on the bony side. Holly was lean, too, but vivacious, always full of energy, full of color and fun.

"You're . . . quieter, I guess," Evelyn continued. "More reserved."

He shrugged. He'd been off-Earth for nearly six whole years. He'd seen massive Jupiter, giant of the solar system, up close; he'd repaired scoopships that dove into that planet's swirling, multihued clouds. He'd nearly been killed out there. He'd lived in a huge space habitat that carried him unwillingly to Saturn, with its bright gleaming rings. He'd left Holly in that habitat that was now orbiting Saturn. He'd promised her he'd return. But the government had refused to allow him to leave Earth again, wouldn't even let him send messages to her.

He'd received no messages from her, either. Was the government blocking them or had Holly already forgotten about him?

Messages. He'd expected the local news media to make at least a little fuss over him. Back home after traveling halfway across the solar system. None of his old buddies had ever gone into space. But nothing, not a peep in the news nets, even though his brother worked for the local TV center. Just like I've never been away. Nothing. Everything here's the same, even the friggin' never-ending war against terrorists and drug cartels. Except for Mom. She's a blonde now, for chrissakes.

But it's not the same, he told himself. Or I'm not the same. Evvie's right. I've changed. Six years off-Earth changes you. Has to. What I took for granted before I left looks . . . strange now. Stifling. It's like coming back to kindergarten after six years of being on my own.

"Before you left," Evelyn was saying, "you were sort of a wise mouth. Now you're . . . well, quieter. Guarded, sort of."

"I'm older," he said with a cheerless smile.

"Aren't we all?" she replied.

Tavalera gestured toward his brother, still juggling, with a silly grin pasted on his face. "Andy's exactly the same as he was the last time I saw him."

"Oh, Andy!" said Evelyn. "He'll never grow up."

Somehow the quiet buzz and restrained laughter seemed almost desperate. It's like everybody's afraid of making any noise. Like we're all back in Sunday school. It became too much for Tavalera. He pushed his way toward the back door.

"Where're you going?" Evelyn asked, right beside him.

"Outside. I need some fresh air." I need to get away from these zombies, he added silently. And I don't need a clinging vine smothering me. He wanted to tell Evelyn to go away and leave him alone, but he didn't have the nerve, didn't want to hurt her feelings.

She came with him as he shouldered his way through the well-wishers who pretty much ignored him in their determination to have a well-behaved good time. Except for his mother, whose eyes followed him every step of the way, looking—not worried, exactly. Concerned. Maybe she's hurt 'cause I'm not enjoying the party, he thought.

Outside it was twilight. The sun had just set; the sky was deepening into violet. Not a cloud in sight, Tavalera saw. The sky fascinated him, after years in spacecraft and artificial habitats. Everybody here took it for granted, that big blue bowl that turned red and gold and deepened gradually into black, dotted with stars that twinkled at you. It isn't that way aboard spacecraft. Even the *Goddard* habitat, big enough to house ten thousand people, didn't have a sky or even a horizon.

It was warm enough outdoors to be comfortable in just his shirtsleeves, even though spring didn't officially start for another month or so.

The neighborhood looked subtly different from the last time he'd seen it. The backyard seemed smaller than he remembered it, the stubbly grass worn down in spots where Tavalera recalled playing ball with his buddies. But now there was a tall aluminum pole in the far corner of the yard, anodized olive green, with another one of those red-eyed security cameras atop it. That was new. The camera turned slowly, slowly, then stopped for a moment when it aimed at Tavalera and Evelyn. He grimaced; then the camera resumed its slow sweep of the area.

Rows of houses stood along the wide, slightly curving street, equally spaced. Just like before I left, Tavalera thought. Maybe a little more crowded, new houses where there'd been open lots and playgrounds before. Or maybe they've shortened the backyards so they could squeeze in some extra houses. Otherwise nothing seemed changed. Except for the poles and the cameras every third house. Who are they watching? he wondered. Who's doing the watching?

Most of the lawns looked half-dead, a sick-looking brown caused by the warming. The new high-rises poked above the screening line of struggling young trees out behind the houses, where the park used to be. Tavalera had played baseball in that park and pedaled his old bicycle until it fell apart. Now the area was a refugee center, housing for people driven from their cities by the greenhouse floods. Hispanics, mostly. And some Arabs or Armenians or something like that. They didn't like to be called refugees, he'd been told: they preferred to be known as flood fugitives.

I guess the world has changed in six years, Tavalera

thought, even though most people are doing their best to ignore the changes.

He walked around the house and down the driveway in silence, Evelyn step-by-step beside him. She made him feel nervous, edgy. No cars in the driveway. All the partygoers had either walked to his house or taken public transportation. Driving individual autos wasn't forbidden, exactly, he had learned since his return. But the city frowned on unnecessary driving. And the fuel rationing kept people afoot, as well. Rationing hydrogen, Tavalera thought. They get the stuff from water, for chrissake. Why should they have to ration it?

Something flickered in the corner of his eye. He looked up, and his breath caught in his throat.

"Jesus H. Christ! Look at that!"

Evelyn looked shocked. "You shouldn't take the Lord's name in vain! They might hear you."

"But look!" Tavalera lifted her chin to the heavens.

Long ribbons of shimmering light danced across the sky: soft green, pale blue, white, and coral pink. Like trembling curtains they moved and shifted while Tavalera stared, goggle-eyed.

"What is it?" Evelyn asked in an awed whisper.

"The Northern Lights, I think."

She broke into a nervous laughter. "Not the end of the world, then?"

Shaking his head, his eyes still turned skyward, Tavalera murmured, "Aurora borealis."

"But why's it showing this far south?" Evelyn asked. "We never get the Northern Lights in Little Rock."

"Must be a really big flare on the Sun," he replied. "Or something."

TOR

Voted

#1 Science Fiction Publisher
20 Years in a Row

by the *Locus* Readers' Poll

———•———

Please join us at the website below
for more information about this
author and other science fiction,
fantasy, and horror selections, and to
sign up for our monthly newsletter!

www.tor-forge.com